What makes Gabriele Kosack's and Günter Overmann's novel *Trümmertänzer* an especially worthwhile read, is its gripping narrative. While reading, you can literally feel the dust from the rubble mountains being blown straight into your eyes.

—Claudia Cosmo,
on the radio show Büchermarkt,
Deutschlandfunk

• • •

In *Trümmertänzer*, the two authors describe the experience of living in those few weeks right after the war in such vivid scenes that you can instantly see the ruins of Berlin before your inner eye or have the distinctively intense smell of cigarettes in a basement jazz club hit your nostrils. An impressive achievement for the writing couple from Cologne.

—Kirsten Gnoth,
in the newspaper Der Westen

• • •

The authors have succeeded in writing a magnificent piece of historical fiction.

—Robert Boucard,
in the literary magazine Im Lesesaal

A DANCE
IN THE ASHES

A DANCE IN THE ASHES

A NOVEL

GABRIELE KOSACK
GÜNTER OVERMANN

Translated from German by Roger "Skip" Wightman

English version by Kenneth L. Fitts

Published by
Elster Publications and distributed by
RockStar Publishing House
32129 Lindero Canyon Rd.
Suite 205
Westlake Village, CA 91361
www.rockstarpublishinghouse.com

Originally published as *Trümmertänzer*, © 2013 by Elster Verlagsbuchhandlung AG, Zürich

English edition © 2014 by Gabriele Kosack and Günter Overmann

Translated from German by Roger "Skip" Wightman
English version by Kenneth L. Fitts

Manufactured in the United States of America, or in the United Kingdom when distributed elsewhere.

Kosack, Gabriele and Overmann, Günter
    A Dance in the Ashes
    ISBN
    Paperback: 978-1-937506-80-3
    eBook: 978-1-937506-81-0

Cover design by: Terri A. Boekhoff
Cover photo courtesy of: Elster Verlagsbuchhandlung AG
Interior design: Terri A. Boekhoff
Author photos by: Ulla Wiberny

Authors' URL www.guenter-overmann.de

In memory of Roger "Skip" Wightman,
without whom the English version would not exist.

ONE

Quiet. Sudden, peaceful, eerie quiet broken only by the crunch of her steps in the rubble.

The sun shone brightly on her; the sky was blue with fleecy clouds, and cherry trees blossomed pink and white, perhaps lured by the silence to come out early. Forsythias gleamed yellow, and beech hedges shimmered with green buds conquering the omnipresent sallow dust. But, no bird sang; no insect hummed.

No bird, no insect, no people. None. No car, no streetcar, no thundering guns. No rockets howling from Stalin's Organ. No martial songs whose cadence still set the rhythm of Mathilde's steps. The city was quiet, quiet as never before. Few dared to venture out, even though the Russians had pushed forward taking the war with them. Mathilde could hardly believe that they had vanished and taken their smell and noise with them—the clopping of their horses on pavement; the tinny clanking of their trucks; the soft, uneven sound of their speech; and the odor of their cabbage, vodka, and papyrossi. All had vanished.

What remained was silence and dust. The smell of fires and smoke blended with putrefaction and rot that even the fragrance of those brave blossoms in this breath of spring could not offset. What remained was the odor of death, at least for Mathilde and others in Kiepholzstraße in Steglitz.

Mathilde carried a bucket in each hand walking toward the only pump in the neighborhood that still worked. It was not far from home but still a difficult walk past houses that no longer stood. She no longer wished to be here, no longer wished to be at all. She blanked them out, no longer saw them, but they remained. Those houses. The rubble.

"Ow," she cried at a stabbing pain. She had stubbed her foot on a grotesque fragment in the narrow pathway—all that remained of the street. Watch out woman, she scolded herself, you cannot be wandering the neighborhood daydreaming. How often had she heard that? "Mathilde, our little dreamer," they had said—her sister, her mother, her father; yes, even her father, the Captain; Johnny Head-In-Air, that was her, that was who she had been and still was.

Mathilde stared at the offending stone at her foot, a sooty black metal clump fused with shards of wood and plaster. What was it, she wondered, as she rubbed her sore foot against her other leg? Her sandals weren't suitable for walking the rubble strewn path, she thought, absently looking toward coal black walls, splintered trees, and the beat-down hedge. Suddenly, far off in the silence and barely audible, she heard a solo trumpet playing music filled with sweet emotion. Instantly she knew the Lustige Laube once stood here. The clump must have been a part of the bar tap fused by the bombs, explosions and fires.

Here at the Lustige Laube she had danced without a care, happy on a June afternoon so many immutable years before in another time. In peace time. Schmidtke, the leader of the brass band and solo trumpeter, had played his solo as she swept across the grass with her new husband, Franz, and Schmidtke winked at her. She danced so lightly and glowed so that even Schmidtke, who had seen so many beautiful brides in his lifetime and was rarely charmed, had winked and played just for her.

Heidrun, Mathilde's older sister and a pastor's wife, naturally had disliked Schmidtke's playful attention to the bride, as had her mother, Emilie Lisson, the officer's widow who insisted on being called Maman—accent on the second syllable, mind you—in the French manner rather than simply Mommy, but Mathilde's Franz had not cared at all. He was proud of his bride, and pleased that she was so pretty and excited, and he adored her, waiting on her hand and foot.

Heidrun, looking like she bit into a lemon had said, "That just takes the cake," and Maman replied, "You cannot expect much from him," her lips pinched in a frown. To them he was merely Franz Tegge, son of a streetcar conductor, merely a constable, a mismatch. Mathilde, a

Lisson, daughter of her father, the Captain, who had been honorably wounded in war and holder of the Iron Cross, deserved better. "It is lucky," Maman said to Mathilde while straightening the wedding dress, "that your father did not live to see your wedding."

Heidrun, who always played the role of big sister with passion, had planned the June wedding to be held in their big, dark preacher's manse with its even larger, darker garden, and had mapped out the details before Mathilde could say as much as one word. But this once Mathilde had prevailed; she stood up to both Maman and Heidrun. It was her day, her wedding day; neither Maman nor Heidrun would ruin it for her.

Mathilde had beamed and gone hand in hand with Franz following the band which, at a proper distance from the church of course, changed their tune to upbeat polkas, waltzes, and her favorite, the spirited polonaise. She recalled childhood Sunday school outings, and the polonaise, and the moment when the dignified band had broken into dance music. Her wedding day had happened for her, only her, and when they arrived at the Lustige Laube she danced so sprightly that even the jaded Schmidtke winked at her.

Without noticing, Mathilde stepped into the ruins of the former garden before the Lustige Laube, standing almost on the spot where the dance floor had been, and she smiled. Hermann, her brother-in-law, had, in fact, spoken to Schmidtke, but did not throw him out of the band for no one but Schmidtke could make the trumpet's sound seem like sweet flowing honey.

Mathilde tore herself from her daydream memories and moved on, but she continued to hear Schmidtke's honey sweet sound, which made everything around her more pleasant. The stench, the tumbled-down walls, the fear, and even the weariness in her bones was almost bearable until, just in front of her, she saw a dark figure bent over something. She knew, but did not want to know what was happening. Greedy, grasping hands were plundering a lifeless corpse of anything of value right down to his underwear. She turned her head, quickened her pace through the rubble, and the memory of Schmidtke's sound faded into the silence.

Schmidtke had fallen in those first days of the war. Perhaps it was better that way, to be spared all the destruction and misery.

She finally arrived at the pump where only a few people, like herself, had found the courage to leave their homes. They stood among shabby arbors and derelict gardens and no one spoke in the impenetrable silence. Only the squeak of the jerry-rigged, broken pump handle, worked with surgical precision by a team of three men, broke the silence. They mutely pumped water into wash basins, cans, jugs, anything that had survived the last days of bombs and inferno.

Mathilde looked at the dirt and debris on ill-fitted men's trousers and on the clothing of the women in line. She looked down at herself, realizing she was just as dirty, and unconsciously brushed plaster dust off her dress. It was her good dress, a deep-blue velvet with Brussels lace trim. She wanted to leave it in the closet, but everything else was soiled or torn and in need of mending and washing. Washing? When would she be able to wash again, to sew, and iron?

Reflexively she tore a loose button from her sleeve. In a few weeks she would be thirty-five, but she felt like a hundred. Her scalp itched, her once curly brown hair was dull and hung from her head like a mop. She longed for a visit to the hairdresser, a little care, and above all sleep, true, restful sleep. Her once full lips had become tight, not from unhappiness but from exhaustion and despair—a despair of war, and fear, and bombs, and battles, and screams. Despair from the horror of it all.

Once she had been elegant, now she was thin, almost haggard. Fatigue, deprivation, and hardship cast their shadows on her once round face, deep dark lines were etched around her little snub nose and her green eyes, eyes that were once limpid pools in summer, in peace time, oh, so many long years ago.

A piano of her own, that was her dream, but she could not afford it. There had been one in the grand apartment where she grew up. It stood in Maman Emilie's salon, an heirloom from her father's side of the family. Mathilde's father, the beloved Captain, descended from a Prussian-Huguenot line of officer families where sons learned to fence and daughters learned the spinet or piano. Maman finally sold their piano to pay the staff. They had to have staff even though they starved more than lived on the Captain's small disability pension. Their soup during the week became ever thinner, their underclothes and dresses ever more threadbare, but Captain Lisson still invited guests and their spouses for Sunday Souper. So it had always been, and so it would always be; so, fat floated on the consommé served out of fine porcelain tureens by maids wearing white sleeves and starched aprons.

1923 had been the height of inflation when a loaf of bread cost a billion Reichsmark, and they sold their piano for more money than they could count. Mathilde, at thirteen, had leaned against the Captain's chair as they watched it being moved out.

The Captain had returned from the First War with a wounded leg and never left his chair except to go to bed or the bathroom. Maman Emilie covered worn spots with hand-knitted coverlets so the chair could remain in the alcove of the only room facing the street that she had not sublet. The salon was necessary, even though the family had to crowd into two tiny maid's rooms. The larger, much nicer rooms with street views at the front of their stately Berlin residence in its most prestigious Wilmersdorf setting, had been rented to respectable single men.

Mathilde and her father, the Captain, together in the communal embrace of that fatherly easy chair mutely watched the calloused hands of strong men move the piano, her father's heirloom, out of the salon. She had played that piano and taken lessons from Miss Nebenich every Monday at three thirty for three years, and at a reasonable price. "Because the child is so talented," said Miss Nebenich, "and because artists do not look to filthy mammon." And because the dear lady, Maman, invited Miss Nebenich regularly to Sunday Souper where she enjoyed slightly watered-down sherry and offered learned discourse about Schubert's piano music.

Schubert or Mozart. Mathilde got a lump in her throat when she thought of Mozart and his famous A Major Sonata with the "Turkish March". She never finished learning it because Maman sold the piano and she could no longer practice. Then, as the piano money had dwindled, they could no longer have Sunday Soupers in the salon, and Miss Nebenich lost interest in Mathilde's talent.

Later, after Heidrun's husband, Hermann Steinhoff, had been ordained a pastor, she was allowed to play the organ at his church. She and her husband, Franz, had no money for a piano of her own, nor was there space for it in their modest apartment. She could have made room by moving the buffet to the attic, but she would not talk with Franz about it. To Franz her music was a frivolous whim of a Lisson from prestigious Wilmersdorf. No one paid good money for such a whim, no one. He had no sympathy for her whim even though he was a caring and, within limits, generous man.

Was? No, Mathilde thought. Not was, but is! He is still alive. She hung on to that hope, like an animal, instinctively. She prayed for him every night. It didn't hurt to help that hope a little.

Franz was right about the piano, more than he knew. It would have been destroyed by now, splintered into firewood by the Russians. She felt a chill recalling the Russians who were gone now, probably just for a little while, but at least they were gone.

Feeling the a chill she forced herself to look toward the spring sun, forced herself to think no more about the Russians while the sun shone warmly on her face. "Hey, are you asleep standing there?" The typical bark of a Berlin woman's voice, a heavy blow, a stab in the back.

Mathilde picked up her bucket and pushed up to the others who mechanically took a step toward the pump as the first in line filled his receptacles. They all stood silent, mute, and withdrawn as though unconscious. Keep going, keep on doing, thought Mathilde, and simply keep on.

So it had to go, waiting without illusion. Just as it was a few days ago, when they had been bunched together in holes, bunkers, sitting in cellars, surrounded, bound up, almost suffocated by the crashes, noise, the deadly din of the war; then, just as now, they retreated into silence. Each had turned inward for a little separation, for a little freedom from the unbearable closeness, from the horrible coerced community of the war.

Silence and fear. Wordless screams, mute whimpers, supressed sobs. The drone of airplanes came closer day after day, night after night. Louder, always louder. Sirens screeched, flak beat a staccato rhythm into the ceaseless cacophony, each sound layered one on top of the other, pitiless, unceasing, hurting more than fear. Drowned the cries, sobs, and whimpers. Drowned the silence.

"What are you waiting for, Mathilde?"

"Yeah, come on, Mama."

A hand tugged on Mathilde's arm. The hand of her only daughter, Karla, yanked Mathilde out of her stupor with all the force of her fourteen years. Finally she resisted the deadly cacophony outside that seemed to paralyze her and followed Karla down the cellar steps. Her older sister, Heidrun, was already at the foot of the steps with her youngest in her arms. Heidrun, the pastor's wife and Mutterkreuz awardee, marched toward the cellar door, and with a voice as clear and distinct as on Sundays in the choir where her voice was always recognizable, she asked Mathilde, "What were you thinking about?" Church choir, choir of sirens, choir of bombs.

Mathilde just shook her head. "Gerhild, give this to me." Her niece, Heidrun's six-year-old daughter, could barely lift their all-in-one bag, as the family called it, which held all the papers, savings books, everything of value; it was always close at hand and usually carefully hidden under the bed. Mathilde took the heavy bag from the child. She didn't know where her thoughts had been. Apparently nowhere, in a void that was more bearable than its opposite, life. It happened more and more in these, apparently, hopefully, last days of the war. These were endless days of "waiting for the final victory" that no one believed in anymore. They waited for the desired, feared end that wasn't quite there even though you could taste it, feel it. It forced itself into Mathilde's thoughts and pushed everything else out, pressed the pathways of her brain against the inside of her skull so that she could hardly move.

Karla and her younger cousin Horst, Heidrun's ten-year-old, stormed past Trimborn, the building's super who was posted in the cellar door, almost knocking him down.

"Hey, be careful!"

"Pardon, Mr. Trimborn, you know they didn't mean to." Heidrun nodded reassuringly to Trimborn.

It always amazed Mathilde just how many voices her sister had—

her singing voice, speaking voice, a voice that went from hard to soft, from sharp, domineering, or shrill to whining, ingratiating, sincere. Or polite and friendly, as now, but piercing no matter the situation, always piercing. A voice that even cut through the rumbling, the clattering, the screaming. A voice that unceasingly, inevitably, soared to a cloying crescendo. "Yeah, yeah," muttered Trimborn.

The pastor's wife was okay even though she and her brood spread out as if they were still in their pastor's house. She was brazen but at least she spoke. You could talk with her, unlike with her sister, Mrs. Tegge, the real renter in his house, who came down the narrow steps after her. She was so quiet that Trimborn thought she was a snob who felt better than everyone else, and he knew others thought the same of her. He knew all his folks, from the fifth floor on the right down to the ground floor on the left.

Heidrun shifted little Heinrich to her right hip, blew a strand of blonde hair out of her face that had come loose from the immaculately pinned up knot, and reached out for Gerhild who went down the steep stairs in front of Mathilde, holding tightly to the wall in fear. "Hurry, child, don't you hear the thunder?"

In fact, the all too familiar rumble outside got ever louder with the clatter of flak mixed in. An explosion came very close. Plaster dust drizzled from the walls, the house shivered, and quaked.

"In with you!" Trimborn shoved the two women with the children in front of him into the cellar, banged the doors shut, first an outer one, then the reinforced inner one, and slammed the bolt home.

The cellar was crammed full. It could hold no more. In truth, there were too many already. Everyone had taken someone in—friends, relatives, bombed out neighbors and refugees, during these last days since the firestorm raged over Berlin, and the allied planes dropped Christmas tree flares that glittered like very un-Christmas-like gifts.

Heidrun tugged her two youngest behind her through the thickly packed people in the cellar, greeting them left and right. Not everyone smiled at her, but they respectfully made way until she got to "her" corner, the corner in which Karla, Mathilde, and Franz had crouched during the air assaults on Berlin.

She reached her corner with her family, and stuffed the valuable bags under the little bench. "Make room," she said, squeezing between Karla and Horst. She shut her eyes, and held her breath, and waited. Waited like all the others sitting in the cellar.

Muted growls, harsh whistles, dry coughs of thousands of guns pressed in from everywhere. Mathilde could only guess where the bombs and the shells actually hit. She had learned to tell the difference between regular and incendiary bombs by their sound. She knew how an artillery shell sounded and could tell the difference between a Stalin's Organ and their own artillery. Friendly artillery grew weaker from month to month; their growls, bellows, rattles became fewer week to week. But so long as one still heard it, there was a battle. So long as the battle continued no one could surrender, not until the bitter end. If the SS discovered a white sheet in the window of a house . . . traitors to the Fatherland were still hung.

No one in their cellar dared to think of surrender. The building's super, Trimborn, had hung the Swastika flag out a window just a few days before, on April twentieth, Hitler's birthday. They feared Franz, Mathilde's husband, too, because of his position even though he had been drafted into the militia. Inwardly, Mathilde laughed at them. He was probably a rear echelon soldier just doing his duty, and if one was not guilty, what was there to worry about.

They sat in the cellar and waited. Even as the Russians pushed through the streets, they sat and waited. Hidden from the muffled sound of fighting that pressed in on them, the rattle of machine guns, the firing from tanks that sounded so different from bombs, they cowered, pressed together in the cellar. Each was alone in their own space despite their unbearable nearness. All were silent.

Elegant Heidrun, shrunken from exhaustion and cold and fear, held Heinrich in her arms. The two-year-old could sleep despite the noise, despite the concussions. Gerhild, who should have started school on Easter, sat on Mathilde's lap staring at her aunt with eyes wide with fear. Horst, too, had given up trying to be the strong man of the house and clung to Karla, his older cousin. Karla sat, eyes alert, her chin thrust forward checking on her family over, and over, and over again.

Heidrun prayed unceasingly, a pastor's wife's duty. She prayed for herself and all the people in the cellar, and for Frieder, her oldest, who was away in an Adolf-Hitler-School in Thuringia. She had not heard from him in weeks and prayed that her fourteen-year-old had not been drafted into the militia like her brother-in-law, Franz. She also prayed for her husband, Hermann, because it was her duty even though there was little reason to worry. The pastor had volunteered for chaplain"s duty in the army. Despite not hearing from him in months, she wasn"t worried because he did not have to fight. He was on the western front with troops pushed back from the Ardennes. What would it matter if he were a prisoner in either a British or American POW camp?

They huddled, pressed in, despite the distrust that had pulled them apart, separated, and divided them. They forgot their unseen borders as the noise of battle finally died down.

The unknown came close and their eyes went wide with fear. Boot steps and strange voices were heard outside. The cellar door, with its bolts and locks, was blown open.

Two Russian soldiers stormed in, strong farm boys. Machine pistols at the ready, their backs to the wall just inside the door, they glanced over the rows of fearful people. Other than Trimborn only two other men sat in the cellar, but they were both far over sixty, shook with fear, and presented no danger.

The Russians relaxed a bit. "Stay where you are!" one of them ordered and turned to go out with his comrade. Then Gerhild began to bawl.

The Russians turned back. The inhabitants of the cellar shot perplexed, angry glances at Heidrun and Mathilde, thinking their first danger was almost over and now . . . One of the two Russians looked suspiciously at the fearful, upset faces, the other fumbled around in his jacket pocket. The cellar mates hardly dared to breathe. Only Gerhild cried and screamed. Mathilde sought to calm the child, stroking her, whispering, kissing, but to no avail.

Heidrun shoved Heinrich to Karla, tore Gerhild from Mathilde"s lap. "Quiet or you'll get it."

The little girl shut up. Her fear of her mother's threat was greater than her fear of the strange men.

The second Russian found what he was looking for. He took a morsel of raisin bread out of his pocket, broke off a piece, tossed it, and Gerhild quickly caught it. Tensions relaxed. The Russian appreciated the child's quickness and laughed before he and his comrade vanished.

Heidrun took the sweet bread out of her daughter's hand and cut off Gerhild's protest. "First I will hear how quiet you can be, quiet like a little mouse." The child shut up again. The bread stayed in Heidrun's pocket. For later. For all. A little portion divided by four. Four hungry kids. The two mothers always went without, always gave up their share, yet it was never enough.

Hours later, during which time those who sat in the dark of the cellar whispered feverish rumors about "The Ivan" and waited without knowing what to do, the two Russians came back. One, who could speak a little German, advised them that the immediate danger was over. They could return to the apartments. But, the cellar occupants stared at the young soldiers. Could they trust these sub-humans? No one stood up, no one left.

The two Russians did not care. They brought more bread, a little bacon and cabbage, and gave it to Heidrun.

"Cooking," one said and grinned. "For children."

Heidrun nodded her thanks, held the food tightly, but made little move to get up. Their cellar mates looked over at Mathilde, at Heidrun, and their children. Mathilde knew what they thought; the constable's wife, the pastor's wife, those two always had it better. Now they got gifts. They won't share. "Love your neighbour" and Christian charity doesn't hold that much sway, not for them.

Even if charity had ruled, Heidrun would not have thought to share. The soldier who spoke a little German signaled Heidrun with his machine pistol to leave the cellar to go up to the apartment. Mathilde's apartment.

"*Dawai, dawai.*" the Russian ordered. Heidrun did not react. He repeated the unintelligible syllables, "*Dawai, dawai.*" His voice sounded angry.

Mathilde and Heidrun looked at each other, unable to move. What should they do? What did the Russians want from them? The second one made a commanding move with his head and rumbled something impatiently; slowly, resigned to their fate, the sisters stood up.

Heidrun dumped Heinrich on Karla's lap. "You stay here."

The two-year-old cried, "Mama, no!"

Gerhild also began to cry again, quietly this time, and Karla's eyes were dark with fear and defiance, glancing questioningly from her mother to her aunt while she held tightly to the struggling little boy who would not let go of his mother's sleeve.

With a jerk Heidrun tore herself loose from Heinrich and scolded. "Be quiet, everyone, stay together! Quiet!" She gathered up the food from the Russians, and started to follow them out to the cellar door, but Mathilde could not move her feet, could not move anything; it was as if she were paralyzed.

"What are you waiting for?" whispered Heidrun. "Let's go, out of here, before they want the children too."

"Children come with us," commanded one of the two Russians, one with a rosy face and blond forelock. "*Dawai!*"

Karla did not stir. She just looked at him as though she wanted to devour him and vomit him up at the same time. Gerhild and Horst clung to her making themselves a large mass, a clump of children no one could touch, move or carry away.

The Russians lost their patience and raised their guns. "Children too!"

Instinctively Mathilde put herself in between them, "Yes, yes, we are coming." She did not need to look at Heidrun to feel her repressed anger scalding her as she took Gerhild into her arms, "We are coming, yes."

She threw Karla such a decisive glance that she suddenly, quickly moved as if she had been on a spring. With Heinrich in her arms and Horst clinging to her skirt, Karla followed Heidrun behind the other Russian soldier, the thin one with dark hair, holding the Russian food in front of her like a shield. The blond soldier brought up the rear behind Mathilde and Gerhild.

It was as if they were going up the center aisle to the altar for a Thanksgiving service; the image popped into Mathilde's head. Heidrun carried the offering in front, the children followed eagerly, and they were thankful for the food that God gives them daily. This day God was named Ivan. Mathilde almost giggled, but she felt a poke in the back from the blond's gun barrel that shoved her toward the cellar door; so painful, so close, much too close.

A poke in the back, a hand shoving her toward the pump.

"We can't have that, a proper dreamer. Now, pull yourself together. You aren't the only one who hasn't slept in days."

It was the same coarse voice as before. Still Mathilde was thankful for the shove and the scolding. The interruption. She did not want to go any further in that little procession up the stairs to her apartment when after the meal . . . Yes, they had eaten, cabbage with bacon, potatoes, raisin bread, so rich tasting and warm which they had not had for a long time, but after the meal . . . Mathilde slammed that door in her mind shut. She forgot, she buried, she sealed up what had taken place. She turned around and looked into a pair of cloudy blinking eyes that were the only light in a face made dark tan from ill humor, consumption, and exhaustion. "You are right," she said, "I beg your pardon."

The woman muttered obligingly, surprised at the apology, pointed with her chin at the pump. "Go ahead, you are next."

Mathilde filled both buckets. She nodded goodbye to the lady, who paid no attention, and stepped by the three that worked the pump handle. At least she broke the silence with her remarks, thought Mathilde, this unbearable, insidious silence. Silence that ruled since the Russians had moved further on, without explanation or goodbyes a few days after they had rolled over the city, the neighborhood. Now they were gone, apparently, probably only for a short while, and had left behind them uncertainty. Uncertainty and fear.

They had awoken this morning to an unfamiliar silence, and had looked through the blown out windows into empty streets. Anxiously they asked themselves what it meant, what would happen now? The war was not officially over, the Germans had still not surrendered, even though "the Führer had fallen in the battle against Bolshevism." Russians trucks and tanks and troops were gone, out of their streets, out of their neighborhood, fighting somewhere else. The people remained temporarily alone in defeat, but the Russians would return soon and occupy the city.

But today they were alone, thought Mathilde. She would sleep on the sofa tonight. Alone. She wanted to sleep, sleep, nothing but sleep. She picked up her buckets and started home. The water splashed on her hands, but that did not bother her. She passed by the robbed corpse with its pale naked limbs, the shadow of unshaved cheeks with clouded eyeballs. It almost didn't bother her anymore. A cherry blossom floated into Mathilde's bucket to be pushed around by wood splinters that swam on the surface of the water from the broken pump handle.

Spontaneously, Mathilde put down her buckets, took the blossom and laid it on the face of the dead man, and closed his eyes. The cloudiness vanished. She gazed at the blossom, rosy white on dark blue shadows, and suddenly it seemed to her that she heard a bird sing in the silence.

TWO

The man standing in front of the house looked like an animal, alert, about to leap, ready to fight or flee. He cautiously scanned the area, pulled his wide-brimmed, coal-colored hat down over his face to obscure his olive complexion and black hair. Powerful hands were thrust deep into the pockets of his worn suit trousers as if they might betray him before he stepped into the entry, yet he wore a colourful patchwork vest over his white shirt, its sleeves rolled up revealing muscular arms. The vest spanned his powerful shoulders and wide chest and seemed about to burst. He knew the vest would stand out but did not care. The danger, for him, was over. He wanted to be recognized. The dangerous game of hide and seek was over, at least for the moment.

He stretched, and spit. A smile crept over his sharp-featured face with thick black eyebrows. It was much easier to get the address than he had feared. He asked at the post office, and in the midst of all the destruction, the house had remained intact. He didn't have to track the man he hunted. He didn't have to search the little notes, pieces of wallpaper, chalked directions that were hung, pasted and scrawled on the stubs of the ruined walls for relatives, friends, and spouses to follow.

If his good luck held, he thought, it was even possible that his man was home, that he would only have to climb a few stairs and knock on a few doors. Possible but unlikely. There weren't many men left in Germany. The few that were still alive roamed around, distraught, lost, and weak. He grinned. Finally weak.

He stood, undecided, before entering. There was no name bell or name plates, not even a front door. Before he could go in, the super, a sixtyish-year-old man in a dirty undershirt and stained pants accosted him. He looked so much like a super that Zille could have drawn him.

"What do you want here? Go on. Off with you," the old man grumbled, "Soon as the cat's away, the mice dance on the table." Trimborn must have been waiting behind the door.

The man used all his will power to control his anger, like a wild horse chomping at the bit. He had to stay reined in. "I need to find someone."

"No one you could be looking for lives here." The super stared at the stranger, at the hat, the vest, the olive skin of his arms and hands, but could not make eye contact. "Go on. Get out of here."

The raging wild horse strained at its reins. He knew this look, knew it from birth. He had to run from it for years, to hide, to disappear because of this look. This look had become his life, and for this look, for this life, he would now claim revenge. But not yet. Now he had to control himself. It was too early to show his hand. Honest anger has a long life.

He turned without a word and left the house, left the super standing there muttering. Across the street he sat down on a pile of rubble, took out a pack of Camels and smoked, forcing himself to be calm. Forcing himself to think of the next step, and the next. That is how it would be done. That was part of his job. It was necessary for survival. It was how he had survived all through these last years.

The cardboard that covered the glassless window moved, and he could see the super's face staring at him from behind it. He laughed to himself knowing the super feared he was being watched. He knew the super was afraid, afraid of him, and that he envied the man's cigarette.

No doubt the super was asking himself, how did this guy come by American cigarettes? The Amis were holding on the Elbe and may or may not come into the capital. He must have used trickery. That's how his kind got everything. So it had always been. So it would always be.

The man grimaced contemptuously. He knew that envy, that confusion, that fear. He sat. He waited.

Two, three cigarettes later he saw a girl about six-years-old and with spiky blonde hair come out of the house. She went down the street with her milk can. If I'm lucky, the man thought, I will learn what I need from her. He stood up, followed her and caught up to her. He walked beside her for a few steps until he spoke up, "What do you think, are we going to get anything today?"

The girl looked up at him with large uncertain eyes. Fear, he thought, fear was all he could see in the eyes of the children, but he had no pity. It was only fair that the German kids had learned fear just like the children of his people. The girl looked at him a moment with her fearful eyes, shrugged her shoulders and went on.

"Yeah, well, they might be out already, you think? If they don't have milk, then maybe at least some curds?"

The girl shrugged her shoulders again and kept her face straight ahead.

"Look there," he said looking skyward. The girl automatically looked up and saw nothing until he thrust his hand into the air and, like that, he had a bonbon in his hand. He extended his hand to the girl. "Please, for you."

Just as the girl went to grab it, it disappeared from that magic hand.

The girl looked baffled as the man reached behind her ear, pulled the bonbon out again, and offered it to her anew. "There it is!" he said.

The girl smiled shyly and carefully took the bonbon, unsure whether it might disappear again. She quickly unwrapped the candy and stuck it in her mouth.

"What's your name?" the man asked.

"Gerhild. And yours?" She slapped herself on the mouth. "Excuse me please, and 'yours, Sir' I meant to say."

"You don't have to call me sir."

"But I must. We are not related at all."

"Then I am not allowed to call you Gerhild but Miss So-and-so. What would it be?"

The girl laughed, an open, bright child's laugh. "You cannot call me Miss Steinhoff either."

"Why not?"

"I am a child. People use the familiar to children and the formal to adults."

"But one can change it around."

"I don't know." Gerhild thought, shook her head, her spiky hair whipping back and forth. "No, that is not allowed, that is what my mom would say."

The man did not answer. They stumbled a few steps beside each other over the rubble, slid down, dug in their heels. Then Gerhild peeked over at him, wanting to ask something but didn't dare.

"Now I am sure you want to know what my name is."

Gerhild nodded.

"I don't have a name."

"Not possible. Everyone has a name." The girl chewed the rest of the bonbon and looked at him amazed.

"Do you want to give me one?"

Gerhild looked at him doubtfully. "Didn't your father and mother give you one?"

"No, they must have forgotten."

"But because of that, they gave you magic. Are you a magician?"

The man shook his head sadly. "No. I only wish, but in reality I am no magician."

They approached the milk store in the basement of a house that was three quarters destroyed. A line of people stood in front of it, but it wasn't yet open. Gerhild and the man joined the line. "And, do you live over there?" He indicated the direction from which they came.

The child nodded seriously. "Not really, but we were bombed out and we're staying with my aunt."

"Is she also a Steinhoff?"

The question seemed to amuse Gerhild. "No, she has another name. She is married to Uncle Franz after all."

"Uncle Franz?" The man raised his thick eyebrows. "Okay, that explains it." He laughed. "That was dumb of me. Does your aunt have children?"

"Only one. Karla, my cousin."

"And you, do you have siblings?"

"Three brothers."

"And you all stay with your aunt?"

"Yes." Gerhild didn't look too happy about it.

"It must be pretty crowded there, with so many in one apartment."

Gerhild nodded vigorously.

"And when Dad and Uncle Franz come home . . ." She shivered, seemed to picture what it would be like then, but she thought of something else. "Can you do some more magic?" She smiled at the man with pleading eyes. "Even if you are not really a magician?"

"Another bonbon?"

"Oh, yes, please."

The man motioned to her. "Look in the milk can."

She did, and cheered. Five bonbons lay in there. The woman in line in front of them turned around and looked suspiciously at the man but didn't say anything. Her child stared enviously at the bonbons.

"One is for you, the others for your brothers and your cousin," explained the man.

Gerhild put the bonbons in her pocket. "I will save mine for later. Otherwise, they will all have one and I won't anymore."

The man nodded. "Good idea."

Suddenly Gerhild's eyes got even bigger than before, she looked up at him seriously. "I completely forgot to thank you."

"No big thing. I saw that you enjoyed it." He stroked Gerhild's head, and by doing so stroked away his own embarrassment that the child's warm trusting look had raised in him.

"And you are still a magician. Even if you don't admit it. Your eyes twinkle funny."

The man smiled wryly. He had brown eyes with amber flecks. The child was not the first to comment on his eyes, but before he could continue, Gerhild was pulled away. A boy, about fourteen years old, pulled her toward him. "What are you doing?"

"Leave me alone." Gerhild turned around so forcefully that the boy momentarily lost his grip and stood there surprised. "The man is a magician, Frieder," she said gaily. "He did an amazing trick with bonbons! One for you, too." She pulled the sweets out of the pocket of her little dress, and held them out to him.

Frieder was over his surprise and knocked them out of her hand. "You know that you are not allowed to speak to strangers. And that you shouldn't take any bonbons. You know that." He pulled her further and shoved her down the street toward home even though she cried, hit, scratched, and bit him.

The man saw the woman in front of him nodding her head and guessed what she was thinking. The boy did right. Had it gone on, this vagrant would have done whatever he wished. Even so, she did not mind that her child grabbed up all the bonbons.

He smiled disgustedly. That's the way they were, these Germans. Then he lit another Camel in sight of the envious woman and left.

* * *

Mathilde could understand Heidrun's anger, but most of all she shared her fear. Still the way Gerhild bravely, miserably tried to hold back tears in front of her mother, and brother, tore at Mathilde's heart.

"How many times have I told you not to talk to strange men? How many?" Heidrun was in the middle of scolding as she sacrificed a little of their costly kindling to heat some oil in a pot. "Lucky for you that Frieder came by just then. Who knows what would have happened?"

"He was a Gypsy," said Frieder. The fourteen-year-old had suddenly appeared at the door two days ago. The Adolf-Hitler-School students were sent home by a teacher who had the foresight to see the outcome of the situation and sent them away with the strict order to not undertake any Werewolf activities. They would be called if necessary. The boys gritted their teeth, obeyed, and set out on the long dangerous journeys to their parents' homes through the brutal apocalyptic landscape that had once been the German Reich.

"Gypsy," Frieder went on, "or Jew. Either way he didn't look normal."

"That's great!" Heidrun stepped to Gerhild and boxed her ears. The girl began to howl, making Heidrun even angrier. "Child, how could you be so dumb?"

In the background, the radio broadcast announcements from the Soviet Supreme Commander. The quiet had not held. After the first wave of Russians, the frontline troops had moved on and were followed by a second wave—the occupation troops. And a few months later in July, the Americans and Brits would follow and set up defined occupation areas.

"Did he give you anything?" Heidrun had to turn back to the range as the oil steamed, bubbled, and sizzled while she kept up the interrogation. Gerhild could not answer, sniffling, and gasping for breath. "I asked you something!" Heidrun raised her hand to strike and with the other hand threw some peas in the boiling liquid.

Through her tears, Gerhild nodded. "Bonbons," she sniffled, "but I wasn't allowed to keep them." She threw a glance at Frieder.

That prompted another scolding. "I told you a thousand times, you should never take anything from strangers, a thousand times! And quit howling. That doesn't get you anywhere."

Gerhild sniffed her runny nose and tried to swallow her tears.

Heidrun shook her head again, and again with bitter disappointment, and Mathilde saw Maman in front of her. She reacted just like that when they were kids. Maman never struck her children as Heidrun did, but her displeasure, the bitter disapproving pinched face and angry lips hurt more than any slaps could have.

". . . and since you came home with no milk," Heidrun scolded on, "you will go to bed without supper."

Gerhild's eyes pleaded for pardon and wandered to the simmering pot from which rose an unusual aroma that spread like a poison cloud throughout the kitchen. "But I am so hungry," she said.

They were all hungry, always hungry. Since the Russians, with their bacon, bread, and vodka had been gone, the family relied on scant greens from the backyards and rations the Russian Kommandatura passed out. Rabbit food, the kids called it. They would rather have had the rabbits and fed it to them. The greens did not stretch far enough, and even if they could get some meat, it was often spoiled like the rancid oil Heidrun tried to make usable again with the help of the pea trick.

"Off you go, quick march!" The tone of Heidrun's voice allowed no back talk. Gerhild trundled off, sobbing, even though she tried not to.

"You did well." Heidrun turned to Frieder.

"Not at all," Karla shot back. Mathilde had noticed her daughter was starting to boil for several minutes, like the oil on the stove. Now she boiled over in an angry fountain.

Heidrun was shocked. "What? Should Frieder have let Gerhild just stand there? With a Gypsy?"

"How does Frieder know he was a Gypsy? Or a Jew? Maybe he was only being nice."

"I learned how the races look in school, and that's how they look."

Karla chided him derisively. "Oh, really? Which was he then, Gypsy or Jew?"

"I didn't see him long enough," said Frieder defiantly. He was only a few months older than his cousin, Karla. Those few months, and the fact that he was male, made his opinion worthy, so to speak, as far as that went, but Karla would have none of that, not her, and not now.

"But he was no German, of that I am sure," Frieder went on. "And there was no guarantee he was nice."

"Regardless, it doesn't matter," interrupted Heidrun raising her voice, gesturing with a wooden spoon. "A girl takes nothing from strange men. That is much too dangerous."

Mathilde attempted to mediate. "Perhaps he did really just want to be nice, but you just can't tell. What Frieder did was right."

The boy tossed a "see, I win" glance at Karla. They had always vied with one another, not just since Frieder had joined them after making his weary journey home from Thuringia. They fought when they had first met as small children. To equal Frieder's greater strength Karla relied on her wit, sarcasm, and sneakiness. Like that time a couple of years ago when Frieder joined the Hitler Youth; he was a Pimpf, their lowest rank, and the youngest in the Pack. Karla had secretly sewn a cloth heart on his uniform so he would get teased by his comrades. Frieder's father, Hermann, had made a special visit to threaten her with a sound thrashing because, beside being the butt of jokes, Frieder also had to endure a reprimand from his Pack master for not paying attention to his uniform; a tirade Hermann immediately passed on to Karla. The uniform was a holy icon, not something to be trifled with. Franz had to step in to keep Hermann from hitting her, and Karla had been grounded for a week. Frieder swor eternal revenge.

Karla was never one to give in. "What could have happened? Other people were standing there. But you had to trumpet yourself like some great knight."

"Karla, please!" Mathilde wanted her daughter to stop. It had already gone on long enough, her incessant bickering with Frieder on top of the seven of them living in one small apartment. It was too much.

Karla went on, oblivious. "If the man was so unbelievably dangerous, Frieder should have stayed with her. At least then we would have milk, and nothing would have happened but no. Sir Knight just had to be a hero."

Mathilde saw Karla's cheeks flush as she tensed, leaned forward and glared at Frieder. That girl sometimes acts more like a cat than a girl, her mother thought.

"It was not his job. It was Gerhild's," Heidrun said, lifting the pot off the fire as if she wanted to cool down the heat of the sparring as well as the oil, "and that she did not do."

"Frieder didn't do his either. He was supposed to find wood. . . ."

"Stop, now!" Heidrun held the seething hot oil pot in her hand, almost a threat. She wanted to drum some respect into her niece, but had to control herself.

Mathilde realized Heidrun had gotten to the point that she wanted to box Karla's ears, as she had with Gerhild, and became unusually fearful. No, not that. She wasn't going to let Heidrun beat Karla. "You two," she said emphatically to her daughter and her nephew, "go together to find wood."

A pause . . . Heidrun put the pot down, and Mathilde breathed again in the quiet.

Karla's glance became more obstinate. "I'm supposed to take care of Heinrich."

"I'll do that myself," Heidrun said. "You help Frieder, and hush! Oh, and take little Horst with you."

Horst pleaded. "Mom, please no. My feet." The ten-year-old had outgrown the last pair of shoes he owned and couldn't wear them no matter how hard he tried, not even with the toes cut open. He had taken to running around barefoot and promptly stepped in a bunch of broken glass. Sorrowfully he pointed to the blood soaked bandages on his feet.

Heidrun offered no pity. "Pay better attention where you walk in the future. I tell you all the time, he who runs barefoot must pay special attention. So, now go to the line at the baker. Trimborn said there might be bread today." Heidrun cut a few food rations out of the book, put them in Horst's hand, and looked at Karla. "Take care that he doesn't lose them. And you, Horst, don't say a word to anyone you don't know, is that clear?"

"Why should I have to look after Horst? Frieder can do that. He is his brother after all."

"But you are a girl." Frieder grinned.

"Go now!" Heidrun ordered.

Karla glared at Heidrun without moving, and Mathilde almost expected she would attack her aunt, but then she appeared to have thought better of it. She took Horst by the hand as he hobbled along, and the three children left.

Mathilde watched her daughter go, and something like envy rose within her. She, herself, had often disagreed with Heidrun but had said nothing.

Heinrich began to fuss because he was hungry, and Heidrun rocked him slowly in her arms.

Mathilde said, "Karla was right. Frieder would have done better to wait with Gerhild at the milk store."

"Now you are going to pick on the poor boy," Heidrun shot back, waving her free hand through the steam that came from the oil so she could sniff it. Ah, she thought, the pea trick that Mrs. Trimborn had told her about seemed to really work. The spoiled oil was indeed useable again. The peas and firewood were not wasted, and her anger slowly faded like the rancid odor. "Frieder has it hard enough. He is the only man in the house for all of his fourteen years."

Mathilde looked irritated at her sister. Frieder, the man of the house? Not from where she sat, he wasn't.

* * *

Mathilde went to find Horst, expecting him to be in line at the bakery, but he was nowhere in sight. Her worry quickly became fear. Maybe he met a molester just as Gerhild had. Worse, there was no sign of either Frieder or Karla. She asked others in line if they had seen them, but no one had. She forced herself to swallow her anxiety as she searched through the rubble, the ruins and yards, asking anyone she found if they had seen them, but no one had. No one knew anything.

On a corner at the border of their neighbourhood, where the children were not supposed to go, she saw a man leaning on the remains of a streetlamp post. He was smoking and looked Italian, or maybe a Spaniard. Could this be the Jew or Gypsy that enchanted Gerhild? Or the molester Heidrun feared? She calmed herself with the thought that, were he such a man, he surely would not be hanging around casually smoking.

The man straightened up from the lamp post, flipped his half-smoked cigarette away and walked over to her as though he had heard her thoughts loud and clear. Unnerved, Mathilde could not look at him.

"Something wrong?" he asked. He stood close in front of her and seemed not at all unfriendly.

"No, no, nothing. I was only . . ."

An unexpected smile came over his face revealing glistening white teeth. He must be healthy, she thought. Healthy, powerful, full of life. No German man was like that these days. And he wore that colorful vest. Without realizing it Mathilde looked down at herself, at her stained, spotted, much-mended everyday dress whose colors were so faded and dust covered. It mirrored how she, herself, felt.

"You looked as if you wanted to ask me something."

Something unusual rang in his voice, in his manner of speaking, something unknown, yet familiar to Mathilde. Familiar, like music.

"I am looking for children." Mathilde pulled herself together. "Two boys, ten and fourteen. The younger one is barefoot. And a girl, fourteen, with brown hair. My daughter. Have you seen them?"

He nodded. "They have been past here. The little one stands over there at the bakery."

"Thank you." Mathilde looked in the direction he pointed and felt a weight lifted from her shoulders as she saw Horst in front of a bakery they didn't usually go to.

"Thank you so much," she said as she left, knowing he watched her as she ran to Horst. She felt his presence behind her. She recalled Schmidtke, how he had winked at her as he played the trumpet for her, for her alone. Mathilde trembled with a sudden chill.

The man went back to the light post and watched with contented satisfaction as a passer-by knelt to collect his discarded cigarette butt, taking a deep pull on it before moving on.

Mathilde reached her nephew. Worry and anger fought within her. "What are you doing here? Why aren't you where we always go? Don't you know how much I worried about you? How come I find you here?"

"Karla told me to," stuttered Horst.

"Yes, and? Why are you standing here?"

"Because Frieder said the line was shorter."

Mathilde shook her head, still angry. "How could he know that? He has only been home two days."

"That is what Karla asked him, but he said that he simply knew and she should keep her mouth shut. Then they started arguing." Horst looked at his aunt pleadingly. "I can't do anything else, really. And my feet hurt."

Mathilde patted him on the head.

"I know. Where are they off to now?"

"Gathering wood," he said, pointing to a patch of rubble a couple of hundred meters down the dismal remains of a street. "Frieder said that they could get pieces of a roof frame."

"Wait here a bit! Sit down and scoot forwards when it is your turn to move. I'll fetch them here."

Horst dropped down between the legs of those standing in line, wincing as he did so. Mathilde went in a quick march in the direction Horst had pointed. She soon heard Karla and Frieder shouting in the distance, arguing, of all things, over a piece of wood.

"I have already figured out how long and thick the piece must be to burn best in our stove," the boy said and handed his cousin a saw. "So do it."

"You lie."

"If it is exactly so," he said, extending his hands, "it burns just long enough for Mom to cook, and we don't waste any wood."

"Did you learn that at your wonderful school?" Karla's scorn was unmistakable.

Frieder ignored her. "Ordinary physics," he said, "as any True German would know."

"There aren't any more 'True Germans'," interjected Karla. "The Amis got them all, or The Ivan."

"How can you say something like that? You are a traitor to the Fatherland! Do as I told you. Now."

"So you want to boss me around? Mama's boy!"

Frieder turned pale. "What did you say?"

Karla knew she struck home. "Mommy's boy! Afraid of the Bad Uncle, so he grabbed his little sister and ran home. Mommy, mommy, the Bad Uncle gave us bonbons. . . . "

"Say that again!" Frieder, furious, raised his fists, but Karla would not give an inch.

"Sure," she taunted, "beat up on women. You should be good at that. But something useful? No, not you."

She pointed high up to an attic apartment in a building whose front side had been sheared off by a bomb. Part of the kitchen floor hung suspended over destroyed floors and a stairwell. It was held up by two outer walls at right angles to each other and looked ready to fall at any moment. Oddly the kitchen table was still covered by a tablecloth, scorched and fluttering in the wind.

"What do you think a person could find up there? Coal probably, maybe even coffee, or preserves, lentils, barley, sugar, but not for you, Mama's boy. You are afraid of heights, you coward!" Frieder quaked and grimaced, and Mathilde understood his caution, but Karla's teasing continued. "Tough as leather, fast as a greyhound. Didn't they teach you that in your fancy school?"

Frieder turned and stomped up to the house.

Mathilde tried to call out, "Frieder, no!" The words stuck in her throat, and Frieder began to climb. The boy was agile, and strong. He climbed to the first floor, then the second floor, and held there for a moment, looked around, and latched onto a sewer pipe that ran along the wall up to the third floor. He stopped, unable to go further. The sewer pipe was broken off, and the third floor was a just meter-wide masonry ledge spanning the side walls overlooking a gaping hole all the way to the ground. Opposite was another pipe that went up to the attic apartment, but to reach it he had to leap the abyss, or scale the tile wall. He studied his options, but with all his courage and skill it seemed an impossible task. He steeled himself against the ridicule Karla would heap on him and reluctantly climbed down.

"Thank God," whispered Mathilde, happy the spat was over.

Frieder had hardly gotten back to the ground when Karla started mocking him. "See, you couldn't do it. Were you afraid, Mama's boy?"

"It can't be done." Frieder thrust his chin out. "Impossible. No one can get up there."

"Sure it can be done. If you aren't a fraidy-cat. It was right there within reach, you Wolf cub." Karla laughed at Frieder's balled fists. "You pink-fisted coward."

Frieder decided that his manhood fared better if he stayed calm and lowered his fists. It was not right to hit girls. "Well, if you are so brave, you show me how. *You* show me how!"

"Gladly." Karla quickly started up.

Mathilde glared and called out, "Karla, no! What has gotten into you?" Karla seemed to not hear her mother as Mathilde ran after her, grabbed her arm, and held her fast. "I forbid it, stop this child's play!"

Karla wrenched loose, out of her grasp, and stomped away. "I don't need permission from you. You give in to everyone every time. Well, it is time that someone shuts his mouth and Aunt Heidrun's as well."

"Please, Karla!" Mathilde's voice broke. "That is foolishness, dangerous foolishness." Mathilde was left frustrated, and angry that Karla would not mind her. She watched, surprised at her daughter's agility, as she went up the same way as Frieder and made it to the third floor. There she grabbed a hanging electric wire and tested its hold. Mathilde held her breath. Surely Karla would not . . . but she did.

Karla put her weight on the wire, testing it again without taking her feet off the ledge. It held. Using the wire, she swung over the gaping hole and grasped for the pipe on the other side, but missed.

Mathilde's mouth went dry. Her scream was hardly more than a rasp.

Karla swung back and this time she made it to the ledge and clambered back onto it.

"Karla, please!" cried Mathilde. "Come back. You can see it won't work. You will kill yourself."

In the meantime, a few other people joined Frieder and Mathilde and stared at the girl more than ten meters high above the jagged, sharp and tumbled rubble beneath her.

"Karla!"

Karla heard Mathilde's voice break but paid no attention. She would not give up. She grabbed the wire, took a few running steps this time, jumped again . . . and this time it appeared she was actually going to make it, but at the apex of her swing, as she was about to grab the pipe, there was a jolt. The wire tore about two feet out of the deck.

The crowd groaned. Mathilde stuffed her fist in her mouth to keep from screaming.

Karla was just able to reach the pipe and grab it to hold on, but she was out of breath, hanging in the air by her fingers hardly able to hold her weight. She dangled a little, back and forth, like the wire which she had let go to grab the pipe. To pull herself up on the pipe and climb to the attic apartment as she wanted was impossible from this position.

Karla tried to find a perch with her feet and finally found a protruding stone she could brace herself on. She tried to pull herself up but could not. At least she could relax her hands a little. The onlookers released a sigh. The imminent danger that the girl would fall passed for the moment. But only for the moment.

Karla looked to the left, to the right, up and down. She realized just what a mess she was in. No handholds. No chance to get back on her own power. She called for help. The people who stood below just looked up and gaped. There was no way they could help her unless someone could do the impossible, and scale along the sheer tile wall.

Mathilde held her breath, and almost fainted, unable to grasp what was happening. They had made it. They made it through the war, they survived, they made it past the Russians, and now this? It was not possible, it could not be. Someone must do something.

Someone must stop the catastrophe. Karla feared for her life, and Mathilde suffered with her, but no one could help.

The spectators looked on helplessly. One cried out to get the fire department; they might be able to reach her with a ladder truck. Another answered, "They have more important things to do." A third chided, "It's all nonsense, she could not hold out until they got here." Frieder stammered, "I didn't want this, I really didn't want this."

A murmur went through the crowd, the sound of astonishment. Unbelieving Mathilde took her hands from her face. Could there be some hope? She looked up and saw a figure slowly working his way from the ledge on the third floor along the wall toward Karla who was holding on with her last strength. The man, wearing only dark pants, clung to the wall like a fly, his fingers forcing themselves into joints, his bare toes finding holds in the narrowest cracks. Centimeter by centimeter he crept closer to Karla.

"I can't hold on any more," Karla gasped in the suddenly breathless silence and was clearly heard by those standing below. The mood changed. A voice called to the girl to hold on, that rescue was close, only a few moments more for her to hold strong. Mathilde bit her knuckles bloody and shivered, her eyes riveted on the figure moving high over the rocky jagged ground. Who was he? Please, she prayed, please save my daughter.

The climber was just a few centimeters away from Karla. Her grip was slipping. Her hands were losing strength. Millimeter by millimeter she slipped, no matter how hard she tried to hold on. It was seconds before she would fall.

The man, whose face was pressed to the wall, had reached the pipe, grabbed hold of it, and held fast. Karla screamed as she slipped a little further, the last little bit. The man held himself with one hand on the pipe and grasped Karla's hand with the other. Now the full weight of both bodies hung on his one hand holding onto the pipe. Effortlessly, he pulled Karla up high enough that she could get her elbow onto the pipe, and then she put her knee on it and could climb up. Approval roared from the crowd, and Mathilde could not stop murmuring, "Thank you, Lord, thank you, Lord, thank you, Lord."

"Can I let loose for a moment?" asked Karla's rescuer. She nodded. He used his second hand to help and swung himself high like he was a gymnast mounting a horse from a standstill. He pulled himself up next to Karla on the pipe, took her by the hand, and guided her gently to her feet. Slowly, step by step, they balanced themselves on the pipe and climbed to the remainder of the attic apartment's kitchen.

Tears of gratitude ran down Mathilde's cheeks. Cries of "Bravo!" rang out, many applauded. When they reached the top the man seated Karla on a chair. She put her head in her hands, breathing heavily, and stared out into space. Shudders ran through her body. The man walked to the edge of the floor and stood there a moment, looking down. They would not have been surprised if he had waved an imaginary hat, or bowed, but he didn't. He called down to the watching crowd telling them to find him a rope, and throw it up to him. Mathilde recognized him. He was the same man she had met a few minutes earlier, the man who directed her to Horst.

Frieder murmured, "That is the one with the bonbons."

The rope was fetched. Frieder climbed once again to the second floor and threw it high. The man broke off a chair leg, clamped it across an empty doorway, tested the strength of the construction, tied the rope around the chair leg, and took Karla on his back. She held tightly to him and slid with him down the rope to the ground.

Mathilde held Karla in her arms. She was much too elated to scold Karla, and Karla leaned heavily on her mother, sobbed and sniffled in relief, as her mother softly stroked her hair and patted her back. Over Karla's shoulder, Mathilde's glance fell on the man who had put his shirt and vest back on and lit a cigarette. He hardly noticed the praise, the slaps on the shoulder from thankful bystanders. He looked as if he thought he had made a mistake instead of performing an heroic deed. The remarkable amber-colored flecks in his brown eyes did not flash, they were dim, quenched.

Mathilde let go of her daughter and walked up to him. "Thanks," she said. Only a word, yet her word made the man shiver as if chilled; within her word was an unreal warmth that he had long since quit expecting from anyone, much less a German.

"I would be honored if you would come dine with us," Mathilde said, paying no attention to the strange look Frieder threw her. She expected his attitude; that the Gypsy had rescued Karla was well and good, even if it was the little snipe's own fault. In spite of that, she should just not bring him home. But Mathilde had other concerns. "We don't have much. I will try to round up something, but you surely know how the times are," she said, suddenly astounded by her own courage. How could she invite someone when she had nothing to offer? And a stranger at that. She looked at him, and he no longer looked so powerful but rather conflicted, alone, lost, and, with that, somehow no longer so strange. He seemed to really need the company of other people.

He didn't answer.

"Excuse me please. I should have introduced myself first. I am Mathilde Tegge and that is my daughter, Karla."

Karla smiled at her rescuer. "Thank you," she said, and she meant it, too.

"It was nothing." He smiled back at Karla and his eyes lost some of their clouds. "Camillo Baumgartner." He held out his hand to Mathilde. The hand that had saved Karla's life.

Mathilde took the hand, sinewy and strong, but not as hard or calloused as she had expected. "Will you come, this evening?"

Still Baumgartner hesitated. "Only if you allow me to contribute. Only if I can bring something, too."

"No. That's not necessary, really."

"But why not?" Camillo Baumgartner smiled easily. It was as if he found new strength from Mathilde's touch, and amber-colored flecks sparkled in his eyes.

THREE

He stood staring at the entrance. The sign by the door was new, its colors brighter. The old one must have been somewhat larger. The holes from which it had hung shone darkly over the corners of the new one. The Stars and Stripes now waved from the flag pole where the Swastika flag once fluttered. The former city hall which he assumed had been the seat of Nazi party leaders was not damaged. Allied bombers had not attacked this small town where he now stood. He had reached his goal, had arrived at the provisional headquarters of the American Army for this region, somewhere between Magdeburg and Halle.

He had asked directions along the way. People answered even though they were worried, doubtful, and mistrusting. He knew why. The coat. It was a thick black wool coat in relatively good condition. Even though the shoulder epaulets and insignia had been ripped off it was easily recognizable as the uniform coat of the SS. Franz Tegge could not bring himself to discard it even though it was hot and sweaty in the spring sunshine, even though it might put him in danger. While he was growing up no one could afford to throw anything away if it was at all usable, and that was even truer in these times. Who knew when you could ever get such a good warm coat again? For that matter, who knew when you could get anything at all?

People looked at Franz, and at the coat. They were still intimidated by him, and by this piece of clothing. What nonsense, Franz thought. It was over, long over. It was over for him just as it was for them.

At least he could find his own way—wherever his path would end. It had been hard enough, but so far he had survived. He had been able to make his own choice to get to where he stood right now, in front of the American headquarters, instead of being dragged to the Russian Kommandatura. If that had happened, if the Russians had found him first, he would have been shot immediately, at best, or imprisoned and tortured to death. At least the Americans would not do that. They would not ship him off to Siberia. That was all he could hope for at this point.

He had done it, but hesitated to go in. He enjoyed his last moments of freedom, enjoyed the sun which, like an ironic commentary from a God he didn't believe in, shone unhindered this May. He was policeman enough to know he must give himself up. He knew that he could not escape, not that he had been such a bright light that there would have been an intensive hunt for him. No, not for him. He was only a minor official that had the bad, good luck to have worked in Berlin. He had just done his duty.

No, he was no great prize, but he knew what it meant to be wanted for prosecution, and he knew himself well enough to know that he wouldn't be able to handle the fear of being discovered. He would never be free of the fear that he would be rousted out of bed by the American, Russian, or English military police. Of course he knew this fear only from the other side of the coin, but it had screamed at him through every pore of those he had arrested, even when they had let themselves be taken quietly.

Franz looked around. Only a few people were on the street. They hastened by, pale, exhausted, eyes lowered, shoulders hunched forward. Some had their collars turned up even though it was not cold. Some kids crowded around a black GI who was passing out chewing gum. Franz was disgusted at the mere thought of the sweet sticky stuff and popped a licorice lozenge in his mouth. He savored the sharp taste on his tongue. Not for the first time, he thought, the Führer had been right. Such people did not deserve him. Not the Führer, and not victory; a victory that black apes and Russian peasant dolts had achieved.

As for himself, there was another advantage of his position: The war had by and large passed him by. He only really got into it right at the end. Again his luck was such that while he was defending the homeland at the edge of Magdeburg the Russians overran Berlin. It did not take much imagination to know what they had done there. Franz gulped, his worry about Mathilde, about Karla, about his little family, stuck like a lump in this throat.

He could not change that now. It was too late. He took a deep breath, steeled himself, and went up to the building.

The GI sentry stopped him. "Stop. What do you want?"

Franz couldn't understand what the GI said. "Police . . . ," he answered in hopes the soldier had asked what he wanted. "I want to speak to the police." Franz spoke carefully, word for word, as he had rehearsed.

"You can't get in here. There are no police here. Fuck off!" The GI waved him away with one hand and raised his weapon in a threatening manner with the other. His buddy came out. "You need help?" he asked. The first GI shook his head.

Franz took out his ID, his police identification, and gave it to the sentry. The GI glanced quickly at the paper, saw the SS insignia, and grabbed Franz by the arm. "This is a fucking Nazi!"

The other one also grabbed him and brutally pulled his arm behind his back. The two then shoved him into the building, past an empty monument alcove that had held a Hitler bust just a few days ago, into a small room. The window was barred.

"You stay here, okay?" The soldier's voice sent icicles up Franz's spine. The bile of fear again burned, leaving the after taste of vomit in his throat. Yeah, he would stay, he would not run away. Why would he? He wanted to be here. The two GIs left the room. Franz heard a key turn in the lock. There was no going back. He was here now, in an office emptied of its regalia and cupboards and made into a cell. He sat down on the only chair in the room and waited.

* * *

Peace had come four days ago. Four days since the German Reich went under, collapsed into chaos, into a confusion that Franz had not imagined possible even in his worst nightmares. Four days since it was officially over. Four days since it was "peace." Four days during which he was isolated. Four days in which he decided for himself what he should do.

Five days ago he had been ordered to defend a village in Sachsen-Anhalt. Franz Tegge, chief detective, automatically had become Unterscharführer in the SS and a sergeant in the Volkssturm, the last reserves of fifteen-year-old boys and grandfathers. He and three others, had been ordered to defend a brook in the middle of a meadow against the Russians who had already surrounded Berlin and most likely had long since taken it.

They all knew that it was over, but they could not disobey an order to defend the homeland, they had to fight on. They dug in to the left and right of a little wooden bridge that went over the brook. Franz was the youngest, except for a sixteen-year-old who could hardly carry a rifle, but he was in command because of his rank. It was his responsibility to carry out orders; under no circumstance were they to allow the Russians to cross the brook, even if it cost them their lives. The others with him, one a disabled veteran of the First War and the other a worker from a munitions plant who, up to now, had been considered indispensable.

A new little command, the old constellation, the last unit; really young, really old, and once upon a time important. It was almost like the group Franz had commanded in the Oderbruch to defend the Reich's capital not that long before. They were ripped up, blown apart. Franz had no idea how the others were, but it didn't matter. They were all in the same mess.

The young ones understood too late that war was something more than a scouting game or weapons practice like they did in the Hitler Youth. How could they have known better? They only knew the war through radio and newsreels or maybe from one of the boy-soldiers their own age who, after the phone and electric lines were down, acted as town criers as they rode bicycles carrying messages throughout the city.

The eyes of youth were still bright and shiny, they believed in the Endsieg, the final victory, just like the boy who had been detailed to him now. None of the three adults chose to dissuade him. You never knew who the young zealot might tell what you said. The boy dreamed of heroic deeds, like the tales told by wearers of the Knight's Cross, or the fictions of novels and movies. He was the first to die. He tried to stop a Russian tank with only a single panzerfaust, but the tank's machine gun fired before the kid could get his weapon ready.

The munitions worker took off shortly after that. Franz should have shot him as a deserter, but the veteran held him back.

"Come on, let him go. We can't stop The Ivan anymore. With him or without him. Why should we dirty our hands with the likes of him?" He threw his rifle in the brook. "I'll see if I can get back home. Otherwise, I'll end up in a POW camp, and I have already been there, done that. . . ."

It was nonsense. Nonsense to arrest the veteran, nonsense to follow the worker. The death of the youngster was nonsense, like Franz's own life. Nonsense. Everything had become nonsense. Everything he had once believed, once trusted, was gone. Destroyed, killed, vanished.

He sat down on the edge of his foxhole and stared at the brook and the land. The meadow was green, the fields planted, the farm house in the distance unharmed with smoke coming out of the chimney. Tears almost filled his eyes as he wished to be in that house, wished to sit in the kitchen where the farmer's wife was probably serving food to her husband, her children, and maybe a maid from labor service. He imagined they sat together for an hour or two after eating and before going to bed. The wife would be mending socks or letting out the kids' pants, the farmer smoking a pipe. Franz wished he were home with Mathilde and Karla in their little modest comfortable apartment. He didn't even know if the house still stood. Everything had been okay up to the point he had been drafted into the Volksturm at the beginning of the year. What if the Allies had carpet-bombed it? They feared that most. He didn't know. They always believed the cellar to be safe.

After a while fog rose up over his legs and he got cold. The brook splashed, the birds twittered. He heard only the rumble of artillery in the distance. The front, the fighting, had gone on past him without him really noticing. He was hungry. He had to think. He couldn't stay where he was, that was clear. He couldn't go back to Berlin. The Russians were there. At the last briefing the lieutenant spoke of the counter offensive in the Reich's capital. Counter offensive? No, he couldn't go back to Berlin. Berlin would be certain death. What should he do? He ate his last portion of rations, drank water from the brook, and thought further. He considered his shrinking supply of licorice lozenges in their little tin box. He stifled the urge to pop one in his mouth and carefully hid the box in his inner pocket. Finally he made up his mind to push west toward the Amis. Hopefully they held the ground on the other side of the river.

* * *

The bars threw long shadows across the room as the warm May sun sank slowly behind the tended vegetable garden Franz could see through the window. He had done it! He was sitting under arrest in an American cell. The icy cold in his spine numbed his feeling for anything else. He still worried about what they might do with him, about the interrogation, the prosecution, and the verdict that awaited him whether prison or worse. He remembered the overwhelming fear he last felt when crossing the Elbe at night in a stolen rowboat. It did not matter who caught him, Ivan or Ami—they would have shot him on sight. He had been lucky. No one saw him. He rowed across the river to the opposite bank, pulled the boat up to firm ground, a reflex from his training that he only recalled later, and grinned as he vanished into the darkness.

Here in the storeroom he felt no fear. Here it was clean, orderly, and smelled like dust and floor wax. He felt safe here. He could breathe deeply here. He heard noises outside, noises he recognized. He listened to noises of a normal business day. Footsteps, the clattering typewriters, and voices he could not understand but whose tone was nonetheless calm, unexcited. This was the routine of business as usual. He could breathe freely, he had done it. Now where? Now what? Again he saw the blood, heard the screams. A woman had reached her limit as she had squatted and peed on the curb. A German woman. She didn't even wear panties any more. Shameless. A private hit an officer who had given him an order and bloodied his nose—a German soldier, in open mutiny, had not been immediately shot! But he was allowed to leave unmolested while the stunned officer stared after him. A wild mob stormed an army depot, overran the custodian defending it, and left him lying in front of the door screaming, his arms and jaw broken.

A woman held a stolen sack of flour to her breast like a baby protecting it even as a soldier—a member of the German Wehrmacht, no

Russian, no subhuman—threatened her with his bayonet trying to take the sack. The mob pushed and shoved them, she fell onto the bayonet holding the flour sack. Blood and flour mixed into a sticky brew. The soldier pulled his bayonet out, ripped off her shoes, and began going through her pockets.

"The flour is done for, sorry to say," he said, disappointed, and continued searching her coat. He found cigarettes in the pocket, a lighter, and other little items. He lit a cigarette and handed the pack to Franz behind him who declined—and would have even if he had been a smoker. Franz shuddered in disgust. It had gotten to this point with the German people. It would never get that far with him.

Franz stuck his head in his hands, his elbows on his knees, staring into the darkness. He had done it. He had survived. He had made it through to where he could hope for the best. To what purpose? To what purpose for anything?

He heard a key and straightened up. Two GIs came in, grabbed him, this time without overwhelming force, without trickery or hate. Franz knew the difference, knew the technique. They stood him up and led him outside, through the hall that was now empty. A dim bulb lit their way past the empty, proud, towering monument alcove and out into the street. A truck stood waiting. Franz climbed up into it and discovered a few other German soldiers of undetermined rank. "Do you know where it is going?" Franz asked. One soldier laughed.

"To the POW camp. Where did you think?" The soldier glanced at Franz's coat. "The times when your kind would have had a reserved room in the Ritz are over," he said. The truck started and drove on.

FOUR

The leather straps cut deep into Mathilde's shoulders; jars of preserves pressed painfully in her back, her neck hurt. The rucksack she carried had not been made for such a load, but rather a couple of sandwiches, a water bottle, warm jacket, and an umbrella in case the weather changed. Their vacation is what the rucksack had been for. Back then . . . thought Mathilde. She couldn't believe that it was only seven years ago that they had made their trip. Back then in the peaceful past. Only seven years and yet an eternity, an eternity of war.

She slunk weak and tired along the imitation of a street, she wanted to cry. Her feet and legs hurt despite the hiking shoes that she had saved through the war. Now, because of the burden on her back, she was forced to wear them on the long tiring march from Steglitz to Moabit, Moabit to Steglitz, two and a half hours there, almost three back. That was what it had really come to on the streets that had become narrow beaten paths through the rubble. She had to clamber over fragments of cobblestones left by burned-out tanks, eviscerated cars, tipped over advertisement pillars. She carefully balanced herself on improvised catwalks over unexpected water or clefts in the cityscape.

The path to Moabit, Hermann's old parish, was particularly difficult. That part of the city was an island, ringed by the Spree and many canals. There were no longer any bridges, only jammed barges or improvised crossings she had to crawl across to reach the other side.

Mathilde was sweating, thirsty, and the unavoidable overpowering dust clogged her pores, her eyes, her ears, and nose. Every few days the sisters went on the endless march to Hermann's former parish. They went from house to house while Heidrun spoke of their horrible fate, their frightful need as a bombed out wife with four children without a husband, and who knew where the pastor was stuck, or if he was even still alive?

A horrible fate, thought Mathilde bitterly. Why does she exaggerate so? It wasn't that bad, there were many a lot worse off out there, many bigger horrors, a lot more misery. As soon as the thought occurred to her she felt like choking, burning, like falling apart so she shoved those thoughts aside as quickly as possible. It was embarrassing for Mathilde to stand beside her sister like a vagrant and beg for help. Heidrun did not beg, she demanded without a single bit of self-doubt.

Her success proved her right because hardly anyone wanted to send the pastor's wife away empty-handed. Many helped willingly, readily, piously. That's when it was really embarrassing for Mathilde. Today, besides the rucksack, she carried another two bags, filled with potatoes, flour, and sugar. Her fingers were cramped around the handles, almost numb from the pain and strain, they were so heavy. And while she carried the stuff that Heidrun had gathered in today's rounds, her sister stayed in Moabit drinking a little liqueur with the wife of Schmelzer, owner of a lamp-making factory and head of the Presbytery from whom she would get still more groceries that she would bring later.

These were groceries that they needed, Mathilde had to admit, since what they got with the grocery ration cards was not even close to enough. Without help from Hermann's parish they would be starving just three weeks after the Third Reich had capitulated. Without food obtained by their begging there would only be nettle soup, as for so many. At least it was spring, at least nettles were growing, Mathilde told the hungry children. In spite of that Gerhild once asked whether they could get Russian cabbage with Russian bacon. Mathilde could not blame her. She, too, longed for a real meal.

Still, the Russian. Her stomach cramped shut if she thought about it, how . . . She hurried her steps as if she could outrun the memories.

Two men approached her. Skin and bones, the clothes flapping around their bodies, the eyes deep sunk in the sockets, they supported each other side by side—prisoners of war, slaves, concentration camp inmates on the desperate search to see what once had been their home. The two survivors, hardly living men, evoked an image. A picture that had shocked Mathilde into a silent scream. A picture that she had seen a few days ago on a placard posted on a house wall showing a bulldozer shoving a mountain of bodies into a mass grave. Starved corpses, emaciated bodies. People who had died in German camps. Miserably treated, starved. Hung, shot, gassed.

Gassed. Mathilde would never have believed it. Heidrun still considered it nothing more than evil propaganda from the enemy. Mathilde suspected more than she really wanted to admit that what their enemies, the occupiers, the victors said was true. The German people had murdered millions of Jews, Gypsies, communists, homosexuals, and the mentally retarded. Gassed and cremated. Mathilde retched.

Franz had never spoken about what he did, but Mathilde knew him, knew it must have been something awful. She had noticed how Franz's expression had become ever starker, empty, depressed. She noticed how he spoke less and less when he came home from work, noticed that he often sat for hours and just stared straight ahead but didn't dream. He just stared into emptiness. Into an emptiness that frightened her. She never asked what was wrong. She did not want to know.

Mathilde hurried further along, out of sight of the two freed *KZ* inmates. Her shoulders ached, her arms needed rest, would gladly have rested if she could have set down the bags for just a little time for relief, but she ran further. She had to get home; the kids were alone. She had to protect the kids. At least protect the kids. Since the climbing escapade in the ruins of that house she was always in a panic, afraid that something could happen to them. Probably, certainly they were arguing already. They argued unceasingly or tried some other nonsense. They could not stand the hunger, the misery, the crowding as well as the adults could.

Finally Mathilde could go no further, she set the bags down carefully between her legs and clamped them tightly so no one could grab a bag. Public morals had become raw and brutal. She stretched as much as the rucksack on her back would allow and watched thoughtlessly as three kids sat and played in the middle of the twisted pieces of destroyed beams as if in a sandbox. She gave herself a moment's pause, a moment of forgetfulness, forgetting hunger, misery, rubble, bulldozer, piles of bodies.

An old woman shuffled past Mathilde, hollow-cheeked wearing a filthy and torn coat that had once been fine. The old one tried to hide her envious glance at Mathilde's bags, tried in spite of her hunger, in spite of her need. She tried to keep her dignity but did not succeed. She could not lie about her misery.

Mathilde gave her a packet of sugar. Perhaps she should have given the released prisoners something as well, but she had not thought about that at all. The prohibitions of the old regime still held sway.

The old lady took the packet and her lower lip trembled. She could hardly speak for thankfulness.

Mathilde murmured, "It's okay, it's alright." She picked up her bags and went on. She had almost hugged the old one and patted her on the back. Heidrun would scold because Mathilde gave away sugar while they themselves did not have enough. Mathilde felt they should share the groceries as the people from whom they had begged shared with them. Otherwise, how could the soul be calm?

Mathilde passed the railway station near the zoo, the Bahnhof Zoo, a lot more like piles of rubble than the Bahnhof Zoo it had once been. Only the entry portal of the ticket offices remained. The roof over the platforms had fallen in a shower of glass, steel beams stuck in the air like giant pick-up sticks. What an idea, thought Mathilde. Everything was a great game. But the platforms were cleaned off, and she could hardly believe that already some stretches of track had been repaired. There were a few trains again, not on schedules, sporadic, but they ran. They ran through train car cemeteries with bent metal sculptures and torn seats. They brought back refugees, bombed out people, and children who had been sent to the country. Still more war prisoners, forced laborers, and many others; DPs, "displaced persons" as the Allies called them, who all tried to come home.

Only the men, the German men, were still in the war. Either in graves on the battlefields or, at least one hoped because there were no reports about them, in custody. Mathilde hoped as well. She had heard nothing from Franz since the end of February. Heidrun felt, to be sure, that no news was good news. If something had happened to Franz, Mathilde would have known long before now. Maybe Heidrun was right. Hopefully she was right. Certainly Franz was tucked away somewhere.

Even so Mathilde worried. What would become of her without Franz? Heidrun was optimistic but she had reason. Hermann had written a postcard from an American POW camp. Hermann was alive. Heidrun had information, good, hopeful information.

Still the soldiers did not come home, not even Hermann. Only the fifteen-, sixteen-year-old children, who shortly before the end had been thrown into the fight to save the fatherland, had not been put into an internment camp by the Allies. Mathilde saw just such a youth at what was left of the train station entrance. He looked around helplessly, without orientation, hoping to get picked up, but there was no one there. Perhaps, probably, hopefully because no one knew yet that he had arrived.

But maybe there wasn't a home any more. Maybe the house, furniture, and family had all fallen victim to the bombs, flames, and explosions. Mathilde knew of a case in the neighborhood where a girl in the Arbeitsdienst had been sent home. When she got there the house had vanished and everyone was dead, her parents and her two little brothers. Mathilde had comforted her, wanted to take her in, into the little apartment, but Heidrun had taken her somewhere else. They really did not have any more room. And naturally Heidrun was right, as always.

A cripple hobbled on crutches along the cleared path through the entrance. He was perhaps thirty, had lost a leg and wore a bandage on his head. The women who waited in front of the train station held out placards to him, "Do you know this man?" Underneath a photo, almost always someone in uniform with a few items: name, rank, unit, when and where the last report came from. The one-legged man shook his head sadly. He knew none of the missing. Maybe Mathilde would have to search for Franz in this pitiful manner at some point, but it was too soon for that. She could still hope that he would simply come to the door one of these days.

Suddenly a young blonde woman came out of the waiting group and ran up to the one-legged man. She hugged him so hard she almost threw him to the ground. Mathilde unconsciously smiled. Sometimes there was a little hope in all the confusion and this woman got her man back. Even if he was an invalid. The boy who had been searching for his family turned, and started out on his way. Mathilde hoped he would find his lot. Mathilde prayed for that and she was suddenly almost certain he would.

As she got to her house with her wounded shoulders, aching back, and cramped hands, Frau Trimborn called out to her from the super's apartment. "Yeah, you won't have so much time in the future to play the hoarder...."

"Why not?"

"... They've already been to your place." The pity in Frau Trimborn's cold voice barely disguised the curiosity and malicious delight that Mathilde saw in her eyes.

"Who came by to see us?"

"The Russians. They were here, in our house."

Mathilde's heart plunged through the floor, panic spread through her gut, she wanted to go immediately up to her apartment and check on the children.

"They have gone again. They were in civilian clothes, no soldiers."

"What did they want?" That the Russians were in mufti was no comfort to Mathilde. Quite the contrary.

"I heard that they are picking up former party members and everyone who had anything to do with the Regime to get help with clean up. And I thought . . . ?"

"Did they come by your place?"

"They wouldn't bother with us." Frau Trimborn shook her head. "Thank God we are too old. It is different for you."

"But I still don't . . . only because of my husband . . ."

"Relatives count as members, too." Frau Trimborn's voice sounded like she was sucking on a bonbon.

* * *

Mathilde was afraid and very nervous as she went to the construction site that she had been assigned to, still feeling she was in a precarious situation. After talking to Frau Trimborn, she immediately stormed up to the apartment. There were no Russians and there had been none, assured Karla. When Heidrun got home it turned out she had heard about the disturbance, too. It was only a matter of time before the Russians would appear for Mathilde and, because she was the wife of a Gestapo official, put her on forced labor.

Heidrun vigorously and loudly wondered what they should do. Mathilde did not ponder, she did nothing. She wanted to do nothing except sit there and wait for the Russians to come. Somewhere inside her she felt a paroxysm, a spasm of painful barbs, a feeling—no, not that: a premonition, an intuition of guilt that held Mathilde in its sway, sitting and waiting for her fate.

Heidrun spoke against Mathilde's paralysis like a self-confident powerful, unceasing river. Franz had only followed orders, Heidrun repeated again and again. Mathilde had nothing at all to do with it but instead needed to care for her own family as first priority. That was their duty, their only duty as mothers and wives.

Mathilde, like always, had let herself go with the flow, but even so, the unending barbs inside her remained. Yesterday morning she had gone to the city hall where the Russian administration resided and voluntarily reported in without saying who or what Franz had become. She was issued a ration card for the hard labor she would be doing, just as Heidrun had hoped, so the family had a few more calories. Above all, Mathilde had no idea how long she could get through this charade.

She was really feeling uneasy as she got to *her* rubble field. She didn't know what awaited her, neither what the work would be nor how she would be treated. She was ashamed of her husband and at the same time hoped he was still alive. She loved him but could not let go of the image of those bulldozers. The piles of corpses. She could not comprehend it. Could not believe that the man with whom she shared table and bed, the man who had always been good to her, had hardly ever raised his voice to her—that *he* could have been involved in such a monstrosity. It probably had been so, but she could not comprehend it at all. Perhaps the work would do her good, at least distract her from her, according to Heidrun, unhealthy musing. Perhaps.

A few women at the worksite were laughing as Mathilde approached. She stopped for a moment afraid they were laughing at her because of her clothes. She really was something to laugh at, but they stopped laughing as she walked by and she realized that they were not laughing at her, their clothing was in just as bad shape as hers. In fact, she was just a little better off than most with her hiking shoes. Some had only rags wrapped around their feet. The women were talking among themselves and had laughed out loud at a joke. Mathilde could hardly believe that one could tell jokes in such dire circumstances, but apparently one could.

She looked around. There were about a hundred women and very few men on a huge mountain of dirt and rubble that had once been houses, apartments, and shops. Not too long ago people had lived here, had loved, worked, felt safe here. People who had left traces in the rubble, reminders of their lives—shattered pots, broken toys, scorched pieces of clothing. On one wall that still stood was a picture of a non-commissioned officer with mourning crepe on it. Ripped out wires hung down, remnants of burned balconies, blackened floor tiles, plaster covered pieces of furniture lay all over the place. Amid all the clutter, flies swarmed around countless piles of excrement.

The men, mostly really old or really young, and a few among them slightly injured in one way or other, stood high in the rubble with picks and sledgehammers and broke large pieces of wall into manageable pieces. One group of the women formed a long row passing bits of trash from hand to hand down the pile. Mathilde was surprised when she heard automatic mutterings of "Thank you," or an occasional mechanical "You're welcome," as if the women were giving gifts to one another.

Those women passed the stuff to another row of women who sat next to each other and broke up the chunks with hammers to examine the stones looking for good ones that could be reused. They knocked off the mortar and put them up in stacks behind them. The unusable remainder was thrown on a trash pile. A third group shovelled the trash into a horse-drawn wagon which they had to pull with their collective power because there were no horses.

A fourth group dug out steel beams with bare hands or with a few tools. Metal and everything else that appeared worthwhile was separated and put with the usable stones. Supposedly, the destroyed houses would be rebuilt with this material. Later maybe, sometime in an unforeseeable peaceful future.

The sky was postcard blue, the sun shone, but it was too hot for this time of year. The women had stripped as far as was modest, except for the headwear made of shawls, tablecloths, and bibs that everyone wore. Their faces, their bare arms were covered with dust that ran with rivulets of sweat. If they wiped the sweat away, a streak of lighter skin remained on their face. Because they often wiped their sweat, the streaks took on a wild look, like Indian war paint. At least that is how Mathilde had imagined it when Franz had related the famous stories of Karl May's travels to her and Karla, stories Karla could never get enough of.

Mathilde stood there with a note from the Russian administration that she was to come to this worksite near Innsbrucker Platz, almost a half-hour foot march from home. She was lucky because others had to go a lot farther to work. She looked up the mountain of rubble and thought if they had to take it down this way it would take a thousand years. Perhaps that was God's punishment for what had happened. Thousand-year Reich, thousand-year punishment.

"Do you intend to join us?" A man suddenly stood next to Mathilde, mid-fifties, unshaven, with a fearsome face and eye patch.

Mathilde awoke from being mesmerized by the hurry-scurry on the pile of rubble, nodded and handed the note from the occupation forces to him. "Can you tell me where I can find Mr. Schall?"

"You found him, Heinz Schall, that's me. Have you already worked on site?" He let his glance wander over Mathilde, stayed a moment on her hands. "No, of course not. Well, come along." He wrote her name in a notebook and stuck the note in it; he rumbled as he looked at her shoes and then scrambled up the mountain of rubble. "Work starts at six thirty, breakfast at nine, lunch at twelve. At three we take a little break, quit at five thirty. Everything else you will learn fast."

He said nothing more which was alright with Mathilde who thought his manner too familiar toward her. She was unaccustomed to being bossed by a strange man. Unaccustomed and uncomfortable.

About halfway up, Schall showed Mathilde to a place in the row of women that handed the pieces of rubble down. Another, a young girl whose face showed the strain, was sent down to the sitting group, and in a quarter of an hour Mathilde wanted to trade places with her. She could hardly breathe for the dust, and her hands were cut despite the gloves, and hurt. She kept stumbling, since she could not find a firm footing despite her shoes. She hit her knees and shinbones because she tried to save her shoes. The first pieces that she passed on down she had found to be light, but after a short time they seemed to get thicker and ever heavier. When Schall finally roared "Breakfast!" the women joined a spontaneous flowing stream down to where she had stood before to take their break. Mathilde felt like she would never again stand.

Then it came to her that she had only brought two slices of bread, sticky and at the same time dry because she had nothing to spread on them; above all she had nothing to drink. She should have brought more than something to eat.

"You've got no water, huh? I forgot that the first time, too." A woman who worked a little above Mathilde, held out a beer bottle full of water.

"Then you won't have any . . . ."

"Back there, on the corner, is a pump."

"But can we go there during the work?"

"The Pirate doesn't say anything if we disappear for a few minutes. He doesn't want us to collapse permanently."

"The Pirate?"

"Yeah, Schall, the one-eyed guy." The woman pointed with her chin at the foreman who sat at the foot of the rubble pile and ate his breakfast.

Mathilde nodded, took the bottle, and drank a careful gulp. "Thanks."

As she handed the bottle back, she looked more closely at the woman. She was in her mid-twenties, small, slender, had short blonde hair, like the fashion was at the end of the twenties, and determined bright blue eyes.

The woman returned Mathilde's look with interest, examining her.

"I believe I saw you the day before yesterday at the Bahnhof Zoo. You are lucky. Your husband came back," said Mathilde.

"Huh?" replied the woman.

Mathilde nodded, looked down a bit and wished she hadn't said anything and that the conversation was over. At the same time she wished the opposite.

The woman kept looking at her. "Robert is not my husband, he is my brother."

"Oh, okay." For some reason Mathilde felt embarrassed. She chewed on her bread, took another drink from the bottle. She was so thirsty. "I would have thought he was your husband."

The woman laughed out loud with a clear laugh. "I am not married." She stuck her hand out to Mathilde. "I am Lene."

"Mathilde." She shook hands after a little hesitation. Just like with the foreman, the familiarity that was everywhere in the work site was hard for her to accept. On the other hand she was happy that no one pressed her for her last name. She had decided to talk about Franz as little as possible. Not only because she was afraid of losing the extra rations card, but she was mostly afraid of what would happen if the others discovered what Franz had done, what organization he had been in.

Lene had noticed Mathilde's hesitation. "We use the familiar address here in the work site because it would be difficult to say, "Madam, would you please be so nice as to take this?" Lene mockingly played the gentile lady.

Mathilde had to chuckle, "Oh, yes, but even so a few still say please and thanks."

Lene mulled this observation a bit; she answered, "The human is an animal of habit," and changed the subject. "You are married of course, aren't you?"

How did Lene figure that? But Mathilde nodded. "No idea where my husband is. I haven't heard from him for quite a while."

"Yeah, that's clear. We are the poor swine who have to suffer."

Mathilde needed a second to understand that Lene also meant her when she said "we." She was included. She—Mathilde! Shame washed over her.

Lene didn't notice and continued. "Robert, for example, was a little weak in the lungs. Sports and stuff like that was not his thing. He would much rather sit in the corner taking things apart and putting them back together." She laughed briefly, but it died immediately. "But naturally, they still drafted him. . . ."

Mathilde watched Lene and simply listened, happy that the conversation was no longer about her husband, the secret policeman Franz Tegge.

". . . and not until nineteen forty-three. Robert was placed as an engineer in factory 'vital to the war effort.' Then they accused him of sabotage and sent him to Russia in a penal company." The bitterness and emotion in Lene's voice was crystal clear. "That was after they worked on him so hard in the Prinz-Albrecht-Straße that he looked like he had gone ten rounds with Schmeling. Damn bastards!"

Prinz-Albrecht-Straße, the headquarters of the Gestapo. Franz's work place. The brother of this woman who sat and talked like they had known each other for years was one of his victims. Perhaps Franz had not personally tortured Robert, but yet—the image of the bulldozers flashed before her again. Tears and nausea and horror filled her throat. Tears that she swallowed only after a long pause and could ask, "And . . . Had he . . . ? Or was he innocent?"

"Of course he did it, what do you think?" Lene laughed an astonishingly cheerful laugh. "He wanted nothing more than that this shit of a war ended."

Mathilde nodded slowly. Lene's brother was a cripple because he did not want the war to continue. A cripple that had been prosecuted by men like Franz. Prosecuted and tortured by men only doing their duty, following orders; by men like her own whom she still hoped lived and for whom she hoped all was going well.

FIVE

Franz, like all prisoners in the POW camp, was not allowed to keep anything except for what he wore on his body. An American GI who stood at the entrance murmured in bad German, "Just toss it. In America everything new." So they took his rucksack, his razor, and his wristwatch. The only thing he was allowed to keep, rather miraculously, was his little tin of licorice lozenges, his own personal relic. He laid the other stuff on various piles without regret or the feeling that he was losing something or that he was being treated unfairly. Even when he had to give up the twenty-year silver pin for his service in the police force, it meant nothing to him. The policeman that he had been for so long no longer existed.

They were given a blanket and were designated a sleeping area that was in the open air at first. That was no problem since he had been allowed to keep his coat. He was warm in those first still cool spring nights. Warmer than the others, he was left alone. His fellow prisoners recognized that coat and stayed away from him. They wanted nothing to do with the former Nazi, even other Nazis that were possibly, probably, certainly among them wanted above all to hide who they really were. They stayed away from him, from each other.

It was nothing to Franz, he liked being left alone. He had always been happy to be alone. He stayed here in the internment camp like a lone wolf who needed no one else. He gave his first ration of cigarettes to a fellow prisoner who was a trained barber. Even if he smoked, he would have traded it for a haircut. It was important to him to be well-groomed. Important for himself. What the others thought didn't matter.

The barber cut his hair, but was not allowed to shave him since blades were forbidden. They might be used as weapons, but by hook or crook the barber had gotten hold of a pair of scissors.

His already small face had become smaller and more pointed, even though that impression had been softened by his beard which the barber could only trim and not get rid of completely. His hair was still thick and naturally blond, a muddy, street-dog blonde as Heidrun, his pastor's-spouse sister-in-law called it, though it was now streaked with gray. He was forty-two and disappointed, distraught, burned out, as hollow, empty, and black in his soul as a building that lay in ruins.

He had deep furrows in his cheeks. The stress of the last years and the hardships of the last months had left their mark on him. In the mirror his tired and disillusioned pale gray eyes looked back at him from behind round glasses. Eyes that expected nothing anymore. Whether the Amis executed him or put him prison forever, what was the difference?

In the SS he was industrious, reliably completing assigned duties, and proving he was determined to be successful, showing less mercy than anyone ever expected from him, the son of a modest streetcar conductor from the slums of Prenzlauer Berg.

And Franz followed his orders here as well. The prisoners built their own camp, put up tents, dug out latrines, and built a mess hall from green wood. Franz liked the work, even though it was difficult for him since he was not used to hard physical labor. He was satisfied. There was enough to eat and an orderly daily routine, a clear structure into which they had to fit.

Fit in, plan, and survive. Adjust himself. That is what he must do. He missed Mathilde, missed Karla, but he forced himself to not think about them. He didn't think he would ever see them again. They were characters from another world, another life that had nothing to do with here and now. They were, it often seemed to him, the wife and daughter of another man, someone almost unknown. A person he once knew well, but now they had lost touch.

Unlike all the others, he did not write the permitted postcard where he could say where he was and what had happened. It wasn't important. Everything earlier than the instant he turned himself in to the Americans slowly sank into the fog of his memory, even his wife and his daughter sank into the blessed fog that swirled around everything that had happened to him in the last years. That was how he protected himself from sorrow and doubt.

To him morning roll call was an unbelievably sloppy formation. To be sure, they had to get into rank and file, but no one cared about their posture and alignment. Still most of the prisoners stood at attention out of habit. This morning, after the count, the sergeant called out, "Tegge? Franz Tegge? Come on."

Franz stepped out of the rank and went forward. He felt their stares on his back and sensed their thoughts.

Those looks did not matter to Franz. He had done his duty, followed orders, nothing more. He wasn't responsible, at least not personally. They just wanted to make him responsible, he was sure of that. Was it right? He didn't care. It was the way it was and there was nothing one could do about it. Nothing that people like Franz could do at any rate.

After a long and uncomfortable ride on the bed of a truck, he sat on a wooden bench in a vestibule. They hadn't cuffed him, they trusted him, or more likely, they were sure he wouldn't escape, and they were right. He crouched there and looked straight ahead. Their naiveté, that they would try to wear him down by having him wait, astonished him. He was a policeman, a Gestapo official, part of the most effective, relentless arm of authority. He had interrogated hundreds of prisoners and was accustomed to such tricks. It was futile to use such tactics on him.

After a while he was led into a room. A German office with a double desk, rolling shutter chest, regalia on the walls and wooden chairs. Yet a German office would never look like this. Not only that there was no picture of Truman hanging on the wall, or no calendar with pinups from Coca Cola, that wasn't it. No, such disarray would have been unthinkable in a German office. Open files lay everywhere, coffee cups were here and there, and empty plates with used cutlery on them. It was unimaginable that a German official would be lounging in his chair with his feet on the desk like the

American soldier to whom Franz had been brought.

Franz figured the man was a little older than him, mid to late forties maybe, bald and portly. The uniform was tight so he had undone his belt and the top button of his pants, again, something unthinkable for a German official.

He inspected Franz with remarkably small brown eyes. Franz waited in the doorway for the man with his feet on the desk to tell him what to do. He was probably an officer, but Franz was not familiar with American rank insignia. The door closed behind him.

Still the man said nothing, just looked at him. He looked at him like a scientist would at a rare reptile, not without interest, but with noticeable loathing. Franz returned the look and ignored the rejection it bespoke. He was prepared, had already figured that he would be interrogated and just wondered why the Amis had let so much time go by. He wanted to tell everything, admit everything. He wanted to cooperate. Why else had he turned himself in? But the soldier appeared to have not understood that. He just looked at him as if he wanted to further unbalance and weaken him so as to get a confession. Or information. So, what was this silly game? Still the soldier made no move to begin the interrogation.

Franz got tired of waiting. "Please. I will speak. I am here to speak. What want you to know?"

"Sit down." The American abruptly took his feet off the desk, stood up and buttoned up his pants. He cleaned files off one of the chairs. "I am Lieutenant Herter."

It sounded like "Hörrtörr" to Franz. The man spoke a somewhat rusty German but it was clear that his roots were in the Ruhrgebiet. Franz didn't dare to ask how an American lieutenant had acquired a *Ruhrpott* accent but he would sure like to know. He was surprised and curious which, with him, was an occupational hazard.

Herter sat down as well. He set more files, an ashtray and an empty glass to the side, fished out another file from under a pile after some searching and leafed through it. He looked at Franz who was sitting on the edge of the chair. "You are Franz Tegge, born 20 April, 1903 in Berlin, last known address in Berlin-Steglitz, Kniepholzstraße."

"Yes, Sir."

"You share the birthdate with the Führer." Herter smiled wryly.

Franz shrugged his shoulders. "Happenstance."

"But still an honor?"

"Oh, wonderful honor. I almost always had to work. . . . There was always some sort of a parade for the Führer's birthday."

"As my grandfather always said, 'Every job has its burdens; every job has its trouble.'" The lieutenant did not bother to hide the sarcasm in his voice.

His grandfather must have been German, thought Franz. Apparently the lieutenant himself was born in Germany. It was only a question whether he left before thirty-three or afterwards.

"You became a policeman in 1920 from the midlevel of police academy candidates?"

"Yes, Sir."

"Your last rank was that of chief detective?"

"Yes, Sir."

The American's smile changed from scornful to sly. "Was it not earlier that of junior squad leader?"

"That was the same thing. In thirty-six the entire police force was brought into the SS. Overnight we were all SS people."

"So, suddenly overnight."

"Yes, overnight. Through a simple federal law."

"You were not a volunteer? No, no one did that. No one was convinced, no one was inspired. It was just everyone's luck to have been forced. Could do nothing about it. "

Franz became angry. "No, in that case we really could not. We could do nothing against that, all police became formally SS people." He calmed down. "That had no impact on me, it changed nothing for me. We still kept our old rank insignia. I was a detective before then and the same afterwards. That should be in your file."

"Detective?"

"Yes, in the burglary section. I hunted thieves."

"Only thieves? Until you were drafted into, what was it called? Volkssturm, a people's militia?"

"No, not until after my transfer to the Gestapo. But I'm sure that is all in the file." Franz felt a vein pounding in his temple. Anger, he felt angry. Not fear, not uncertainty. He was angry because, apparently, he was not being taken seriously. It was a familiar tactic; ask questions about what you already know in order to find inconsistencies. However, that method would not work on a colleague. Surely this lieutenant knew that. Something that was part of Franz's occupation, something that he practiced, would not work on him.

"How did your transfer happen? Can you tell me about it?"

Herter did not notice Franz's discomfort. Franz had to stay controlled, there was no other way. "There isn't much to tell, they needed people. And after thirty-three, the rate of property crime clearly fell."

"Because people feared the draconian punishment?"

"Because the economy improved. At least that is my theory. Punishment for those crimes was not made harsher under the Führer."

Herter nodded. "When was that? Your transfer to the Gestapo, I mean."

"Thirty-eight."

"Couldn't you avert it? Didn't you still want to catch thieves?"

Franz fell quiet. Couldn't he have stopped it, averted the transfer? "Yes, probably," he finally answered quietly. He was here to speak; therefore he should not hold anything back.

"But it would have led to disadvantages?"

Franz needed a moment to think. "Disadvantages probably not, but I would have lost advantages." He looked at the floor unable to return Herter's keen look.

"What kind of advantages?" The lieutenant remained stiff- necked.

"Promotion, raise, entitlement to a larger apartment. The three of us had lived in a single room before that."

"An apartment from which you had driven the Jews. That you got for a song, fully furnished and with all the other inventory."

Herter's accusation returned Franz's dignity. He tensed and sat upright, "I don't know who lived there earlier. The apartment is small, and when we moved in it was empty."

"Good."

Herter hesitated, but seemed satisfied with the answer. He apparently knew from his documents that Franz had not lied.

"What other advantages did you get yourself?"

"I was promoted, they granted me and my family a *Kraft durch Freude* trip for a vacation, special rations of food, that sort of thing." Franz looked at Herter straight in the face. He asked himself why this game played on. He was embarrassed by the other's primitive interrogation tactics. Or was Herter trying to sell himself to Franz as stupid? No, that wasn't it, Franz suddenly realized. Herter was an amateur. He got his knowledge of police interrogation from crime novels and movies. Apparently he had been picked for this duty because he spoke German. Herter could do no better, he tried but tried in vain. This was useless, and Franz almost felt pity for Herter. "May I make a suggestion?"

"Yes?"

"Why don't you take me to a cell, give me paper and pencil, and I will sit down and write down everything from my life and work history? Everything that I know about the actions of those I was involved with."

"You mean deportations! Prosecutions! Show executions!" Rage almost choked the lieutenant's voice as each word hit Franz's ears like the crack of a whip. "Don't pretty up your horrific deeds with a concept like 'actions.'"

Franz nodded. Herter's rage confirmed his impression that he was no trained interrogation specialist. "I will write about those horrors in which I took part. That simplifies the process and saves time. I am ready to make a full confession. Please do not forget that I came here of my own free will. I did not hide, I did not disguise myself. You can rely on me."

"Trust you?! A Nazi, a butcher?!"

"Whatever." Franz leaned back and waited for further questions.

Herter thought a bit, apparently suspecting that he was not Franz's equal. Finally he rasped, "Okay, we'll do it that way. At least, what the facts are, but despite that I'm still interested in something else. You came in voluntarily. Why?"

The question surprised Franz. A chill washed over him, shook him for the first time since he sat on the bench in front of this cluttered room. Should he tell the lieutenant the truth? And if not the truth, then what? He felt hot. He wiped his brow with his sleeve. "I would not have survived," he finally answered. He had to swallow a few times before he could continue. "You would have found me eventually. Or the Russians would have. And so this is better, or is it?"

Herter nodded, and abruptly became friendly, almost courteous. "Why did you believe that you would not have survived? Didn't you have an old buddy who would have helped you? Someone in the passport office who would have given you false papers, for example?"

Franz slowly shook his head. No, he had no such buddy. He never had had one. "And even if I did, one still can't hide your entire life long." The sentence sounded sadder, more true and lonely than Franz wished. All at once he felt defeated because the amateur was just a person, like Franz. And this person, this amateur, seemed to know what went on inside Franz.

Herter looked at Franz for a while, jotted down something, and looked back at him. "Do you believe you made a mistake?"

"Didn't we all? If one just looks around our country . . ."

"I mean a personal mistake. Do you feel personally guilty?"

Franz was immediately alarmed. He had to be careful; he couldn't allow himself to fall into Herter's trap. Even if he was an amateur, he was still dangerous. He had managed to tap into Franz's emotions. That was truly astonishing. "I followed orders," he said, and immediately shut up again.

Herter nodded, as if he had expected this answer, and kept quiet. But in that silence there lay renewed resentment, suspicion, even hate. Also an emotion, thought Franz. The lieutenant played with his pencil as if he had to make a decision. A decision based on hate? That wasn't good. One had to be clear in decisions, clear, precise, and necessarily cool.

After a while Franz asked, "Do you want to know anything else about the facts?"

Herter slowly shook his head and continued playing with his pencil.

"Then I suggest that I write first. Whatever decision the prosecutor arrives at . . ."

"No," interrupted Herter, suddenly decisive. He paused before he went on, a pause during which he inspected Franz again, and again Franz did not in fact know what he felt—anger, fear? No, what he felt was hope. Absurd hope. Because the hate had disappeared from his opponent's eyes.

"I am not sure if the prosecutor will take up your case."

Franz hadn't thought of that and, again, felt surprised and uncertain. He reacted more strongly than necessary, than advisable. "I thought that the Americans were so proud of the fact no one was imprisoned without a fair trial?"

Herter look at him piercingly one last time before he took a deep breath and relaxed somewhat. "We won't lock you up, although I think you more than deserve it." He stroked his chin. "You are not with the police here. Or the prosecutor, but with the OSS."

"OSS?"

"Office of Strategic Services. The army's secret service. Even if it is hard for me, we need men like you."

SIX

Dust. Dust in the ears, dust in the nose, dust clogging eyelashes, bringing tears to their eyes, dust forcing its way through clothing into their every pore. And pain. Pain in the neck, pain in the arms, pain in the back, in calves, in the feet; and fatigue, exhaustion. The women worked to the point of insensibility. And their hunger. Even with the little extra food they earned with their ration cards, it wasn't enough. It was never enough. It was harder than anything Mathilde had ever done in her entire life, and yet she became used to it.

Work had become almost fun. It was just as hard as it was at the very beginning, but over time she had grown callouses on her hands and become much more adroit, working like all the others. When she first had started she would cut her hands on sharp edges of concrete and protruding nails. She got splinters in her fingers and rubbed her skin raw. Her hands bled all the time despite her gloves which had become rags after only a few days.

Now she learned how to grab pieces of rubble without hurting herself, how to hold the shovel so she could use the handle for leverage. She learned how to get mortar off the bricks which wasn't as simple as it might look; hit it too hard and the stone broke, hit it too softly or in the wrong spot and the mortar didn't pop off. Still, she learned how to do it. She had to learn.

She was one among many at the worksite where everyone seemed the same, yet she did not fit in. She wanted to but could not. She stayed apart during breaks, didn't gossip with the others, laugh at their jokes or trade tips about where you could get what you wanted or needed on the black market. She tried, whenever she could, to be inconspicuous and stay separate from her co-workers.

Above all, she dodged Lene, or tried to. Lene always squatted next to her during breaks and looked out for her. She had taken Mathilde under her wing.

Oh, how Mathilde wanted to return the friendship Lene gave so freely to her, but she couldn't. A terrible foreboding rose from deep inside her keeping her apart—dread over what Franz had done. She couldn't become a close friend with this woman whose brother had been crippled by men like Franz. She simply could not. She could not, did not, would not allow herself to lie forever. She chose to keep to herself, shut herself out, rather than live a lie.

She worked without talking and kept to herself during breaks, day after day. Slowly it became routine for Mathilde's life, for all their lives. That is if, after everything that had happened in this here and this now, there could be anything like normal.

After work she stood in line somewhere, like most of the others, to get groceries or something else they really needed. When she came home to the little apartment she quickly ate what Heidrun had cooked—*if* there was electricity that day.

Since there most likely was no power, she often ate cold mush made of some unrecognizable substance, or water-soup, veggies in cold water, because Heidrun hoarded, saved, and strictly rationed what little kindling they still had. Then she immediately fell into bed dead tired. She was too tired to take care of anything else. Too tired to talk to Karla about how her daughter stood in line, helped around the house, took care of the kids, too tired to review the little spats Karla had with Heidrun and Frieder; even too tired to think about Franz. Since Karla slept on the sofa with her, Mathilde didn't once miss his body next to hers. Short and deep, a sleep of the dead, and thank God for small favors, a nightmare free sleep that shoved the memories of her husband and what he might have done, probably did do, into her subconscious.

She was glad he wasn't home, even though she worried about him. She was afraid of him, her husband! She was afraid of meeting him again just as much as she longed for him. She lived and survived. Exhaustion, hard labor, starvation, doubt, sorrow, and worries built a cocoon around Mathilde, an iron corset she could escape only in those few moments she had to herself, only for herself, like sometimes at noon if she could find a little place where she could be alone. Mornings, and evenings too, if she could steal the time, she visited a stand she had discovered one day amidst the dusty piles of debris. It was cobbled together from splintered boards and ripped plywood, a stand where an old couple sold flowers they had picked themselves. Some people bought or bartered for flowers to take home to bring a little life, color, and freshness to the oppressive gray destruction outside and the gray misery inside. Mathilde tried to go there every day and stay a moment or two. She greeted the couple, who returned her greeting, and stood quietly. They knew she came to look, not to buy.

"Krespe is on sick call, Mr. Schall." Roswitha Starworski stood with her hands on her hips as she spoke to the Pirate. She had earned her nickname, Warhorse, because she was a large rough woman who was married to an innkeeper and beer wagon driver who had been missing since Stalingrad. "If she can, she will be here this afternoon," she said in a tone that brooked no argument. It would cost Minchen Krespe, Roswitha's closest friend and quiet as a mouse where the Warhorse was loud, at least a half day's pay and hard labor ration no matter how sick she was or whether she got to work this afternoon or not.

"Krespe can do what she wants as far as I am concerned. It seems she doesn't need the extra food." Schall tried to turn away, but Roswitha stepped into his path.

"Krespe is not sick through any fault of hers." She emphasized every single word and stared meaningfully straight into the foreman's eyes. "I said, she will be here this afternoon if at all possible."

Schall understood. He understood immediately. He understood only too well but didn't want to show any weakness. Who made the decisions here? Who had the say-so? He rumbled, "Yeah, okay, if she is here then she's here, and we'll see what happens." The Warhorse remained standing in his way. He barked, "That's all, Starworski." Shoving her out of the way, he clapped his hands and yelled, "Come on, come on, get to it. It is long past seven." Then he marched off.

Roswitha sneered as he stomped off and took her place in the bucket line a few women above Lene and Mathilde.

"Who is doing it to Minchen?" asked Helma, a thin lady with a rat-like face that Mathilde had decided was some type of criminal, though she didn't know for sure *what* she did.

Roswitha answered tersely, "The same woman who did it for me. She doesn't have any problem doing it, and Krespe will recover quickly."

Mathilde tried not to overhear. She didn't want to learn who had done it to Krespe or where she had gone to have it done. She tried to push the voices into the background and concentrate on something, anything else, on the buckets handed to her from above as she handed them off down the line. The buckets, the handle, grab and grab and grab, but it didn't work. She could not put it out of her mind.

"It is a disgrace that the high-ups have outlawed it." Lene was mad, fighting mad. "At least they could have spared us the shame of having to sneak around to the black market doctors. Of course the Ivans deny it's even happening, and the Reds in city hall want to cover it up so they don't ruffle the feathers of their Moscow pals. If it's not happening to you, why worry about it?"

The Warhorse always felt no one except her had the right to speak about things like politics, and answered to the whole group, "Do you know the epitome of shame? Rape." Muffled huffs and puffs and some snickers too. Even Lene grinned a little. Mathilde had the feeling that her skin bled red, her face burned so.

"Exactly. Better a Russki on the belly than an Ami on the head." The remark came from Elfriede. She was, except for Lene, the most pleasant to Mathilde of all those in the group that went up the rubble mountain day after day. Elfriede was one of the few that had survived a cellar collapse and never tired of telling how an old man next to her had bled to death without her noticing. The old fellow had always brought a framed family photo. "Dead, all dead, everyone in the picture except me, dead wife, dead children, dead," he would say. With every alarm he single-mindedly took it with him into the cellar and protected it by leaning it on the wall behind him. When the people in the cellar were buried alive, the glass in the frame shattered and stabbed him in the back and throat.

He was in shock and didn't realize what was happening. He just became very quiet, and Elfriede, though she had wondered why his chanting had finally stopped, didn't notice either. At least not until it was too late and the geezer had bled out. Every time she told the story Elfriede ended it saying, "Because of a picture. A photo of his dead family; dead wife, dead children, dead, dead, dead."

The words stayed in Mathilde's head like a refrain. She tried to banish the noise, the stories, but the women around her talked on and on, their voices always painfully present, always chattering about the subject that affected all of them, the subject that Mathilde knew too well and did not want to hear about because the more they talked the more it pained her.

"Did you all hear about it, too?" Roswitha was in her element. "Apparently everyone who carries a Russian brat gets a grocery ration card Number One. Hard labor rations. From Stalin personally." The snorted snickers became laughter.

"Ask yourself how to explain the little one to your hubby so that whenever he comes home he will say 'Amen,'" Roswitha went on loudly, buoyed by the excitement, "I know a woman whose husband already came back, and she had a big belly, and he immediately felt she had shamed him, so he ran off, straight back to the army."

"But who is so pregnant that it already shows?" Elfriede shook her head not understanding.

"It's true, the bulge did not come from an Ivan, so the fellow should be happy about that, but their horns don't carry a sign saying who put it there."

With a knowing smile Helma handed the bucket further down the line. "Surely he'll come back when he gets hungry."

The Warhorse shouted "Hopefully not, is what I'd say. That way she can have more room in the house."

The women laughed again, but laughter stopped when Schall yelled angrily, "Enough gossip. You're not here for the fun of it!"

Deep sighs came from some of the women with memories of the

husbands they missed and cared for and waited for.

Mathilde's mood became stony. She shut herself off from them as much as she possibly could.

Lene did not want to let Roswitha's scorn go unchallenged. "I bet when you cry for your hubby at night that you're just as whiny as the others."

The Warhorse answered back as she handed down the next bucket, "Are you jealous because you don't have one?"

Lene shrugged her shoulders not wanting to answer. She kept quiet and handed Mathilde the bucket, and Mathilde handed it quietly further down the line; she could not, did not want to take part in the conversation. She was uncomfortable with the coarseness, the shamelessness, the carelessness of the talk. Not long ago none of them would have thought such talk possible, even the Warhorse with her loose tongue would have been shocked. Mathilde knew that it helped, but even so she could not talk about it. She was ashamed and thought about Maman—and please don't forget the accent on the second syllable— who had always said, "If you act modestly, nothing will happen to you."

Well, she had acted modestly, and still it happened to her. She knew that Maman was wrong, yet she was still ashamed, so ashamed that she buried the events deep within the inner sanctum of her subconscious behind an iron door so that light would never again shine on it. Never again. She had gotten through it relatively unscathed, and after a few days she knew she would not be one of those who had to find a doctor and beg for help. At least that hadn't happened. The Russians had left nothing behind, nothing but memories.

"I heard about someone who got caught twice at the same time. She got the clap, and when the doctor did it for her she almost bled to death," added Helma.

"Yes, and think about the poor, poor young girls, their first time . . . . They will never enjoy love again, not ever." That came from Gerda, the professor's wife, who occasionally recited poetry and had a hard time not saying "thank you" and "you're welcome."

"Yeah," said Roswitha who threw a suggestive look at a young, unusually buxom, and almost indecently good-looking woman, "and others have been well cared for thanks to their admirers. So it goes in life, isn't that right, Inge?"

Inge would not let herself be provoked. "What should I have done? Shame myself to death?"

Many had no other choice than to take a Russian, preferably of higher rank, as lover and provider to at least halfway protect themselves from the usual brutal violations. Mathilde's Russians had not been officers, for sure, still they had . . . Mathilde felt like she was going to throw up when she thought about how those two had created something like family life with Heidrun, her, and the children.

Lene laughed. "I just climbed up high under the roof. The Ivans didn't trust going up more than two flights."

So that was how Lene had escaped the worst of it. She and two others in her house hid without food or light and only a paltry amount of water. They stayed all day bent over, squatted, perched in a narrow partition in the furthest corner of the attic. They crept up there after other, rather flabbergasted Berliners realized their "guests" from the East did not like to go above the second floor. They seemed to find it unimaginable that anyone could live so high, like birds in a nest. High-rise buildings were unknown to them and made them feel imprisoned since every escape route could be easily cut off. That would have left only jumping to their deaths. Unthinkable. Yes, in the norm the Russians had gone no higher than two floors, thought Mathilde. In the norm.

* * *

Papada-pàda . . . her fingers flew over the keys, light, floating, dancing, and Mathilde's head felt just so light, floating, yes, almost dancing because of the hunger she had completely forgotten, because of the notes that ran together to make the melody, the harmony, the music, from the papada-pàda at the beginning to the "Turkish March" at the end of the piece. Playfully, happy, yet almost fumbled, almost cautiously wafted into space, much less stern or serious than in the record by Wilhelm Kempff that was next to her record player at home. It was like Mathilde had always imagined the A Major Sonata should sound. How she would play Mozart, though she would never have that chance.

The "Finale à la Turca" shone brilliantly in clear triumphant counterpoint to the sorrow and despair of the opening movement; papada-pàda papada-pàda . . . —this slow, solemn, in spite of all lightness disillusioned and lonely beginning that evolved, towards the end of variations on the theme into happiness, into life. Life that after the minuet, the middle movement, fairly exploded in the march of the last movement. Mathilde sat there, played and heard. Totally absorbed, happy.

The world around her was lost as she lost herself in the music. She crouched and played in the middle of the rubble surrounded by despair and destruction. Soundlessly she played on a keyboard broken off at each end leaving only a mass of wires that had once been its strings. The wood body of the instrument no longer existed, taken for the stove of some fuel-hunting rubble dweller. Mathilde had found what remained in a niche, a small niche as impossible as the piano itself, a gap, a little cave formed by the walls of some destroyed apartment where the piano had been in its time.

A niche, a hole, any hideout, a place Mathilde sought for her noon break. Today, after all the talk of rape throughout the morning, she had even less desire to be around the others so she fled and hid herself. Here she had found a gift from heaven, a piano. Her fingers caressed the keyboard, she played from her soul, but without sound, mute, yet full of tones; she was one with the instrument. She forgot that her hands had lost agility because of work in the rubble.

Mathilde froze. Someone was whistling the melody along with her; her rhythm, her phrasing, exactly as she played it. It was as if the whistler could actually hear her. Impossible. It absolutely could not be. She tore her hands from the keyboard and the whistling stopped. Frightened, she looked up and noticed the entrance to her little cave had darkened.

"Play on."

Mathilde stared at the outline of a man who stood in the breech.

"Please play on. Mozart could not sleep without the final chord."

Mathilde remained still. The light was behind him so she couldn't see his face, but she immediately knew who stood there. Surprised, she was momentarily distressed, uncomfortable with physically painful memories. She had invited him, invited this man on the same after-noon that she had taken the silver place setting from her dowry; her dowry that despite everything had not been sacrificed to their need for money. She had not been able to take that from herself and Heidrun; it should be handed down to their daughters, Karla and Gerhild, car-rying on the family tradition. Yet without this man Karla would have been dead and in no need of a dowry. Mathilde took a complete set—knife, fork, spoon, dessert spoon—from the family's silver and went to *Kolonialwaren Färber* who she knew had a few precious things, valu-ables, stored away. She bought a can of beef from German army supplies, a bottle of wine, eggs, flour and sugar for a cake, and a few potatoes that didn't have many black spots at all. Färber wasn't a profiteer and added a jar of preserves. From all that Mathilde fixed the meal to which she had invited this man.

"One evening at the Mozarts'," the man went on since Mathilde said nothing. "The lad, Wolfgang, was already in bed, and his father played the piano downstairs in the parlor when the doorbell rang. Leopold, Wolfgang's father, interrupted his playing without ending the piece and went to the door and visited with his friend who had come by. Suddenly Wolfgang appeared in the parlor, played the last part, played the coda and went back to bed. Without the conclusion, without the harmony fully closing, he could not sleep."

"How do you know so much about Mozart?"

"Someone probably told me the story." The man, Camillo Baumgartner, Gypsy and tightrope walker, as he had told Mathilde at that lamentable meal that should have been a celebration of Karla's life, shrugged his shoulders and was for a moment distant, resentful almost rebellious. "Perhaps it is not even true."

Mathilde understood what he said, but what she didn't understand was why he said it, why he would even speak to her. That meal had been a catastrophe. It was true that Heidrun had said nothing. That is she chose not to argue with Mathilde about taking the silver to buy gro-ceries. Naturally one must thank Karla's savior. Heidrun knew her duty as a Christian. Even so, Heidrun did not agree that she should have invited "such a person"—a social inferior, that's what Heidrun thought of him—to her apartment. Mathilde had silently protected herself from Heidrun's reproachful sighs by reminding herself that, after all, this was *her* apartment. Even when this Gypsy, this subhuman, had brought more groceries than he ate and gave them cigarettes, even then the artiste's generosity did nothing to alter Heidrun's mistrust, her aversion, and scorn. Of course that didn't keep her from hoarding the expensive gifts in the kitchen cabinet, her treasure chest.

Nothing and no one had interrupted Heidrun's monopoly of the conversation at the table, not Mathilde's glance, Baumgartner's silence, or Karla's comments. She talked incessantly and in excruciating detail about how hard her life was, the struggle to get the children through it all; worries about her and Mathilde's husbands. She spoke sanctimoniously about the sorrow of the unnumbered widows, and the mothers who'd lost their sons. She complained so long that Baumgartner finally stood up, tersely said his thanks for the meal before turning to Heidrun and adding, "I have the deepest sympathy that your people suffered so much." And with that he had left.

"What are you doing here?" asked Mathilde surprised, puzzled, and a bit unsettled to meet him again.

"I wanted to know who was playing the piano so marvelously here."

Mathilde was flattered, a little embarrassed, and smiled unwillingly. "Stop it."

"No, seriously."

"Seriously—you could not have heard me at all." Mathilde pointed at the pile of junk that had once been a piano. "And if you had heard me, it most certainly would not have been marvelous." As evidence, she held her hands high. Calloused, swollen hands, stiff, puffy fingers.

The artiste nodded casually, almost indifferently, as if it did not matter if she could actually play the sonata at all, whether soundless or audible. His eyes rested on her.

Mathilde felt exposed, vulnerable, and intimidated by this look. "What are you doing here?" she repeated finally. She retreated to the conventional, the ordinary, the everyday.

"I am looking for a place where we can perform. And we have decided that if we can span our cable between the ruins here, there will be enough of an audience."

"They won't be able to pay to see you. None of us have anything."

"But we must perform. What else should we do? We don't know anything else." His tone held a mixture of pride and resignation.

"Tegge, where are you hiding?" Schall's voice, the voice of the Pirate. It sounded angry. "Dammit, the break is over. Put an end to your laziness!"

Mathilde smiled at Baumgartner, embarrassed, took her water bottle and pushed past him through the entry. She made herself small so as not to touch him. She did not know why, she just did it. "I must go," she said quietly, quickly.

"Your foreman?" Baumgartner nodded a little in the direction of Shall's voice. "I want to speak to him."

"Do that. Although I doubt he will let you play here."

"It doesn't hurt to try."

"Perhaps." Mathilde shrugged her shoulders and hurried back. Back to work, like every day yet it was not like every day. The notes of the A Major Sonata still rang inside her, the music stayed with her, and she wondered how Camillo Baumgartner could sense, could know what she played, be exactly in tempo and start in exactly in the correct spot. How he had even found her. What finally shot through her mind was that she must have unconsciously hummed the tune. That would explain it. He had heard her and followed along. The notes had called to the unexpected, unusually pleasant strange man out of the rubble.

The reunion and the music together made a remarkable oscillation, a unique floating, and a peculiar mixture of sadness, confusion, and joy. Mathilde had been amazed at Heidrun's tirade that evening. She had run into the hall after Baumgartner, apologized, and thanked him again for saving Karla. He merely nodded curtly before he vanished without saying goodbye. Mathilde had understood that.

Despite the memory and the tension it raised in her, the afternoon's work went well, much easier than usual. Schall yelled, "Quitting time," much earlier than she expected, and the women hastened away from the work site. For all of them there followed a second, and a third job, standing in the lines in front of the shops, in their kitchens, at their sewing machines, at their children's beds. So it was for Mathilde. Today she had heard there should be rations of barley at Färber's, and even though she didn't really want any barley she had to be there anyway because you had to get whatever you could, whenever you could. She hurried down the street. It looked like rain; the sooner she got to Färber's the sooner she could get home, and with luck she might make it without getting wet.

"Come with me, I'll show you something." A voice behind Mathilde stopped her abruptly. She whirled around and looked in Baumgartner's face. Close, very close to her. For the second time today she was startled as if she had seen a ghost.

"Come on." He took her arm and pulled her along. She would have resisted, but his eyes betrayed him. A smile shone in those eyes, a roguish smile danced on his lips. Quickly he led her over a path around a barrier to a side street and into a rubble-filled house. Almost before she knew what was happening, he led her toward the basement. Just as he was about to take her down the steps she became afraid. What was she doing here, what did he have in mind, what was he going to do to her? She started to protest, but the artiste laid his finger over her mouth. "Shh," he said as he calmly, softly touched her.

Mathilde angrily pushed his finger away. She was not budging an inch. She stared at Baumgartner. "What is this?" She was furious and indignant but she whispered.

"Don't worry. I won't do anything to you. I just want to show you something. Come on." He took her hand, lightly, almost tenderly, like a cavalier leading his lady to the dance floor. Mathilde could do nothing but follow him down the steps, even though a starburst of panic spread through her.

*   *   *

And suddenly she was no longer going down the stairs, but up—the steps that led from the cellar of her house to the apartment in that little miserable, laughable, Thanksgiving procession on the day the Russian came.

Heidrun held the food tightly, almost as tightly as Horst held onto her jacket. Karla carried little Heinrich, and Mathilde had Gerhild in her arms. The girl smiled sweetly at the soldiers who had given her raisin bread until Mathilde turned her niece's face to her and pressed her head against her chest. Don't make friends with the enemy, the strangers.

Still the one soldier, the sandy-haired, the happy one, noticed Gerhild's smile and how Mathilde tried to hide it from him. He threw her a glance whose meaning she didn't understand, yet cut her to the quick. There was something in it, something like, how could it be, like saying hello. Hello? Gerhild squirmed wanting to get her head free, but Mathilde held her tight, putting her arms around her if she could provide protection.

Two women, their children, and the soldiers climbed up floor after floor. The stairwell was covered with fine white dust, cluttered with splinters and pieces of mortar, but it seemed to have come through alright except for the blown-out windows in which slivers of glass remained as the little group passed by. At the second floor, the Russians stopped and indicated a blown-out door.

"That is not our apartment, we have to go higher." Mathilde went on. The two Russians followed hesitantly.

"Thanks, many thanks, here we are," said Heidrun as they stopped in front of their door on the fifth floor. The door was intact and the lock even worked. Mathilde turned the key with shaking hands and let Heidrun and the children enter. "Thanks, it is okay," Heidrun said again; her tone was such that under normal circumstances would have dismissed them like slamming the door shut, but the Russians didn't care and pushed in behind them into the apartment which instantly seemed even smaller. The soldiers stood there astonished even though the apartment really was nothing special. It was just two little rooms and a halfway spacious kitchen, but with furniture, proper furniture—beds, sofa, table, chairs, pictures, a grandfather clock. . . . Even a bathroom. The Russians had apparently never seen anything like it.

Just like the stairwell everything was okay, but covered in a white chalky dust. It looked like a powdered sugar landscape, almost decadent in its undisturbed state. Still, if you looked closely you could see glass fragments everywhere. Heidrun carefully made a path into the bedroom with the children and sat the three on the bed. "You don't move from this spot, understood?" The anxious children nodded.

Karla dropped down beside them on the bed. "Should I tell you a story?"

Heidrun stood firmly in front of Karla. "Not now. This is no time for lounging around. You need to sweep and clean up. But be careful that you don't hurt yourself and the little ones don't hurt themselves. Clear?"

Karla pouted. "I am not your servant girl."

Heidrun raised her hand threateningly. "You do what the adult tells you to do. We all have to work together. Understood?"

Karla stood up, threw back her ponytail and strutted to the door just as Mathilde stepped into the room. She put her arm around her daughter's shoulders, "It is best if you stay in here, okay, because of the Russians."

Karla grinned mockingly over at Heidrun. "Now what?"

"Sweep!" said Heidrun just as Mathilde, not understanding, asked, "What do you want her to do?"

Heidrun explained it to her, while the grin danced wider over Karla's face. Mathilde opened her mouth to argue with Heidrun, closed it again, and said nothing. It was as if she was caught between sister and daughter. She quickly pulled Karla to her, and just as quickly Karla pulled away. Mathilde sighed, "Your aunt is right, child, we all need to help as best we can, but just do it quickly. Do you understand?" Karla went to get the whisk broom and dustpan without looking at mother or aunt.

The Russians watched the whole scene from the hall through the open door and ogled Karla as she passed them. In a fluid, almost soft movement Karla spat in front of them and went on without hesitation. Their lusting eyes grew small and predatory as they followed her, and Mathilde got frightened. She smiled helplessly at them, "She meant nothing by it, please excuse. . . . She often forgets herself."

"Often?" Heidrun appeared in the bedroom door. "You are way too protective of her. If I were in your place . . . ."

"Please. Not now. You'll make things worse."

Karla banged around in the kitchen with the dustpan. Mathilde was close to tears. Then one of the two Russians, the one with a few bits of German, stepped up to her and put his arm around her shoulder. Mathilde froze though the lad did not seem to notice. With a motion of his machine pistol he sent Heidrun away. "*Dawai*, cook." Heidrun pushed past Mathilde and went into the kitchen.

She ran into Karla at the door. Who spit in front of Heidrun as well, a gesture Heidrun judiciously overlooked. The other Russian grinned. He seemed to enjoy the rebellious girl.

Mathilde held her breath. "So go get the sweeping done. And close the door behind you." Mathilde's chin pointed quivering at the bedroom door. Karla understood the quivering better than the words and vanished into the bedroom.

Hardly had the door shut behind her daughter than Mathilde could no longer hold back her tears. The young Russian who still had his arm around her shoulders pulled her to him, and for a moment Mathilde actually laid her head on his chest. She pulled back as she felt the rough uniform material on her cheek. The Russian held her close and looked into her eyes, straight forward and earnestly. His buddy glanced interestedly over at them.

"You husband?" asked the Russian.

"Yes," stammered Mathilde.

"Where?"

Mathilde shrugged. She hoped that Franz was far off, as far off as possible, in order that he did not fall into the Russians' hands.

"Then I your husband?"

"What?"

"I your husband." The Russian beamed at her. He let Mathilde go, took off his cap and twisted it in his hands. Suddenly he looked like a farm boy expectantly asking for the hand of his betrothed. His blond hair stood out from his head in a strawy mess. He had green eyes and thin, almost silvery facial fuzz on his healthy ruddy face. He was most certainly not yet twenty. "I your husband, okay?"

"Don't even dare to dream. . . ." Mathilde put her hand over her mouth. Why did she say something so idiotic? But the Russian had, luckily, not understood and asked happily once more, "Okay?"

The older one, who had brown hair and was way less good-looking and pleasant *and* seemed very decisive, said something in Russian that Mathilde did not understand. The blond soldier nodded and went into the kitchen. Heidrun had unpacked the food but sat at the kitchen table not doing anything.

"*Dawai*, woman, cook . . ."

Heidrun turned around and looked straight at the soldier. "With what?" She pointed to the empty coal scuttle next to the range.

The brown-haired Russian who had followed his comrade understood without translation. He turned back into the room, broke apart a chair and a second one and carried the wood in the kitchen. Mathilde had to hold herself up with a hand on the wall. The Russians did what they wished, took whatever they pleased knowing full well they were the victors.

The dark one threw the pieces of the chairs to Heidrun and sat at the kitchen table. Heidrun began to heat the stove. The blond Russian leaned against the wall next to Mathilde. He offered her a cigarette which Mathilde took under Heidrun's disapproving gaze; German women did not smoke. Mathilde stood there and smoked while a stony-faced Heidrun cooked. Mathilde knew that Heidrun expected her to help. So what? She leaned her head against the wall and enjoyed the light dizziness caused by the unfamiliar nicotine. Enjoyed standing there, thinking about nothing, doing nothing.

The quiet was a no-man's-land into which the clatter of pots and the sizzle of the burning chairs pushed. The brown-haired, older Russian finally pulled a bottle of vodka out of his pocket, took a deep gulp and gave it to his comrade who also took a drink, then held the bottle out to Mathilde. She didn't want any. The dizzy feeling from the cigarette was enough for her. Heidrun rejected it indignantly. German women did not drink, just as little as they smoked. The sisters exchanged a glance, and Mathilde turned away. The Russians shrugged and drank in great gulps.

They drank quietly until the bottle was empty. The blond had another bottle with him; they passed it back and forth while Heidrun cooked and Mathilde sat and the sun gradually went down. A rare warmth spread throughout the apartment carrying the smell of bacon and cabbage that finally enticed the children out of the bedroom. Karla carried Heinrich in her arms, Gerhild and Horst clung tightly to her legs. Four large pairs of eyes stood focused on the simmering pot. Heidrun and Mathilde wanted to get the children back to the bedroom, but the Russians, as if understanding the kids, made room at the table. They all sat there packed together like one big family and ate; silent, uncertain, yet, in some strange way, together.

After the meal the vodka ran out. "Schnaps?" asked the dark one. Suddenly he could speak German. "Schnaps?"

"We don't have any," answered Heidrun.

The blond boy looked at Mathilde. "No schnaps?"

Mathilde shrugged. Maybe Franz had a bottle somewhere. She had never paid any attention to anything like that. She went into the living room. The brown-haired, thin one stood up and followed her with heavy uncoordinated steps and watched Mathilde search. She wasn't quick enough for him. He tore open the doors of the living room cabinet and started throwing everything out, tablecloths, cutlery, along with Mathilde's sheet music.

As he grabbed the good plates, Mathilde cried, "No!" She shoved him aside with some force, which amazed her, and carefully arranged everything on the table. "That was a wedding gift, Karla will inherit that."

It meant nothing to the Russian who didn't understand a word she said, stood unsteady on his feet, looked at her impatiently and belched. His mood brightened as he saw a bottle of rye. "Schnaps," he growled satisfied. He took a drink and passed the bottle to his comrade who had come into the living room, and he drank, too. His young farmer's face glowed from the alcohol.

His gaze fell on the gramophone that Mathilde had bought from her household allowance. At least she could listen to Mozart even if she couldn't play his music. The blond grimaced at Mathilde with glassy eyes. "What that?"

Mathilde didn't know how to explain it to him. "What *that*?!" repeated the Russian, upset. He staggered over and stared at it. "Gramophone, music." Quickly Mathilde took a record out of its sleeve and laid it on the turntable under the angry gaze of the two soldiers. It was one of Franz's records with Zarah Leander. Schlager music seemed to stand a better chance of pleasing the Russian than Mozart. *Ich weiß, es wird einmal ein Wunder gescheh'n* rang through the air. Now the Russians understood. "I know there will be a miracle someday . . . ." The blond said something in Russian that sounded like "music" and nudged his comrade with his elbow before he started to whirl around. Dancing bears come from Russia, the thought shot unbidden through Mathilde's head. She had seen one in the circus before the war. He had worn a fur cap on his head, and they could smell him even in the fourth row, Mathilde and little Karla.

The dark-haired bloke drank some more and wanted to dance with Mathilde. She hesitated but the determined Russian grabbed her, his hands like painful clamps on Mathilde's shoulders. The blond got in between them and after a short argument pushed his comrade away while the fluting sounds vibrated on Mathilde's breastbone, her ribs, and her heart. The brown one staggered and fell, causing a great din and almost knocked the dishes off the table as they clattered, clanged and swayed, but remained standing. He saved his bottle from the fall and seemed satisfied to sit in the corner and drink. The blond threw his arms around Mathilde and tried to kiss her, his alcoholic breath like a clinging haze over her face. She had to work to keep her balance because the Russian held her so tightly. "I said I husband," he mumbled with a thick tongue.

The music and noise had alarmed Heidrun. She appeared in the door with Heinrich pressed to her breast. "I said, I husband," the blond slurred once again and whirled Mathilde in a parody of dance steps.

Mathilde was forced to go along and looked to her sister for help. Heidrun returned the look and instinctively pulled her little one closer. The brown-haired one emptied Franz's rye, slid slowly on his side and suddenly began to snore loudly.

The song ended. Mathilde wanted to get loose, but the drunken farm boy clung to her, breathing heavily. "Music," gasped Mathilde, "I'll play some more music."

The Russian let her go. Yet Mathilde did not run to the gramophone but to the door. Heidrun was still there, now joined by their kids. Heidrun and Karla tried to clear a path for Mathilde, wanting to shove the kids aside, but they got confused, stumbled over each other, and actually blocked the path. The blond bear chased after Mathilde and pulled her forcefully back by the wrist. "I now husband," he said, not at all angrily but with astonishment in his voice. He was astonished that she ran from him. He pulled her down on the sofa and kissed her with an open mouth. Mathilde screamed softly, Heidrun pushed the children out of the room, "Disappear. Off with you, into the bedroom!"

Karla tore her aunt's watch from her arm and cried, "Take this, take this too! We have more, everything you want."

Neither of the two soldiers reacted. Heidrun grabbed the watch back, "That is worth nothing."

"But we have to help Mom," pouted Karla as she ran to the blond trying to shove him away from Mathilde. The Russian slowly turned around, like an animal interrupted while eating, and shoved Karla back. She fell backwards against the other, the sleeping one, who angrily snored louder but did not wake up. The sandy-haired bloke fell on Mathilde again, and again Karla got back up and went after him. "Karla, don't!" begged Mathilde, as she twisted and turned under the heavy man. She held her head away from the wide-open mouth and the drool that tasted like tobacco. Heidrun stormed into the room and pulled Karla away just as the Russian had drawn his machine pistol sensing that Karla was in attack mode about to go after him again. He fired into the ceiling and plaster spurted and drizzled, the lamp wobbled and the blond farm boy grabbed Mathilde under her skirt.

Heidrun shoved Karla out of the room, shut the door, placed herself against it and let Karla hit and scold her. But she did not let the girl back in the room.

Then, on the other side of the door, it was quiet, very quiet, and Karla was suddenly silent. She stared at the door knowing what played out on the other side, what happened to her mother, what she had to go through. Karla had often heard the whispers and talk, the horror stories about The Ivan.

Heidrun's face mirrored Karla's fears, she looked sympathetically at her niece and wanted to hold her hand, wanted to take her away from what happened behind the closed door, but Karla shook off Heidrun's hand with a jerk. Heidrun shrugged, "Stay here, either help me wash up or go into the bedroom. We can't do anything now." As she walked away she said, "It will pass. Everything passes. We are in God's hands." With that, Heidrun disappeared into the kitchen.

Karla stayed in front of the door, the whole night. She kept vigil over her mother's horror like a faithful dog. At some point Heidrun brought her a blanket. Karla did not stir, just kept staring at the door.

The next morning the Russians disappeared, but in the evening they came again just as Heidrun and Mathilde, with lots of elbow grease and little water, had cleaned and straightened up the apartment. They appeared after Mathilde, with a guilty conscience for using a precious quarter bucket of water for herself, had finally taken a bath and washed as best she could.

The two soldiers brought more food with them, Heidrun cooked, and they all ate together, men, women, children. Dinner, then rape. This time it was the brown one's turn. "He husband," said the blond bear and drank while the dark one threw Mathilde on the sofa.

So it went along, day after day, night after night. The two Russians left in the morning, came back in the evening, had their food cooked, ate with the regularity of office workers, and, just as routinely, fell on Mathilde, taking turns, one on one night, the other the next as each one raped her. And every night Karla slept in front of the door to the living room.

The Russians did not bother Heidrun. She always carried Heinrich around with her, as if he were a part of her own body. It was said that the Ivans left mothers with little children alone, and that seemed to be true since nothing happened to Heidrun with the child in her arms whether she was in the apartment or outside where she heard about many who had been raped like Mathilde.

When Karla saw how Heidrun protected herself, she scolded her aunt until she gave Heinrich to Mathilde and tried to protect herself with Gerhild, but the Russians didn't go for it. "Child Mama," said the sandy-haired one and forced Mathilde to give Heinrich back to Heidrun before he pulled Mathilde into the living room and shut the door. As Karla took her place in front of the door, Heidrun said, "Your mother is a heroine. She is saving us all."

On one morning Mathilde woke Karla from her sleep on the threshold and looked into her eyes, the eyes of her daughter no longer a child and not yet a woman. She saw that Karla knew but didn't understand or couldn't grasp what was happening. She saw pain and rage. She hugged her, wanting to mother her with warmth and hugs but could not put Karla's pain into words despite needing, wanting to console her. But Karla broke free, seemed inconsolable and defiant.

Mathilde knew that she had to speak though she really wanted to bury what had happened deep within herself. She knew that no matter what she said or how she said it, she could not ease the pain or heal the wounds, still she had to speak. "I'm not the only one. And that helps. Really."

Karla rejected her mother's words. "Child, please . . ."

"Only because everyone talks about it . . ."

Mathilde interrupted, more firm and certain than she felt herself. "You are so young. You shouldn't even know what it is."

"Nonsense, Mom, I am old enough."

Mathilde turned away and stared at the wall, unable look at her own child. "Maybe . . . this war . . . you have grown up way too fast." Mathilde stared at the wall without moving, so fixedly, so unnaturally, so far off that Karla grew uneasy.

"Mom? I . . . I don't want it to happen to *you* . . . even if it happens to a lot of others. . . ." Tears trickled and she sniffled, quickly wiping her nose.

Mathilde faced Karla realizing her unruly child could cry about it, too, and somehow that almost consoled Mathilde.

Karla tried to squelch the bitterness choking her with rage. "And why you? Only you? And not Aunt Heidrun?" Karla's tears flowed uncontrollably.

"Only God knows that," answered Mathilde quietly. "And much, much better me than you, dear. Better me than you," she repeated gently.

Mathilde's gentleness soothed everything, the pain, the bitterness, the wrath as Karla cried and buried her face in Mathilde's neck and Mathilde held her daughter tightly. Very tightly.

* * *

Mathilde was scared, holding herself tightly, hugging herself with both arms. She stood in a dark cellar room; how had she come here, why was she so afraid?

Her eyes followed uneasily along the beam of the flashlight that Baumgartner shone through the darkness. And there it was again, the object that had frightened her. It stood in a corner, fat, covered, massive, and threatening.

Without noticing Mathilde's fear, Baumgartner went over to the shapeless thing, took off the tarps and cords that covered it and shone his light on it. Mathilde recognized what it was. A grand piano gleamed black and polished in the light of the flashlight. A grand piano! With an elegant, demonstrative movement Baumgartner pulled out the piano bench that had been stored under the instrument and invited Mathilde to sit down with a fluid motion of his hand.

It was a real grand piano, a Bösendorfer, perhaps one that had played in concerts, philharmonic concerts that Mathilde might have attended if she somehow had had the money. It was a noble instrument she had never let herself dream of playing. "Come, trust yourself."

Mathilde hesitated, then went to the instrument and softly stroked over the cover. Finally she sat down carefully. "But this is a break-in, we aren't allowed to. . . ."

The artiste smiled an open and clear smile for the first time today, like a warm radiance. "We're not going to harm anyone or anything. Besides, who knows if the owner is even alive?"

And it seemed to Mathilde that a cloud passed over his face as if for a short moment he felt sorrow. As if the smile had brought the sadness with it. "Please, play."

"Won't it be too loud?"

"We will leave the cover down."

Mathilde nodded and flipped the keyboard cover up. Her fingers floated a moment over the keys almost as if she was afraid to unlock the tones of this instrument, almost as if she feared to wake an ogre, a monster. She glanced once again at Baumgartner who nodded to her. Finally she struck a note, tenderly and carefully. It dragged a bit, clanked a little, and was a little off key. She tried a fifth chord. It sounded somewhere between a fifth and a major fourth. Even so, one could hear and sense what a wonderful instrument this was, with a mellow and full sound. "Play Mozart."

"But I can't do that at all. Besides . . ."

"Try it."

Mathilde stared at her hands uncertainly. "At least the beginning . . ."

Was she wrong, or was Baumgartner imploring her? "Okay. It is on your shoulders." Mathilde tentatively began to play the beginning of the A Major Sonata, but before she could finish even two measures both of them grimaced. She tried to play a bit further as they looked at the expression of each other's face, and both were smiling, beginning to giggle. Suddenly they were carefree children playing in this forbidden place, torn between their courage and high spirits, and the fear of getting caught.

The piano was totally out of tune, it sounded wrong, awful, something to run away from. Mathilde stopped playing. "Should I really continue?"

Baumgartner shook his head. "The thing has probably been left standing too long down here. It is a shame." He shrugged slightly.

Mathilde saw the disappointment in him. She could feel it. She felt it in her own body, and then she turned back to the piano with an inspiration. She improvised with her rusty, work stiffened fingers a few notes of a little awkward melody, at first dull, often too slow, and again too fast, neither its rhythm nor its notes fit, but nothing mattered since the piano was so out of tune—whatever she played would sound wrong and false. Still she went on improvising. A syncopation unconsciously slipped into the melody, her left hand unconsciously found a running bass line and after a few measures, the bass line and the syncopation melded into a ragtime tune. It was a piece that Mathilde practiced at home as a piano student over twenty years ago. It was a piece that Miss

Nebenich had not been allowed to know about because she considered such music fit only for nightlife. It was a piece that she could only practice if Maman was out of the house since she considered it Negro music, which was true, but her Captain father in his velvet chair, who did not like the endless strumming of Czerny etudes or Robert Schumann's "Kinderszenen", had nodded, agreed and kept time with his remaining foot like Baumgartner now softly kept time. The piano was out of tune, but even so the notes that Mathilde coaxed from the instrument sounded right, happy and lively, off-key, crazy, and in spite of that harmonious. It was a harmony of false notes. Baumgartner soon kept time with his body as well as with his foot. The music pulsed through him, completely through him. After a bit, he took off his vest, kept his hat on, and began to drum the rhythm on the housing of the piano, at first softly, as he followed, supported and served Mathilde. Then, by and by, Baumgartner took over the rhythm and Mathilde followed. Baumgartner got faster, ever faster, Mathilde got more certain and played endless variations on the same theme. Baumgartner spurred her on to ever more wild and daring melodies. At some point he took more and more of the solo part, changed the rhythm, led her away from the straight eighth notes of the ragtime accompaniment to the freer, wild, confusing rhythm of his people's music. Mathilde followed along, involuntarily but happily.

Mathilde yanked the kerchief off her hair and shoved it up the sleeves of Franz's old shirt which she wore to work, all the while playing with one hand regardless of what she did. She threw her head back, and her brown locks flew, as did drops of sweat. Mathilde laughed. She stole her laugh from the rubble, the heavy pressure deep within her, the need to escape what had happened; stole it from the fear. Stole it from the shame.

Suddenly, completely unanticipated and unexpected, Baumgartner stopped drumming. He let his hand sink and looked at Mathilde as if he saw someone else. A stranger, nearly an enemy. It took a few seconds before Mathilde even noticed that Baumgartner had quit, and she sensed it more than she heard it. She jingled a few more notes, slowly, ebbing, before she really understood what had changed. And finally she stopped playing and stared at the keys. She could not grasp it anymore. She was suddenly drained of all feeling, purposeless and empty. Sweat ran down her arms, and she breathed like she had been running. Mathilde's panting was the only noise in the dark cellar. Other than that, silence reigned, impermeable and heavy.

At some point—she didn't know how long they had sat and stood there, perhaps minutes, perhaps hours—Baumgartner pulled out a pack of Camels from his pocket and offered her one. She took it and they smoked silently. Finally, Baumgartner said, "I thought I heard a noise. But I was probably wrong."

With that he broke the magic spell completely, chased the music which still hung in the room to full flight. Mathilde jumped up from the piano bench in a start, "Shit, I still have to get to Färber's. . . ." In a rush she put on her kerchief, shoved the bench back under the instrument that Baumgartner was quickly covering by the light of the flashlight. It was as if the two could not leave the cellar fast enough.

As they left the house it was dark. The streets were wet. It must have rained heavily. They had not noticed anything while down in the cellar—an empty, silent space separate from a world filled with rubble.

Wordlessly, Baumgartner accompanied Mathilde home. He didn't touch her although it seemed to her that they went hand in hand. It seemed as real as the notes at noon had been, when she played and he whistled.

They ran by *Kolonialwaren Färber* which had naturally been long closed. Mathilde pursed her lips, thought about her mother and immediately relaxed them. Heidrun would be the one now not to understand; incomprehensibly, reproachfully refuse to accept that she did not bring home barley. And her sister would worry about her.

Mathilde had no idea how late it was, but it was dark, it was night. Unconsciously, she hurried her pace.

Arriving at the door she stopped and her eyes met Baumgartner's. She found the courage to quickly touch his arm with her hand. "Thank you," she said, smiling shyly at him, "thank you for letting me play." He looked at her and for a moment gazed directly into her eyes. Then he abruptly turned and left.

He hurried off. Almost as if he was fleeing something. Almost as if he had something to hide, thought the man, who came out of the shadows of the rubble slope across from the entrance to Mathilde's house. Yes, he has something to hide, thought the man, who wore a black coat, a coat that could not hide its heritage from the SS clothes cupboard. Indeed, he has something to hide. Evidently that man with the funny-colored vest, which made him look like an exotic bird, a dandy, a buffoon, had flirted with a married woman. With Mathilde, his wife.

Mathilde glanced after Baumgartner, looked around a bit, and quickly disappeared into the house.

That went fast, thought Franz. Pretty fast. But the times have changed, the wind has turned. He stared stone-faced for a moment at the entrance as if he thought about following his wife up into the apartment, his apartment. Then he turned and walked away with resolute steps.

SEVEN

As quietly as she could Mathilde turned the key in the lock, slowly opened the door, slipped in, shut the door, and stepped toward the living room. Suddenly she heard a match strike, and a candle flickered to light illuminating Heidrun's disapproving face. She had been waiting in the vestibule just like Maman, her expression a carefully tuned mixture of anger and anxiety. Even though she expected it and wasn't startled at all, she gazed strangely at her sister. "Why are you coming home at this time?" Tone and words, the same as always, as if Mathilde was still sixteen and had dawdled on the way home from choir practice. She tore herself from Heidrun's gaze and pushed past her into the kitchen, washed her hands, bent over the sink and drank great greedy gulps of water directly from the faucet. They no longer needed to go the pump in the Schrebergarten or to the hydrant on the next corner to get water. A few days before the water had begun flowing from the plumbing, even on the fifth floor. "Use a glass." Not advice but an order—just as if Maman had left her old-folks home in south Germany and suddenly appeared, about thirty years younger, in Berlin.

Mathilde straightened up, dried her hands and mouth, and looked at her sister. She did not feel like arguing. She wanted to go into the living room. She wanted peace, not conversation or arguments. The rough, off-kilter and out-of-tune notes from the piano she had just played echoed in her skull like it was a great cavern. Unconsciously, she nodded in time to Baumgartner's drumbeat as she took a glass from the cupboard and drank more water. Suddenly she realized how hungry she was, realized she hadn't eaten anything since the sticky rolls with dry yeast spread for lunch. "Farts with caviar paste," Lene called them. She looked in the oven to find it empty. Empty? She looked at Heidrun confused. "Didn't you keep anything for me?"

"The kids were hungry and you were supposed to get barley." Heidrun didn't even think of apologizing, her tone harsh and accusatory, as was her face when she glanced into the empty shopping bag Mathilde had set down next to her.

Mathilde couldn't believe Heidrun had given her portion to the children and laughed out loud. "I couldn't have eaten the barley even if I had it," she said, pointing to the candle in Heidrun's hand. "No power, no cooking."

Heidrun continued pressuring her, but her voice was tinged with disappointment, almost sorrow. "Why didn't you bring any?"

Mathilde already felt guilty, and not just because she'd forgotten about the barley. She quickly began to make excuses for herself. "Färber's was already closed."

Heidrun had done what she set out to do. She enjoyed waiting for her sister to come up with an excuse for getting to the grocer's so late.

"We . . . we had to work late," Mathilde continued. "A wall broke down and a whole floor fell in. Schall was worried that everything would come down and wanted the rubble moved away, as long as we had light, so nothing happened."

Heidrun looked at her sister skeptically, doubtfully, but seemed to let it go and accept the explanation as she started to leave the kitchen. Mathilde hung up the hand towel and looked to Heidrun as she went to open the pantry cupboard. "Give me the key, please?"

"Why?"

Mathilde stared at her sister while her anxiety and bad conscience changed into bewilderment, irritation, and anger. "Why?!"

Heidrun's hand wandered to her jacket pocket but stayed there. "There's hardly anything in there. I go to a lot of trouble to apportion it and if you take something . . ."

"I'm hungry, Heidrun. I've worked the whole day . . ."

"And you should eat as well." Karla marched into the kitchen and put some pieces of zwieback in her mother's hand. "Where did you get these?" Heidrun and Mathilde asked at the same time, both of them flabbergasted.

Karla made an evasive gesture.

Frieder had followed Karla into the kitchen. "She stole the stuff, what else?"

"From where?" Heidrun managed despite her confusion, looking rapidly from one to the other. "And if you knew that your cousin stole, why didn't you stop her?"

Mathilde agreed with her sister. "No matter how bad we have it I don't want you to steal."

With that she considered the matter closed and started into the living room, but Heidrun stopped her, glaring demandingly at her, but Mathilde could do no more.

She longed for peace and quiet, finally some peace, finally some sleep, finally to be alone with Mozart and ragtime. She yearned to be all alone with the memory of keys not really struck, with sounds that never really happened, that lived only in the emptiness of air, in a vacuum heard and shared only between two people. She needed to be alone with the memory of the Russians intermingled with the memory of the "Turkish March" and ragtime. Maybe sometime, one day, the memories would be disentangled.

Looking at Heidrun's silent demand, she turned to Karla to give her back the pieces of zwieback and scold her. But her daughter preempted her. "What? Do you think I should return something?" Karla exchanged a look of disbelief with Frieder. That was absurd. On this they fully agreed. Whoever didn't take a little advantage now and then didn't survive in these times. You had to sail a hair's breadth on the border of what was allowed, or just a little across it. Everyone did it.

Nailed by Heidrun's glare, Mathilde began to scold, "Just because everyone does it . . ."

Karla again interrupted. "I didn't swipe the zwieback anyway. Not really," she said, staring hard at Heidrun, challenging her so that, again, Heidrun's hand unconsciously went to her jacket pocket. The key to the pantry cabinet was still there, good and safe but . . . Heidrun threw a questioning glance at her niece who just as emphatically challenged Mathilde. "So eat already before you fall over."

Her mother automatically took a bite out of a piece of the zwieback and began to chew while Heidrun with a dismissive gesture and determined face unlocked the pantry to inspect its contents. Reflexively, Frieder and Mathilde push nearer and watched the inventory over Heidrun's shoulders. There was half a loaf of paste gray bread, two or three hands full of peas, a final precious jar of plum preserves, ersatz coffee, a little salt, a little sugar, and five wrinkled potatoes. Karla had in fact retreated a few steps toward the door and folded her arms in front of her expecting the coming thunderstorm and oddly amused by all this.

Heidrun found what she expected. "You took the zwieback from the pantry. You have stolen from all of us. Us, your family." With each word, Heidrun stepped closer to her niece who leaned against the door casing for support and protection, her smile never leaving her lips.

Frieder examined the pantry like a detective. He was astonished. "Mom, I don't see how." He asked his cousin, "How did you manage to do that?"

Karla enjoyed his incredulity, his envy, that she had pulled it off, for how often had the kids stood there in front of the pantry like organ pipes from F to H, from Frieder to Horst, and wistfully thought how fine it would be if they could share only one thin slice of bread with perhaps a few sugar crumbs on it. What a delicacy that would be. "You'll never know."

"Don't you ever do that again, Karla!" Heidrun's voice would have turned boiling water into ice. "I won't punish you now because you wanted to do something good for your mother. But that won't ever happen again, do we understand each other?"

Karla nodded, surprised. A cold Aunt Heidrun was much more impressive than one hot with anger. "Come, Karla, we are going to bed. I am dead tired." Mathilde took her daughter and led her through the vestibule to the living room. Heidrun and her children had taken the bedroom because they could all sleep on the wide nuptial bed. "You want to bet I can figure out how you did it?" Frieder called after Karla.

"You can be sure I'll get something out of it, too."

"Stop that, Frieder! Don't be so childish," ordered Heidrun. "Don't be like your cousin."

Karla followed her mother savoring her small triumph as Heidrun scolded Frieder. "Now eat the zwieback, Mom. Shall I get you a glass of water so it won't be so dry?"

Mathilde shook her head and closed the living room door, "Please don't take anything more from the pantry." Hungrily she stuffed the zwieback one after another into her mouth. "She wouldn't have given you the key. And it is our cabinet." Karla shook her head, amazed. "Heidrun knows what she is doing. If we don't severely ration the food …"

"You always defend her. Always. You let her get away with way too much."

"What would it accomplish if I started a fight? I still wouldn't get anything to eat."

"No, that you would get from me," answered Karla with triumphant defiance.

Mathilde had to smile at that, even if unwillingly, and plopped down in a chair. "Well, I don't want to hear any more about it. Please try to bear with Aunt Heidrun," she said after taking a breath. "I know it's not easy, but, please, try. Don't make it any harder on us."

Karla nodded. She wanted to help, and besides, there remained the fact that she'd taken the zwieback, stole it and knew she shouldn't have. She laughed quietly to herself. Frieder would never figure out how she'd gotten things out of the pantry without leaving any clues. Never. The thought made her feel a little better.

The sofa, table, and floor were littered with Heidrun's sewing kit, and Frieder's and Horst's packs, so Karla began to clear all of it up; Heidrun insisted the kids study regularly since there were no official schools. Karla also picked up the few playthings for Gerhild and Heinrich that she had voluntarily pulled out from her own little "treasure chest" after her younger cousins had moved in. And with what result? Heidrun and her family spread out into the living room as if it belonged to them, too. Apparently it wasn't enough that they already occupied the bedroom; Heidrun insisted that a bedroom was for sleeping only, you didn't play in a bedroom.

"Shall I help you?" asked Mathilde. Still she made no move to get up.

Karla shook her head. "Stay there, you have done enough for today." She covered the sofa with a sheet and fetched the featherbed and pillows from the cabinet that used to contain Mathilde's records which had been moved. Heidrun's opinion was that the bedclothes did not belong on the sofa all day. How would that look if someone came to visit?

When Karla finished, Mathilde shuffled directly over to the sofa and groaned while stretching her back, massaging her feet and sticking her legs in bed. She lay down and thoughtfully studied her calloused hands before pulling the covers over her.

"Where were you really?" Karla asked her mother.

"We had to work longer, I already told you."

"Then you would have gotten wet because it rained pretty heavily. But you're not."

Mathilde had already closed her eyes but was suddenly wide awake. "We got under cover, what did you think?" She heard the sound of her own voice and the lie she told, and she knew that Karla also heard it.

"Mom. Oh Mommy," Karla said pitiably, almost amused that her mother would try to shrug her off with something so simple and easy to see through.

"It is none of your business where I was."

"Aha." Karla nodded to herself. Mathilde heard the amused understanding in her voice and quickly became a little angry. "Come to bed and sleep."

"Okay, okay." Karla undressed and snuggled in the covers.

Mathilde soon heard the peaceful regular breathing of her daughter beside her; she, who on any other day fell into bed like a dead person and slept without being able to think about anything, tossed and turned. Her fingers danced across an imaginary keyboard, playing the Mozart sonata once again. This time it did not sound like it had at noon in the rubble field. Again and again she clearly heard Wilhelm Kempff in her imagination, regardless how hard she fought against it, again and again she fell into the tempos of the phrasing on the Kempff recording that was now buried in a corner of the broom closet with her other records and sheet music. It almost seemed to Mathilde as if the freedom of how she played on the destroyed keyboard and the ease and deftness with which she later improvised on the grand piano in the basement had its foundation, it's beginning in Camillo Baumgartner. The Gypsy tightrope walker who had met her so unexpectedly, so puzzlingly, so unreal. And now he had met her once again. Coincidence?

Mathilde reluctantly shoved the thoughts aside.

Nonsense, you're imagining things. Little dreamer. Now go to sleep. You have to go to work in the morning. You need your strength. But it didn't work. The music, pictures, thoughts shot through her head like little shooting stars that went out before she could grasp them, before she could figure out what to wish for.

EIGHT

It smelled like before the war, the scent of silver fir and spruce that got a bit mustier the closer you got to the water. This was so different from the city where you smelled the destruction and it smelled just like it looked. All it took back there was a little wind or someone walking in the ruins to stir up clouds of cement and mortar dust that hung like ghostly pillars amidst the rubble. The dust carried the stink of burned wood and decayed life over the debris. Here, where the sun shone through the pine needles, it smelled like before, like on walks with Mathilde. Mathilde. Franz shoved those thoughts and let them dissolve in the light.

Faint cries of the bathers came from the Krumme Lanke. Karla had screamed and shouted with joy when he had brought her here to swim on Sundays after church long, long ago. For a moment he could see her, how she played in the water instead of practicing. Somehow she had learned to swim faster than he had expected but completely without discipline or order.

He pushed these thoughts away as well, decisively, almost angry that they kept coming to the surface. He freed them in the deceptively serene air. Who knew whether Karla and Mathilde were watched or not? He would have ordered it if he had to search for himself. Who knew what the deal was with the guy in the colorful vest, the one with whom Mathilde had recently come home. He could hardly believe that Mathilde . . . no, she would not have done that. Absolutely not. Still, Franz felt a pang when he thought about it . . . his wife, another man . . .

But no matter what was going on between them, the stranger's presence could possibly signal a danger to Franz. A danger to his freedom or danger for his family. He shouldn't have gone to his apartment, he thought, but then he would not have stumbled upon that man in the first place. On the other hand, he needed to know how things were going for Karla and Mathilde, whether they were living in the old house—*if* it still stood.

After seeing the two of them together, Franz had quickly and quietly fled. He spent an uncomfortable, restless night in the Tiergarten area of Berlin between burned bushes, raw refuse, broken and explosion splintered trees. Seeing the trees in this state of destruction, he thought, was almost harder to bear than it was to see the bomb-gutted buildings. He didn't find a place to sleep anywhere, but he would not have been able to sleep on the finest eiderdown quilts given his painfully empty stomach. He prayed for good luck the next morning, luck when he was going to the neighborhood where a colleague had lived. And his luck was good, for purely by chance he took his place in line behind the wife of the colleague he sought and spoke to her.

"Isn't that something?! I just happen to come by here and I find you, just like that, after all that has happened."

The woman started to sob and wipe tears from her eyes with a dirty hanky before Franz had even finished his greeting. Her husband was dead. He had been drafted into the Volkssturm later than Franz, in the last days of the war, and detailed to the defense of capital. He had fallen at the end of the battle fighting to his last breath against the Bolshevism. Like the Führer. The only difference being that he was torn up by a Russian machine-gun burst.

Franz tried in vain to contact other colleagues who he knew had been in Berlin at the war's end. He found houses destroyed with no sign that the people who had lived there survived. Others had been captured by the Soviets and immediately had been sent to Siberia, or so everyone thought since none of them were heard from after their capture. Still others seemed to have simply disappeared or fled. In any case they had vanished without a trace and even if someone knew where they had gone, no one said anything. Not even to him, a former colleague.

He had to be careful. Were the houses watched? Were the wives and children watched? Each time he met mistrust. What did the man want, who was asking about their father, husband, neighbor, customer? He felt that he knew those who had known him, mostly the wives of his comrades, wanted nothing to do with him. He represented the disaster that had taken their husband, mate, bread winner.

The others—even though they did not know him—noticed, smelled, felt what he had been and still was—a policeman, even without the black coat. With a heavy heart, he had finally parted with it, so as not to be identified. On the morning after the night in the Tiergarten, before he began his inquiries, punctually at eight, just like he was still a clerk, he had carefully hung it on a stub of a branch, like at home in the closet. Only he would not come back to take the coat off this hook. He did not have the strength to overcome the desire to turn back around after a few steps. The coat hung in the spring sunshine. Lifeless. A limp sad sack. Resolutely, he turned away.

Even without the black coat Franz was still a policeman. The people he questioned did not know why he asked about the men and they worried. No matter who sent him, like the SS before, people had to be cautious. It had been ingrained in them to be on guard. They would rather have bitten their tongues off than say what they really thought, knew, or meant. They would not talk, at least within hearing range of anyone like Franz, someone who was obviously in the same circle as those he asked about. If someone asked about any of those men, it could bode nothing good.

Even so, Franz learned what he needed. He had enough experience to be certain that people, at least most of them, did not lie to him. He could tell that they really did not know anything, that the men he looked for had told no one where they were or what they did. Franz had done the same, exactly the same. Karla and Mathilde had no idea he was back in the city. It was too dangerous. How easy it was to overlook someone following you, how easy it was to let the cat out of the bag when someone asked about him like he was doing now especially if they had to deal with skilled questions from an experienced tracker, a man hunter like he had become, like he had been.

So here in the fir-tree dappled sunshine stood an almost hopeless Franz looking at the home of Rudolf Borg, his former supervisor. It was a duplex with a classic gabled roof, brick façade and traditional windows divided into four panes. A real house, he thought, not like the unimaginative, cookie-cutter box apartments and homes built in this neighborhood, Zehlendorf, during the twenties. Thank God that "modern" nonsense had stopped.

Franz would have liked to live in a place like this. He dreamed of owning half of a duplex, just like Borg's, more than any of the other styles of single homes and duplexes. Homes like that were unattainable for him. Even Borg could barely afford his. More than once Franz had seen how the monthly mortgage weighed on him.

His family would not have fit in anyway. Higher SS officials and their families lived here. Not the really big fish but still those above the rank of Sturmführer. A simple policeman like Franz could not belong to that circle.

The war seemed to have gone past this place without a trace. No bombs had fallen here. It had not been fought over. Surely the Russians had come through here, seized houses and cut trees for firewood; but all in all it looked like it had a few years ago when he and Karla walked through after swimming and dreamed about such a semi-detached house for a half hour.

Finally, after he had stood there long enough to be sure that nobody watched the house, he rang the doorbell. Surprisingly, even the doorbell worked here. No response. He rang again and heard sneaking shuffling steps. Then it was quiet again. Franz looked around, but nobody paid any attention to him. There were only a few kids romping and playing through the development, happier and more carefree than he had seen anywhere else in the city.

It was still quiet behind the door. Franz could almost detect the other person who, he knew, was standing behind the door listening like he who stood in front of it. He hoped that it might be Borg's wife, Monika. Franz knew Monika Borg; she had brought her husband a warm lunch every day, a part of their frugality so they could pay for the house. And Mrs. Borg knew him. Borg was a courteous man; if a coworker sat in his office when his wife came in, he introduced them.

"Mrs. Borg, open the door, please. I am Franz Tegge." Franz whispered more than he spoke out loud, but he was certain that the woman on the other side of the door understood, and that she would open the door. If it really was Monika Borg.

The door opened a crack. In the shadows, Franz saw a dull, lusterless eye. He smiled at the eye. The door was shut again Franz heard her take off the chain, and Monika Borg opened the door.

She had once been a beautiful lady, a lively lady. Borg and she had billed and cooed like teenagers and paid no notice at all to the ridicule that billowed up after them as they went down the halls. A pretty, lively lady who did not exhibit the German ideal at all. She was small, slender as a wand, with black hair and sparkling dark brown eyes. Now the sparkle was gone, gray streaked through her hair, her cheeks were sunken and wrinkled. Franz's first impression was that she must be well over fifty as she stood there without makeup, her face taut from recent hardships, from worry and sorrow.

"Franz Tegge. Come in."

She led him through the small vestibule into the living room which was painstakingly clean, painstakingly put in order. Either the Russians had not been here, or all traces they had left behind had been meticulously erased. Nothing in the room was reminiscent of the occupation, the lost war, and the destruction all around. Nothing, except for the bright spot on the wallpaper where a picture had hung before. Certainly a picture of the Führer. Franz took in every detail. This was the way he would have loved to live.

As Franz sat down, Monika Borg offered him coffee. She whispered conspiratorially that it was real bean coffee that she had saved for special occasions.

Franz smiled to himself. I am therefore a special occasion, he thought. He didn't say anything, but waited. Mrs. Borg apparently needed someone with whom she could talk.

"May I ask you something? I mean, you are a colleague of my husband . . . you may know," she said, while laying the table with delicate porcelain and fine silverware. And although she apologized for not being able to serve cake, she understandably laid out dessert plates and forks. Mrs. Borg honored the tradition even if everything had collapsed around her. Franz understood and appreciated her effort. "Do you think I will be allowed to stay here? Or will they throw me out?"

"The house belongs to you, doesn't it?"

"Not yet paid off, not by a long shot. But otherwise, yes."

"No one quartered here?"

Mrs. Borg shook her head. "Until," she shivered, it was apparently hard for her to say the word, "until the collapse, Rudolf could prevent that. And afterwards no one had thought about it. Hopefully it will stay that way."

She went into the kitchen and returned with sugar and milk in a small silver service. The Russians had not been here, thought Franz. It was hardly imaginable that they would have allowed the Borgs to keep their silver. It would not surprise him if he awoke and it was all a dream, yet the little silver pots and little silver cans shimmered on the tray in front of him, and Franz thought he would never have imagined that a gleam could be so real. A shimmering, bright, incomprehensible silvery luster.

"I would advise you to bring a couple of people into the house, refugees, friends, who have been bombed out. You must have a few people in your circle of acquaintances that are on the streets. Fill your house before the occupiers do. Whenever the government functions again, at least provisionally, then you will have people here that you don't know, and who you would perhaps just as quickly want be rid of."

Mrs. Borg nodded. To be sure the prospect was not happy, having to share her home with strangers, but she saw that Franz was right. She went one last time into the kitchen and returned with the promised coffee. Franz smelled the coffee all along, real coffee beans, a fragrance he had almost forgotten. And the pot. It was really made of Meissen porcelain. Borg must have come from a well-to-do family background.

"What does your husband have to say about it?" asked Franz while she poured. It was a seemingly completely innocent question, just an expression of interest, but, of course, it was asked in hopes that he could learn something about his old boss.

Mrs. Borg sobbed. "If only I could ask him." She put two spoons of sugar in her cup and stirred thoughtfully.

Franz savored a sip. Borg was gone. It is a shame he thought, disappointed. Borg disappeared and she knew nothing, just like all the others. It was unfortunate, but the search was worth doing, and at least the coffee made it worthwhile. The coffee and the fact that he got to enter his dream house for the first time, but it had led only to a dead end.

"Rudolf is so far away, so unreachably far. He couldn't stay here to be sure."

Franz nodded, and perked up his ears. Something in Monika Borg's tone, in the art and manner with she spoke about her husband told him that she knew where he was. Where he hid himself. He looked over the rim of his coffee cup and glasses and waited.

She was quiet and seemed to ponder. "I am so worried," she finally said. "Rudolf is not the strongest. And he is not the youngest any more either." Borg was over sixty. A thin bald man with a crippled hand from the First War. A planner, a strategist, who would rather sit at a desk and hatch plans for arrests and raids than take part in them. And if you saw how Monika Borg cared for him, you got the idea he could not butter his own bread.

"If I can help in any way . . ." Franz suggested, trying to bait the hook.

"Thanks, you have already helped me a lot." Mrs. Borg did not bite, not yet at least. "I will invite a husband and wife who are friends to live here. That would surely be Rudolf's idea too."

Franz nodded. "Do that."

There was a pause. She finished her coffee. His cup was empty long ago. He knew that the conversation was over. He really should stand up, thank her for the coffee and leave but he just sat there. Mrs. Borg was his chance. He had to be stiff-necked about it.

"How do you manage?" she asked after a while, more out of politeness and not because she was really interested. She had been given the advice she sought. She didn't want anything more. She didn't offer a second pot of coffee.

Franz shrugged his shoulders. "I struggle through. It is not easy."

"Don't you have anyone where you could go? At least hide long enough until a little calm is restored?"

"I don't believe that will happen for us, Mrs. Borg. It will be a long time before there is enough peace that will let people like your husband and I lead a normal life."

"But Rudolf wanted only a few weeks . . ." She broke off frightened and looked Franz straight in the eye. "You are a friend, aren't you? Rudolf has strongly forbid me to speak about that."

"Then don't do it. Your husband is right to be cautious. Better to be a little too careful, to be too untrusting . . ." He left the sentence hanging in the air, the desired impression made without concluding it.

Franz waited until the recognition that their troubles were not yet over was firmly planted in Monika Borg's consciousness. He had not expected her to be this naïve. Still, Borg had apparently tried to calm her fears, and she believed what she wanted to believe.

"Can I still trust you? You were with him? You were in danger, too?"

"In great danger. I can't stay here much longer, I really need to find a hiding place. They will find me sometime." Now it had gone so far that he had to play out the rest of the script. "That is why I am here. We old comrades have to hold together. But if your husband . . ."

"He did not mean you. I am sure of that." She shivered anew and played thoughtlessly with the useless dessert fork that had the shimmer of authenticity and the embellishment of reality. "If I tell you where he is, would you give a message from me?"

* * *

"Don't move, don't make a fuss, or I'll blow your brains out of your skull." Franz felt the cold steel of a muzzle on the nape of his neck. He had no doubt that the voice meant what it said. Any argument would cost him his life.

Slowly, very slowly he raised his hands. "Don't you recognize me, Kriminalrat Borg? I am Obermeister Franz Tegge."

"Go two steps forward and turn around. But slowly. And nothing stupid."

Franz did as he was told and looked at the face of Rudolf Borg, Kriminalrat Borg. Untersturmführer Borg. He was, if at all possible, still thinner, unshaven and unkempt, his suit stained, no necktie, all in all a disheveled, neglected appearance. And that was not due to the war or the chaos but no, it was due to his habits. This amazed Franz even more since Borg had paid so much attention to a well-groomed appearance. It really was as they had joked behind his back, that he could not cook an egg without his wife.

Borg clutched a double-barreled shotgun in his crippled hand, his good finger on the trigger. Amused, Franz thought, I could overpower him with a quick jump. He could tell Borg was not an experienced shooter from the way he held the gun. He would never be quick enough to get Franz. Nonetheless, he stood still with hands in the air knowing Borg would not do anything to him. And Franz would never attack his boss, or former boss. Not even now that there was no longer a boss or underling, no longer any police as Franz had known it.

"Tegge, what are you doing here?"

"I have a message from your wife for you."

Borg nodded. He nodded bitterly, it seemed to Franz, nodded disappointedly as if he had expected nothing less, nodded angrily as if he should have known better. "Because of that . . ."

"Yes." Franz waited a moment more and then asked if he could lower his hands.

"Certainly," rumbled Borg and made an unwilling movement with the shotgun. "If you had wanted, I wouldn't have had a chance against someone like you. Someone who stood in the front lines and did not spend his life behind a desk. Sorry."

"But you didn't know it was me. And we can't be careful enough."

Borg nodded again, set the weapon down behind him and said nothing. They stood on the veranda of a little house, more like a hut, and looked at each other without saying anything. Behind them stretched one of the many little lakes in Mecklenburg. It was encompassed by trees, a solitary idyll in the middle of the pinewood. A small boat dock stuck out in the water from the hut with a rowboat, which hardly looked seaworthy, dumped on it.

Franz knew such huts; often enough he and Mathilde had spent the night in one while on their hikes. They usually had only a single room, and you could rent one from the local forester for a couple of Groschen. This one had a little chimney, so it would have a stove or perhaps only a hearth. And it was apparently not for rent since it stood on private land; the lake and woods were widely fenced in, apparently for a hunting reserve.

Living in such a hut would be primitive, jumping into the lake to wash up, fetching water from it to cook. A few meters from the house there would be a hole in the ground with a privy over it for a toilet. Franz would have given a lot to be able to go back in time and spend a few days in such a place with Mathilde and Karla. Unconsciously Franz's face became a smile or just a furrow as it occurred to him that for the second time in forty-eight hours he stood on a dream place. How different the dwellings were, here the little hut in Mecklenburg and there the fancy duplex in the big city, and yet they were the same in at least one way—both were unattainable for him, as far away from him as the moon.

For a moment Franz wasn't sure what to do anymore. He remained motionless as if he had all the time in the world which, God knows, he didn't. He took off his glasses and rubbed the lenses on the dirty sleeves of his gray flannel shirt, rubbing as if he could clear away and erase the images, and above all reality. Before him stood Borg so helpless that it hurt. What of himself? Suddenly Franz saw himself, clear and sharp, mirrored in Borg's resigned eyes and his miserable appearance.

He knew he looked as bad as Borg. Not only were his shirt sleeves dirty, but all his civilian clothes—a "gift" from the U.S. Army—stank from the nearly one hundred kilometer hike from Zehlendorf which had turned into a roundabout tour. He had to avoid road blocks since no one was allowed in or out of the city without permission; and with few cars—the few which were passing by belonged to or were commandeered by the Russians—and no trains running he had no choice but to walk or hitch an occasional ride on some farmer's horse-drawn wagon.

Borg took his time, apparently reflecting on what he should do about Franz, what his visit meant, but he could come to no conclusions. Clearly he was not elated that Franz was there. "What do you want?" he asked. "I didn't know where to go. I didn't know what to do. The Amis captured me, but I escaped. And then I thought . . . I mean, we are old comrades, we have to stick together."

"But why did you come right to me?"

Franz shrugged. "Coincidence. You are the first one I have found. A lot of us were captured by The Ivan, and we will probably never see them again. Others have disappeared without a trace. Still others died in the last days of the war."

Suddenly panic flew over Borg's face. He became threatening and defenseless at the same time, like a flock of gray birds in a pale sky. Brusquely he asked, "No one saw you come here? No one saw you when you spoke to my wife?"

"Superintendent, I am an old rabbit."

Borg nodded almost motionless, but the flock of birds remained.

"Do you have something for me to drink?"

"Good. Fetch some water and then disappear."

Franz took a bucket out on the dock and dipped water and drank while Borg watched impatiently. Something wasn't right here, thought Franz. Borg had always been a sociable supervisor and proud that he was like a father toward his people. That Borg dismissed him like that amazed him. The man was afraid of something, or someone. And it was not discovery by the Russians. Franz presented no danger of that.

While he went back up to Borg, Franz glanced into the hut through the window. Only one room, just as he thought. It was disorderly, the bed wasn't made, and a few books lay next to it. Pieces of clothing hung on the only chair, cups and cutlery lay on the table, a pot on the stove. There was an indefinable mass on one of the plates. He had surprised Borg while eating. At least he could warm up his food by himself. Next to the plate, half hidden in the shadows, lay a piece of bread and behind it stood a half-empty bottle. Only with a second look, Franz could identify it as French cognac. Someone was taking care of Borg, and very good care at that, better than most who could only dream of French cognac. Maybe Borg was not afraid of anything but rather had something to hide. But what?

"You were lucky to find such a hut." Franz floated a trial balloon as he got back to Borg on the veranda in front.

Borg immediately parried, "I'm sorry I can't help you. You see how I live." Borg's unhappy conscience engulfed him like a light-filled fog that illuminated instead of obscured.

Franz wondered for a moment whether or not he should grill Borg as he had been trained. He could tell that Borg wouldn't resist for long, but no. It was unimaginable, for Borg was his supervisor. He just could not jump him like a common criminal. Instead he said, "Your wife sends her best wishes."

"Oh, yes, my wife . . ." Borg appeared to have completely forgotten her, and completely forgotten that Franz brought a message from her. It was another signal that something was wrong since he and his wife were always of one heart and soul. "What does she want?"

"She is worried about you," Franz began, "and doesn't know what she should do. I got the feeling that she thinks the whole thing will blow over, that you just have to hide for a few weeks and everything will be back in order. I think that is, to put it mildly, very optimistic."

"Did you tell her that?" Borg spit out the words between clenched teeth.

"Yes."

"You idiot. You damned idiot."

"Why? What did I do wrong?" Franz acted like he couldn't comprehend Borg's anger at all. "You don't really believe they won't be looking for us for longer than a few weeks?"

"No, naturally not." Borg regained his composure. "But, Monika. She was completely distraught after the collapse. She didn't want to let me go. She was afraid. And I couldn't stay, so . . ."

That was not the whole truth. Were this an interrogation Franz would have . . . But, this was no interrogation, and Borg was no criminal so Franz let it go and begged pardon for his awkwardness and excused himself but did not move. He tried the same tactic that had worked with Borg's wife. He simply stood there and waited it out.

But the superintendent had regained his authority. "Like I said, I unfortunately cannot help you."

Franz nodded disappointedly. "Do you have any advice as to where I might go or where I might find help?"

"No. I am sorry. I avoid contact with old comrades. It seems safer that way. So I would like you to go now as well." He turned to the door, hesitated a bit before he went in. "Good luck," he said, and suddenly, unexpectedly the old real sincerity that had differentiated Borg from the other higher ranks came through. "I always liked you, Tegge. You were a good policeman. And you have nothing to feel guilty about. You only did your duty."

"I am afraid the Russians won't see it that way. Just like the Americans."

Borg nodded, opened the door. "Please go. Stay safe." With that he disappeared into the hut.

Franz stared at the door for a moment, and then he, too, turned and went along the path through the woods back to the wood rail that separated the private path from the public road. He thought about what he should do now. What should he think about Borg? Was he afraid of something? Did he have something to hide? Or was Borg's strange behavior simply due to the fact that he, like everyone, had everything taken away from him and didn't know what was going to happen. But he was the old Borg at the end, the one that Franz knew. Had he just been startled? On the other hand, he was well supplied. French cognac? No, Franz's instinct told him something was wrong, and he had always relied on his instincts.

But the question remained, what? And what should Franz do with this knowledge? Should he stay with Borg? Franz was certain there was something to be gained by that, but on the other side of the coin, because he felt an almost ingrained aversion to spying on his supervisor or to pressure him, he asked himself if it would be worth it. Maybe by observing him he might find a way that gave him protection and eventually freedom. If Borg knew such a way, he would be long gone. If Borg knew where to go, he would not live in that squalid hut. If Borg had a plan, he would never leave his wife alone, not just because of love, but because she could be a security risk. If Franz had found him through her, then so could others.

Noise from a motor tore him from his contemplation. He stood still and listened carefully, but he could not tell if the noise came from the road or from the path he was on. In a minute it got quieter, the motor only murmured, as if it were in neutral, then it got louder. The gears ground and the car shifted into a lower gear. That could only mean one thing: The driver had opened the gate and was driving down the private forest lane towards him. Franz pulled back into the undergrowth.

A car did not bode well for poor Borg, he thought. It could only mean the Russians or their German henchmen had been sent to arrest the former Untersturmführer. Under cover of the bushes and the shadows of the trees, Franz worked his way back to the hut. Maybe in some way he could help Borg when he attempted to flee.

The noise got closer. The car would soon overtake him. Franz stood still, and ducked low as the noise got so loud that it meant it was right behind him. He did not want to give himself away by movement. He carefully peeked through the branches about fifty meters from the hut where he could see the entrance.

Borg had heard the approaching car and was standing in front of the hut. To Franz's amazement he stood quiet and erect, and made no effort to flee. It was as if he had expected the car.

A moment later a German army truck appeared in the little clearing in front of the hut. Franz had not seen one in such good repair for a long time. How and where had that truck escaped the war, he wondered? From which depot, which hiding place had the Russians commandeered it? Borg obviously expected the Russians without worry or fear. Was he collaborating on something? Was Borg a traitor? That would explain a lot, maybe even the idea that all this would be behind him in a few weeks. But, if he worked with the enemy his wife would not talk about it, certainly not to Franz.

If that was the case, thought Franz, then it was almost an act of friendship, of comradeship, to have sent him away, so he would not fall into the hands of the Russians because he would have been required to turn Franz over to them.

In the next moment Franz saw that he was completely wrong in every way and certainly about Borg. Two men jumped from the truck. Not Russians but Germans. And men that he knew!

Sturmbannführer Matthus, not a trained policeman but an SS man that Himmler had placed as an observer right in front of Borg. A thickset, uncouth man in his mid-forties with a full head of blond hair who Franz immediately recognized even though, understandably, he did not wear a uniform. A man who, as Franz knew from experience, took unholy pleasure in personally torturing and killing prisoners. One didn't soon forget that.

The other one was Rottenführer Kleinmann, a wiry youngster, probably not yet twenty-five and a very low rank in the SS who was ambitious and had absolutely no criminal talent whatsoever. He was a hundred and fifty percent party loyalist who had landed in Franz's section to protect party interests. He was one of those guys the oldsters, like Franz, were very glad to see assigned to someone else.

Matthus went directly to Borg. The two greeted each other heartily, almost affectionately. They were so confident with each other?! Franz hadn't expected anything like what he saw. He was flabbergasted. When the greeting was over Borg grabbed Matthus by the arm and spoke animatedly to him sharing something of importance.

Franz understood only scraps of the conversation that the wind carried over to him. Still he believed he heard his name. It was clear that Borg warned Matthus of him. Finally Matthus motioned Kleinmann over and handed him Borg's shotgun. Kleinmann posted himself in front of the door while the other two disappeared into the hut.

So this is what the Kriminalrat had to hide. How did he ever get the idea Borg was involved with the Russians, thought Franz shaking his head. It was absolutely the opposite. Borg, who had always been skeptical and kept his distance from the Nazis, who had only reluctantly accepted them when adherence to the party line was more important than technical expertise. Borg had sought allies where he needed them. Franz wondered why he wondered about that. In times like these everyone sought to survive as best he could, just like himself. To be sure he didn't know what Matthus and Borg had in mind, but one thing he did know—he had made a direct hit. Someone owned a truck and had enough gas to drive around in these dangerous times. Someone was able to get the necessary approvals, permits, passes. Someone who had connections Franz could only dream of, and that someone could help him move forward if only Franz was cunning enough. If he was careful and shrewd enough . . .

He thought about sneaking into the truck, hiding in the cargo bay, but that seemed as improbable as getting close enough to the hut to listen to the group without getting caught. Kleinmann knew what he was doing. He had parked the truck in full sight in the clearing. And anyone who wanted to get near the hut would have to cross the clearing.

Suddenly something crackled next to Franz in the underbrush. He jumped, crouched low, as low as he could, and attempted to disappear in the bushes. There, again! It could only be a few meters between him and whatever crackled. Were Kleinmann and Matthus not alone? Had they dropped off a few comrades at the gate to secure the area? Were they now advancing to the hut? Would they stumble on him in a minute or two? Carefully he peered around. He wanted to know how many there were, how many would soon be on him, but he couldn't see anything.

Another noise. This time not a crack, this time it sounded more like a bough being ripped from a tree, a noise that Franz could not pin down. Slowly he raised his head a bit higher and—saw a large roebuck that stood in peace and browsed close to him. Franz stared at the deer fascinated. He had never been so close to such an animal except in a zoo. At the same time he felt the pangs of hunger in his gut, but he had no gun. Even if he did, a shot would have been impossible. No roast for him. Then he had an idea. Slowly, carefully he reached around him, checking the ground until he found a stone that fit his hand, not too big, not too little. He lifted the stone and aimed carefully knowing he had one chance. He aimed for the animal and threw the stone as hard as he could. He hit it in the flank, and the big buck jumped, looked around anxiously sniffing and took off through the underbrush.

Kleinmann heard the noise and raised his shotgun aiming in the direction of the woods, but he couldn't find a target. His shotgun swung hectically back and forth without a chance to shoot. With danger behind it, the roebuck broke from the trees and ran directly at Kleinmann who reacted with admirable presence of mind and shot immediately. The buck reared up, staggered, blood frothing from its throat, made a couple of helpless uncoordinated leaps and collapsed. Kleinmann is an excellent shot, thought Franz; you have to give him that.

Startled by the shot, Matthus and Borg came out of the hut. Matthus had his pistol drawn; Kleinmann pulled Matthus's arm down and pointed to the roebuck that lay dead on the ground a few meters away. As Matthus saw the reason for the shot he got red in the face and shouted at Kleinmann so loudly that Franz heard every syllable despite the distance.

"Are you crazy, man? Everyone within ten kilometers heard that shot! Do you know what that means? In a few minutes the Ivans will be here. Do you know what will happen if they find us with weapons and ammunition? They will haul us off before we can say *drushba!*"

So it went for a few more moments until Borg put his hand on Matthus's arm and said something that seemed to calm him a little. He nodded, sent Kleinmann to recover the buck and disappeared with Borg into the hut. This was Franz's chance. He had waited for this moment. He ran quietly, with quick steps, to the truck. Carefully, slowly, his gaze hard on the ground so he would not step on a branch and give himself away, Franz slipped to the clearing. He reached the edge of the woods, stayed in the protection of the trees, looked, and listened.

Kleinmann had reached the roebuck and looked at it thoughtfully. The animal was covered with blood, and he obviously didn't want to get his suit dirty. Matthus and Borg were in the hut. There was nothing to be seen of them, nothing to hear. Franz hurried over the open stretch from the edge of the woods to the truck. He was breathing heavily when he made it to the truck and ducked behind a tire and took a moment to assess the situation. It worked. No one noticed. Up to now, at least. Kleinmann had grabbed the buck by the legs and tugged it towards the truck, but in the hut it was quiet.

He didn't have much time. Franz opened the tarpaulin just far enough that he could push through, climb on the tires, pull himself up and get over the tailgate. He clamped his glasses to the bridge of his nose with his finger and rolled to the other side of the truck bed. He stifled a cry as he cracked his head on the benches that were mounted on the bed. This truck had been a troop transporter.

There was no time for pain. He heard Kleinmann reach the truck and he quickly looked around for a place to hide. He was lucky, and lucky again, because he found a pile of stinking dirty blankets under the bench. He almost laughed thinking he should secretly rename himself "Hans in Luck", like the guy in the fairy tale. He was thrown by how easily such abstruse thoughts came to mind in this situation. Thoughts for which he had no time. Thoughts that could cost him his life.

Kleinmann started to open the tailgate. Franz pulled the blankets over him not caring how disgusting they were. He crumpled himself up and hoped, prayed, begged that Kleinmann would open the truck just enough to tug the roebuck onto the bed and, in the twilight, not notice the man under the blankets.

Kleinmann had untied the tarpaulin, lowered the tailgate, and heaved the buck onto the truck bed. "Damn shit, what a mess!" The SS man was not successful in keeping his suit, still creased from the cleaners, clean. Angrily he tried to brush away the blood with a cloth, or so Franz sensed. He could not see from under the blankets.

Then he heard footsteps and voices as Borg and Matthus neared the truck. Franz barely breathed as he peeked out from under the blankets. Apparently they had packed everything they could move from the hut. Borg carried an old pigskin suitcase, Matthus a cardboard carton.

"What a damn mess. What kind of idiot are you?" he scolded when he saw that Kleinmann had simply thrown the animal on the truck bed. Everything around it was smeared with blood. "I told you to make the animal disappear."

"Sturmbannführer . . . I thought, the wonderful roast . . . !"

"Nonsense, don't feed me such foolishness, Kleinmann."

"Perhaps he is right," interjected Borg. "If the Russians have heard the shot and look for us, they will see the tracks and think it was a poacher."

"Hmm." Matthus was not convinced, but he did not want to discuss it. He wanted to get out of there. "Okay, put the stuff in the truck." He scornfully inspected his assistant. "But be careful that you don't wind up with Mr. Borg's luggage looking like your suit."

Kleinmann cut off any answer, climbed up in the truck, stepped over the dead buck and took the suitcase and carton that Borg and Matthus handed him. He put them on the bench across from the one Franz laid under and looked around for a rope to secure them.

Franz held his breath. He was running out of air and black stars swam between the lids and eyeballs. He imagined he was looking through Kleinmann's eyes at how that bundle of blankets, even when he held still, gently rose and fell under the bench. The flickering stars exploded into a frantic dance, freed themselves from his eyeballs and climbed in the direction of the horrible stinking blankets over his face, his motionless body.

Kleinmann didn't even notice the bundle of blankets. Not yet. He didn't find a rope, felt under the bench upon which the suitcase and carton stood and found nothing. He groped further, under the bench there and on the other side. The hand came nearer and nearer to Franz.

"Come on, how long does it take you?" Matthus's voice sounded more than angry.

Lucky Hans, my guardian angel, thanks to you, prayed Franz. Kleinmann stopped and pulled his hand back just before he reached Franz. If he had felt him it would have been the end. Instead, Kleinmann stood up, pulled his belt from his pants, and bound the suitcase and carton to the bench across from Franz. Then he jumped from the truck and closed the tarpaulin.

And Franz closed his painful eyes. In spite of the breathless fireworks, he had stared through a small gap in the blankets as the searching hand crept toward him. He shut his eyes, breathed deeply and audibly. But nobody heard him since Kleinmann had started the engine, the doors had slammed, the truck jerked to a start and began to pick up speed.

Franz grabbed ahold of a rail on the bench as he was painfully bounced around. He prayed that the entire way would not be so bad, and his prayer was heard. After they left the forest path behind them and travelled on the road, it got better, much better. So good that after a time of constant swaying on the road he dozed off.

Wild pictures shot through his head in the half sleep, half dream. He was hit, kicked, stabbed and attempted to protect himself, but when he held his arms in front of his face, they hit him in the ribs, punched him in the belly. Suddenly big machines came, half tank, half crane, toward him, unstoppable. He wanted to get away, run away, crawl away, limp away, simply get away, but he was held fast. Now, it could only be seconds, milliseconds, the machines were only centimeters away from him, now they would roll over him, now . . . He woke up.

Something had changed, he could not immediately tell what. It was quiet. Quiet? That was it, the silence. No noise. The engine was shut off, he wasn't bounced around. The truck stood still! They had arrived. He rolled up like a fetus, attempted to make sure that a foot or a hand didn't stick out from under the blankets, or a piece of clothing. He pulled the blankets around him but left a gap very close to the floor of the truck bed. It was his visual umbilical cord to the outside. He wanted to, had to know what happened, no matter what it was.

He lay there and waited. Lay motionless and waited for the tailgate to open, for Kleinmann to off-load the suitcase, carton and deer. He hoped that the army truck would be parked and left alone for a while so he could get out. He lay there and listened carefully. Voices. At first he thought they came from the truck cab and that Borg, Matthus and Kleinmann carried on a conversation.

Then he made out one voice that was louder than the others. The voice moved and finally stopped, next to the side of the truck where Franz hid, separated by the thin tarpaulin which covered the cargo bed. The voice had a Russian accent. They weren't at the end. This was a control point on the city border. Shit, how could Kleinmann and Matthus be so dumb? They must know that the Russians guarded the entry roads into Berlin. Maybe they had tried to go around the checkpoint and were still up against a control point. No matter, it was too late. The Russians would search the truck and then . . . Franz didn't know who he feared the most, Kleinmann and Matthus or the Russian soldiers.

Slowly Franz began to understand what the Russian said, the one next to the truck. "Your papers are in order, comrades." Comrades? Had Matthus suddenly gone over to the Russians? Well, when in need the devil eats flies. "Still," the Russian said, "we would like to look in the cargo bay. You know what Comrade Lenin said, Trust is good. . . ."

Franz felt a bottomless pit open inside him. The inevitable was about to happen; he would be discovered, and it would all be over. "Okay, comrade. But please hurry up." That was Matthus's voice. What was he up to? They must believe they have nothing to hide, thought Franz. The suitcase and carton apparently have only a few personal items without any indication of Borg's real identity. Had they forgotten the big deer? Or would Matthus sacrifice it? As a bribe for the comrade? "Your thoroughness and watchfulness against the class enemy is exemplary, comrade," Matthus went on. "But as you saw in the papers, we are on an important mission to rebuild the Communist party in Germany. And we are in a hurry. So please allow us to proceed so we can go on."

Silence. A pause. At any moment Franz expected the Russian would open the tarpaulin, climb in the cargo bay, and discover him. "Here, we just commandeered this from a fascist asshole." That was Matthus's voice again. "That should suffice to release us, or?" A squeaking pop. A cork had been pulled out of a bottle. "Take a little break."

Again a silence. Then the Russian laughingly said, "Due to the importance of your mission, we can disregard the search."

Franz sighed. He marveled at Matthus who had played this little act so cool and sly, and unknowingly saved Franz's life.

Matthus and the guard said their goodbyes; Kleinmann started the engine and the truck jerked into motion again. They acted like German Communist party members who wanted to rebuild the party. And they had papers allowing them freedom of movement. But how did they get those papers? What connection did they have with the occupiers? And what were they after? Did they just want to hide? With what was obviously at their disposal, they would have long since had new papers or even be out of country. No, there must be something more to it, and he wanted to find out what it was.

A short half hour after the checkpoint they stopped again. Franz had not left the shelter of the bench since the risky stop at the city border and he used all his energy to stay awake. Now, he scrunched up again and made himself just as small as possible.

Borg and Matthus talked while getting out. "It was lucky that the guard did not look in the back. Otherwise he would have known that the papers had been forged," said Borg. The truck door slammed shut. I was right, thought Franz. No cooperation with the Russians.

"They are not forged. They are real." Matthus laughed. Franz couldn't understand what more was said because their voices dimmed as the two moved away from the truck.

Kleinmann opened the tarpaulin only as far as he had to in order to tear the suitcase and carton from the bench and then disappeared. He returned a few minutes later to fetch the big buck. Their hiding place must be nearby. Franz waited a little longer until Kleinmann had time to disappear into what Franz imagined to be a cellar or whatever the hiding place was. Then he crept to the tailgate and peered carefully out. He was in a more or less destroyed street that he did not recognize right away. It felt like he was somewhere in Wilmersdorf or Charlottenburg, but the city sectors had lost their individuality. Just like the streets they all shared one identity, rubble.

Franz looked towards the right and the left as far as he could. Nobody was to be seen. There was a path cleared between two destroyed houses leading to what looked like an intact rear building. Franz was sure Matthus and the others had gone in there. He jumped from the truck, ran around to the other side and ducked behind a wall in a house entryway, which was all that still stood. A short while later Kleinmann, just as Franz expected, returned from the direction of the undestroyed rear premises to the truck, turned it around and drove off.

The sun crept slowly over the sky and up the sharp-edged peaks of the rubble piles. That meant it was now—the middle of June—about eight thirty. Franz did not want to do anything more. He'd had enough for today. He was very hungry, desperately needed something to drink, and had to find a place for the night. He waited another five minutes, and since nothing more happened he left the entryway and started slowly down the street on the hunt for survival for this night.

"Uncle Franz? Is that really you? Uncle Franz?"

Franz believed he had imagined the voice at first. Then he discovered the fourteen-year-old boy who suddenly ran up to him. Frieder, his nephew, the son of Mathilde's sister. Shit.

"Uncle Franz?" he repeated, clearly as surprised about the encounter as Franz himself. He overtook Franz and stood in his path. "What are you doing here?"

"I'm sorry," he murmured, "but I don't know any Uncle Franz." In that moment Franz Tegge, the former policeman, the former SS officer and Gestapo man, no longer knew who he really was or if he really was named something else. He pushed the boy aside and stormed down the street.

The boy watched him for a while, surprised and confused. Then something dawned on him and he gathered the incomprehensible. "I will not betray you, Uncle Franz," he murmured. And as he walked away he hummed quietly, "The drums beat to battle, we fight side by side . . ."

NINE

Mathilde figured she would be here for at least an hour as the line moved slowly forward. If she had bad luck, the store would close before she got there, or their stock would be sold out. After long hours standing in line she would finally reach the counter and be put off with an indifferent, at best sorrowful shrug. "Sorry. All gone." She had chits and her hard labor allowance, but it made no difference, it was all the same. If there is nothing more, there is nothing more; the new Berliner practical wisdom.

Mathilde waited. What else could she do? As usual they had barley, which no one wanted, and sugar and oil. They needed those. They needed everything. She hoped to get some at least.

Mathilde felt especially sorry for the children. In the lines, "might makes right" ruled. There were various tussles with sharp elbows thrown wide and bodies recklessly shoved around. A child was easily hit, stepped on, or knocked down. Even so she and Heidrun sent Horst and, on occasion, Gerhild to stand in the lines. Without the help of their children they simply could not cope.

Mathilde was beyond tired. Deep within herself she was irritated, stressed, and jumpy dealing with the world she lived in. She did not take part in the customary chatter in the lines. She saw the meaningful looks that her second floor neighbor, Else Berners, and the super's wife, Irmi Trimborn, exchanged. Typical Tegge, she was sure they thought, she doesn't talk to anyone, probably thinks she is too good. Their judgmental glares cut like a knife, but she made herself not care. She knew what they thought of her, of the chatter, and of her reputation.

She preferred to listen quietly to how the news reports were swapped, all the while soaring around her own head like an idle dragonfly. Today the talk was all about how the Americans and English would soon march into the capital. The speculation and rumors swapped around concerned what would happen under the new occupiers, what they would change and what would stay the same.

The Allies had divided the city into different sectors, and the Western powers would come the first of July to take over Steglitz and even Kniepholzstraße. The tales told in line were mostly fantasies about the Americans. Great hope rested on the Amis who, for the Berliners, were shining victors. They were so different from the filthy, lousy, noisy, and dumb Russians. The rapists. Naturally the women in the line talked about them with the same merciless frankness as in the workplace.

"... this man told his underage daughter, 'Honor lost is everything lost.' And what did the girl do? She hanged herself from a beam in the loft."

"It was lucky the beam hadn't been burned." A voice from further back. A voice like glass shards.

Mathilde did not realize how the cynical remark had registered on her eardrum, gone to her brain, and elicited a reaction. Suddenly she had turned her head and with vigorous, forceful, and reproachful voice said, "Was that really fun? To blaspheme the bad luck of someone else?"

Else Berners and Irmi Trimborn exchanged astonished looks. Mathilde was just as astonished with herself realizing that the music—playing the grand piano in the basement—had blown open the stone bunker in her mind where she had locked her rape by the two Russians; that really was true what she had told Karla, back then—it helped that she wasn't the only one.

The speaker, a pretty brunette with burn scars on her throat and arms, answered spitefully, "Thanks, but if I want to hear a sermon, I'll go to church."

Scattered, unhappy laughs. Others in the line were eagerly looking forward to a little spat, an altercation, the more so as the brunette stared at Mathilde defiantly. But Mathilde did not want to continue. She had said what she thought. She dropped her gaze and broke the connection with the brunette who turned away with a shrug and a spiteful smile.

Mathilde examined the toes of her shoes. I must polish my shoes, she thought, so they will last a little longer; but with what? Her stuffy head pounded from hunger, exhaustion, and pain. If only somebody would come to take my place, she thought. Frieder, perhaps, or Karla? Mathilde looked around, still no one appeared, none of her family. She had to hold on. Carry on. She moved a further snail's pace forward.

Then he came around the corner. It was Irmi Trimborn, standing a few places in front of Mathilde, who saw him first. "This prick again already," she whispered so loud that everyone could hear it. "What keeps him hanging around here?"

Mathilde's head snapped up. She knew exactly who the super's wife meant by "prick." She knew exactly who was coming. She forced herself to not turn towards Camillo Baumgartner with his hat pushed back on his head and his vest a splash of color against the rubble gray. She tried not to stare at him but could not help herself.

She had to turn around, had to look at the man. She had not thought of him since that remarkable evening in the cellar, and the piano. It took all her strength, not to think of him. It was torment for he was always present in her thoughts. She would love to be able to run from there, to flee, but she could not; she could not give up her place in line so she tried to act as if she didn't see Baumgartner. She tried to act as if she didn't know he existed.

He went straight to her, touching the brim of his hat in greeting. Mathilde felt the disapproving glances from Trimborn in front of her and the others boring into her back. She literally knew their thoughts. What does Tegge have to do with that Gypsy? Look at that, how she has so quickly become comfortable with him. She knew them only too well.

Others in line looked at the artiste with distrust. They were instinctively uncomfortable with this man being around Mathilde. They had heard much about the Gypsies; that they were filthy like vermin, they stole, they kidnapped children. No one had asked or even noticed when these tramps had vanished and no one missed them. Now, here they were again, at least some of them. They were everywhere, and now Berliners had to be nice to them; they weren't allowed the thoughtless pleasure of chasing them off like before. No. Now the pleasure lay on the other side with Gypsies full of impudent pride strutting through the destroyed streets.

"Mrs. Tegge," he said, "is everything going alright?" His warm dark voice with the light strange accent seemed to come out of the distance, even though the man stood directly in front of her.

"Yes, yes, certainly." Mathilde forced herself to look in the amber-flecked brown eyes of the tightrope walker. She immediately felt light-headed. "You look pale. Are you not well?"

"Just work and hunger and . . ." She tried to act normal, but it did not work. Suddenly she heard Mozart, papada-pàda, and then suddenly Mozart was no longer her friend, her comfort, no more her playful break. Instead it was an enemy, a threat, anxiety, danger, reminder of an unbearable, unthinkable world that tried to entice, illuminate, seduce. Mathilde stormed past Baumgartner and ran away.

"Mrs. Tegge!" He called after her. "What is it? Are you coming back? Should I hold your place?"

Mathilde hurried wordlessly on, and the artiste took her place in line.

"Hey, what is this? Breaking into line doesn't go." Else Berners, who had stood directly behind Mathilde, promptly tried to shove Baumgartner out of the line. The woman, who was corpulent in spite of the hunger, pushed mightily with practiced knees and elbows, but the hated Gypsy stood like a tree, a powerful tree, full of life, against whose bark the woman scraped her skin.

"What have you done that scared Mrs. Tegge off?" Irma Trimborn started in. "What happens now? If everyone does that, threatens someone to take their place at the front of the line . . ."

Others in line murmured agreement then; as if a spell had been broken quiet anger became an alarm for self-justification. Shouts arose: "Get out of here!" . . . "Go on, git!" . . . "Damn bunch of Gypsies!"

Baumgartner was not impressed by the little tumult in the line.

Instead he pulled out a packet of cigarettes from his pocket and calmly lit one. The scolding weakened to envious looks, ebbed away, and stopped. No one chose to really go against the Gypsy. A diffuse, never admitted consciousness of guilt created an aura around him that would have taken a lot of confidence to break through. More than the Germans could muster.

Berners backed off first and solemnly told the woman behind her, "It is okay. After all, he did save her daughter's life."

The defiant brunette spoke up again. "Yeah, but that is the worst part. A true Christian does a good deed without expecting a reward."

The one Else Berners had spoken to, the one who had been happy that without Mathilde at least one fewer hungry, needy shopper stood in line in front of her, looked angrily at the Gypsy. "She did not give up her place to him of her free will. It sure didn't look that way."

Baumgartner inhaled a last time and tossed the half-smoked cigarette right in front of her feet. Immediately a tense silence came over those standing there. The woman looked uncertainly from the glowing butt to the striking, powerful man in the colorful vest and back again, but before she could give in to the overpowering impulse to reach for it and withstand humiliation for a half a cigarette, a half-grown boy passing by grabbed the little treasure.

"Thanks," he grinned at the woman over his shoulder as he went on.

She wanted to scream at him, but quickly thought the better of it. She had seen the gloating expressions of her neighbors in line, but what really stopped her was the condescending look she saw in Baumgartner's eyes.

Finally, in the quiet that lingered after the fruitless skirmish, Irmi Trimborn said, "In any case, it is good that poor Mrs. Tegge has a man in the house again." Some of the women nodded in agreement. In spite of all the critical gossip, they all hoped to soon have a man at home again to protect them from the intrusion of depraved people. A real man, not an oldster, a child, a cripple. For a moment, they all hung their thoughts on that.

They were so busy with their wishes, their hopes, that none noticed the lightning in Baumgartner's eyes as Irmi Trimborn spoke about a man living with Mathilde, and none saw the triumphant smile in the corners of his mouth.

* * *

A few corners away from the line, a distraught, confused, and upset Mathilde ran into her daughter's arms. "Mom, what are you doing here?"

"I wanted to come. To let you go." Karla was disappointed, both disappointed and irritated. Irritated by her mother because she couldn't wait another five minutes. After all, Karla was already on the way to take her place in line.

And she was even more irritated with Frieder. It was his turn to replace Mathilde, but that didn't happen. No, not Frieder. The elegant young man had come home with, at best, an arm full of wood that had taken all day to gather, and worse, he wouldn't say where he had wandered off to all day. No one but Karla even asked. Now Heidrun had sent her again after she had worked the whole day at home, and just because Frieder, the idiot, had not shown up in time, again.

Karla had finally left. Horst would have been the one to go, but he had just hobbled back home from another line, because he still had to go without shoes. And her mother should not have to stand there any longer. There was too much resting on her shoulders already. She drudged without pause at the work site taking care that she got their food rations, and then had to stand in line to bring the food home with her after work while Aunt Heidrun always just went begging, with high expectations, but ever smaller success. Her pastoral flock didn't have anything anymore. There was hardly anything left to give. They depended more and more on Mathilde, and on Karla.

"I won't abandon you, Mom," said Karla, "you know that."

"Yes, of course." Mathilde lovingly caressed her daughter's head and cheeks. She saw the disappointment, irritation, and bitterness in her eyes. She wished the schools would open again. Then at least Karla would have mornings out of the house. "But I couldn't last any longer," she went on. "I was about to collapse." Then Mathilde collected herself as much as she could, not wanting Karla to notice her confusion, hoping her daughter would blame her condition on fatigue and exhaustion, both of which were more or less true.

"Where did you stand? Maybe they will let me back in."

"In front of Mrs. Berners," Mathilde answered. "I can't imagine . . ." She was about to say her place was held open by Baumgartner, but she didn't. She half hoped he had, that he stood in line and could be replaced by Karla, but she also half hoped that he had gone out of the line, and out of her life.

"I'll go anyway. The old bag doesn't bother me." Karla headed out. "I had better hurry."

Mathilde watched her daughter for a moment. Suddenly she swayed and leaned against a wall for support. She knew that her dizziness was caused by lack of strength but told herself she didn't have time for sympathy. I have to get home as fast as possible, she thought, and rest. I must not break down. Karla needs me. She isn't nearly as strong as she acts. Not at all. With that, Mathilde started to trudge across the rubble, looking for an easier way, a shortcut over the rough paths.

Moments later, after Karla had taken a few steps, she suddenly remembered she wanted to tell her mother something—something important—and turned around, but Mathilde was nowhere to be seen.

TEN

"Surprise." The child's hands covered Frieder's eyes before he could enter the apartment. Gerhild had secretly waited on the stairs that went up to the attic and jumped on his back just as he was opening the door. She clung to him like a backpack and kept his eyes closed. "Guess who's here?"

"Uncle Franz?"

Gerhild giggled. "Cold, very cold. Why did you say that?"

"I don't know." Frieder bit his tongue. How could he talk about Uncle Franz? He simply could not make mistakes like that. He had to learn to keep his mouth shut. Grimly he tugged at his sister's hands. "Let me go now."

Gerhild held on. "Tell me first," she squeaked.

Frieder had no desire to play games. He was tired, hungry, and he needed peace and quiet to think like a grown-up, like a man. There was no doubt it was Uncle Franz that he had met earlier. At last a ray of hope. Even if Uncle Franz did not want to be recognized; no, that wasn't it—it was exactly *because* he did not want to be recognized that Uncle Franz acted as he did. To Frieder that could mean only one thing; Uncle Franz was still fighting. And that was what Frieder had yearned for all along.

Since he had been back in Berlin, he and two classmates from the Adolf-Hitler-School patrolled the streets whenever they could, looking for anyone who had not yet given up the fight against Bolshevism and the Jew-infested Americans. They were looking for anyone who could give them, the young Werewolves, orders. Frieder had finally found such a person. This was not time for child's play.

"Try again." Gerhild didn't let go.

Frieder did not want to play this game, but he knew his sister would never give up until he had at least played along for a while. "Do I know him, or her?" He asked.

"Of course." Gerhild gurgled in sheer pleasure. "Very well."

Frieder thought about for a moment. Perhaps it was one of the women from Dad's parish who maybe, hopefully brought along something to eat. That would be nice, but not really any reason to get his sister so excited. "Miss Gräuler," he guessed, considering the problem seriously, but with more hope in his voice than he really felt. If it was that unmarried thin-as-a-rake librarian, then there surely would be a little extra to eat. She always brought something with her.

Gerhild giggled. "No, no, completely wrong."

"Is it a woman?"

Gerhild giggled some more. "No."

Suddenly Frieder sensed that something was different; Gerhild was not only childish and silly, she was really happy, from the bottom of her belly and her heart. Suddenly, he had no idea why, whether from a smell or something from Gerhild herself, he knew—it had to be Dad. It could only be Dad! If it were Miss Gräuler or any other woman from the parish, Gerhild would definitely not make such a fuss. "No …! Are you telling me it's Dad?" he asked incredulously.

"Yesss!" his sister cried in jubilation. She finally jumped off his back and stormed into the apartment. "Daddy, Daddy, Frieder is here!"

The boy slowly followed her as if he had bet he could get closer to the edge of a cliff than anyone else and was testing his footing with each step, hesitating then retreating the closer he came. Frieder knew he was afraid of his father. He feared the familiar searching gaze of those brilliant, cold blue eyes that gave his father a mysterious ability to see through and know about everything. He feared his father would ask where he spent all his time and why he came home empty-handed. Uncertain what would happen, he entered the living room to find his father waiting for him with open arms.

There was no trace of accusation in his father's voice. "Boy, you are finally here!" He seemed to be very happy.

"Dad!"

Frieder flew into his arms, and the large thin man with his full, prematurely gray hair hugged the boy tightly. "I am so happy, I am so happy," he murmured over and over.

Frieder thought he saw a tear sparkle in his father's eyes, but he knew his father never let his emotions show. Maybe he believed that because he felt his own tears tickle the bridge of his nose. He tried with all his might to hold the tears back. Most of all he didn't want his father to see him cry. He pressed his face against the rough shirt, but it smelled strange, like cheap soap, and not at all like the smell that he remembered. Before the war, in peacetime, his father always smelled of his pungent aftershave, but no matter. He was here again, thought Frieder, as he burrowed his head closer to his father's chest to push his tears back into his eyes. It didn't help when his father stroked his hair. It was an unaccustomed gesture.

Heidrun came in the room without "her two men" noticing. She stood still for a moment, said nothing and watched calmly, happy and smiling at the intimate hugs between father and son. God has been good to us, she thought. He has spared my family. They were all back together; healthy, alive and—together!

"Supper will soon be ready," she said. "There is isn't much, to be sure, but we must be thankful."

Father and son sprang apart as soon as they heard her voice, embarrassed to be discovered in a display of tenderness and trying to restrain their tears in front of Heidrun, and each other. They were surprised, unable to speak, as they looked at this tall woman with her rich blonde hair, but she had already turned away.

Heidrun stood in front of the cabinet, tall and straight. For the occasion, she wanted to use the good tableware—Mathilde's good tableware—because Heidrun's own service, her inheritance from their grandmother and the heart of her dowry, was a victim of the bombs that destroyed the parsonage and everything else around the church. And of course, with the good table service went the silver cutlery—Mathilde's silver which was no longer complete because her far too generous and often misguided sister had traded a complete setting to Färber for a little food and a bottle of wine so she could invite that Gypsy. Heidrun sighed. The silver originally came from their great-great grandmother and had been handed down from generation to generation. She would have taken better care of it. . . . Oh, well. So long as Franz wasn't home again and Heinrich was still too young to use a fork and knife, no one would notice a set was missing. Still, it was a shame.

"Did you escape?" asked Frieder with so much hope that Heidrun had to smile. Her oldest wanted to see his father as a gallant hero, and he was right. Hermann was a hero. He was a hero because he had come back to them.

"No," answered Hermann, "I did not escape. I am a man of God, the Americans treated me well. They are upstanding Christians, the whites at least."

"But we learned in school that international financial Jewry had the Amis fully under their control." Frieder sounded worried; as if what he had been taught might no longer be true.

Hermann nodded slowly. "Yes, apparently it is so. On Wall Street in New York. But the little guy, the individual soldier, he was just like us, a common, civilized human being."

"That means you will like it, Daddy, if the Amis come," interjected Gerhild, drawn in by her curiosity.

"Oh, yes, compared to the Russians in any case. Naturally, it would have been better if our beloved homeland were not occupied at all."

"But then we shouldn't have lost the war."

"Then we shouldn't have lost the war." Hermann repeated the happy words of his saucy daughter with melancholy, sorrow, incomprehension, and horror.

"Then why did we lose? The radio always said . . ."

"The people were not worthy of the Führer." Frieder cut his sister's words off. "We failed. All of us."

"But I didn't do anything," protested Gerhild.

"You also didn't fail." Hermann stroked her lightly on the head. "Come, help your mother set the table."

A little later they sat at the table, and Hermann said the blessing. The children were happy to hear his tenor voice again. Their father could sing so wonderfully in church, yet that same voice could so angrily scold that it almost hurt.

The prayer ended traditionally as they all held hands and said "Guten Appetit" in unison. Suddenly it was like it had always been, especially for Heidrun. So intense and powerful was her emotion at this moment that it took Heidrun out of the present, out of the reality of everyday life, the war and the rubble, and into her home, the parsonage, where those whose guests they were in this cramped apartment had once been her guests.

For a moment it was like it had been, everything like it should be, the family ritual, the fancy table setting, her mother's silver; familiarity overpowered Heidrun. She dissolved in it, lost herself and the times in their voices, the smells, the motions of her loved ones, and in their own unique and comfortable long-practiced gestures and words.

She took Hermann's plate and served him first just as she had before he went into the military. Then followed Frieder as the oldest son, then the others, and at the end she helped herself to what remained. As always that was little enough even though she had virtually begged food from former parishioners to celebrate a festive meal. "Something to eat for the pastor who has come home today," she had said. "Praise and thanks be to God."

She had even gotten a piece of smoked meat with bacon rind and edible potatoes that weren't too rotten so she could cut out the bad spots and with starch and water stretch them enough to make mashed potatoes. To mask the unpleasant smell and foul aftertaste she made a gravy. Heidrun was very proud of that gravy because she roasted substitute coffee instead of bread crumbs in the salty fat of left over bacon rind. The best of her luck was that there was enough electricity for her to cook and roast on this joyful day.

Hermann and the children waited until Mother was ready to eat although it was hard for them to contain their hunger and eagerness. Still, if they were to eat together, that is the way it was. They waited because it was what they had to do until Father opened the table talk.

"Very tasteful!" Hermann declared with his first bite. "I can easily tell that I'm home again. Right, children? Nowhere else does food taste as good as it does when it's made by our mother." After a fleeting smile in the direction of his wife, Hermann turned to his oldest. He wanted to know how things had gone with Frieder, what the teachers in his Adolf-Hitler-School had said, and how he had made his way back from Thuringia to Berlin.

After he and Frieder talked he wanted to hear how Heidrun and the children had survived the bombs, the loss of the parsonage, the war's end and the first weeks of peace. Heidrun didn't want the children to go into sordid details so she quickly spoke up telling much of what happened but not all. It was not the right time to speak of horrors. Today was a lucky day, a day of happiness and togetherness. They didn't need to burden today with any evil.

Hermann told about being in the American prisoner of war camp in the Rheinland, his release and his journey back home. There wasn't much to tell. Since he was a chaplain the occupiers gave Hermann a train ticket so he had travelled across a devastated Germany to Berlin comfortably. There were interruptions, of course. Many tracks were not yet repaired, many engines were missing and those that did run frequently broke down.

He could not believe the enormity, the ferocity of the violence that had broken over his home city like an apocalypse of the Lord, and in this case the Lord wore a very human visage, the visage of their conquerors. He was enraged and despaired for the destruction, and he was disconsolate for the loss of the church and parsonage, but he was happy and lighthearted, perhaps too happy, because he found his loved ones unhurt. The whole family was happy, and the longer they were together, the more they talked, the happier they became.

Heidrun felt relief that even little Heinrich wasn't at all shy and chattered along sitting there beaming at his father and wanting to talk like the grownups. He had already called him "Daddy." The fear, horror, burdens, and hardships they endured had all been suspended. In their high-spirited chatter they became stories of adventures overcome, harmless anecdotes.

"One comrade," Hermann said, "Willy he was called, Willy Mertens, occupied himself with everything and anything the Amis threw away, and they threw away everything, things that you could make something good and useful from. It was unimaginable. Such waste would be unthinkable under our command. Mertens was pretty good at handiwork, so he made all sorts of things like pots, cutlery and tools out of old cans and all sorts of other odds and ends.

The Amis were so excited about it that they bought things from him. They paid him with cigarettes, corned beef, soap, and I don't know what all. Things we had never seen before. And Willy naturally traded everything he was paid. He got rich in the camp since he had everything he could want—cigarettes, liquor, and food. In no time he had so much that he didn't need to work any longer and looked for others who could make the things for him." Hermann shook his head in admiring amazement. "German industriousness."

"What did the Amis want with the things?" Horst asked. "Didn't they have their own utensils? And tools of their own?"

Hermann laughed. "Sure, more than enough. Most of them better than ours. But they collected souvenirs. Mementos to take home," he explained to Gerhild's questioning look because she did not know what souvenirs were. She had never heard the foreign word that had been used in the time before the Third Reich.

Frieder, on the other hand, nodded knowingly, nodded condescendingly. He not only knew the word but had long understood that you could make a profit from the hated occupiers with the proud memorabilia of the unjustly defeated Reich. Even better, you could, if you were slick enough, not only enrich yourself but use their own weapons against them.

"They went wild for such things," continued Hermann. "If you had a decoration or, like many, a copy of *Mein Kampf* in your rucksack, the Amis tore it out of your hands."

Frieder triumphantly declared, "See, Mom. We shouldn't burn the book. We have to trade it like I've said all along."

Horst had told them what he had overhead about burning *Mein Kampf* while standing in line for food. Someone said, "With five copies

I could prepare a hot pot that would serve six people." Another added, mockingly, "Well, Old Adolf left us something good after all." Ever since, to save it for the kindling pile, Heidrun had locked Franz's copy of *Mein Kampf* in the kitchen cabinet where she also guarded their ever dwindling supplies of food treasures like gold.

". . . and one fellow, a lieutenant in the Luftwaffe," Hermann went on, ignoring Frieder's remark, "he did not give up his pilot's watch like he was supposed to do. The Amis took everything from us when we were processed into the camp," explained Hermann. "But the lieutenant managed to keep his watch and sold it to an American officer for a carton of cigarettes. A whole carton—a fortune! After that he was almost as rich as Willy."

"The Russians always wanted watches too," said Gerhild. And the conversation abruptly went silent. Suddenly the Russians were still there, the Russians and everything that had happened behind the colorful curtain of the stories they had told. Suddenly the memories were there even though nobody wanted to let them in. Heidrun glared at her daughter, thinking: Can't you just keep your dumb mouth shut? But it was too late. Once spoken, the memories could not be banished. Gerhild innocently went on, unaware of any offense. "It's true," she repeated.

Although she had no such intention, she got support from Heinrich. "*Ura, ura,*" he joyfully squealed, "*Ura, ura.*" Without understanding what he said, he repeated ever more proudly the demands of the two Russian soldiers that had made themselves at home in their apartment. With that he unabashedly scratched his head so that his lice fell on the tablecloth. The child had lice, like all the kids in the city, and their mothers simply could not overcome the pests. There was no medicine, no remedy, nothing.

"Heinrich, quit scratching, that's not polite," Heidrun turned on her youngest. "And Gerhild, you quit saying such horrible nonsense." All at once the happy mood was gone and a heavy, uncomfortable, oppressive silence lay over the table.

Hermann looked at his wife with an anxious question in his eyes. Had she too . . . ? Before, when Heidrun had told their story, he heard only what he wanted to hear, what he had hoped to hear. He took no notice of the undertones and omissions in her story. Heidrun shook her head slightly, signaling Hermann wordlessly, No, nothing happened to me, but let us not talk about it here and now, not in front of the children. Hermann breathed easier and said a silent prayer of thanks to God the Creator that He had protected his family from disgrace.

The easy-going mood was gone, torn away by the memories of the Russians and their horrors.

Heidrun gathered plates and empty dishes together. "Horst, Gerhild, you do the washing. But don't use too much dish powder or water, do you hear me?" Neither Horst nor Gerhild moved but looked, apparently absently, at the door behind Heidrun. "Now get up and do what your mother told you."

"Mathilde!" Hermann stood up and spread his arms.

Heidrun spun around. Mathilde stood in the door and stared at them around the table. Her table, with the family of her sister and brother-in-law around it. She felt as if she stood outside herself, as if she were seeing a film in which she played a lonely stranger.

Heidrun was terrified. Her sister loomed before her, a bad omen, a punishment from God for the good fortune she enjoyed because of her sister. Mathilde had sheltered her and the children, even sacrificed her own body when the Russians occupied the apartment; she was, in this moment, a reprimand from God, a vivid reminder that God had granted Heidrun the blessing of her husband's return instead of Mathilde's. She was His punishment because in her moment of exceeding joy Heidrun had forgotten her sister's sorrow and that of so many others who waited, worried, and hoped without hope.

Mathilde was God's punishment because Heidrun had not saved anything for her sister to eat. Mathilde, who worked for all of them, to whom she owed everything including what she and the children wore right down to their underwear. Heidrun had simply forgotten her during the rapture of Hermann's return. Now she stood there in front of her sister, paralyzed.

Herman, unlike his wife, had no bad conscience and went to embrace his sister-in-law. "God bless you, Mathilde. Let the heavens praise you because you have taken us in!"

Mathilde was mute, staring at the scene with empty eyes. She moved slightly toward her sister just before Hermann could touch her and she began to sob.

Hermann's arms fell to his side as he looked quizzically at his sister-in-law. He didn't understand. Heidrun and Frieder kept quiet, one frightened, the other tense. Silence. Only Heinrich babbled softly to himself. "Aunt Mathilde, what is wrong?" asked Gerhild finally.

Horst was as surprised as his sister. "Aren't you happy that Daddy is here again?"

"Sure," said Mathilde and tried to stop the tears. "But still, it is only … This is all a bit too much for me. I am so happy, I have to cry."

Heidrun shook her head quietly, sympathetic, and worried. She knew better. Frieder also knew better. He was old enough to understand why his aunt cried. He was just about to say, "It isn't at all that bad, Aunt Mathilde; Uncle Franz is alive." But he couldn't say anything, above all not here, not in front of the others. To do so would endanger Uncle Franz, endanger his mission. Maybe he could speak with his father later. Maybe Dad would know a way to signal Aunt Mathilde that she didn't need to be sad, everything would be alright. But in no way could Frieder say anything now. Not now, not here.

Frieder stood and went toward the door without helping Horst and Gerhild clear off the table. Horst protested but Frieder went on. He had to go. He couldn't look at his aunt. He wanted to push past her in the door but she stopped him.

"Where do you always hide the whole day?" she asked.

Frieder didn't know where to look or what to do with his hands. He knew he had to answer but had no idea how. He stammered some incomprehensible generality. He couldn't say anything. He had to keep his mouth shut. He had to!

"I stood in line, waiting," she said, "and you didn't come." Mathilde dried her tears, her sorrow turning to anger. Anger at this boy who left her waiting and was now acting like a pasha. On top of it, Hermann had come back! She knew her brother-in-law well enough to to predict that he would smother her and Karla with his well-meaning rules just like he did with his own family, justifying himself by saying he was only supporting her and Karla, and how good it was to have a man at home again. Heidrun would try to calm her by repeating his argument. Mathilde pressed on, "It was your turn, Frieder, but you didn't show up. Instead Karla had to."

"Leave the boy alone. After all it isn't every day the father comes home." Hermann defended his son. "It won't hurt your daughter to stand for an hour once in a while."

Mathilde's whole complaint against Frieder flooded out. "He wasn't even here when Karla left to take over for me in the line, after she already had worked around the house the whole day. . . . That is to say . . . he didn't know that you were back. He is simply negligent and lazy."

"I fetched wood," Frieder defended himself helplessly and hoped that no one noticed the lie because he most often came home without even a small piece of wood. I have to get out of here, he thought. Sooner or later she will ask me what I have done all day, what I do at all. Then I'll have to lie again, lie in front of Dad. And that, he knew, he would not be able to do.

"I am going to fetch water," he said. "You will want to wash up, Aunt Mathilde." Secretly he thanked God the water service had been interrupted again.

Frieder's unexpected willingness to help was so astounding that—a startled Mathilde moved to the side just far enough that Frieder could slip by her and flee.

"See, the boy is not lazy. And he is caring as well." The pride for his son was unmistakable in Hermann's voice.

Mathilde nodded. It should not have surprised her that Hermann defended his son. He had always done that. Why should she expect it to change? Nothing ever changed with Hermann and Heidrun. Nothing. Only for her did everything fall apart.

Horst walked toward the kitchen balancing a dangerously high tower of plates. "Be careful with the dishes," Mathilde shouted, letting her anger that should be directed toward Herman, Frieder, and Heidrun loose on the exhausted looking barefoot boy. Mathilde knew she was wrong, and it was made worse by the fact that Franz hadn't come home.

As Horst pushed past her with his chin and the tower of dishes quivering Mathilde lit into her sister. "Couldn't you have at least waited supper until Karla and I could be here?"

Heidrun's guilty conscience caused her to rage like a mad tigress, growling, trying to tamp down her anger by speaking precisely, loud and clear, accenting each syllable as if she were speaking to someone hard of hearing. "Hermann was hungry after finishing his long trip, and so were the children. Besides, we never know when you will get home."

"If Frieder had relieved me like we agreed, you would have." Mathilde's anger rose like a pot of milk ready to boil over. "And besides you always want to wash up before eating."

"Frieder could have already fetched the water instead of filling his belly."

"How so? If he stood in a line somewhere?"

"That is enough." Hermann interrupted the sisters' fight. "Let us go through this day in peace and thankfulness that God has led us safely through these times. And in prayer that He will hold his protecting hand also over Franz."

Mathilde nodded slowly and wiped her hand on the green checkered cotton dress she wore to work. It was her last dress except for the blue velvet. She wanted to save both, but her only other option was to sweat to death in the wool pants Heidrun made for her from an old blanket. Mathilde really had no choice but to wear the green one so she could at least save the blue velvet.

Hermann was right, she thought. We should be thankful, thankful and trust in God. "Okay," she said. "I'll just have something to eat. At least there's still enough water for me to wash my hands, isn't there?"

Then she saw the look on her sister's face—and knew. "No, tell me it isn't so,'" she said, even though she knew without a doubt. "Please tell me it isn't so."

Again Heidrun had not saved anything for her to eat. It wasn't possible. It couldn't be. Mathilde, the hard laborer, was dumbstruck. And Karla—what about Karla? The girl would be beside herself.

"We thought you would bring something home," Heidrun defended herself helplessly. "Besides which we had another mouth to feed, and

I got most of it from the members of the parish, when they heard that their pastor was back. . . ."

Mathilde turned silently away. Heidrun followed her. "I still have a few peas that I can cook, and maybe there's still some fat in the pan to pour over them." She flipped the light switch to test it and the hall lit up. "And look, we even have electricity. I can whip up something for you and Karla."

Mathilde slammed the bathroom door on her sister, shutting out the hall light and the querulous voice. A little later Frieder came with two buckets of water. Mathilde took them in and heard him quickly leave the apartment. It was all the same to her. He could wander around wherever he wanted. If his parents let their golden boy wander, was it up to her to control him? To warn him against the dangers that threatened straggling children and youths in the rubble-strewn streets, the remnants of the war and the double-dealing of the occupiers?

Tired in every pore, every cell, and every drop of blood, Mathilde undressed so she could bathe but sat on the edge of the bathtub instead and stared blankly in front of her. She was too tired to move, too tired to cry, too tired to be angry or disappointed. The scorn, which she had just felt, collapsed, petered out, and vanished. As quickly as it had flared it changed into sadness, despair, and pure, almost tender exhaustion. She could do nothing more, and wanted to do nothing more.

She didn't know how long she had sat there without moving when she heard a ruckus from outside. Hermann's tenor voice, that cutting, painful, piercing noise. "Are you crazy? Get that man out of my apartment immediately. What has come over you to bring such a person here?"

It was Karla's voice that loudly answered back. "Your apartment? *Your* apartment?! It is Mom's apartment. My parents' apartment. And mine. Be happy that you can stay here."

"How do you talk to me? You have forgotten what respect is." Hermann's voice was loud and shrill. "Whosoever has no respect for adults, has no respect for God—and you two get back into the kitchen and clean up. Now!" That was probably aimed at Gerhild and Horst peeking in to see what the fuss was about.

"If you want to preach, go to your church." Karla replied in the scornful tone that Mathilde knew too well. Girl, girl, she thought, you're talking yourself into trouble. But she could not bring herself to move while Karla went on. "But you can't, can you? Because it is gone! Why doesn't the dear Lord make the church whole again so you can preach?"

That was too much for Hermann. "Don't you blaspheme the name of the Lord!"

Mathilde heard a smack. Hermann had hit Karla. She knew she should jump up, run out and confront, stop the shocking behavior of her brother-in-law, but she clung fast to the edge of the bathtub, held there not just by her exhaustion or her nakedness. Something kept her from opening the bathroom door. She didn't know what it was. Did she not want to know? Did she not want to recognize it?

Karla cried out in anger, but did nothing else as far as Mathilde could hear. "Mr. Baumgartner wants to see my mother. And she is here in *her* apartment; she can decide who she wants to visit and who not."

Baumgartner? Camillo Baumgartner? Mathilde was startled. What was he doing here? Had he followed her? Was he calling on her? She didn't know which was worse, which she was more afraid of. Outside the door the fight between Karla and Hermann grew louder. Thoughts shot through Mathilde's head. She had to do something, she had to take control, otherwise it could become a catastrophe. But what? And how? She looked down at herself, naked and unwashed. She glanced in the mirror; she looked terrible. So what, she thought, this is no time for vanity.

Outside Hermann and Karla screamed at each other with undiminished strength. Then suddenly Hermann must have raised his hand against Karla again because Baumgartner's warm, smooth and yet somehow dangerous voice cut through the shrill, sharp tones, changing the melody. "Do you really want to lay violent hands on the girl again?"

Silence reigned. A tense silence. The general pause before the crescendo.

At lightning speed, Mathilde dressed and tore open the bathroom door not caring how she looked. Baumgartner and Karla stood by the apartment door and Hermann by the door to the living room.

Baumgartner's presence seemed to fill the vestibule to bursting. With his hat cocked back on his head, the colorful vest and powerful limbs the Gypsy looked larger, much larger than the gray, shrunken, stubborn-looking holy man, although Hermann overtopped Baumgartner by a head. No one said a word, the only sound a rattle of tableware from the kitchen, and Heidrun rummaging in the living room making a loud, clear, an accusatory staccato. But she did not show herself.

Hermann's face was very flushed as he struggled to get himself back under control. He glared at Baumgartner with hostility, and Baumgartner returned his look with equal antagonism, but Mathilde saw something more in Baumgartner's eyes, something other than hostility and hate. It almost seemed to her as if it was a look of disappointment. Disappointment at the pastor? No, that couldn't be, she thought. She must be wrong. It had to be anger. Anger at this self-righteous German man who had groundlessly scolded him; who had slapped Karla and seemed ready to throw the Gypsy out of the apartment.

Hermann forced himself to be calm. "I don't let anyone talk to me that way," he said. "And certainly not someone like you. Leave now. Before I forget myself."

Mathilde felt his anger, bitterness, and dislike for Baumgartner so completely and clearly that she felt her face flush as if liquid fire coursed through her veins. She shut her eyes, opened them again, took a deep breath and said with a decisiveness that surprised even her, "Please, Hermann. Mr. Baumgartner saved Karla's life. He is always welcome here in my apartment. Always. Do you understand?"

 Hermann looked disconcerted and taken aback. He held his silence motionless. "Besides he kept our place in the line for us after your dear son once again failed to come," said Karla poisonously.

Mathilde turned on her daughter, "Please hold your tongue."

Karla was not about to hold back, lashed out at her uncle, "And you are sure to not have anything left for us to eat. I know you. And it is *my* mom who works for all of you."

"Heidrun made a mistake. I apologize for her. It will not happen again."

Mathilde could do nothing but marvel at her brother-in-law. He seemed to have no trace of a bad conscience, not even a small acknowledgement of guilt. He could admit the mistake, not his own naturally, and go on with the matters of the day.

"Not happen again? Don't make me laugh." Karla's voice poked, bored, and pricked. She would have loved to use her finger to poke, bore, and prick; she would like to go at her uncle's face with ten fingers.

"Karla, enough." Mathilde spoke softly but with determination and so clearly that her daughter pulled in her claws, albeit slowly, threateningly, one sharp fingernail at a time, one after the other.

"Excuse me," Mathilde said, turning to Baumgartner. She looked in his eyes, looked at the tiny smile that had stolen up to his eyes to mingle with bitterness, hate, and exhaustion. "Come on in," she said with a sweeping movement of her arm toward the kitchen. "Unfortunately I can't offer you anything but in spite of that I am happy that you are here."

She was startled at what she had said, startled at what she had done, and almost relieved that Baumgartner made no move to accept the invitation.

"I would just be a disturbance," he said and reached for the door handle. He turned once more. "Ah, I have brought you something." From his pocket he produced a can of beef and a loaf of bread and shot a sarcastic glance toward Hermann. "Just so you also have something to celebrate."

Hermann could not take his eyes off the can revealing his longing and revulsion, hunger and disdain almost audibly drooling as his mouth watered. Still he said nothing.

Baumgartner parried the look like a fencer in battle. "I did not steal it," he said. Now for the first time you could clearly hear the anger. With hardly disguised hate in his voice he continued, "I have only taken what belongs to me."

"Stop lying. That can came from the Wehrmacht supplies, I see that clearly." Hermann raised his shoulders, thrust his head forwards, went into attack posture.

"There isn't any such thing anymore. The German army has been disbanded. To whom does whatever is left belong?"

"The German people." Hermann spoke with dignity and conviction, a soldier coming at attention.

"Therefore, to me too," countered Baumgartner. And before Hermann could argue he continued, "I am a German," pulling out his passport on which a large "Z" for *Zigeuner* was stamped and laughed sarcastically. "We Gypsies originated in India. And the Indians are purebred Aryans."

"Aryan or not, right now I speak," Hermann's voice echoing the authority of thousands of accusingly raised fingers, "only of the present. He has survived at the cost of others. This meat and this bread are certainly not his first theft."

Mathilde watched Baumgartner who didn't move and looked proudly in Hermann's face, his fists clenched. It was as if he wanted to hold onto the vacuum left by the death of his race, his people, as if a vacuum was better than nothing.

"What would happen," Hermann went on, "if everyone took for himself what pleased him? There must be a rule of law, otherwise everything falls apart. One can clearly see that. But your kind has never understood it."

"As opposed to you?" Baumgartner became ashen and lost his almost arrogant dignity, his calm, and his power. Mathilde clearly saw anger in his eyes, his fists ready to let loose that vacuum, death and nothingness on Hermann, like a flood. "The girl here spoke the truth. You have taken everything from my tribe. Everything. The horses, the wagons, and the children." He took a bitter pause. "And now you talk about a foolish can of meat?"

Mathilde and Karla followed the exchange of words between the two men spellbound and tense as Baumgartner set his hat correctly on his head in order to not let loose at Hermann while his other hand clenched the door handle to hold himself back. Otherwise he would have catapulted his indignation, despair and anger against the German who self-righteously had crossed his arms across his chest. Instead Baumgartner said, "Goodbye," and opened the door.

Karla cried, "Mommy!" helplessly protesting, exhorting.

And at the same time, Mathilde put her hand on the Gypsy's arm,

"Please stay. You can't leave in an argument."

The artiste hesitated. "You call that an argument?"

Mathilde sensed real scorn in his voice. And once again she felt exposed without knowing from what, and shamed without knowing why.

"You must be crazy, Mathilde. You can't get involved with someone like him. No matter if he saved Karla's life or not," murmured Hermann. He fled to his wife who had appeared behind him at the doorway and watched the scene in the vestibule, thunderstruck, disapproving, resigned.

"Yeah. It's all the same to you, just as I thought," bawled Karla behind Hermann who shoved Heidrun into the living room with a woeful commanding gesture and slammed shut the door.

Baumgartner stood there, the door handle in his hand, hesitating; hesitated like Mathilde whose invitation and polite words she would have loved to stuff back in her mouth even if she choked on them because the truth was she agreed with what Hermann had said. What had she done? The question went around and around in her head. What had she said? And then, not only did she not take back her words, she repeated them.

"You can't just go," she said. "I would like to share the meat with you. I insist." She went in the direction of the kitchen and waited in the door. "Please come."

Karla stood next to her mother and beamed at the Gypsy. "Yes. You kept my place in line so you must share our food." She held up the shopping bag in which the barley rations were, as well as sugar and a quarter liter of oil.

Baumgartner spoke to Mathilde rather than Karla, his voice sounding as pale as his face beneath his brown skin. "I don't care for barley." Finally he shrugged and followed the two into the kitchen. He could not withstand their invitation, determination, and friendliness.

"Go on," Karla said to Horst and Gerhild. "I'll dry the rest."

Gerhild said, "I want to stay here with the magician." But Horst, who was looking at Baumgartner with wide eyes, quickly pulled her out of the kitchen.

Mathilde put plates on the table, fetched knives and glasses. "I am truly glad that you came by," she said to the Gypsy.

He slowly sat down at the table, slowly rubbed his hand over his face. He heard, felt, and knew that what she said came from the heart even though she was a *gadsche*, a foreigner to his people. And he wondered about himself, because he was happy about that.

ELEVEN

Only a few fires glimmered through the dusk over the wide space, like frightened fireflies driven together; they burned in the furthest corners of the great plaza, as far as possible from the bombed-out ruins of the former police station, the former school building the boys and men of the travelling people had to erect. Back then in the brown, still peaceful brown past, not more than ten years ago. As far as possible from the burned remains of the shed that had belonged to Schelenz, the former Platzmeister, the supervisor of the whole compound.

Schelenz, who had gone up in flames with his shed, had been a brutal scoundrel. He struck out at everything and everyone who had the bad luck to come into his view. But Schelenz and his kind did not bother the travellers beyond that. Such treatment was nothing new, and they had become used to it. Unfortunately. They had not taken it seriously, neither the strikes nor the hate. They had just shrugged their shoulders at it and laughed and joked about it. Until it was too late.

A faint odor of feces hung over the whole plaza, which even the smoke from the fires could not mask, because it was in the middle of sewage drainage fields where sewer water from the metropolis was sent after treatment. They had been forced to settle on this piece of land and had become used to the stench after a bit. They had to. After a while they didn't notice it anymore. Now it almost made them feel at home; washing up the memories of happier times like iridescent fragments of mussels. It was the stink of the living, not the dead. The dead did not stink, they only rested.

Meadows on the other side of the plaza near the church and the village cemetery were lost in the gathering darkness. For as long as they had been allowed to own them, Gypsies had pastured their horses in those meadows. A farm lay on the edge of the meadow that belonged to the *gadsche*, non-Gypsies, who were always friendly. Partly because they earned a lot of money from them; and because the Sinti, the Roma from the drainage fields, bought from them. Always bought, never stole.

On the other side there was a railway track on which in earlier times a train rattled by every few minutes. Now it was quiet in the plaza. That stretch of railroad had apparently not yet been repaired. The quiet was frightfully stagnant as it had never been before. Gypsies are normally loud; always chattering, fighting, laughing, singing, scolding, and telling stories. They are always playing fiddles, shoeing horses, cooking, and fixing their wagons. Without the voices, without the noises of work, without the music, a quiet had settled over the plaza that made it hard to breathe. It was a terrifying, ghostly quiet without the clamor, the cries and joyous romping of their children. The lack of children was the worst. They were the most fragile, and almost none of them had returned.

It had been, back in the peaceful brown past no more than ten years ago, not an inviting place to which they had been consigned and shipped. The sun burned in the summer and nowhere was there a tree or a shadow. In the winter the wind blew over the plain without any undergrowth or settlement to stop it. But still, they had lived. Almost a thousand people had been here at one time, not here by choice, but nevertheless here—in the world. They had lived. At least they lived. Their kind, and in their custom.

Now there were perhaps still twenty or thirty of their people on the wide, dark, inhospitable field. They had returned to the place where they had last seen their relatives, their friends and brothers, their Gypsy tribe, their *kumpania*, for the last time, and where they had to leave their most beloved. If there was a chance to again meet the lost ones, the missing ones, the ones taken from them—then it would be here. For that reason the little group of people endured and waited. They had been forcibly settled on this dirty, stinking field more than ten years ago, part of "the battle against the Gypsy plague" to ensure the Reich's capital looked proper for the Olympic Games. This place was an insult to every Gypsy soul, and even though they wanted to leave, the sooner the better, to be where they really belonged, out on the open road under the high free sky, they could not.

Others from their *kumpania* left the field and moved around, asked here and there, followed leads, sought and even found some survivors of the horror. Not so Camillo Baumgartner. He and a few others stayed and waited. They had agreed upon that with their families, as in *The Good Soldier Švejk*, as Švejk used to say, ". . . after the war in the *Kelch*, 'round six." They wanted to, had to keep their agreement even though they suspected or in some cases were, in the truest sense of the word, dead certain that they waited in vain. Still they did not, could not give up.

Now and then, though seldom, one would return. But none who returned were those for whom the tightrope walker longed for and waited.

He had the gray hat pulled down low over his face and stared, lost in thought, into the fire. The flames laid a red glow over his mouth, nose and forehead; only his eyes lay in the shadow of the brim.

A young woman stepped out of a tent behind him. He had not had a wagon for a long time. The Nazis had confiscated and destroyed it. The tent was a shaky, fragile construction out of two old army ground cloths. Camillo had to stretch them over a rickety wood frame and anchor them to the ground with improvised tent pegs. The tent would withstand an occasional shower in summer, but it would not survive the coming winter. Until then, time stretched endlessly to the horizon. Until then there was something worth doing, something to settle, which was greater than all time.

The woman was in her late twenties, somewhat younger than Camillo, and six feet tall; she had a delicate, round face in which one could hardly see the privations of the last years, in which the horrors, trepidations, and fears hardly left a trace. Thick black hair fell down to her hips; black-brown eyes looked at the world through a melancholy veil. Her face was dominated by a large, very large mouth with full lips which simultaneously radiated attraction and terrifying sensuality. She wore several layered blue and greenish skirts made of threadbare velvet, a yellow blouse, and no jewelry. Her bronze brown feet were bare.

She walked nearer and softly laid a hand on Camillo's shoulder. Then she took the pot that hung over the fire on a tripod and poured boiling water in a container. After a moment she stirred in some sugar that she took from a hidden pocket in her skirts and poured an enamel mug full of sweet black coffee that the tightrope walker thinned with a good shot of schnaps.

"Thank you, Keja."

He raised the cup to his mouth, but before he could drink Keja quickly took the mug out of his hand again and poured a few drops on the ground. "This is for you," she murmured.

Camillo stared for a moment at the self-willed group of drops, then took the mug back unenthusiastically and drank. "You do that as if they were all dead." He had emptied the mug in one draft.

"They *are* dead. And you know it."

Camillo said nothing, just maintained his silence. He was full of bitterness, full of hate. After a long silence he said, "Tell the story. Tell the story about them. Their *mule*, their spirits, are with us as long as we remember them." He looked at Keja with a despondent plea to tell their story to counter forgetting them so his wife and his son would not sink into the fog of forgetfulness, into the fog of nothingness. He waited, lit a cigarette, and drank another swallow of schnaps from the bottle.

Keja took a short pipe out of her pocket, lit it, took a swallow and suddenly began to orate in her harsh alto voice. "My sweet, blessed God, there once was a young Gypsy who was called Philomena. She was so beautiful that you could more easily look into the sun as upon her, such a light shone from her, so much gold flowed down her body. Her hair was as black as ebony. It had a silky gloss and smelled like a thousand roses; exactly like her soft velvet skin into which every day she rubbed the salves and oils that her father, Pulika, had gathered from faraway lands just for her. Her clothes were made of the finest silk, her coat velvet and rare furs. Her jewelry was made of pearls and gold pieces as large as saucers."

A stream of words flowed from Keja's mouth, rhythmic and monotone and unceasing, rushing through one and another rapids, through one and another whirlpool where it turned around and around on itself but with the unwavering certainty that, while it might spill over its banks from time to time, it would never stop. The stream would always flow. And as it flowed, on and on, it held the memories of life. The memories, the *mule*, of Philomena herself and Sandro, her son. Camillo's son.

Camillo sat there and listened to her. He smoked, drank, and listened to her. Listened to how Keja recited about Pulika, Philomena's father, who had become fairytale rich. A true millionaire for he had spent his millions, which was the only way the Roma would truly consider him a millionaire. How she recited about the gleam of his wagon, about the magnificence of his horses on which he based his riches, for Pulika was a horse trader. Philomena, the only and idolized daughter among five sons, a wild girl who recognized no rules and was pampered much too much by her father in the eyes of the others in the *kumpania*. She was pampered so much that she refused to take care of the household and instead stayed out in the meadow with her brothers and the horses. Not that she had to cook, clean, wash, and iron herself. There were a whole host of poorer relatives around Pulika for those chores. But Philomena should have overseen them because women were responsible for the household. They were not to disregard that responsibility.

Camillo listened carefully, smoked, drank, smiled and—recognized his Philomena. The rebellious, fearless, and unbridled Philomena. The only one who might have been able to rein her in was Camba, her mother, who had been killed by a *gadsche* years ago. Camba had predicted while telling a fortune to a woman that her husband would betray her. When the wife confirmed her husband's betrayal not too long after the prophecy, he took his revenge out on Camba.

"Pulika's love for Philomena," Keja continued, "was immeasurable. And since no one could put the brakes on that love for Philomena, it was little wonder that her name was seldom spoken when the men of the tribe gathered to discuss the marriage of the young people. No one wanted to lie, no one wanted to embarrass Pulika, and they would have to do one of the two if they talked about Philomena because they all considered her to be a spoiled, moody, untamable girl with high, unattainable expectations and a wild temperament that would certainly make her future husband unhappy."

Camillo nodded. Tears ran down his cheeks. It was as if Philomena could step out of the tent at any moment, kiss him, joke with him, and laugh with him.

"Philomena also inherited her mother's talent for seeing into the future," Keja went on. "Fortune telling was a service that other Roma women provided to the *gadsche*, but they didn't really believe in it themselves. They did it just to make money. Philomena, like her mother however, really saw more than one could guess. While the other Roma women knew precisely how to tell what the *gadsche* had in the way of wishes, hopes, and fears through their conversation and then read those exact same things in their hands, eyes, coffee grounds, or animal entrails the *gadsche* provided, Philomena looked deeper. Philomena looked into the soul. It was a rare gift and a dangerous gift. A gift Philomena learned to control with difficulty.

"She had help from an old woman named Lyuba who was also blessed with, afflicted by this talent for second sight, and recognized it in Philomena. Philomena learned from her that her gift was also a curse. She learned from her how she had to manage it. She learned not to flaunt her valuable and rare ability but to hide it because the truth often released rage and hate.

"With the years, Philomena knew everything she had to know. And, since she presented a striking appearance when she strolled through the streets, a young, beautiful, desirable woman adorned with gold and in rich clothes of velvet and silk, she was soon named queen of the fortunetellers."

The night had fully descended on the campgrounds. Very few fires still burned, most members of the *kumpania* had retreated and slept. Only Keja and Camillo still sat in front of their tent. And Keja told the story; told it as solace, as a desperate barrier against the black night of death. And Camillo knew that the painful part would now begin. The part in which Keja spoke about her and—him.

"Philomena enjoyed her work and liked strolling around to amuse herself at their annual fair. As she was leaving the mouse circus tent her glance fell on a small crowd standing in front of a tavern and staring upward. Interested, she walked closer. She heard the music of an accordion, guitar, and fiddle playing a slow melody that sounded not sad but like a dance tune. Suddenly a shock went through the crowd, a collective inhalation, and then everyone held their breath as if on command. Unconsciously, Philomena reacted along with them, inhaled with them, held her breath along with the others.

"Like the others, she stared up in the air. Up there she could make out a man dressed in black pants and a red-and-white banded shirt who wore an outmoded hat, a bowler, and seemed to float in the air between the gables of two houses. Completely free, detached, weightless as a bird. What was that? Amazed, Philomena blinked and looked up in the sky. But that surely could not be . . .

"She could not believe what she saw. The music swelled and it looked as if he wanted to jump into the depths, but he sprang into the sky, made a pirouette, a second one, spread his arms out wide and ceremoniously bowed. He danced. He danced through the air to the music of the three musicians who sat in the middle of the crowd. Philomena watched the dance in the clouds with her mouth wide open. Then, finally, as the man again landed after the umpteenth dance she saw that he did not float. She finally saw the rope that bent a little under his weight.

"Philomena's incredulous astonishment turned to admiration. What elegance, what confidence, what beauty on such a thin rope. And how dangerous it was. How easily he could fall, she thought.

"But the act wasn't over yet. A second person joined the man on the rope, a woman who carried a parasol and wore a snow-white dress as well as a similar hat; and after the cloud dance there followed a clown number.

"The man fussed about the woman, wanted to dance with her. He asked and begged like a little dog, but the woman always rejected him. She had no appreciation for the elegance of his movements and pushed him away. What a dumb cow, thought Philomena. Still, even though he had no expectation of success, the man did not give up. His jumps became ever more daring, his dance steps even more so. He came close to falling more frequently but caught himself each time at the last second, and the audience followed with baited breath and the frenetic relief of applause.

"Suddenly the number changed and became a fight. A fight between the man and the woman, a fight for their lives. The man became more agitated, ever more desperate as the woman's rejection became more and more harsh. The boundaries disappeared until Philomena, like the other onlookers, could no longer tell what was real and what was acting; whether, up there on the rope, they watched the gruesome reality of a lovesick man who would fall inevitably into the abyss. Or were they watching a virtuoso performance?

"Then, suddenly, it seemed clear; it was bitter reality. After a last, desperate attempt to win the love of the one he worshiped she forcefully shoved him away so that he lost his balance. The startled audience screamed or threw their hands over their mouths in terror. The man wavered and fell, certain to plunge into the bottomless depths but, at the last second, he grasped the rope with his hands and hung there like a gymnast on the horizontal bar.

"Philomena boiled with rage, burned with unconscious hate. Suddenly she glimpsed a dark cloud around him, an unhealthy aura. She was frightened because normally she could recognize an aura only through great concentration and effort but this was clear. The man on the rope was surrounded with death, destruction, and distress. What was also clear was that death, destruction, and distress emanated from the woman.

"Unconsciously, Philomena murmured *armaya*, a spell to protect the man from the woman—and it seemed to work. The words seemed able to command the woman to stop. Seemingly horrified at what she had done, the woman held her quivering parasol out to the man trying to pull him up but he disdained any help, turned in a giant wheel around the rope and swung himself up again.

"Relieved, Philomena took a breath; the *armaya* had worked but perhaps it was not needed at all since, as the other members of the audience suddenly applauded, the cloud disappeared. The two tightrope walkers smiled at each other and curtsied together, and Philomena realized in overwhelming horror and shame that everything, the entire fight, the entire drama, had just been an act.

"The two gave an encore and then exited with an elegant harmonious *pax de deux* in the air which made the show in which they had fought comedic. Still, Philomena had seen the clouds. They were as real as the ground on which she stood. Even if no one but her believed in them, Philomena knew that the man, the tightrope walker, had been in danger. The danger emanated from the woman who had danced on the rope with him, and Philomena knew that she had to protect him."

"She wanted to protect me." Camillo interrupted Keja's narrative with a bitter laugh and a hoarse voice. "If only she could have looked out for herself. . . ."

Keja didn't comment; she filled her pipe anew and drank. She looked questioningly at her brother-in-law, the husband of her husband's sister. Should she narrate further? Should she tell of how Philomena had gone to him after the show wanting to get acquainted, to be with him in order to avert the danger that came from the other woman who she soon learned was Camillo's sister? Should she talk of how they had fallen in love and how Camillo's friends, the musicians, had talked to Pulika about giving her hand to him since Camillo's father, who by tradition should have done this, was already dead? Should she recall, after Pulika finally agreed, that Philomena said yes, but with the stipulation that she be allowed to dance with Camillo on the tightrope because of her mistaken belief that she had to protect him from his sister, Djidjo? Should Keja tell of the marriage celebration which was the most opulent the *kumpania* had ever seen or how, in the end, Camillo kept his word and walked the tightrope with Philomena?

Camillo shook his head imperceptibly. No, he didn't want to hear anymore; could not stand to hear. With a lifeless look he took the last swallow from the brandy bottle. "No *mulengi dori*, no mourning ribbon; no farewell; no forgiveness. They didn't even leave us a corpse." Bitterness, hate, agonized fury made Camillo's voice hard and angry.

"Do you think a *dori* could still accomplish anything?"

Camillo shook his head slowly, sadly, conscious of all those he and they, the *kumpania*, had lost. Earlier—before an unimaginably long peace-and-war-brown time, not even more than ten years ago—when they had to measure a dead person in order to build the coffin, the Gypsies did not use a tape measure. They used a small strip of cloth, and when the coffin was finished they cut it into little pieces. These pieces were knotted together into the *mulengi dori*, the bond with the dead. The *dori* was said to have great magic. One guarded it carefully, wore it next to the skin, and used it as a last defense if danger from the *gadsche* threatened. Then one opened the knots and murmured the name of the dead and asked him to open the noose around one's own neck just as he himself had opened the knot of the *dori*. Surely many Gypsies had a *dori* in their pocket when they went into the gas chambers. But such a ribbon had no power against the insanity that covered those years like putrid slime that would last for all eternity.

They stayed quiet for a long time. From the other Gypsies in the camp there was only the occasional groan, snore, and tortured whimpers of memories as they slept. Otherwise, it was quiet. No laughter, no talking. No night bird sang, no animal cried.

Camillo lit a new cigarette from the old one and smoked without talking. He smoked hurriedly as if nicotine were oxygen that he had to have to survive. Keja packed her pipe yet again and pulled on it slowly, thoughtfully, and exhaled a smoky cloud as if she made an offering of incense.

But the old rites, and with them the help and release they offered, were gone. They had died with the many who had been lost. Those they no longer had with them could be forgiven—but who could forgive the living? "I should have listened to her," said Camillo, after he had thrown the quickly smoked cigarette butt into the fire. "She always warned me about Djidjo. She said Djidjo is not bad but dangerous, even if she means well."

"You don't want to tell me in all earnestness that Philomena was right? That she really had foreseen the disaster?" Keja's voice sounded full of resentment.

"Philomena was right," persisted Camillo. "Djidjo finally dragged us all into ruin."

"Only because she wanted to stay in Berlin. No one could have known. . . ."

"Philomena knew it. I unsettled her, made her doubt herself, laughed her off. I should have trusted her."

"You didn't want to go either after Sandro was born. You wanted your son to have the good life. And nowhere else could anyone make so much money as in Berlin in the *Wintergarten*. Add to that the possibilities we had at the UFA in Babelsberg. They always needed acrobats and artistes. We lived well, lived really well."

"Too well."

"And besides," Keja was not to be held back any longer, "who could have known what they would do to us? We are Aryan. Many of us had fought in the First War."

"We are not Sinti but Roma. Travelling people. It is not good for us to stay too long in one place. . . ."

"Then why are we still here?"

Still Camillo paid no attention to Keja's angrily interjected question, ". . . it kills us," he continued. "Besides which, you are wrong. It wasn't about the money. We could earn that anywhere. It wasn't about Sandro. He would have gone with us in any event, like any Roma child. Rather, Djidjo had fallen in love with a *gadsche*. That is why she wanted to stay. And I did not force the issue. Therefore we all stayed. We stayed much too long. And I could not protect her. I could not protect any of us."

Quiet. Silence. Hopeless, bitter, sorrowful silence.

In time, Keja broke the silence. "Let us leave," she said, returning to her favorite theme.

"No."

"Why not?"

"We stay."

Keja shut up as she saw Camillo's face. The dead live as long as we think of them, she thought. The dead live as long as we think about them.

"We will play again," he said. "You are crazy."

"They will report about us. I have seen reporters in the ruins, even people with movie cameras from the *Wochenschau*, the news reels. If one of us is still alive, he or she will hear about us. That is much better than wandering around like blind people in the neighborhood." After a long pause filled with unending sorrow he said, "And we are here if someone still comes. Like we said we would be. In case anyone returns."

TWELVE

Lene looks bad, Mathilde thought, worse than everyone else. Everybody's skin was chapped from the endless dust, and all their clothes were patched and threadbare. Their hair, what you could see of it from under their kerchiefs, was greasy and dull; but for Lene, Mathilde thought, it was something more. Lene seemed to have a dark, evil cloud hanging over her. Her once determined blue eyes peered through a dim, wan film. The wrinkles of her forehead, the creases of her mouth seemed deeper. Though hunger had dug into all their faces it seemed more severe on Lene.

Lene had always kept her optimism and spirits high despite their problems. "Children," she would say, "we have survived this cursed war. Is that not a miracle, a damned wonderful miracle?" She had overcome Mathilde's reserve with her demand for friendship, and in the end Mathilde's shyness and fears gave up to Lene's overwhelming affability; but now, her friend had not been herself for a few days. No longer was she the vigorous Lene who one day found a squashed rubber ball and convinced all the women, normally unwilling to get involved in any playfulness, to play dodge ball. Instead she wandered around, listless, careless, and miserable, not speaking, distant, and irritable. Even the half bar of soap Mathilde had given her on her birthday as a timid token of their beginning friendship was greeted with a cheerless thanks, and Mathilde was disappointed. That half bar of soap was valuable, a treasure she had hoarded since the end of peace and the beginning of war. She had even hidden it from Heidrun's eagle eye, and it was genuine. It was a lightly perfumed soap you could use to wash your hair. There was no comparison to the caustic lye soap they had to make do with for washing everything from clothes to dishes to people, but to Lene it merited only a fleeting smile. She remained withdrawn, closed, and melancholy, disinterested in celebrating her birthday anyway.

At first Mathilde was disappointed, but she understood from hints, half sentences, and bits of conversation what the problem was; Lene's brother, Robert, was not doing well. His amputation wound had turned septic, unable to heal. On top of that he had diabetes and needed insulin but, even if they could find a doctor to treat him, Robert had nothing to barter and without insulin there was little a doctor could do. Insulin wasn't available legally, and a black market purchase was so expensive Lene never considered it.

Robert also had to have regular meals so Lene carefully divided the little she had into halves. They had been alone since their parents died in the hail of bombs so Lene made sure Robert got the larger half. She then divided her portion into thirds so Robert could have an additional ration while she ate the second third and traded the rest for bandages. She starved so Robert would have enough. At least the wound was kept clean, but Lene knew she was fighting a losing battle. Without insulin the amputation wound would not heal.

Lene didn't talk much about Robert or how things were going for her, and no one asked even when they knew about her problem. Nothing was secret at the worksite, but everyone had troubles of their own; their own children, their own families . . . and they did not, could not take on someone else's trouble, even if they wanted to. Not so with Mathilde. She offered help and support with the same unquestioning friendship Lene gave her to help Mathilde overcome her own reserve, but Lene fended off her offers.

"Only a miracle can help me," Lene said, "and you can't produce one of those, can you?"

Mathilde tried to bring back Lene's joviality with a joke, but it was unsuccessful; always unsuccessful but Mathilde remained just as tenacious as Lene had been with her before. Knowing that Lene had brought nothing to eat for days, she sat down next to her and offered her a piece of bread, but Lene declined, as she did each time. "You won't have for yourself."

Given her concern, Mathilde was forceful, almost brusque. "Just take it. You're about to collapse."

Lene glanced doubtfully at the bread, at Mathilde, then suddenly grabbed the bread and jumped up. "Excuse me, but . . ."

Before Mathilde could say anything, change anything, Lene had traded the bread to Helma the Rat for a butt. Helma always had cigarettes, Russian, known as "Stalin's revenge" to Berliners. Lene simply had to have one even if it was just a few puffs. She needed it more than bread. Sitting back down next to Mathilde, she inhaled greedily, deeply, furiously.

A dour Lene stared straight ahead and shrugged her shoulders. "Forget it," she said, guessing what Mathilde wanted to say. Lene knew that what she had done was irrational. She tried always to be rational, but sometimes it took a determined effort.

Mathilde started to say something, but a woman screamed at the other end of the pile cutting her off. Others called out something Lene and Mathilde could not understand, and still others motioned for the foreman.

Mathilde craned her neck and anxiously looked in the direction of the screams. "Something has happened over there," she said.

Lene concentrated on getting the last little bit of nicotine out of the cigarette. Nothing, not even an accident, could rouse her from her morose and melancholy lethargy. Suddenly her eyes gleamed with an idea. "Maybe it was not an accident. Maybe it was a dud."

Unexploded allied bombs, Russian artillery shells, and German grenades lay everywhere throughout the rubble waiting to explode at any moment if the workers were not careful. Luckily that had never happened in their workplace at Innsbrucker Platz, but a couple of kilometers away in Kreuzberg, not far from Lene's apartment, five children were blown up while playing with a grenade.

"If it's a dud, everything will come to a standstill for a while," Lene said hoping that it would be a long time before they started work again, and Mathilde knew she was right. "Until the clearing service has come and defused the thing," Lene continued, "there won't be any work done so it won't matter if I go off to be with Robert for an hour or so."

"And if not?" Mathilde didn't like the idea.

Lene winked at Mathilde. "You will think of something," she said as she ran off.

Mathilde looked after her and worried. What would she say to Schall if he missed Lene? For a little while she could say that Lene had gone to the toilet, or that she was filling her water bottle at the pump, but how long would that hold up? She could only hope Lene would return soon, so she wouldn't have to make up any story for her at all.

Mathilde looked around and joined the women around her who were streaming to the other side of the rubble mountain where the commotion had arisen. As she got closer, she was relieved to see that it had not been an accident. No one ran for a stretcher, no one cried in pain. But it was not a dud either. The women stood around a little group of colorfully dressed people, and in the middle of them all Schall was in an animated discussion with a man. A man who wore a colorful vest and anthracite colored hat. Camillo Baumgartner had announced he needed to speak with the foreman.

Mathilde slowed her steps unsure whether or not she wanted to meet the artiste. How should she greet him, how should she act? She hadn't seen him since Karla invited him in at dinner provoking the ugly argument with Hermann. After the three of them had dined in the kitchen, Baumgartner had vanished abruptly as always, silently, more phantom than person. Mathilde wished she could do the same now, but she knew she could not run away. She had to work, the break was over, no bomb had exploded and she could not hide. She had to cover Lene's back. She could hear Schall talking.

"I don't have anything against you playing here. The main thing is you don't start before the end of work."

Mathilde was surprised that Schall, the Pirate, had no problem with the Gypsies using the already cleared area between the rubble piles as a stage. The few conditions that he had Baumgartner readily accepted. Above all, Schall did not want to interrupt the work.

The two men sealed their agreement with a handshake during which the Gypsy noticed Mathilde and winked at her with half a smile over Schall's shoulder. Mathilde returned his greeting stiffly, but at the same time she felt a tingling sensation moving up her spine, a pleasant feeling that sent goose bumps all over her. He would perform. She would get to see him at his art.

Mathilde watched as the man in his colorful vest went over to a wall, set his hat firmly on his head and nimbly climbed to an iron hook near a hanging and fused electric cable that projected from an almost undamaged building. The cable was done for, but the hook held up when Baumgartner stood on it as a test.

Meanwhile, Schall turned back to his women rubble workers. "Come on, girls, back to work, the show is this evening and you all are invited, but till then we must accomplish a little bit."

He clapped his hands. "Tegge, the invitation includes you, too. So, back to work, quick march!"

To set a good example he started back, back to the rubble heap. Mathilde tore her eyes off Baumgartner and trudged after Schall while worrying what she should say if he asked about Lene. She knew he would ask, it was inevitable since he would try to control "his girls" much more strictly as long as the artistes were there to tempt them away from their work.

Schall, however, soon had other things to worry about as word of the Gypsies' arrival spread like wildfire. More and more people, children, adults, and old folks came streaming in. All were curious to see these strangers as they set up their stage. There was a rumor that some of the artistes had performed in Berlin's most famous vaudeville, the *Wintergarten*. None of them had ever been there even though the theater was close by. None of them could afford the price of tickets or the cover charge, but everyone knew the *Wintergarten*. Whoever had played there was good. Very good.

Schall had his hands full trying to corral the gathering crowd that stood around everywhere and gaped. They got in the way of the workers, endangered themselves, the women and the artistes. But he fought a losing battle. The people didn't want to leave. They were repulsed and attracted, fascinated by the strangeness of the Gypsies. They were also hungry for entertainment and yearning for a little fun. Fun they enjoyed even while the tightrope for the later presentation was still being prepared.

Two Gypsy boys, about sixteen-years-old, performed little tricks, jumped vaults and backward handsprings, walked on their hands and lifted each other into acrobatic poses. Two girls about the same age juggled colorful balls as children stared wistfully wondering how and where they got those. They did magic tricks with cards and marbles and during all of this, accompanied by two older men playing a fiddle and accordion, they danced short merry dances like little pantomimes that made the bystanders laugh.

Meanwhile Baumgartner, bare-chested but still wearing his hat, fastened his rope on the hook he had previously tested and worked to set up an iron pole with a small perch on it about thirty meters away. Two young men, also shirtless and sweating heavily in the bright sunshine, were busily pounding large stakes into the ground with sledgehammers so pole and perch could be secured with thin metal cables. Behind the iron perch Baumgartner drove another stake into the stony earth; it would later anchor a winch that would stretch the rope taut so he could dance on it.

While the men worked and the youths entertained the bystanders to make them curious about the show to follow, Gypsy women wearing colorful dresses, and bright kerchiefs and chains scattered around their black hair, offered their services as fortunetellers. They didn't find a lot of customers because the Germans were uneasy with these women who looked so different, spoke so different, smelled so different. They were wary almost to the point of being fearful, and watched everything from the safety of a distance.

Mathilde hurried to follow Schall's order and gone right back to work. She didn't want to do anything that would call attention to her and cause him to notice that Lene had disappeared. She was positioned about halfway up on the rubble heap with a good view while she worked relaying buckets of debris. She could follow the work of the Gypsies and watch to see if Schall approached or Lene returned. There was still no sign of her and, thankfully, Schall was busy.

"Hey, Tegge, you always stick together with Behrendt. Where is she? We are wearing ourselves out here and she is slacking off."

Roswitha, the Warhorse, was the first to say out loud what the others were thinking; they had to do Lene's work. They often did it for a few minutes because they all had to go to the toilet or take a moment to catch their breath; they all had a bad day now and then. A few minutes were okay but not more than that.

As soon as Roswitha said something the others naturally started to grumble. Gerda, the professor's wife, whose once lyrical tone of voice no longer bothered with the niceties of please or thank you and who knew the practices and patterns of the workplace as well as anyone, yelled out, "She's probably back there staring at the Gypsies with her eyes bulging out of her head while we work here like fools."

"Now, that I can understand. Those boys have sexy butts, for sure." The Russian's sweetheart, Inge, gave a loud and lascivious laugh.

Roswitha shouted, "Why should Lene have all the fun? Where is she?" She dropped her bucket bringing the whole line to a standstill and stomped over to Mathilde despite the rumbling of protests. "Well? Where is she?"

Minchen Krespe, Roswitha's mousy little friend, followed right behind her. If the moment had not been so threatening, Mathilde would have laughed out loud. It was just too funny to watch the little delicate woman attempt to imitate Roswitha's coarse, intimidating pose. "Yeah, where is Behrendt hiding?" Minchen's voice was a faint echo of Roswitha's.

Mathilde didn't know what to say. Everything was going wrong. She had feared Schall but he wasn't the problem at all.

"How dare she expect us to cover for her goofing off?" Minchen's outrage hit Mathilde in the face like a wet rag, but she couldn't say anything. She just glanced helplessly from one woman to another.

"Schall sent her back there. There, where the Gypsies are." Mathilde didn't know where she came up with that idiotic idea. Even if the women believed her, Schall would know she'd lied; but that didn't matter yet since the women didn't believe her anyway. They clustered together with Roswitha and Minchen in a circle that closed ever tighter around her.

"So? Why didn't you say that right off?" the Warhorse shot back.

"And when exactly did he do that?" Mathilde recognized Gerda's glare as the same unsettling look her husband, Franz, said he used in his police work when he suspected someone lied. "I don't know anything about it," she said, hesitating slightly. "Just as he sent us back to work. I think he wanted to have a few people over there in case there was trouble."

Mathilde looked for help toward the street corner where she hoped Lene would appear and defuse this tense situation, but Lene was nowhere to be seen. Instead she saw Karla holding Heinrich in her arms and Gerhild by the hand as they were running up to see the Gypsies. The excitement had spread as far as Steglitz, but there was no time for that now as Inge spoke in a rage. "She's in for it when she comes back and you, too, if you have lied to us. Why should we have to carry all the load?"

Everyone murmured agreement.

"That's easy for you to say. You're a fine one to talk." Finally Mathilde got a little support from Elfriede because Inge was the one who took the most frequent and the longest breaks, and groaned loudest when she had to take an occasional half step more to pass her bucket down the line.

Yes, Mathilde thought, Inge was not one to accuse her of being lazy. "I don't lie," she said.

"Yes, you do," cried Inge who was about to go after Mathilde as Roswitha and Minchen nodded in agreement.

Gerda restrained Inge and smiled knowingly at Mathilde. "We'll soon know," she said. "Here comes the Pirate now." The foreman noticed that work was interrupted around Mathilde. He gave up trying to herd sightseers and he came up to the group scolding, "What is the matter with you? Don't stare. Work!"

Seemingly innocent nods, assenting mumbles, indifferent shrugs and false smiles came from the Warhorse and the Rat as Gerda, Inge, Minchen and the others started back to work. They purposely left a big gap next to Mathilde where Lene should have been. Elfriede unconsciously started to step in to fill it but stopped as Roswitha glared.

Naturally, Schall noticed. He looked up and down the row, once, twice, and figured out who was missing. "Where is Behrendt hiding?"

Mathilde was hot and cold at the same time, thoughts chased, swirled, shot through her head. Now it was in the open, the Pirate had asked the question. Now it would happen. Now it had to happen. Mathilde stayed quiet and waited, anticipating judgment.

"You sent her over there with the Gypsies," said Roswitha with her malicious grin aimed at Mathilde. "At least that is what Tegge told us."

Schall seemed confused. "Did I do that?" He turned to Mathilde, "Did I really do that? So that is why she's missing here." He was not angry, not accusing, just confused. He simply wanted to know if he had done such a nonsensical thing.

"Yeah. We were surprised, too." Mathilde seized her chance, surprised by the firmness in her voice and surprised at how easy the lies came from her.

"Really?" The Pirate still didn't understand.

Mathilde tensely watched him. "Well okay, then." He shrugged. "Move up a little," he said to the others, "and close the gap." He turned away, wanting to go back to the other side, to the Gypsies working and the idling onlookers, but he just wasn't sure. "You wouldn't be lying to me, would you, Tegge?"

Mathilde could not stand up under his look. Fate had only given her a little reprieve, and now it would come down hard. She imagined Heidrun's accusations, Hermann's disproving gaze, and felt Karla's sympathy because she had lost her job. However, fate was kind to Mathilde. "No," Schall said, "you can't lie," as he walked away.

"Lucky," whispered Helma.

"Yes," smiled Elfriede.

Relieved, Mathilde watched Schall go. She could hardly believe it, but her story actually worked; she survived again, she pulled it off. Pleased, for a short time, with her success she didn't notice how the women closed the gap and returned to work.

"Hey, Tegge, don't bore holes in the air. Grab hold." Gerda gave her a sharp poke in the ribs and brought Mathilde down to earth. She was made painfully aware that the women weren't done with her. Not by a long shot. They were angry and bitter that they had been hoodwinked, and they were going to take it out on her.

Mathilde took full buckets from above and empties from below and passed them along the line. Each time Gerda, standing above her, passed a full bucket she banged it against Mathilde's shinbone. Roswitha, who stood below, ripped the bucket from her hand so that if she didn't let go quickly the skin on her hand would split, and if she let go too soon the bucket fell with its contents spilling on the ground and Roswitha would yell, "Can't you watch what you're doing?"

After this happened a few times Roswitha, with her malicious grin, threatened to sic Schall on her again. But Mathilde decided quickly it was better to put up with their torment without complaint than have Schall come around again and get suspicious. There was nothing for her to do but accept their spitefulness, taunts, and dirty tricks, and hope against hope that Lene would return. But, Lene did not come.

* * *

While Mathilde worked, Karla and Heidrun's two youngest watched the Gypsies' preparations for their temporary theater. Enticed by the antics of the performers, the two little ones toddled innocently among the acrobats and marveled at their amazing feats and magic tricks and laughed at the merry songs performed by girls hardly older than Karla.

Gerhild didn't know what to think when she discovered yet another amazing detail on the Gypsy women's clothes: shimmering pieces of fringe, two or three jingling bracelets, even a few gold pieces sewn on a sleeve or jacket hem. She gaped in wonder. Where had these strange women and girls gotten all these expensive pieces in times like these? How could they have preserved their colorful exotic clothes and sumptuous jewelry, those vestiges of a long past, better, more glorious time?

Soon Gerhild discovered Camillo Baumgartner and crowed happily, "Can you make magic bonbons again?"

The artiste was just ready to erect the pole and shook his head smiling. "You don't have your milk can with you, where should I slip them?"

The boys stopped their performing and, together with Baumgartner, began raising the pole little by little. At the same time the young men who had driven the stakes secured thin metal cables on the pole so they could anchor it later. The rope hung loose and would be tightened after the pole was in place.

Despite the exertion that made his forehead veins swell as sweat rolled down his neck, Baumgartner managed to nod to Gerhild. "Besides," he said, "what would your brother say if you got bonbons from me again? He'd be upset with you for sure, and your father, too."

"They can't say a thing. You aren't a stranger any more." Gerhild proudly held her head high, her pigtails bouncing saucily, and Heinrich babbled, "Bonbons, yes, bonbons, Heinrich get too."

"Hey, you two, stop that." Karla felt embarrassed by the little ones. "Mr. Baumgartner has already done enough for us," she said. "You can't beg for more."

"No doubt you'll find a few bonbons," Baumgartner consoled them, "just not now. I can't let go here right now." With that his face became a mask of such a comical grimace that Gerhild laughed out loud while Heinrich began to whine.

"Come on. We'll not disturb Mr. Baumgartner any more," Karla said pulling the children away with her, but she didn't get far. Gerhild's laughter suddenly stopped, and Heinrich's whining broke off as he stood wide-eyed and about to cry.

"Karla," Gerhild stammered, "who is that?"

They stood in front of a gigantic woman, at least a meter eighty tall, with long black hair and a very large mouth, her eyes drawn to narrow slits. Keja smoked a pipe and had listened to the conversation between her brother-in-law and the three *gadsche* children.

Unexpectedly she beamed, reached down to stroke Heinrich on his cheeks and smiled at him. "You're a sweet one," she said with a somewhat smoky, yet friendly voice.

Still, Heinrich began to cry, and Karla lifted him into her arms while Gerhild pressed close to her cousin. "Look, Karla!" she cried out as if the strange woman held a dagger or pistol, "the lady smokes a pipe!"

"Did I frighten you? I didn't mean to." Keja took the pipe out of her mouth, knocked it out, stuck it in her pocket and pulled out three bonbons from the depths of her skirt, which she held out to the children.

Karla shook her head, Heinrich turned away and pressed his face into Karla's shoulder; even Gerhild didn't trust enough to take one though her gaze hung wistfully on the sweets.

"Take them, I have enough." Once more, Keja's hand disappeared in her skirts, came back with more bonbons and held these out encouragingly to the children.

Gerhild hesitated and took one. "Can you do magic too?" she asked shyly.

"No." Keja laughed. "I can't do magic. I just have bonbons in my pockets."

Gerhild nodded, got the bonbon out of the paper and almost reverently stuck it in her mouth. Heinrich took courage from Gerhild and turned his head to look at Keja. His eyes bounced back and forth from the woman to the bonbons in her hand. His lust for the sweets finally overcame his fear, and he stretched out his hand. Keja laid a bonbon in it; with clumsy child's fingers he clawed the wrapping paper off and stuffed the bonbon in his mouth.

Karla put him down. For some reason that she didn't understand it angered her deeply that her cousins had let themselves be tempted to take the bonbons. At the same time she didn't begrudge them the rare pleasure. "Would you like one too?" Keja asked her.

Karla shook her head. The woman had a sinister air about her, and as fond as Karla was of Mr. Baumgartner, as much as she trusted him, this Gypsy lady seemed threatening to her.

Keja smiled and took Karla's hand before she could blink. "No, you don't want any sweets like your siblings, you want something completely different."

"They are not my siblings. Gerhild is my cousin and so is Heinrich," stammered Karla. She was nervous, wondering what this woman was up to. She wanted to run, just get away. "Come on, let's go," she said to the children as she tried to pull her hand from Keja's, but Keja would not let go.

"So, cousins, and you have to look out for them?" Keja seemed surprised.

"Yes." Karla jerked her hand away. She wanted to grab the little ones and go.

"Wait." Keja laid her hand softly on Karla's arm. The girl seemed unable to do anything but stand still. Keja turned to the two little ones. "You stay sitting here and don't move from this place. Watch how they set up the pole. If you are good, you will get some more bonbons."

The siblings nodded earnestly and sat side by side on a fallen steel beam, sincerely, pleasantly satisfied to suck on their bonbons and absentmindedly scratch their louse-plagued scalps.

Keja again took Karla's hand and held it gently, almost playfully, but to Karla her touch burned on her skin. She wanted to rip her hand away, to resist, run away, but something held her. She was unable to move even a millimeter. She was unable to withdraw from Keja's power, Keja's will. It was as if she was delicately dancing, stepping softly away from the little ones. Karla could not look away from Keja as the Gypsy looked deep into her eyes. "You want to know what the future brings."

Karla nodded even though she wanted to scream, "No." She did not want to know. Above all, she did not want to learn of it from this woman, but she was powerless.

"Let me see then . . ."

The lines in Karla's hand seemed to glow red hot as Keja ran her finger along them.

"I have no money at all." Karla tried a last desperate attempt to escape. In vain. She didn't want to but had to. She had to follow this fortune teller, this beautiful, proud, powerful woman who smelled so strange, so sweet and tangy at the same time.

"Then give me something better. Your smile?" asked Keja and smiled herself.

Karla was trapped, completely trapped. She didn't notice that she was suddenly further away; away from Baumgartner's field of vision, away from her mother's sight; far away from them all, as if someone held her in outstretched arms way out over the edge of the world.

She was suspended in silence and quiet. The shouts of the men erecting the pole, the murmur of the onlookers and the music all came from far away, and even farther was the faint rattle of metal on steel, the pounding of the women who tore away the walls and cleaned mortar fragments from tiles. Karla was barely aware of the sounds as if they came through a bell jar; soft, distant, strange, and unreal. It seemed to her as if she could hear Keja follow the lines of her palm, as if she could hear how the Gypsy woman studied her, looked into her, as if she could hear what would come.

After a long silence, Keja began. "You are a tomboy, aren't you? You seldom do what your mother wants, right?" It was a shot in the dark but not really. Keja's hunch was close to the mark having observed Karla's wild eyes, her small closed mouth, her unruly loose hair jutting out in all directions. She no longer needed to mesmerize her quarry with piercing looks and, instead, turned her attention to Karla's hand. As part of her act Keja murmured a few words that Karla could not understand; that she was not supposed to understand.

To Karla the words seemed like a strange prayer. The fourteen-year-old wanted to stay mute, not to speak or reveal anything about herself to the Gypsy lady, yet, against her will, she was compelled to talk. "How do you know that?" she asked. "Did you read that in my hand?"

"Ah," thought Keja—a lucky shot. She smiled secretly but didn't say anything until finally she continued, "Your father was in the war and is still missing." It wasn't an exceptional or bold assumption, and the reaction would be interesting.

The girl nodded but did not answer, and then a hard look came into her eyes. Keja saw it immediately. Something is troubling her, she thought, something more than is normal for a fourteen-year-old with possibly other men in her family who might have been soldiers. "He's missing," she repeated. "Or lost. You are worried about him."

"How do you know all that?" stammered Karla. Unbelieving, helpless.

"It is true though, isn't it?"

"Yes."

Keja paused for a long, silent moment knowing the effect her protracted gaze would have. She could sense how uncertain Karla was and wanted to explore that uncertainty; she had to know.

"There's something else," Keja said suddenly, her smoky voice feeling, groping her way. "I can't tell yet what it is, just give me a little time."

Keja looked deeply into Karla's eyes to confirm the overtone she heard in Karla's "yes" before, and Karla's eyelids fluttered. Keja knew. She was right there. She could clearly see Karla's thoughts as if they were a book opened before her. "You're afraid your father is dead?"

"Certainly," Karla replied softly. "Everyone has that fear."

No, thought Keja, that's not it. She hesitated and waited but nothing cleared up so she decided to take a detour. "You often wish you were not in your situation," she said, stating the obvious for most fourteen-year-old girls.

Karla merely nodded, so Keja continued. "A photo of Hans Albers hangs with your things, and next to it is Marika Rökk," she said. That, too, was easy since Karla would likely admire the handsome masculinity of a Hans Albers more than the subtle charms of Rühmann, Prack, Heesters. And Marika Rökk was the iconic female rebel of popular German films; the one who didn't always do what was expected and follow orders but chose her own path and, to the consternation of others, somehow managed to get out of whatever trouble she ran into. Karla's admiration of her was a simple assumption.

"That's right; that is true." The girl's voice sounded surprised. And Keja could tell that Karla slowly lost her fear and resistance. She opened up like a fresh oyster when the knife hits the sweet spot and the oyster yields.

"The two would go well together, don't you think?"

"I don't know. Next to Mr. Albers, I believe a woman would not have much say, and whether Mrs. Rökk would put up with that . . ."

"Many women gladly take the secondary role."

"Yes, unfortunately." Karla nodded.

"Like your mother."

"She just isn't strong enough to stand up for herself," the girl said, without warning suddenly becoming furious. "She doesn't have it easy, really not. There is no other way, and everything depends on her, but she doesn't like to do it, she's not happy."

"That is not what I meant." Keja attempted to soothe Karla. She did not want to destroy the trust she had uncovered.

"You don't know her."

"No, I don't know her." Keja had no idea where the girl came from or what she was doing here or what she had to do with Camillo. She wondered where this *gadsche* brat knew him from and had no idea, at least not yet, but she would find out. "Be that as it may, she is submissive."

The girl nodded in resignation.

"That won't happen to you, Karla," Keja said, smiling again, beaming even. "I can assure you of that."

"Yes, absolutely not." Karla tried the declaration on like a glove that was too large and completely forgot to wonder how the stranger knew her name.

Keja noted Karla's omission with yet another smile. Trust between them had been created. "Absolutely not," she repeated, glowing in the trust, power, and good will that shone in Karla's eyes. And then all that was gone.

Karla's eyes were suddenly clouded. "Nothing will change, I think." The certainty the girl radiated a moment before disappeared like smoke in the wind.

"You are strong and smart. You're not like other girls, other women. You have often thought about how simple it would be just to run away." Keja almost felt sympathy for the girl, but she immediately stifled the impulse. "You could have run away but you didn't. You know it is not out of the question; you are not far from it, but still you don't do it. Times will change, and then you will be ready. I see that clearly."

Karla let her shoulders droop, almost curling into herself. "I don't know," she said.

Keja watched her closely and bided her time. She wanted to let her talk. She could tell there was too much weighing on her, and that Karla needed to tell someone, sometime. Keja would be that someone. She needed to know what this *gadsche* family had to do with Camillo.

"A few days ago my uncle came home."

Keja recognized the indignation in the girl's voice. Karla didn't realize she was speaking about herself without Keja reading her palm or prompting her. "Those are my aunt and uncle's two youngest children," she said, nodding toward where they'd left the little ones. "The whole family lives with us. They were bombed out, and to make it even more difficult my uncle comes home and immediately gets the largest piece of meat if there is any and is treated like a damn king." The fourteen-year-old smiled at Keja self-consciously, embarrassed. "Excuse me, please."

Keja shook her head. The girl had no need to apologize for raw language. Not to her.

"But it is true! Uncle Hermann pops up and gets everything and doesn't have to do anything for it. Nothing!" Karla paused and sighed. "I don't believe times will change" she added, returning to what Keja said. "If the women would stay alone, if the men didn't come home anymore, maybe."

"You don't really wish that, do you?"

Karla stared at the Gypsy woman with an expression revealing a quiet, rebellious, and wise corner of her mind she had never chosen to explore, much less say out loud. And she had said it. No one but Keja would notice, but Keja knew it from her own thoughts, her own veiled looks. She knew it and understood.

"You hope your father doesn't come home?"

Karla hesitated, swallowed, stared at the Gypsy and said nothing. Slowly, very slowly it trickled into her consciousness what she had just said, what she had just thought. She jerked as if Keja had hit her. What Keja had framed as a question, seemed to her to be a declaration. " Naturally, I don't want that. I really hope he is alive. I pray for that every evening, together with my mother."

Keja looked at her without reaction and listened.

"My father is no worse than most others, certainly not. In any case I like him better than Uncle Hermann. Not only because he is my father. He is simply nicer." Karla spoke quick, disjointed phrases as if she wanted to throw the syllables at ghosts to make them disappear. Ghosts she herself had called up. "He often helped Mom. Even peeled potatoes when he was home. Much different from Uncle Hermann. He is much nicer, a lot easier going."

"You surely had him for only a few days on leave in the last years. Except for that he was somewhere in the front lines."

"No, no. He was called up only a few months ago."

"Is he that old?" Keja asked surprised. "Or was he so important?"

Karla faltered. Became quiet. Her mother had impressed on her to speak to no one about her father. With no one, no matter who asked. And although Mathilde had not said why, Karla knew exactly why. Her father had been a policeman, even a part of the Gestapo. She had clearly seen how much everyone feared him before the collapse. "I don't know," she said. "I really don't know if he was important." She broke off, pulled herself together again and shut up.

Keja considered her for a while. "You are strong, you are brave, and you are smart," she finally repeated. "You will fashion your own way; I see that clearly." She decided to leave the father theme for a while.

"Strong, wise, brave," Karla sang with scorn. Keja recognized her tone only too well from herself. "You can't really see into the future, can you?" Karla continued. "Why do you say that?"

"Because you would know that I am neither strong, nor wise, nor brave. Foolhardy and crazy, perhaps."

"I see the power. What you do with it is your business. And, if you were not wise, you would certainly not know when your bravery turns into foolhardiness."

"Too late. I only realize it when it is too late." Karla stared into space, lost in her own thoughts as if Keja were not there. Nor did she notice that Keja had begun to softly stroke Karla's hand. "If Mr. Baumgartner were not there, I wouldn't be sitting here. I would most likely be dead," she said.

"Ah," thought Keja, hiding a triumphant smile. Now we're getting somewhere. The girl would talk now; and Keja would learn what she needed to know.

"Mr. Baumgartner saved my life." Karla shook her head. "It was really dumb of me, but Frieder, Uncle Hermann's eldest son, is a year older than me and tries to act like a grown-up and just like his father on top of it. So Frieder challenged me, and I know I shouldn't have accepted it. I was just as dumb as he was."

She shut up again. Keja waited a moment and then casually asked, "What happened?"

Karla began to tell about the arguments in the apartment, the quarrels with Frieder in particular, and about their squabble when she had climbed up and suddenly could not go forward or backward. Her tale came like an unstoppable flood as she told about how crowded home was, and how sometimes she felt like she was in jail; how her mother supported them working on the rubble pile, and how thankful they were that Mr. Baumgartner helped them with a few groceries and cigarettes now and then.

Once she started she could not stop. She told Keja about her hopes, her dreams, and her worries. She emptied her heart out to this utterly strange woman, this utter stranger, talking as she could not talk to her mother because Karla always worried about Mathilde and felt like she had to be strong for her.

Karla talked as she couldn't talk with her aunt or any of her friends, and Keja listened. The more Karla talked, the darker Keja's countenance became, the more her brows contracted, the tighter she compressed her lips. It was okay that Camillo didn't let this *gadsche* kid simply fall. She understood that. It was proper. But what other business did he have with this family? Why did he magically produce bonbons for the little ones and give the adults cigarettes and groceries? Why did he help a family of the murderers? Wasn't it justice for them to be hungry? Wasn't it justice for them to take care of their rubble? Wasn't it justice that they now had to mourn their dead?

Hate rose in Keja. Hate for Camillo, hate for the Germans. Suddenly she had an irresistible urge to hurt the girl who sat there so strong and at the same time so desperate in front of her. She wanted to wound her. She wanted to see her cry. She wanted to hear how she moaned and screamed.

"It hurts my soul what I have to tell you." Keja cut off Karla's story like a sword stroke, she spread her arms in despair and pointed to a line in Karla's hand. "That does not look good, not good at all."

"What?" Karla stopped in shock.

The fortuneteller followed the line down again and again until it glowed like a brand. She shook her head, assumed a disconcerted look, and paused, breathed deeply and, after another pause, said, "Your father is dead."

The girl seemed to not understand. She stared at Keja without expression, motionless, and even seemed to stop breathing. "Your father is dead," repeated Keja. Softly, almost sympathetically, almost consoling. The impulse to hurt Karla had disappeared almost as fast as it had struck, but now she had said it and could not take it back. In truth she didn't want to. What was said, was said. She recognized that, and her people had held that thought for thousands of years.

"Dead?"

Keja nodded and waited for the sorrow, waited for the tears. "Are you sure?"

"Yes."

The girl nodded. She seemed to have the result that she expected, but she did not cry. "Perhaps it is better so," she whispered.

I was right, thought Keja; the girl wished her father to be dead even though she said the opposite.

"Now I can tell you, now that he is dead." Karla hesitated; Keja kept quiet, looked expectantly at the *gadsche* girl. "He couldn't be happy anymore. By no means. He was," Karla hesitated, took a deep breath and then said out loud, "He was with the Gestapo."

THIRTEEN

That evening, after he finally got free from Frieder, Franz was too tired, too done in, too hungry to follow the trail he had found any further. He could do no more; he curled up like a tramp and went to sleep—sleep, sleep, and sleep—in a corner between the remnants of a couple of walls that were still warm from the sun of the day. He slept like a dead man.

He woke up in the morning twilight with aching joints, a growling stomach, and sheer unbearable thirst, and knew he had to look for shelter, wash, shave, and clean his clothes. Otherwise he would stick out like a sore thumb.

While searching for a pump Franz found a beer bottle stopper in the trash. When he had worked in the theft department one of his "customers" had shown him how to make a skeleton key out of one of these. After his much needed wash up he broke into a drugstore which had miraculously neither been destroyed nor plundered and stole a shaving kit, soap, and a clothes brush. It amused him to notice a not unpleasant excitement as he quietly unlocked the door, looked around the shop, got what he needed, carefully sneaked back out, and vanished. He almost enjoyed being on the other side, enjoyed doing what just a couple of weeks ago would have been completely unthinkable.

Shortly after fleeing the scene, he stumbled upon or, more correctly, ran into a place to hide out. He expected greater difficulty finding a place since he could hardly go to the housing office for a listing, not to mention that every undestroyed apartment and space, even the smallest shed, was doubly or triply occupied; but good fortune smiled on him and he found a Volkswagen on the edge of the street. Apparently its owner had carefully locked it before a bombing attack, but during the onslaught the car, along with the entire street, had been covered with rubble. Only a narrow path snaked along between the remains of houses so that none but a few rats had discovered the VW until now. The car formed a little arbor in the middle of the rubble. Franz had only to unlock it with the help of his newly-minted skeleton key, drive out the rats, and make himself at home.

When he emerged from his new hiding place, all shaved, washed and outwardly presentable, his stomach growled even louder. How could he get something to eat without money, ration cards, or anything to trade? He realized he should have taken more from the drugstore than he needed. His honesty and decency were a curse. It was unthinkable to expect him to continue surveillance of Matthus, Borg, and Kleinmann in these circumstances.

His stomach ached as he walked through the Volkspark which no longer deserved to be called a park, racking his brain to figure out how to get something to eat. He was surprised to see so many people out and about, seemingly ambling around without destination as if they were just out for a walk. They wandered over trampled down meadows, among splintered and chopped down trees, meeting and talking with another, standing together and then parting to go their separate ways without any obvious purpose. Strollers? In this number? In these surroundings and in this poor excuse for a park? Franz watched all that was going on and suddenly understood what he had found. This was a black market. Now he knew he would get something to eat.

He forced himself to be calm as he slipped between the black marketers even though he was faint from hunger. He studied the crowd until he found what he was looking for, a lady about fifty years old in a tattered yet clearly expensive raincoat.

The woman looked around nervously, made several attempts to speak to different people but hesitated each time, not trusting herself to have the guts to go through with it. Franz followed her until finally someone spoke to her. A man opened his coat and offered her bacon, biscuits, coffee, and an opened pack of cigarettes. Franz's mouth watered when he saw the biscuits and bacon, but he stood back and continued to watch. After a little bargaining, a deal was made. The woman gave up a pearl necklace that would normally be worth a great deal, but right now she needed groceries. Satisfied, the woman left the park.

Franz followed her for a few blocks then quietly came up behind her. "Police," he barked. "Show me what you are carrying." The shocked woman looked at him, her eyes pleading, but Franz remained firm. "I mean now!" he said. The intimidated woman opened her bag, and Franz was pleased his tactic worked so well. She was too surprised and guilty to ask for his badge and credentials, and his professional tone and demeanor sealed the deal.

"Please," she said, "it's our wedding anniversary. My husband so likes to smoke. If he gets a cup of coffee, well, that's like Christmas for him. Please, Inspector, it was my first time, I swear. I will never do it again. Please look the other way, can't you?"

The woman was about to break into tears and almost made Franz feel sympathy for her. She was neither a professional dealer nor a practiced liar, still his hunger drove him on. "I'm sorry," he said. "I have to take you in to the precinct station. Naturally, you will lose the things and have to pay a fine." The woman sobbed. "However ..." Franz paused as if weighing the risks, "perhaps we can work something out."

"Yes?" Hope glimmered under the tears.

"The bacon and biscuits I have to confiscate. But coffee and cigarettes are not food in the strictest sense. I could let them go."

"And what about the fine?"

He took the bacon and biscuits out of the bag. "Run away. And hurry. I had bad luck and you escaped," he said, winking at her. "We don't really have to do everything the Russians tell us, do we?"

The woman beamed thanks at him.

"Greetings to your husband. And, celebrate well. How many years of marriage is it now?"

"The twenty-fourth," she answered and disappeared as quickly as she could.

A short time later Franz was hidden in the vestibule of a house across from the army truck where he had hidden the day before so that he could watch the gateway through which Matthus and Borg disappeared yesterday evening. His belly growled painfully causing him to regret having eaten the biscuits and bacon so quickly, almost before the woman was out of sight. His conscience nagged at him a little, but he knew he would have to feed himself the same way in the days and weeks to come. What else could he do? Sadly enough, the only thing he knew he would probably never get, by force or trade, were his beloved and sorely-missed licorice lozenges. He looked into the shiny tin box with its few remaining pieces before returning it to his pants pocket; a promise, he told himself. A promise of better times ahead.

He kept careful watch on the gateway and the area around it. No one lived in the house anymore. Few outside walls remained and these only to the height of its elevated ground floor. It had been a five-story-high building at one time judging by the nameplates at the entrance. Next to them hung the ever present reports of what had become of the former occupants, where you could look for and perhaps find them—if they had survived the bombing inferno.

A blackened enamel sign for a printing shop hung at the entrance to the courtyard. Next to it was a display box with broken glass in which were still pasted remnants of samples for death and marriage notices that had somehow withstood the fire bombs. No one could know how. At his post across from the entrance Franz waited, sounding out the situation. He would do nothing hasty.

About an hour later, Kleinmann drove up front in the truck. He got out and told the kids loitering around to keep their dirty paws off it and, at the same time, guard it carefully. He disappeared into the court-yard and returned in a few minutes with Matthus and Borg. The three drove off together amid protesting cries from the children who had been playing hide and seek around the truck, all the while singing out the children's rhyme, "*Eine, zweie, dreie, das Haus, das ist entzweie . . .*" Kleinmann shooed them away like an angry farmer scatters birds in a grain field.

Franz had waited for this chance. He had to get in, learn the layout, and get out quickly. He pushed his way past the kids who were paying no further attention to anything but their game as they romped around each other. "*Vier, fünfe, sechse, das war die Bombenhexe . . .*" they chanted.

Once inside the passageway Franz came to another door to a stairwell whose steps led to nowhere. A cellar had collapsed under the weight of rubble. He could smell the faint sweet stench of rotting meat, lighter than excrement yet more disgusting. Not everyone who sought shelter there had survived. Outside the tinny, nerve-racking chant droned on. "*Peng peng krach bum, wer das nicht schön find', der ist dumm.*" Franz shook his head almost envying the children's ability to create a game out of the horror.

The courtyard was yet another huge pile of rubble. Franz crept carefully around the debris, stones, fragments, but could find no other way out. Borg, Matthus and Kleinmann must have gone underground somewhere in the courtyard—but where? He looked around again and again, but he could find no clue pointing to where their hiding place might be. Suddenly he noticed a trail of footprints in the soot leading around a huge pile of stones. He followed them and came upon a steel door that lay even with surrounding stones, but unlike them it was not covered with soot. He noticed it was hung on hinges. Clearly, it had been brought here for a reason. Tentatively, carefully, he tried to open it. Locked. This door led somewhere, hid something. This door led to the hiding place for the men with Matthus.

Franz quietly unlocked the door with his skeleton key and opened it, being careful to stay covered by the door in case someone was in the room below who might shoot an intruder, but nothing happened. After waiting a few seconds, he slowly came around the door and peered into the dark hole. Daylight cut a path through the darkness revealing a metal colossus that gleamed sallow in the opening. A press, he thought. A press the Russians had not found. If they had found it they would have taken it back to Russia as part of their reparations loot. It smelled like printers ink and old machine oil. This, he decided, must be the printing shop that had the display box out front, and it was apparently undamaged.

A ladder leaned against the doorsill providing access to the room, but he refrained from climbing down. It was much too dangerous without a light or a weapon. He shut the door, locked it, and returned to his

VW for a nap. He needed to recuperate, having seen and done enough for the day.

The next day, along with the necessary food, he "requisitioned" a gas lantern at the black market, and as the man—this time it was a man—opened his bag Franz found a bonus—a large breadknife. He hadn't been looking for a weapon but this was better than nothing.

Now, newly equipped, he climbed down into the printing shop after the three had left their hideout for the day. The space was about five meters wide and six meters long. Windows were nailed shut with strong boards, and the ceiling was reinforced with additional wooden joists, the reason why the workplace had not been destroyed. Next to the large press he had seen from above there was a second, smaller one and various cutting and binding tools. Everything was clean and tidy as if the master and journeymen had just quit work a few minutes ago. The machines gleamed with oil. If they had electricity they could start work again immediately.

In the back of the space was a door that Franz figured led to the owner's, the master printer's, apartment. He opened the door slowly, always wary of an ambush, and entered a kitchen whose window and ceiling were reinforced in the same way as the shop. Behind the kitchen was a bedroom and a small landing; it led to an entrance door that had been secured with beams and boards as well. The debris pile must have been behind it since the whole building had been buried.

The bedroom itself contained a double bed, night tables, a wardrobe and dressing table. There was nothing uncommon except for some crude makeshift bunk beds against the walls that provided accommodation for ten people.

Everything was clean, tidy, down right neat. Some candles stood on the kitchen table, two cups in the sink. Franz sniffed the cups and smelled real bean coffee which had been drunk from them. A carbide cooker stood on the cold stove, a large canister of water was under the sink. The roebuck hung in a corner; a few pieces had been cut out.

Franz looked in the cabinets and found a whole warehouse: hard, long-lasting, army bread, margarine, smoked sausages. Almost without realizing it, his trained eye looked for licorice lozenges. He only found groceries, cigarettes, coffee, and liquor. Whoever hid out here could hold out, sustain themselves well, for a long time.

Franz had seen enough and climbed back out. He had just laid the door back on the ground behind him and locked it when he heard voices at the gate corner. He recognized Matthus's, but not those of the other men. He quickly searched around for a place to hide, but where could he go? Where? He could not return to the printing shop where he would be trapped or out into the courtyard where he would run right into Matthus. If he climbed up on the rubble pile he would be a sitting duck. Where? Automatically he crouched down even though it was senseless and ran away from door. About a meter along he saw a small space under a large piece of wall that had remained whole during the building collapse. He crawled inside. And listened.

He heard Matthus, Borg and Kleinmann, whose voices he now recognized, come around the rubble pile. There were at least two other men with them. Franz heard the door open and fervently hoped he had left everything the way he had found it. He heard them climb down the ladder and go through the printing shop into the kitchen. One of the men rubbed his hands together. "Coffee," he said, "I smell coffee."

"And a nice juicy roast," said another who seemed to have just discovered the roebuck.

Franz wondered how he could hear them so clearly and then discovered a pipe that came out of the kitchen ending in the wall in which he was hiding, apparently a ventilation pipe. Whoever set the printing shop had really thought of everything.

Matthus told Kleinmann to make coffee. While the subordinate did that, Franz could hear how courtesies and banalities were exchanged, how the newcomers were shown the rooms, how they were given the "house rules." Kleinmann called one of the newcomers "Sturmbannführer," but before Franz could learn more, Matthus interrupted, strongly forbidding the use of the former ranks. "It is best that each becomes used to their new names," he said. "We are called Müller, Schmidt, Lehmann, and Schulze, understood?" The others murmured agreement.

Franz retreated. He did not need to know anything more. This was Matthus's secret. A group of former functionaries and diplomats met here to hide out, get new identities, perhaps to flee or perhaps to go underground. He took a breath in relief and grinned. This was more than he had hoped for. He would keep them under observation for they were his ticket back into life.

In the following days he observed the men from outside the courtyard, outside the archway. He had made sure there was no other exit and was certain he could keep them under surveillance without putting himself in danger. Outside he had, if needed, opportunities to escape, and if he did run into Matthus, Borg, or Kleinmann he could always chalk it up to coincidence.

Franz knew a few of those that showed up in the next days from having seen them in the old Gestapo headquarters, Prinz-Albrecht-Palais, and was confident they would not recognize him. All were escorted by Kleinmann who seemed to be the man Friday for the group. He handled them with exquisite deference since they were all higher ranks from the now defunct regime. New ones came daily and a few, like Borg, seemed to live there while others appeared sporadically. None of them noticed Franz.

Day after day Franz stood in the shadowed foyer and watched. Twice Frieder had gone past apparently looking for him. A third time Frieder had a friend with him, and the two had a higher ranking Russian soldier in tow. The three were involved in a protracted negotiation, using hand gestures along with fragments of Russian. Franz was amazed at how fast these kids had picked up a foreign language. Soon, he thought, very soon they would easily pick up enough English to conduct the same business Franz had just witnessed with the Americans and the British. And with them, he mused, it would be much more lucrative.

Franz could not see everything, having pulled further back into the shadows, but he could surmise that two medals, worthless insignia of the overthrown ruler, were traded for a considerable amount of cigarettes and vodka. He grinned at the boy's ability to create value out of junk and was almost a little proud of Frieder, but it was a paradoxical pride. Franz got a twinge when he saw his nephew who reminded him of happier days; contented, simple, down-to-earth days in Kniepholzstraße where he could no longer go. It was dangerous. He could be discovered.

At least, that's what he told himself, but he knew it wasn't really that. When he was honest with himself, it was about Mathilde.

Mathilde. When he thought about her an odd feeling crept over him, something smarmy and unnerving coursed through his bones. The picture of her saying goodbye to the stranger that evening was burned into his retina. He forbid himself to think of it. Mathilde was not unfaithful, not untrue, period; and the only reason he didn't go to his old apartment—he told himself—was caution, wasn't it?

His mission, he must not forget his mission. Had to keep watch on the men around Matthus, had to fulfill his task, at least until the Americans marched into Berlin. The mission was perfect for him; it kept him from pondering. And it would not be long now. Day by day he fulfilled his mission. Clockwork. Day by day. No unusual events.

* * *

Until today. Until this warm, cheerful, breezy summer day. Until today they had come a few at a time, every day others arrived and left, but never had they all gathered at once. Franz kept a mental list of names, faces, and the little bits of information he was able to get, but today something new was happening. He had to know what that something was.

Franz had to be cautious. He carefully observed the rubble path that was wide enough for a truck to pass. He peered in all directions; no one else showed up, yet he waited several minutes more until he was absolutely sure the last man had passed him and vanished into the printing shop. Just to make certain he again checked out the street to confirm no one was around. The only thing notable were the shrieks of kids playing somewhere distant, their pathetically audacious songs and rhymes providing an inappropriately high-pitched counterpoint accompaniment to Franz's daily vigil.

Franz slipped into the courtyard and nervously glanced over his shoulder once, twice, and again, his ears attuned to every noise, every step. Was another one coming? No. No one else entered the courtyard. He made it unseen to the ventilation pipe and listened but understood next to nothing since everyone was talking at the same time. Matthus had to work to gain their attention. "Quiet, comrades, quiet!" He had to repeat himself several times before they all settled down. "Yes, comrades, it is true. We must deal with the possibility that we have a traitor in our midst."

An excited murmur erupted and probability was argued. Some were furious and took it as fact; others were sorrowful and didn't know what to do or what would happen now. Still others refused to believe it. "Such a swine in our ranks? No! Impossible."

"Somebody must have told them." Kleinmann's shrill shout silenced the murmuring. "The damn Bolsheviks stopped me, and I thought, okay, no problem. We have gone through control points often enough. Our papers are in order. But the Russki did not even look at the papers. He immediately had me out of the truck, standing with my hands up while a stinking Tartar stood in front of me with his Kalashnikov. Their muckety-muck went straight to the hood and first off checked the engine number against the papers. How did he know to do that?"

"Up to now I thought the Russkis did not know there even was such a thing as a motor number," a clear squeaky voice sounded out with an attempt to make a joke, but only a few laughed.

"You gave up the truck without a fight?" The short military question of a man used to giving orders.

"He was alone against four men. And they were armed. He had no choice." Matthus defended Kleinmann. "We can be glad that he got away from them."

"Don't you wonder about that, comrades?" Again the military voice. Franz thought he recognized the Sturmbannführer but he wasn't sure.

"What are you trying to say?" Kleinmann became angry. "Are you trying to say I might be the louse in the coat?"

"No, he doesn't mean that." Matthus's voice cut sharp in both directions, as much toward Kleinmann as to the other man. Sharp enough to effectively grab the fighting cocks by the throat. "Why would he come back to us if he had betrayed us to the Russians?"

"So he would not raise suspicions. Because he wants to spy on us further," the Sturmbannführer offered up.

"That is nonsense! Not me, never." Kleinmann's voice cracked.

"Why are you so sure that there is a traitor?" a new voice mixed in.

"Perhaps it was simply a coincidence?"

"If it was a coincidence why did that Ivan immediately look at the motor number?" Kleinmann was convinced he had been betrayed.

"If it was no coincidence, if someone really has told on us, why haven't the Russians come and grabbed us?"

"So you are really afraid, huh?" scoffed the Sturmbannführer; Franz was fairly certain that it was him.

"Turned chicken? That is more likely what a desk jockey like you would do," the skeptic said defending himself. One word led to another, the men took sides, the discussion got heated, and the tension invited a fight.

"Comrades, we won't accomplish anything this way." Matthus tried to cool their tempers and took command even over those who, in the dim Nazi past, had outranked him. "We don't know if we have really been betrayed or if it was coincidence, but we must act as if there might be a bad apple among us. That is why I have you here today. We have to be careful, very careful. After tomorrow the Amis march in,"—Franz pricked up his ears—"and take over their part of Berlin including Schöneberg. Without the truck that the Russians confiscated, whether they were tipped off or not, everything will be more difficult. Even if it's obvious to all of you already, let me re-emphasize it: Be careful what you say and with whom you speak. Consider well who you trust." Matthus paused. "As for the traitor, if he really is among us, let it be understood that he is already a dead man. Our honor is called loyalty," he said reciting the SS oath, "and whoever violates our honor, our loyalty, may God be merciful to him."

* * *

Now, where is Karla hiding, wondered Mathilde? She could see Heinrich and Gerhild sitting in Camillo Baumgartner's vicinity, watching with their eyes wide as he and his helpers almost finished building the contraption for the tightrope. Where was Karla? Why did she leave the children alone? What was she doing? The little ones seemed okay but still . . . Mechanically Mathilde passed buckets up the line, buckets down the line, and pondered. About Karla. About Lene who still had not returned; and it would soon be quitting time.

Buckets up, buckets down. Luckily Roswitha, Helma and the others had lost interest in pestering her. So far even Schall hadn't had a chance to look up, so everything was okay. Mathilde decided she would search for Karla right after work and then, as quickly as possible, go to Lene's place. Something must have happened, otherwise she would have returned long ago. Lene would never do something as dangerous as leaving work for so long a time that Mathilde would be put in danger covering for her.

She was happy when Schall finally yelled, "Quitting time, ladies!" She ran over to Heinrich and Gerhild to see that they were okay and had just set off to find Karla when her daughter suddenly ran smack into her. A distraught, flustered Karla stood mute in front of her for a bit and then tried to get past her but Mathilde held her back. "What's wrong, child?"

"Nothing, why should there be anything wrong?" Karla broke loose and ran on to Gerhild and Heinrich. "Come on, you two, time to go home."

"No, I don't want to. They are going to start now." Gerhild squirmed mightily as Karla grabbed her hand. Baumgartner and his helpers had finished their preparations, and the child wanted to see the performance but Karla was adamant.

"When I say it is over, it is over. Understood? Aunt Heidrun will be waiting and worrying. You know there will be trouble if I tell her why we're late."

"Why are you suddenly so harsh?" Baumgartner had come up behind Mathilde and said what she was about to ask. "Your mother is here, so your aunt won't be so mad."

Mathilde was bothered by the voice behind her and unconsciously she turned around to see the artiste who was watchful, almost as if on the hunt. He calmly nodded to her.

Karla looked uncertainly at the Gypsy. "No, that doesn't work."

"Karla, what is with you?" Mathilde was firm. "Tell me, what is wrong?"

Baumgartner just smiled at the girl who did not return the smile, could hardly withstand the look. Still she said nothing further and made no more attempts to leave. She stood there, shifting from one foot to the other. Her eyelids fluttered and her gaze was unsettled. "I . . . I would like to go home right now."

Mathilde looked at her daughter in astonishment. "What happened?"

"Nothing, how many times do I have to tell you that?" Karla became petulant, and Mathilde felt her well-intentioned worry drain away. She did not ask again. Just as so often happened, she just could not keep up with her daughter. They stood undecided before one another for a moment while the kids sat back down.

"Come, we start in a couple of minutes," Baumgartner said. "I have reserved special seats for you." He attempted to lighten the mood and clearly intended to escort all five in front to the first row where he had made a temporary bench out of boards supported by fragments of stone.

Women from the workplace gathered around the performance area, and people from everywhere streamed in. Baumgartner had hoped for a newsreel film crew to find them, but that was perhaps too much to expect for an impromptu performance.

"I can't," Mathilde said reluctantly.

"Why not?" Baumgartner looked genuinely disappointed, which surprised Mathilde like an inappropriate gift.

"I have to go to a friend. She needs me. But you are welcome to stay here with Karla," she added as she saw Gerhild's disappointed look.

"I want to go home," repeated Karla.

"Not me." Gerhild began to whine. "I don't want to, don't want to, don't want to." She stamped her feet on the ground. "I am not going one step."

Karla boxed her ear, and Gerhild was struck dumb with surprise for a moment. Then she began to shriek like a banshee, angry, upset, and so loud that people turned to look at her.

"Do you want another one?" Karla grabbed her roughly by the shoulder. The little girl shook her head and got quiet, sniffling softly and attempting to squelch her tears. She let Karla take her and Heinrich's hand, and followed her large cousin reluctantly but without resistance. She looked longingly at the tightrope, the acrobats, and the musicians as she disappeared with Karla in the wasteland of rubble.

Mathilde sighed. "I have no idea what is wrong with her," she said to make amends for her daughter. She knew that Baumgartner expected her to stay, and she wanted to stay but at the same time did not want to. Because of Lene, she told herself, but also because she felt so odd in the presence of the Gypsy, so torn. "I must really leave, right now. . . ."

"Your friend cannot wait another hour?"

Mathilde hesitated and wavered. Camillo Baumgartner had done so much for them that he didn't need to do; but there was Lene, and Lene lived in Kreuzberg, and the subway was not yet repaired, and there was no gas for busses so she would have to walk. That meant it would take at least an hour and a half to get there, and her return would make it three hours. It was six thirty. Dark would come about nine thirty, and ten was the curfew. If she didn't go now there was no reason to go at all because there would be no time to help her friend. "I'm sorry, really. I can't. Surely you will play again tomorrow?"

Baumgartner looked at the impatient crowd waiting for the performance. Next to the pole that held the rope stood a large, pipe-smoking woman. She looked over at Mathilde and Baumgartner together with an unfathomable dark gaze. "Yes, probably, if we get as many people," he said. "Will you stay tomorrow?"

"Yes, yes, certainly. I would like to watch you. Certainly." Mathilde quickly turned and marched away. Lene was more important now. First Lene, then Karla, then Mr. Baumgartner, she decided. To-night before bedtime, she would talk quietly with Karla. And watch the performance tomorrow.

Baumgartner watched Mathilde thoughtfully for a moment, and then he turned and went back to the people. The music swelled to an expectant level; the spectators sensed that it was starting, quit talking, a few began to clap. Before he began, he beckoned a lad from his troop over and whispered something in his ear. Quickly and silently, like a hunter or lithe animal, the youth set out on the path.

"What are you doing with these *gadsche*, Camillo?" asked Keja. The Gypsy didn't answer. He just climbed the pole, got on the plat-form and bowed.

The young Gypsy broke into a trot away from the workplace, following Mathilde.

FOURTEEN

Mathilde crossed over Potsdamer Straße, struggled over the grotesquely bent tracks that marked the border between Schöneberg and Kreuzberg, along a steel thicket of train cars tumbled helter-skelter as in the aftermath of a spring flood, up to Yorckstraße, to Dudenstraße, trudging awkwardly toward her goal.

Everywhere there were work places like the one she and Lene shared, everywhere there was dust in the air, everywhere there were piles of prepared stones, trucks and horse-drawn wagons waiting to be filled with debris and hauled off. Stacks of steel, beams and shards of scaffolding made grotesque puzzles everywhere. Mathilde got lost in the maze though she knew generally where she was. She asked questions and was sent in the wrong direction and had to ask again until it was almost nine o'clock when she finally reached Lene's apartment.

Remnants of the Kreuzberg rear-housing complex thrust grotesquely into the evening sky. The front and two outermost buildings were bombed out, burned out, collapsed into sooty black skeletons. The third and innermost rear house stood alone, free and light as never before, its rear courtyard—where children had played in the shadows and the lack of sunlight put them at risk for rickets—still bright in the twilight. It was probably brighter there now than it had ever been on a summer's afternoon before the war.

The windows were all broken and covered with paper or Bakelite and nailed with wood. On this summer evening they all stood open, creating a cacophony of whining children, women's scolding voices, and pots clanging in a symphony of everyday life with everyday worries and everyday joys in this last crimson blush of evening light.

Mathilde knocked on a splintered but still intact door off the mezzanine and asked a young woman about Lene. "Third floor left," she said and slammed the door shut. Mathilde climbed the steps to the third floor dodging broken floorboards, past the unflushed, stinking communal toilets on the half landings, past dry water faucets at the corners of two passageways leading to apartment doors. The water lines had not been repaired yet.

The door was open a crack. Mathilde knocked and called out. No answer. She slowly opened the door and looked into a short, dark hallway. To the left was a door that led to the kitchen. Straight ahead another led to the living room, which smelled faintly rotten and somewhat like charred wood. She noticed the varnish on the doors and floorboards that had blisters on them. It must have gotten hot as hell in here when the front houses burned, she thought.

The kitchen was empty and tidy; the stove was clean but cold. Lene had squeezed a cot between the kitchen cabinet and the table covered with an oilcloth table cloth. Chairs were neatly shoved under the table. The noise of the summer evening came in from the courtyard and other apartments.

Off and on, another sound mixed in with the other noises. The sheer tension of the moment had caused her to ignore it, but now Mathilde listened to a hollow-sounding call coming from the only other room in the apartment. She knocked on the living room door and waited. A few moments later, when no one answered, she went in.

"Lene! Where have you been?" A voice seeped out of the dark, eerie and invisible. The windows were closed and blocked with thick particle board, and the foul odor she had smelled faintly in the foyer came from here; the odor of sickness.

"I am not Lene. I am Mathilde, Mathilde Tegge, a friend of Lene's from work."

"Did something happen to my sister?"

The helpless panic in his voice caused a cold chill to run up Mathilde's back. "No, no," she calmed him. "She just left this afternoon to see after you and didn't come back. So I wanted to ask if she needed help; to see if I could do anything for you."

"She hasn't been here," Robert mumbled and went silent so that Mathilde heard only his quiet, rasping, feverish breathing. "Where can she be?" he implored through his weak, anxious rattle.

"I have no idea. She only told me that she was coming to you." Again, the silence. "Should I open the window? The air is very pleasant outside." The room was making her nauseous.

"Yes," he replied in a raspy whisper as Mathilde felt her way along the wall to the shimmering crack where she thought the window was. She released the clasps, pushed open the panels, and took a deep breath before turning to look at the crippled man. He lay in a bed opposite the window. The bedcover was wet and stained with sweat, and she thought she saw spots of blood. Beside the bed was a table with a carafe of water and an empty plate on it, and a chair. A threadbare carpet lay on the floor. Next to the door stood a scratched-up dresser with a vase containing straw flowers and a framed photo on it. Mathilde recognized Lene, and her brother Robert. Behind them stood an older couple dressed in their Sunday finery. Lene's father had the insignia for the SPD, the Social Democratic Party, on the lapel of his suit. It was the portrait of a family in happier times.

Robert's eyes were red-rimmed, sweat glistened on his forehead, plastering his hair to his head. He wore only an undershirt. His leg stump and thin body were outlined under the blanket. He was unshaven and looked at Mathilde with glassy eyes.

"Can I do anything for you?" she asked. "Do you need some water? Or anything else? I'm sorry I didn't bring food."

Robert shook his head wearily. "Find Lene. If she doesn't get here soon . . . I just can't make it anymore. . . ."

* * *

Lene's lips were drawn thin; her angry eyes stared at a point on the opposite wall, her fingers drummed on the wooden bench where she sat. What was that cow doing? Four hours she had squatted in the foyer of this office building, which somehow had escaped the bombs and looked like the war had never happened. Entry required prior permission, yet at this point Lene had already been kept waiting four damn hours for Hedwig Strache; as if Strache were a queen and Lene a pathetic supplicant. Well, maybe that's what she thought she had become—Hedwig Strache though was anything but a queen.

She grew up on the same Kreuzberg block as Lene and went to the same elementary school. Unlike Lene, Hedwig did not pass the entrance test for Gymnasium, the upper secondary school. Their fathers were both on the SPD's executive committee and both had grants from the workers' educational association for their daughters, but even that didn't help Hedwig enter Gymnasium. In 1933, when the Nazis banned the SPD, Hedwig's father joined the NSDAP while Lene's father refused just as Lene spurned the Nazi-sanctioned League of German Girls, the *Bund deutscher Mädchen*.

Therefore Hedwig and Lene crossed paths again in *Hauptschule Kreuzberg*, the public school for those who weren't "good enough" for Gymnasium. For obvious reasons, the local NSDAP leadership had not approved continuing Lene's grant, and Behrendt's father could not afford to pay her tuition for her on his salary as metalworker for Siemens.

Following school Lene apprenticed to an optician in Wilmersdorf. Hedwig Strache wanted something better, an office job or "patent-leather-shoe job" as Lene and her school girlfriends derisively called it. Hedwig's father, a Nazi party member who worked at Siemens like Lene's dad, provided a recommendation along with a little pressure—and lo and behold Hedwig was hired as secretary of the company's internal NSDAP group.

While Lene quickly learned her trade and became irreplaceable to her boss, an elegant old gentleman, Hedwig lacked basic spelling skills and was unacceptable as a secretary, despite prior goodwill, quickly earning the scorn and malice of her colleagues. After two months, she was moved to the telephone center to work as an operator.

Hedwig Strache had full lips, a cute snub nose, brown locks, and a full but not too full figure. She danced well and wore pretty clothes well. Men wanted Hedwig Strache. She soon left the telephone center to become the personal assistant to a senior engineer at Siemens whom she accompagnied to one trade show after the next.

She didn't need to spell correctly for that job, just smile; something she could do very well. Besides, she could engage in animated conversation about this, that, and everything while giving everyone to whom she spoke the impression she was especially interested in them. She wasn't bothered if her conversant forgot what they had talked about five minutes later. She found her calling.

Hedwig Strache got around being conscripted into the Labor Force. Lene was less fortunate. She was taken from her heartbroken boss, the optician, and sent to Jena as a conscript to grind precision telescope lenses for artillery pieces, a replacement for the young men who had been sent to defend the fatherland. Hedwig remained with her engineer and travelled with him throughout the world, and Lene hated her. Hedwig's world got steadily wider, at least until 1942, as she went to Paris, Lisbon, Madrid, and Rome. And everywhere men lay at her feet.

Still, even if Hedwig Strache was, to be sure, *everybody's darling*, she was certainly not everybody's love. Even her senior engineer kept her at arm's length, insisted on separate bedrooms when they were travelling, and more; he insisted that they actually be used. As the engineer's wife had once jealously called her a whore Hedwig could, without lying, point out that fact as evidence that she had never betrayed her with her engineer husband. Never. Even though the whole world believed otherwise.

Toward the end of the war, there were no more expositions and trade shows for her boss to visit. No expositions, no negotiations, no banquets, yet somehow no one ever thought to order Hedwig Strache to some other job. She came to her office at Siemens every day at nine o'clock. She had insisted on an office even though no one really understood why she needed it, and she left in the afternoon around five. Not a soul knew what she did there, but she was there, so they all thought it was okay.

Hedwig's luck held, and with the invasion of the Russians she met Holger John. He also came from their Kreuzberg neighbourhood, was a few years older than Lene and Hedwig, a communist, and had been in Moscow during the war. Now he returned with the Red Army and needed help since he was appointed the provisional district mayor. Hedwig Strache deleted a few unpleasant details from her biography and that of her father—not really deleted, Holger just didn't ask about them—and Hedwig Strache, the worker's child, was predestined for the assignment. She was spared the fate of many other Berliner women, particularly the young and pretty. No Russian soldier dared approach her since she was under the protection of a party functionary.

Hedwig Strache told Holger John heart-rending stories about false and unfair distribution of the little that they had available to distribute. After such gentle manipulation he transferred her to the material logistics office in the provisional district, a position that Hedwig Strache prudently did not use to her own advantage. To the contrary, she was so firm with herself that Holger John had to encourage her to think about herself once in a while. And what did she take? One lipstick!

However, just because she didn't give herself preference did not mean Hedwig suffered from want. Everyone who needed, asked, begged something from her quietly slipped her some of their share. Hedwig, unlike Lene, didn't consider the practice corruption because people did it voluntarily. They would have gotten what they needed without this favor, but it might have been slower in coming due to bureaucratic red tape and delays according to whatever criteria may have been used to determine if there were more in need than goods to distribute.

So Lene had waited for more than four hours for Hedwig Strache. Four hours during which she was tormented by the image of Robert lying in his sweat-drenched bed clothes, feverish, weak, and racked with pain. He desperately needed her help; desperately needed the medicine. More than once she was ready to get up and leave, to damn Hedwig Strache and try for help elsewhere, anywhere else, but still she sat there. There was no other place to go. Without Hedwig Strache there would be no insulin. Without Hedwig Strache, Robert would die.

"You are back already?" Strache had remarked as she met Lene in the office's gray corridor shortly after Lene had entered over four hours ago. Hedwig Strache had swept in wearing a simple dark blue dress with a white lace collar that was very becoming on her, high heel shoes, lipstick, nail polish, hair washed and shiny, soft white skin—even her hands—all of which made Lene envious. "I don't know if I can help you this time."

"Robert will die without the medication."

"There simply isn't enough, and others need it just as much as he does."

"Please." Lene hated to beg Hedwig Strache for anything, but there was nothing left for her to do.

"I will see if I can do anything. But don't hold out much hope."

Hedwig swept away smiling, leaving Lene sitting there; sitting for four hours. Lene had thought it would take one, maybe one and a half. She owned a bicycle, probably her most valuable possession. She had had a hard time grasping her good luck when she had managed to save it from the greedy, insatiable hands of the Russians who left nothing with their German owners. Lene had not even been able to really hide the bike, but it was as if there had been a magic cover over it where it had stood, stored in its niche between the cellar steps and the house hallway.

Normally she could make it from her job site at Innsbrucker Platz to Kreuzberg in less than half an hour. If Strache had quickly stamped the ration coupon, Lene could have fetched the insulin at the hospital and taken it to Robert. Everything could have been done in another half hour, and then she would have been quickly back to work. It would have taken at least that long to take care of the dud. But, not this; not the whole afternoon. Had Mathilde managed to hold Schall back?

It doesn't matter, Lene thought. It's too late now. They all finished work long ago. What was it now, after eight? After eight! Lene was horrified. Strache had probably forgotten all about her, forgotten and gone home; or she had let her sit here in the hope she would go away and not bother her anymore. No, not so, she told herself bitterly. Not her. Not Lene Behrendt. She would not be treated that way.

Lene stood up, knocked on the door through which Hedwig had disappeared hours ago and without waiting for an answer opened it and entered. The room was empty. Exasperated, she leaned against the door frame. Now what? Impotent with rage, she screamed Hedwig's name; screamed her name again and again. Suddenly the material logistics manager appeared in the door to the neighboring office wearing a light summer coat and hat, previous gifts from her senior engineer.

"You're still here?" she said, acting as if Lene had not screamed, or as if they had just met somewhere on the street.

"What do you think?" Lene swallowed her pride, her rage, bile filling her throat and causing a stabbing pain to engulf her body with a bitter, painful agony that burned her ribs. She forced herself, willed herself, to regain her composure.

"I am sorry, I really tried everything, but I cannot give you a stamp so soon again. What should I then tell the others for whom I would have nothing left?" Hedwig looked truly sad, truly dejected. A brilliant actress, Lene thought as her blood boiled again. "Unfortunately, I can't slip you anything this time."

Lene heard the venom in her voice, knew it was unwise to go after Hedwig but couldn't help herself. "What's that supposed to mean?" Immediately Strache bared her fangs.

"I have nothing, nothing left," Lene replied, having given all she owned, the largest part of her heavy labor ration, to the pharmacist in the hospital to get the rations Hedwig allowed to be dispensed. She had even given Hedwig a few gifts, and Hedwig had taken them without so much as a "thank you," with no acknowledgment that Lene had given her anything at all.

"Sad." Hedwig sighed. "Really sad."

What a sanctimonious cow, thought Lene, you conceited bitch. Still, she forced herself to keep calm. It made no sense to get furious again.

"I know that there is too little," Hedwig went on while buttoning her summer coat. "There is too little for everyone. I manage the shortage, not the surplus. I can't keep putting you at the head of the line."

"I don't want to go ahead of others. I only want to get what Robert needs to survive."

"I can't. Really not."

"You left me sitting around here for four hours waiting and hoping just to send me home like this?"

"I didn't ask you to come. I did not promise you anything."

Lene admired Hedwig and hated her at the same time. How did this woman she had grown up with, almost next door to, remain so distant, so calm, so friendly in tone, yet so hard-bitten in deeds? After a long pause during which she looked at Hedwig like she was some sort of strange insect, Lene asked, "How do you do that? How can you stand there in your fancy coat, your fancy shoes, your fancy hat, and just look on as Robert dies a wretched death? You came from the same stall as us. We were in the same class."

"That was a long time ago," interrupted Hedwig. "A very long time."

She seemed hardly able to remember it, Lene thought. "I don't understand. I really don't understand. If your father were my father, if my father had been a member of the Nazi Party, I would tear the clothes off my back and sell myself if that meant one less person would die."

"I cannot help everybody, unfortunately." Hedwig attempted to push past Lene to go out the door, but Lene would not let her go, would not be dismissed.

"What would the fine Herr Volkskommissar say if he knew what you had done up until a few weeks ago?"

"I worked at Siemens as a management assistant. What is wrong with that? Besides, naturally, he knew it."

"Not exactly the spearhead of the working class."

"Holger did not choose his coworkers on the basis of their membership in the German Communist party . . ."

". . . rather by how they looked," sneered Lene as she broke in. "Or because of some other favors?"

". . . but rather by abilities. I have management experience and am not burdened by politics." Hedwig showed no expression.

Lene recognized that she had learned to control her facial expressions, but it took an effort. "And your father, the old Nazi party member, is he not burdened by politics either?"

"My father allowed himself to be deceived and betrayed by the values of his class. I am not responsible for him." Hedwig shrugged her shoulders, and a gentle smile played around her lips. "Besides, Holger said that if he wanted to arrest everyone for simply being a party member he would not be able to do anything else."

"Is that also true for the Betriebsgruppen-Unterführer or whatever your father was within the Siemens National Socialist subdivision, with all that fruit salad on his chest?"

"Lord, didn't they all have some such pompous title and some such pompous post?" Hedwig tried to sound casual, but Lene saw growing anger in her eyes though it no longer mattered. She could live without Hedwig's benevolence. "You didn't say that to your Holger, did you?"

"No. But seriously, I cannot imagine it would especially upset him."

"And if he discovered that your father betrayed a saboteur?"

"Can you prove that?"

"Do I have to?"

Hedwig stared at Lene. "Are you trying to blackmail me?" Her voice shrank to a soft, dangerous purr. "Is this why you waited until all the others had left? Until you could finally catch me alone?"

No, she had not planned it, Lene thought, but now that it was started she could see it through. She smiled a malevolent smile that felt unfamiliar, strange, but its very strangeness spurred her on. "Your father will probably first be put in a camp. That would be hard on him, wouldn't it? And you . . . You wouldn't be able to help him anymore. You will have lost your fine job."

Hedwig Strache scrutinized Lene, and Lene waited, watching her opponent furtively. She waited for the moment in which the scales might turn in her favor, yet that tiny infinitesimal second slipped by as quickly as it had fluttered from out of nowhere and disappeared back into the relentless stream of time. "No, you won't do that," Hedwig announced with finality as if she were reciting a passage from the Old Testament. She set her hat straight and slipped on her soft white gloves. "You won't go that far, Lene. Not you. You know my father did not betray Robert. He even tried to protect him."

"So he says."

"Your brother refused to accept help," Hedwig went on calmly. "Do you really want the murder of a poor old man on your conscience, someone who really has done no one harm? Someone who tooted his own horn a bit and organized a couple of air defense drills? Do you really want to do him in?" Hedwig Strache sympathetically shook her head and pushed Lene gently to the side as she left.

Lene stared after her. Angry tears veiled her eyes. Hedwig Strache was right. Lene Behrendt could not betray anyone. Not if she was uncertain he had really done it. And she was not certain. Not certain at all despite all the rage that burned in her like an artillery shell ready to explode and fly loose, to smash, to destroy. She could not do it even in this matter of life and death. Robert's life, the only person who was left to her.

FIFTEEN

Mathilde was surprised by how many people were out and about despite the curfew. Their shadowed silhouettes hurried along building walls, ducked into entrance ways, dark voids, and bomb craters when they saw the weak beam of a carbide lamp approaching. Russians almost never rode a bicycle alone, but it was best to be safe, just in case.

Mathilde hardly noticed the others. She simply rode without looking left or right. The street here was cleared and astonishingly smooth, Lene's bike was well oiled and ran easily, the tires were good and fully inflated. She felt the air stream in her hair and heard the tires hum on the asphalt. She could hardly see anything, only a few stars shone wanly over her and a small crescent moon. Sure, the blackout had been lifted but the streetlights, those that were left, were switched off in order to save electricity. Now and then a few candles flickered behind windows in the few undamaged apartments. It is dangerous, thought Mathilde, I must be more careful and ride slower, but she did not go slower.

She raced farther through the darkness, enjoying the thrill, the tingling that the speed evoked, and the danger. She raced into the darkness that drew her in and absorbed her. She felt free in a peculiar, daunting way; frightened by the darkness, by the danger, by the freedom.

Mathilde lost herself in the moment hardly noticing the physical exertion. She had a long day behind her, the type of day after which she usually fell into her bed like a stone and slept. Not today. Not now. While she was riding everything seemed easy. She almost sang. She almost whistled even though there was no reason for it. At any time she could be stopped, arrested and have the bike taken away. Or worse. Much worse.

The Russians would assume any woman pedalling through the night was a partisan and shoot her, or just want to have some fun with her; such things still happened all the time. Mathilde had heard about it at her worksite. Just as before, every woman in Berlin had reason to fear, avoid, and detest the Russian soldiers. The memory of Mathilde's own violation tore through her memory, causing horror and disgust to rise like an acrid broth in her throat. But there were no Russians on the street at the moment. Perhaps they were busy packing. They were supposed to pull out of the western and southern districts of the city tomorrow and turn them over to the Americans, British and, later, the French; or perhaps Mathilde had just been lucky up to now.

She had been searching for Lene, as Robert had asked, and easily found her. Her friend was sitting on the steps of the provisional District Hall, crying.

After a despairing Lene had told Mathilde about her confrontation with Hedwig Strache, she shook her head and said, "The worst thing is she has me by the short hairs. I'll never get a stamp from her again." Lene paused staring into nothing, bitter. "How could I be so stupid as to try to blackmail her? That's Robert's death sentence."

Mathilde put a comforting hand on Lene's shoulder and said a few words, a few sentences that were nothing but empty phrases as she so painfully knew. She was acutely aware that her words could provide no solace, and she was ashamed.

Lene continued, "But I had to try, even that way. I simply had to." She paused to look up at Mathilde and whispered, "Robert would not have lost his leg except for me. I'm the one who caused it. It is my fault."

Mathilde sat down next to Lene and listened.

"At the time, I had been thrown out of school for not joining the *Bund Deutscher Mädel* and for my father not wanting to become a National Socialist Party member," she began, "so that was the end of my stipend and with it the end of Gymnasium for me. Robert was four years older and also on a grant from the Workers' Educational Association. But he was in his seventh year already, with only two and a half more until graduation; besides, he had always been a good student and it was certain he would pass his Abitur brilliantly. Against his inner convictions, he had even joined the Hitler Youth and became a Fähnleinführer in order for all those years, all that study, all the learning not to be for nothing, not to be wasted."

Lene sobbed. "But I called him a coward." She threw a glance at Mathilde before going on, "I didn't let up, and we continued to argue almost coming to blows. He wanted me to shut up, and I simply couldn't. Our father was in the middle and understood both of us, forgetting about politics for the time being, his only dream for us being that we would have it better than he did. Well, Robert succeeded. He had done what father wanted him to do and passed his final exams. He went to university, started engineering studies, and because he worked in an essential war support area he was exempted from the draft. Besides, he really wasn't the strongest guy around. Surely they thought he would serve Führer and fatherland better in his research than at the front."

"And they were apparently right."

Lene laughed bitterly. "As long as he actually supported *Führer, Volk und Vaterland*, yes. Still, I didn't stop giving him hell." She took a deep breath. "I needled him constantly, and while he thought it friendly banter, one time I suddenly called him Nazi slave or Fascist pig, called him murderer. I could not stand it. While I sat in Jena and tried to make as many unusable target scopes as possible, he was here in his workplace working industriously for the final victory and even got promoted for good performance." Lene's voice resonated with past indignation.

"So you always quarreled?"

"Always, when we saw each other. Luckily, after I had to go to Jena, we only met once a month." Lene nodded absentmindedly. "And then, as if he wanted to prove to me, as if he wanted to show me, 'look here, I am not the stooge of these swine,' he concealed an alloy he had discovered. But he did it so stupidly that they caught him immediately. Robert is really not a fighter, and he's not a good liar. He lived to make his dumb steel harder, more malleable, more who knows what." Her voice drifted off into a long quiet. "Well," she said with resignation, "that is the story. And now I can't get him the insulin he needs. Now he is dying and I have killed him."

Mathilde had listened silently. Silently and thoughtfully. She decided there was still a chance to save Robert, and that was what she would do. She had to try if she were ever to look at herself in the mirror again. If some needling and a few arguments had given Lene such overwhelming guilt, how much more reason did she have. . . .

"*Stoj*!" Mathilde glanced up over her handlebars and saw a lantern being waved about twenty meters ahead of her. She braked hard.

"*Stoj*!" came the command again, this time sounding more agitated, angrier. Mathilde held her breath fearing what was to come.

"*Stoj*!"

Mathilde brought the bicycle to a standstill with an effort. About a meter in front of her a very young Russian pointed his gun at her. Mathilde looked into his eyes; thank heavens, he seemed to be sober. As she got off the bike, he lowered the gun and said something that she did not understand at all. But she knew what he wanted; the special pass that allowed her to be on the streets after curfew. The special pass that she did not have.

Okay, she thought, here we go. She pulled Lene's donor card from her pocket, a document with a large red cross on it. Along with that she showed the Russian one of the syringes Robert used for his insulin. She tried to explain to the sentry, in German, that she was a doctor on the way to a patient, a child. She pantomimed cradling an infant in her arms. A child would die if the soldier did not let her ride on immediately.

The sentry did not understand a word of what Mathilde said. He looked helplessly at his comrades who sat a little way further along on the curb, smoking. They did not understand either. Everything seemed to be working as planned—and hoped—at least for now; the Russians were surprised and confused and made no move to do anything to Mathilde. So far, so good, but she was still not past the checkpoint.

Be confident, she told herself. Show no fear. Mathilde continued speaking; hoping that the Russians' love of children she had experienced with "her" Russians was commonplace. She talked and talked. She exhorted with words and gestures how the mother was worried to death, how she prayed for the doctor to arrive; how she would cry inconsolably if her child died because the soldiers refused to let the doctor get there in time.

She began to feel relief when she sensed that her gestures, her tone, and her pleading had reached the men whom she knew did not understand a word she said. The attitude of the young sentry softened, his weapon held loosely in his hand, but he needed a further push. He looked to his comrades, and they looked at each other. They had strict orders to let no one, absolutely no one, pass without proper papers.

Mathilde looked at the group of soldiers. The highest rank seemed to be a young, maybe twenty-five-year-old lieutenant. She spoke directly to him. "Her" Russians had always talked about a Major Grinkow, so she boldly threatened to report her delay to Major Grinkow and he would hold the lieutenant responsible if the child died. She didn't think he'd understand a word she said and hoped that the mere mention of Major Grinkow could intimidate him enough to allow her through.

The lieutenant smiled at her. "Major Grinkow returned to Moscow a long time ago," he said in accent-free German. "He won't help you anymore. Even if you ever met him which I sincerely doubt."

Mathilde was stunned. Pretending to be a doctor was an impulsive and reckless plan right from the beginning. Was she so conceited to believe she could ever pull it off? Was she absolutely crazy? What had she been thinking? Oh well, what's done is done. She dropped her head, resigned to accept the verdict.

"We Russians are not brutes, Frau Doktor, even if most of your fellow countrymen believe us to be," the lieutenant continued.

Frau Doktor?! Did he really buy her act?

"I have always admired your country," he said, "the country of Goethe, Kleist, Heine. Well, the barbarians censored them, too." He stood, threw away his cigarette, stepped close to Mathilde and scrutinized her like a sheet of paper on which the truth was written. Mathilde called forth all her confidence and stared right back at him. The silence was interminable.

"Ride on, Frau Doktor," he finally said quietly while he continued to watch her. "Save the child. I hope you didn't lie to me about that." He gave an order to the young Russian soldier who had stopped her. "And get yourself a special pass if you want to visit more patients at night. It's just a formality and you will save yourself, and us, awkward mistakes."

"That I will most certainly do," nodded Mathilde and went back to her bike. "Thank you very much, Sir Lieutenant."

"You're welcome. What does it actually have?"

"How . . . What does it have?" Mathilde didn't understand, and froze. She stood there as if she had taken root, the lieutenant's mistrust like a cold hand on the back of her neck. She slowly turned again to face him knowing that he wanted to read her face, to read whether or not she had lied. "The child, which illness does it have?"

"Which . . ." she stammered. "Which illness?" She faltered, paused for what seemed like hours to her. "Diabetes." The word burst from her mouth. "Sugar. He is diabetic and naturally undernourished. Like most."

The lieutenant looked at her searchingly once more, then nodded and told her, "My best wishes for a speedy recovery."

"Thank you. Thanks very much." Mathilde climbed on her bicycle and rode off as quickly as she could just to be away from there before the lieutenant thought about it anymore; before he decided he should look at her identity card. Just get away but, she immediately thought, it must not look as if she was fleeing. Go only as fast as a doctor hurrying to her patient would. After a few meters she glanced back and saw, with relief, no one followed her. The young sentry stood at attention keeping watch in the night. The lieutenant sat back down.

The further Mathilde got from the checkpoint the more absurd her story seemed to her. Already, today, she saved herself for a second time using an out and out hoax.

She didn't know herself anymore. Suddenly she could lie, could play a role, could run a con. She laughed out loud, wildly and exuberantly, as she rode on through the night. There was someone new inside her. A few hours ago she had no clue that she could do what she had done, that she could be this bold, self-confident, quick-witted woman— a woman she hadn't known existed. And this woman looked like her, spoke like her, and lived in the same body.

SIXTEEN

The air seemed to stand still. Now and then a piece of wood cracked in the embers, now and then a bird screamed, now and then an insect died sizzling in the fire, and for a moment it smelled of burned chitin. Now and then a dry branch flared up and lit the faces of the two who sat there in the firelight. Unmoving faces; hard faces; obstinate, embittered faces. They were silent. A wrathful, raging, implacable silence.

Loud, disparaging, hurtful words, hate-filled sentences had been exchanged earlier. They had broken out like frothing masses of water from a breeched dam. They knew each other well, knew where and how they could hurt the other, how they could hit the mark. That is why they sat there, why they did not go to bed, not yet, even though it was late into the night. They belonged together, in spite of everything. They were a people, a family, a *kumpania*. It was a tie that reached deeper than any conflicts, a tie that could not be severed by any dispute no matter how intense it might be.

"What did you tell the girl that got her so confused?" That is how the argument had started, with a rather harmless question, while she sat next to him, smoked with him, drank brandy with him, and he turned the kebab over the fire. He took good care of her. He took good care of them all. He contrived ways and means to get them what they needed from his wondrous sources, just like earlier in the confusion of the war.

"What did you tell the girl to get her so confused?" The question had seemed harmless enough indeed, but she heard the suspicion that lurked beneath. She had been waiting for this conversation to start, waiting to draw the saber first, and had answered with a counter question, "What do you have to do with these *gadsche*? The brats really adore you."

"I saved the girl's life." A simple, clear sentence without undertones, or so he had thought.

"The little one told me that, too." She felt that nothing was explained and waited for him to go on. But in vain. Only after he had said nothing for a long time did she play her highest trump, shot with her largest cannon. "Do you know that her father was with the Gestapo?"

He stopped turning the meat and turned his piercing eyes to stare at her, scrutinize her. "That wasn't why she was so confused, was it?"

She did not answer, her anger at the *gadsche* family and at Camillo was blanketed in the camouflage of silence. It had begun when Karla told Keja about her father, about what he had done. An unquenchable flame ignited again just at the mention of the girl's name, it was as if the mere word brought it to life. Keja's people, Camillo's people could do that. They could animate things with words; create life from words, life so real to them that it was as if they molded it with their hands. Why didn't Camillo tell her what he was doing and for what reason? Why didn't he confide in her? Did he not trust her? No, she thought, there could be only one reason for that, one single reason.

Camillo broke the silence, his tone hard, clear, precise, and probing. "Still, that is not why she was so upset. What was it? What did you say?"

"A prophecy. I told her that her father is dead." Keja could not, did not want to hide the triumph in her voice.

"What?" Camillo could not believe it.

Keja's hate exploded in an uncontrolled fury, frustration and indignation that had been simmering deep within her. "It's just not right. We are the only ones suffering. We are crying for our dead while everything stays the same for them, just like it was. We can't express our sorrow so we vent our anger at each other, tearing ourselves apart. The damn *gadsche*; they wait a few weeks and they all return, but none of ours, none of our people come back. None."

"But you can't know whether or not her father is really dead," Camillo said, so bewildered by Keja's outrage that it bounced right off him.

Keja's eyes gleamed. Camillo's little protected one, she who did not deserve his protection—Keja had looked through her and was bent on exposing this *gadsche* brat so Camillo could see what beasts he had invited in. "Yes," she said, "but it could be true, even likely, for the girl herself wishes it to be true after all." Keja and Camillo and all their people knew only too well that to think a thing, to say it in words, was to breathe life into it, awaken the demons. Karla's thoughts, her wishes, her hopes, would become truth, reality and life, whether good or evil.

"I believe you." Camillo nodded his head as if agreeing and ignored the glint in Keja's eyes revealing her attempt to embarrass Karla.

He doesn't get it, thought Keja. He is so smart, sees so much. How can he not get it?

"Still, you have no right to tell the child such a lie," Camillo continued, his voice rumbling with suppressed anger, his words tense and forceful. "Not acceptable," he growled, "not acceptable, no matter what."

Keja felt the tense silence between them, sensing what he was thinking, using it to bore deeper, pressure him. "Ah," she sneered, "the holy Philomena." The woman who dominated his every being, the woman he could not protect, could not save from the barbarians that murdered her—Keja laid her finger right on it. Most of the time she would try to comfort Camillo but not now, not today; not until she knew what it was about the *gadsche* woman, Karla's mother, that had riveted his attention.

Camillo's face grew dark, but he did not respond; a sorrowful haze settled in his eyes and encased his being like a shell.

"I know," she said, "compared to her I am only a novice; she was one who really had second sight."

"The truth is Philomena would never have said what you said to the child even if she had seen it in a vision," Camillo replied quietly, softly and tore at Keja's heart. "She knew the responsibility that comes with such a gift, but you have neither the gift nor the sense of responsibility. You don't have the love, the warmth, the soul."

"And what about the girl's mother? What is the truth about her?"

Keja's accusing tone slashed back at Camillo. "You fawn over her like you want something from her."

Camillo caught the aroma of burning meat over the fire and seemed to center his attention on turning the spit. He stayed quiet.

"Now I get it. Now I know why you are so bent on staying here, why you want to play at that damned worksite. It's because of the *gadsche*." Keja's eyes flashed with righteous anger at him. "What of the holy Philomena? Why do you betray her?"

"I will never betray her." Camillo gave her a look that would burn stone, and for a moment Keja thought he would rip the spit from the fire and attack her, but he maintained his self-control. Only his knuckles turned white as his hand tensed around the handle. "Never. Never ever, do you hear me, Keja? Now shut your mouth! You don't understand at all!"

They smoked, drank, and spoke not a word. Later the boy that Camillo had sent to follow Mathilde from the performance at the rubble stage appeared like a ghost out of the darkness. He gave the tightrope walker a little package that Camillo stashed in the tent behind him. He offered the boy a reward of some schnaps, cigarettes, and thanked him. The boy took both, stayed a short while, sitting while he smoked and drank. Then he disappeared into the darkness of the great field to rest among the few friends who remained; his new family, as close as if they were his own blood, his *kumpania*.

Keja had watched the scene play out, her teeth clenched in disapproval. "Something for the woman, no doubt." Camillo's silence was persistent, wearing and nerve-wracking. "Why do you help the murderers? Why take them food, cigarettes and," she nodded toward the tent, "I don't know what all?"

Camillo shook a Camel out of the pack, lit it, smoked it, and turned the meat, then stared into the fire for what seemed like a long time. "That is my business," he said, "not yours."

Keja waited and watched him. He said nothing more. They were both silent. When the meat was done they ate in silence. After eating, she lit her pipe, fetched a new bottle of brandy, poured him some and then poured herself some. She spoke not a word. They sat there for a long time and smoked, and drank, and said nothing. Their silence was grim, angry, and implacable.

* * *

Mathilde neared the campground after finally seeing a few glowing points of light shining weakly in the distance. She sighed with relief realizing she would not have to turn around and carry the bike back over the tracks to the crossing and start out in another direction. A gentle, smoldering fire ahead told her she had reached her goal.

As she got closer she noticed that most of the fires, or what she thought were fires, were merely embers from past campfires. Around the embers she could make out forms, people wrapped like mummies in blankets as they slept. Behind them were silhouettes of makeshift tents, most of them more primitive than what she and Franz had used in their overnight wanderings. A soft breeze wafted across the darkness, and a loose tent flap beat a soft rhythm in the night.

Mixed with the muted noises of the darkened square was the occasional snort of a horse tethered behind the tents. Animal and sewage farm odors became stronger with each step, and there was another odor. Something else, something fragrant, something like a spice, an unfamiliar perfume or an exotic tobacco that engulfed the field; pithier, more resinous, a bit like incense. A wild uncommon aroma, strange and beguiling at the same time.

She slowed a bit with each step, afraid of being chased away and ridiculed, though her thoughts were on Camillo Baumgartner. He had often slipped them something: bacon, a little coffee, a few cigarettes. That was a far cry from the insulin she hoped he could find. And, even if he could find it, that didn't mean he would give it to her; to one of the people who had abused and killed the Gypsies. Lene and Robert Behrendt, she was sure, bore no guilt for all that, but how could Baumgartner know?

Without realizing it, Mathilde had stopped. Anxiety gripped her, wrapped around her like a thousand tentacles filling her with foreboding and a vague sense of guilt. Tentacles of guilt surrounded her; guilt about Lene and Robert who had courageously resisted the Nazis, guilt about the suffering of Baumgartner and the Gypsies caused by the Nazis; her guilt about Karla born into a hopeless world and left alone by her mother on this hopeless night to save a life, one solitary life. Guilt had driven her here to the Gypsy camp, and she had to go on. No matter the outcome, she had to go on.

Mathilde allowed herself one last moment, a few blinks of the eye for rest, recovery, and recuperation. A few blinks of the eye for weakness. Then, resolutely, she grabbed the handlebars of the bike and pushed it to the camp. She pushed it toward the only fire that still really burned; flames licked up from it like playful baby snakes. Two motionless figures sat next to it, apparently not asleep. Mute, remote watchers from a strange world.

The bike rattled softly. The two figures turned their heads toward it, wary and alert but also curious. As Mathilde got closer she saw what she had secretly hoped for. One of the two was Baumgartner. She would not have to wander around the camp looking for him. Next to him sat the strange pipe-smoking woman that had been with him in the afternoon at the rubble worksite.

Mathilde looked her up and down, subconsciously appraising her. She was younger than Mathilde, taller, heavier, almost stately, as someone might have said in earlier times. No one was "stately" anymore. The woman's skin was, as far as Mathilde could tell in the soft flickering light of the fire, smooth and her hair gleamed bronze. A feeling of jealousy caught Mathilde off-guard and was immediately suppressed. She had no right, no right at all, to be jealous of this woman. Ashamed, she lowered her gaze and reminded herself why she had made the difficult trip to the Gypsy camp. She took a couple of steps toward them and cleared her throat because her voice failed her. She didn't know what to say.

"Mrs. Tegge, this is a surprise." Baumgartner stood to greet Mathilde with open arms, giving her a light embrace.

He's only acting astonished, Mathilde thought, even though he said he was surprised. Something resonated in his voice, in his intonation. He was expecting her.

"A pleasure, of course," he said. "But isn't it much too dangerous, a woman alone in the middle of the night? And with a curfew. What if the Russians had discovered you? Here, come sit with us. Would you like something to drink?"

What nonsense. How could he know I would come? He's no clairvoyant she thought as he reached out his hand to lead her to the fire.

Keja let her pipe drop; she stared at him, then stared at Mathilde. She could not believe what she saw.

Mathilde smiled, hesitant. At least, she thought with relief, he didn't chase me right off. He even seems pleased I came. Then she felt the touch of his hand. A sudden tremble came over her, a warm rush flooded through her. The hair on her arms stood up, her skin and body drawn toward him. No this can't, this should not, will not happen. Quickly she withdrew her arm and stepped away avoiding his eyes. She knew he saw through her, knew she would blush.

Mathilde pursed her lips and pulled herself together to plead her cause, hopefully without stuttering, but she didn't get the chance. As if she had seen the spark pass between them when Baumgartner touched her, the astounding woman with the pipe leapt up and charged Mathilde, unleashing a spate of strange, incomprehensible words. Her voice was shrill, enraged and growing ever louder until it was an unintelligible scream of boundless hate spewing forth, her eyes ablaze. Irrational, powerful fear tore at Mathilde's stomach as her fear became a fear of fear itself.

The woman abruptly stopped right in front of her and from behind her back brandished a long iron spit. Slowly, ritually, she raised her arm as if to slash the iron like a club; her caterwauling ceased and became a murmured, undulant, and strange chant.

Time stood still. Mathilde remained motionless, breathless. She could do nothing, say nothing, and think nothing except a silent plea for Camillo to save her and the surprising realization that for the very first time, and only in her thoughts, she called him by his first name. In that timeless moment Baumgartner grabbed the woman's hand, twisted her arm behind her back, forced her to drop the spit, and pulled her away from Mathilde.

The woman fought Baumgartner, punched him on the chest,

scratched at his face, pinched and kicked, but the tightrope dancer was stronger. He gave her an order Mathilde did not understand and sent her into the tent. The woman nodded, seeming to give in. When Baumgartner released her she turned toward the tent, then suddenly turned and, before Baumgartner could move, charged anew toward Mathilde. Without the spit in her hand, she maliciously murmured, threatening her, conjuring with unrepentant hate and anger in her flashing eyes.

Time did not stand still, but raced ahead to a dizzying abyss of height, distance, depth, and width whirling around Mathilde and the Gypsy woman who drew a circle in the air over Mathilde's head as she spoke. She sketched a cross in the circle and spat three times in front of her subject, and Mathilde knew, without understanding or believing, that the Gypsy woman had put a curse on her. Mathilde tried to swallow but could not, tried to gaze away but could not; she was trapped by the woman's gaze, gestures, and words. She could not escape.

Baumgartner stepped in again, tore the woman away from Mathilde and shoved her before him into the tent. The woman no longer resisted. She disappeared without complaint, the curse having sated her thirst for revenge. She had enough and would trust in the power of the curse.

Mathilde watched. She shivered. She was ashen. Slowly, painfully she realized the immediate danger from the woman had run its course, but the curse from outside of time remained.

Baumgartner emerged from the tent in only a few moments. He wordlessly poured a glass of brandy and handed it to her. She drank and took the cigarette he offered her, drew deeply on it and felt light-headed. She sat in the dust beside the dying embers and flipped the ash into the fire.

"Another one?" Baumgartner lifted the bottle.

Mathilde declined wordlessly.

"Something to eat?"

Mathilde shook her head again even though her head ached from hunger and the thought of food cramped her stomach. "Maybe later," she said.

"You have to excuse her." Baumgartner sat next to her and looked at her sadly. "Keja has had a lot happen to her in the last few years."

Mathilde nodded, continued to look into the fire, and said nothing. She could not speak, she could not excuse, but she understood and knew this lady had every right to attack her, especially her. Still, the shock permeated her being where, with all her warmth and forgiveness, she remained in the omnipresent grip of fear, paralyzing, stark fear.

They sat quietly by the fire for a while. Baumgartner fed it with twigs, pieces of cardboard and a precious piece of firewood, then unexpectedly stood up, went back into the tent and fetched a package. "Please . . . this is why you are here."

Astonished, Mathilde looked at the little package that Baumgartner held out to her. "What is this?"

"Take it. It is exactly what you need."

Trembling, Mathilde reached for the little carton. Insulin, ten ampules. Insulin? How could he know?

Baumgartner smiled fleetingly at her look of astonishment. "No, I cannot read minds. I just happened to find out that your friend's brother needs the medicine and thought I could help. I was going to bring it to you at the worksite in the morning, but since you are here now it must be urgent."

Mathilde nodded, turning the precious package in her hands. "Mr. Behrendt is very close to falling into a coma." Should she take it? It was, after all, why she was here, but an uncertain feeling came over her that was akin to the fear which still held her in its rigid grasp. First the enraged woman attacked her with a deadly magic wand, and then Baumgartner had already known what she needed. It was all very unnerving for her.

"Take it. It is no big thing; it really is a coincidence that I already had it here. No witchery." He seemed to divine her thoughts, and she had to believe him; wanted to believe him.

"Thank you," she said. "Thank you very much. For everything." She carefully put the package in her pocket, then went to her bike, climbed on and started to move away, but Baumgartner stopped her.

"Eat something, please. And rest a while. It will be daylight in half an hour. The curfew will be lifted. It will be safer." When Mathilde hesitated he said, "Please take my advice. Please."

She knew she did not hesitate because of Robert Behrendt. A half hour more or less was not critical to him, not at this point anymore, or so she told herself; besides, Baumgartner was right. It was safer to travel in daylight when she was surer of reaching Lene's home. But she wanted to go, to get away from Baumgartner who confused her. He was so friendly, yet so unusual. Why did he do everything he did for them? She had no answer and could not find one because she never dared ask.

She wanted to get away from that woman who had attacked and cursed her. She wanted to leave this fetid smelling place and did not want to eat what Baumgartner had offered her. She was nauseated from the schnaps that made her throat burn and the cigarette whose taste clung to her mouth. "Could I have a glass of water?"

He went to a water barrel, filled a glass and handed it to her. She drank greedily and asked for another. After she had drank again, she could eat, and gradually the sour smells that surrounded her receded. Baumgartner sat next to her, smoked as she ate, and thoughtfully watched her. The pale orange glow of twilight emerged in the morning mist.

They shared a silence that wrapped them in a light yet warming blanket. "You are a brave woman," he said as she rose to go. They stood face to face with nothing between them, no wall, no ramparts, no fortifications. She looked into his brown eyes and saw the amber flecks that danced in the wan firelight, gleamed in the morning sunlight. The Gypsy returned her look, but to her it seemed a gentle caress as delicate as moonlight falling across her hair, her cheeks, her lips. "A very brave woman."

SEVENTEEN

He stretched, raised himself to his tiptoes and performed an elegant full turn, bowed before her, bowed deeply, looked up beseeching her, an almost submissive look in which all his love shone through. She did not turn away, did not reject him. She was not there at all.

He turned a cartwheel on the rope, did a twist dive and a flip while she watched. Over and over again he courted her. He courted her in an old-time romantic style, but she was not impressed even though each acrobatic move could cost him his life. He danced for her, only for her. She knew that but would not let herself be impressed. She was not there at all.

He tried to touch her, to hug her, to snuggle up to her, and she did not push him away. She was not there at all.

He sprang back, felt the stab in his heart, his soul, and his memory; sprang back, stumbled, and fell. Behind him, under him came a single, sharp horrified scream just as he had heard before, a hundred, a thousand-fold times before and, as before, he grabbed the rope at the last second and dangled from it. He waited for the sigh of relief from below, but it did not come. Or was it so soft he could not hear it?

Baumgartner hung on the rope and looked up. Was it Djido he saw, her hand over her mouth, aghast, horrified at what she had done? Was it Philomena who had once danced that number with him? He saw how she held out her parasol to him, but they were not there at all. They could never return. He ignored the phantom parasol, swung himself up with a giant wheel motion and took Djidjo's hand, and Philomena's hand, and bowed. From the direction of the scream he heard the applause of one lone person and turned. There below, in a singed rocking chair rescued from the rubble at a previous performance, sat Karla. He bowed, a deep and elegant bow, and danced an encore for one person. He danced a *pas de deux* even though it almost tore out his heart.

He climbed down and stood before her, and she looked at him and innocently said, "You miss her, don't you?"

"How do you know that?" He snapped at her, sounding more heated and angry than he intended. He was embarrassed and vulnerable. This German girl had peered into his soul and seen his sorrow.

"Anyone could see that." She smiled sadly, not noticing—or ignoring—his harsh tone. "At least if they have eyes to see."

Baumgartner stood stock still and mute. He did not know why he came here to Innsbrucker Platz just after Mathilde Tegge rode away from the camp at dawn, or why he climbed the rope and danced.

Dancing that number was taboo, dead, just as dead as Philomena and Djidjo after the deportation. He never thought of dancing it, never, not once. Until today. He looked down at this *gadsche* girl and suddenly noticed her resemblance to her mother, a thought that had pushed forward from the depths of his subconscious. Now, after he had danced, he felt the emptiness that the deaths of Philomena and Djidjo had left beside him up on the rope. Sadness and hate choked him. Good, he thought. He could not allow himself to forget. He must not forget.

They stood there, both silent, until Karla asked, "Did you happen to see my mother anywhere?"

Baumgartner was lost in thought, his mind meandering through a familiar labyrinth. Karla's voice startled him as if she had just dropped from the sky, and for a second he did not know where he was or who he was talking to. "Your mother?"

"Oh, sure. You wouldn't know," she said, shrugging her shoulders, dejected, weary, and despondent. "She didn't come home last night."

Baumgartner took a moment to be sure he knew who she was and recognized her distress. He considered telling her about last night but decided to keep it a secret though he was not sure why; and by concealing it from her, he was able to keep it hidden from himself. Instead he just nodded and consoled her. "Don't you worry. I'm sure nothing happened to her."

"I know," she replied. "She probably stayed with her friend from work. Aunt Heidrun and Uncle Hermann said that, too." Her voice grew a little husky, and a tone of stubborn defiance crept in as she announced, "I don't believe them."

"But you can. If not your aunt and uncle, then me."

She studied him. "You know something. And you are not telling it."

"Just trust me."

"Why?" she said, sounding skeptical. She was earnest and respectful, but scared, too. "Are you clairvoyant like the lady who was here yesterday?"

Baumgartner laughed joylessly. "You didn't believe her, did you? She has no more of the second sight than any of the rest of us."

Karla was stunned. "What?"

This can't be true, he thought. She actually believed Keja was psychic, a real fortuneteller like his Philomena had been. Philomena, yes, but not Keja. Keja was a con artist, the avenger. "No. Certainly not."

Karla stared ahead as she tried to absorb what he said. Slowly, thoughtfully, she began to calm her tangled thoughts while her head nodded in a rhythmic movement.

Baumgartner laid his hand on Karla's arm. "Very few people can see the future, and Keja is not one of those. She knows no more than anyone else, nor does she know whether your father is dead or not."

Karla nodded, still not quite grasping it and not questioning how Baumgartner knew what Keja had told her which, she assumed, was just how things were.

"Naturally, it's possible," he went on, becoming sadder than he expected. "There are so many dead. So many. So many dead."

Karla felt the tightrope dancer's sorrow as if it flowed in her own veins, pain under her own skin. "You mean," she said, "like the woman you danced with before? Is she . . . ?"

Baumgartner continued to stare for so long that Karla regretted the half formed question, so lost was he in his own thoughts, so irretrievably alone. "Both," he replied finally, his hard voice breaking. "I first danced that number with my sister and later with my wife."

"And they are both . . . ?"

Karla's thoughtful yet timid question transformed itself and became, in Camillo's mind, a malevolent dervish that maliciously danced in front of him. Suddenly he wanted to grab the girl by the throat and choke her until the dervish vanished into the unreachable, hellish depths it came from while at the same time tears that stabbed like thorns rose to his eyes. Channeling all his self-control he turned his will to quell the tears and blood and phlegm.

"The Nazis? Or was it an accident?"

"No, not an accident," he replied.

They fell silent again, and the man was thankful. But the girl was in turmoil with imagined fear of the knowledge that her father—her father, the hunter; her father, the *Gestapo-Mann*; her father who she never wanted to talk about; her father, the . . . No! She had to choose not to think about it. She refused to think about it. Maybe it would really be better if her father was dead. No, she thought. She had to chase *all* those thoughts away. "Why are you so sure about my mother?"

"Why am I so sure?" Baumgartner shrugged his shoulders. "You will see she will show up soon, maybe a little tired but otherwise quite all right."

Karla was surprised by his response. She looked at him and wondered. Could it be? The possibility flashed before her, tickled her, and almost made her giggle. No. It was impossible. Not her mother. Still . . . ? Is it possible that they . . . ? Karla tried to read Baumgartner's face, but he was expressionless.

As Mr. Baumgartner had predicted, Mathilde came into view, and she was riding a bicycle. Where did she come by that? Karla watched her mother's brown locks wave in the breeze, her eyes shining. She was obviously tired but otherwise safe and sound. As she came closer, Karla saw the rings under her eyes and her skin was more pale than usual. Her eyelids were narrowed from exhaustion, but she moved with a light and happy manner, and she beamed with unexpected radiance that, had she thought of it, Karla did not associate with her mother. In this moment, though, she did not think. She ran forward to her, hugging her, crying,

"Mommy! I've been so worried about you."

"I know, I already talked to Uncle Hermann and Aunt Heidrun." She softly stroked Karla's hair. She sought Baumgartner's eyes just as she had a few hours before during her adventure in the night. "I am sorry, I am really sorry."

Karla let go of her mother. "I am alright now. It was only a nightmare." Her voice did not sound as steady as she had wished. "Yes, I know." Mathilde was well aware of the fear she had caused her daughter. "In spite of that, please, forgive me."

"Where were you?"

"At Lene's."

"Your friend from work?"

Mathilde nodded her head. She didn't want to tell Karla about her foray into the night. Last night belonged to her and her alone. Even if she wanted to, she could not share it, not with anyone. Glancing briefly at Baumgartner, grateful that he too seemed to have kept silent, she said to Karla, "It was too late to get home. I would not have made it before curfew. This morning Lene lent me her bicycle so I could stop at home for a moment before work, but you had already left to look for me."

Karla smiled knowingly and tried to sound more grown-up than she was. "The main thing is you're here and you're okay, aren't you? Is Mrs. Behrendt's brother alright? Is he doing well?"

"Yes, thank God. We managed to get him insulin." Mathilde saw Baumgartner moving around out of the corner of her eye and glanced at him again. "It was not a simple thing, but we got it done. And now he is already much better."

"Then it was worth it."

"Yes," she said, taking a deep breath. "Yes, it was." Reflectively, and with just a little pride, she realized she had done something that, for her, was remarkable. She had helped Lene and Robert, but she had almost forgotten her daughter. Now, she looked closely at Karla and wondered if, perhaps, there was another reason she had been so upset. "What was really the matter last night?" she asked, putting her arm around Karla's shoulder and drawing her close. "I really want to talk to you about it."

"Talk with me? Why?"

A bit taken aback at Karla's response, Mathilde said, "Something was wrong yesterday. When you were here to watch the performance with Gerhild and Heinrich, you were upset and refused to stay. Why was that?"

"It was nothing."

Mathilde felt her daughter's body stiffen and draw away. "Really." She could tell Karla was hiding something from her. "Don't you want to talk about it?"

"I'm already over it."

"I saw you talking to the Gypsy lady. Did it have something to do with her?"

Karla fled into a hug, burying her face in Mathilde's shoulder. "It's nothing. Really. The only thing I care about is that you are here again." She nestled against her mother needing to hold her, be supported by her where it had been so often the other way around.

They shared this, for them, rare moment, and Mathilde postponed her concern for Karla's distress. "You can tell me everything, you know. Always." Karla nodded, and Mathilde closed her eyes hoping for, please, just a moment of peace for herself, but suddenly everything began to spin around her. She was woozy as exhaustion overcame her, and she felt nauseated. She leaned on Karla as much as Karla leaned on her, but she should not do that, she told herself. She could not wilt. Not now, not ever. Mathilde gathered herself together and opened her eyes. She needed a drink of water, and she needed to see Karla had something to eat before it was time to start work. She opened her eyes, and the first thing she saw was Baumgartner.

He sat on a block of stone and watched mother and daughter. He felt full of warmth and sympathy but also a dark envy. When he noticed Mathilde looking at him, he stood, grabbed his jacket, and shoved the hat he had worn during the dance lower on his forehead, then nodded to Mathilde and walked away. Mathilde watched him go, her expression full of thanks. Unconsciously she pulled Karla to her.

Karla followed her mother's gaze and suddenly noticed the odor that clung to her clothes. She knew that smell. The fortuneteller smelled like that. It was the smell of the Gypsy lady. She smiled wryly at her mother, a teasing smile. "Why should I tell you everything? You don't tell me everything either."

EIGHTEEN

Franz heard the rumble of motors; it couldn't be the Russians though—nor Germans for that matter, in spite of the few vehicles which had been allotted to their authorities, appointed by the Kommandatura. No, these motors sounded deeper, more resonant. They ran evenly and quietly, they didn't sputter or backfire. Americans. Finally, the Americans. They had better gasoline and better technology. No wonder they won the war, he thought. Finally, the Americans!

He was surprised that he was so happy. Every day, concealed in front of the Nazi hideout watching his former comrades, now his prey, he had yearned feverishly and impatiently for this entry. Just two months before, the mere thought of strangers, conquerors, and occupiers in the Reich's capital, the heart of the National Socialist Great Empire, would have been repugnant to him; yet now he was happy. The Amis would deliver him from the tyranny of Russian control, deliver him from his current diminished circumstances; erase both his present and his past.

The roar of the engines came closer, ever closer, and Franz stopped to lean on the intact wall of a house to watch the convoy. He habitually pulled the tin with the precious last of his licorice lozenges from his pocket and flipped it open and closed, open and closed, as he watched people lining up in a long row on the edge of the street. They were all waiting, waiting for the entrance of the Americans.

Many just stood mute, caught in the quiet of a no man's land between curiosity and exhaustion. A few waved makeshift flags in anticipatory celebration, a few window openings sported flags as well. The Germans were very familiar with flags. The women had to be resourceful and quickly learned to make do with the woeful lack of material.

The Russian flag was easiest. Just remove the swastika and sew a gold hammer and sickle onto the red field. The Star Spangled Banner was far more complicated. Franz saw a young boy, about six years old, having a hard time waving his almost unrecognizable flag made of cardboard. He stood next to a woman who must have been the resourceful seamstress. She must have used whole rolls of the blue and red braiding to make it.

The woman noticed Franz's gaze and returned it with interest. He quickly averted his eyes and fidgeted with his licorice tin. Women and children, children and women, women and youngsters. Except for him only a few men lined the streets waiting for the occupiers, and they were mostly over sixty or crippled. He was just forty-two, well dressed, clean shaven, and worthy of a second glance, especially when compared to those tired remnants of the master race.

A couple of years earlier women would not have noticed him even though he was younger and stronger. So many had died the hero's death that there was a widespread shortage of men. An average looking man like him was attractive especially if he had a future even though the women could not know that. Franz laughed scornfully at himself and thrust the little tin back into his pocket.

A lot had changed in the last few months, and he had done everything right. Turning himself in to the Amis was the right thing to do. It had been right to accept the mission, and he carried it out perfectly. Now he would be rewarded. He would get a new life in a new world, the world of boundless opportunity. Somewhere in the vast expanse of the American midwest he would build a wooden house and paint it white, with red roof tiles and blue shutters. It would have a yard large enough for a garden to grow fruit and vegetables and maybe some flowers. Yes. Absolutely. Flowers, too. Flowers for his wife, Mathilde.

The Amis came around the corner, tearing him away from his dreams. They sidled their vehicles with an enviable elegance that could not be imitated through destroyed German streets, most of which were really just one lane cleared through the rubble, the debris and atrocious waste from the war. The streets were freed for the freer.

At the front of the column was a jeep with a machine gun and two soldiers who checked out the Germans, alert but without blatant suspicion. Following the jeep were trucks covered with canvas. Franz could not tell what they carried, but they were obviously not troop transports. After every few trucks was another jeep for convoy security.

Franz marveled at how the vehicles drove through the bomb craters in the asphalt with such ease as if they were going across the rolling hills of the countryside. They absorbed the rough terrain as if it weren't even there. The German Kübelwagen, he thought, would have long since been stuck. The GIs sat easily at the wheel and lazed about in their seats even though they were in public. In spite of his enthusiasm for America, it was hard for him to come to terms with behavior like this. A soldier had to have manners, discipline, bearing. The Amis didn't care much about their bearing or the correct way to wear the uniform cap. They lounged about like they were at the beach.

To the right and left of Franz, rubberneckers threaded along on a sketchy, bedraggled line watching the convoy pass with shy, curious and skeptical eyes. Like Franz, they hoped life would be better for them with the Amis, and they were happy to live in a district taken over by them.

The convoy stopped to allow soldiers to get out, stretch their legs, and grab a smoke. A few meters from Franz a little blonde, maybe four-year-old girl wearing a dirty little dress stared at a large, strong GI unwrapping a piece of chewing gum. He was black, very black, and the little one was fascinated. He chewed and chewed but didn't swallow, and the little girl thought he was funny. She wanted a closer look and, without realizing it, let go of her mother's dress and took two steps toward the soldier.

The soldier noticed the little girl and grinned broadly. "Hey you, sweetheart," he said as he reached into his pocket and pulled out a chocolate bar. He held the candy out to her, but the girl's courage vanished. She timidly smiled back at him but hesitated when it came to taking chocolate from this strange looking man.

"Come on, take it, don't be afraid." A pink-white smile was etched in his black face, and Franz saw how healthy and strong his white teeth were. Teeth that the average German, in times like these, could only dream about.

The girl did not understand the strange man and looked questioningly back to her mother who motioned and whispered emphatically, "Come. Come back." At the same time the soldier repeated, "Come on, don't be afraid." His smile was so persistent that Franz would not have been surprised if the man's head had begun to wobble like the mechanical Negro at the fair before the war. That was also a chocolate vending machine, wasn't it?

The little one was torn between going and coming. She took a tentative, brave step toward the black man, and he stepped toward her with his hand outstretched to give the girl the chocolate. But before he could, the little one surprised him. It was as if her last step catapulted her into foolhardiness as she suddenly reached out and stroked her hand over his arm. Once, twice. "You feel just like me," she said, and the onlookers broke out into gales of laughter.

For a moment the eyes of the GI and his two colleagues in the jeep shot suspiciously through the laughing crowd, not knowing why they did so. The girl looked around in irritation, also not having a clue as to why the people laughed, but she quickly regained her composure, grabbed the chocolate and ran back to her mother. The soldiers sensed the situation was not dangerous and relaxed.

Her mother took the chocolate from her and examined it carefully but could find nothing wrong with it, nor did she sense either malice or danger from the soldier. She looked sternly at her daughter. "Did you politely thank him?" The girl shook her head. "Well, then go on," urging her daughter toward the GI. The little one trotted back to the black GI, curtsied and said, "Dankeschön."

The soldier laughed, understanding not the words but the intent, and stroked the child's head. A loud command sounded from up front; the soldiers flipped away their cigarettes, climbed back into the jeeps, and the convoy set off again.

Before the jeeps got completely underway, a few of the older boys ran into the street and scuffled for the cigarette butts, some of which were still lit. Franz was embarrassed. It was still an abomination to him when Germans debased themselves by gathering up what others threw away. He was ashamed and yet proud at the same time. He was proud of the riches he would also soon enjoy in his new life in America.

Franz turned away and left to begin this, his new life. He marched out of Schöneberg, away from his VW hideout and the nest of Nazis, down the Schlossstraße, along Unter den Eichen and further to Dahlem where many of the villas and houses had been spared from the bombs. American trucks stood in front of most of them while men in white undershirts ran in and out carrying boxes, suitcases and bags. The Americans had requisitioned the area for apartments and offices. They really know what they are doing, Franz thought. One day he would like to live somewhere like Dahlem.

He had heard a rumor in the black market that the neighborhoods of Dahlem and Zehlendorf had been deliberately spared because the Americans had long planned to use the area, but when Franz looked around he doubted it. There was just too much destruction. It was possible, of course. The Amis prepared for everything, and why not this, too? Back in May, Lieutenant Herter told him where his organization's office would be in July, and here it was. Unbelievable.

An MP with white gloves, white helmet, white belt and white spats stood guard at the front gate of the address Herter had given him. It looked like a park with no house visible from the gate. Franz gave the code word to the MP as Herter instructed. The MP spoke on a field phone to the house somewhere on the grounds, then patted him down for weapons and put him in a jeep. He was driven through the vast park to Herter's office building.

The park looked like there had never been a war. The trees stood rich and full with no missing branches, very different from the Tiergarten or Grünewald where, during the last winter of the war, many of the trees had been cut for firewood because the failing Reich could no longer supply people with coal. Paths in the park were raked, the lawns mowed, flower beds tended with the flowers and bushes in full bloom. The GI driving the jeep deposited him in front of what he guessed was a six-meter-wide outside staircase that led to a classical portico, a gable supported by Doric columns. The entrance door was dark, stained oak, and in front of it stood an additional two white-gloved MPs.

The whole house was done in classical style like the entrance, a massive dark box. In spite of his fondness for Dahlem and how much he would have liked to go for walks in the park, he could not imagine living in a place like this. The thought made him shudder, but he wouldn't have to worry about it.

Franz ran up the steps of the staircase and was granted entrance without having to say a word. He stepped into a hallway that was paneled in dark wood. A wide staircase led to the upper floors. Pictures of hunting scenes, insofar as Franz could tell, hung on the walls, but there were also a few light patches. Paintings had hung there that the new owners apparently did not appreciate, probably portraits of the Führer or the Reichmarschall, or works by Adolf Zeigler, president of the Reichskunstkammer, the Chamber of Fine Arts, who was derided as the "master of the German pubic hair" because of his obsessively detailed nudes. Franz guessed the villa must have belonged to one of the Nazi greats. Otherwise the park would not have been well tended right up to the end.

Herter fetched him after a short wait in the hall and took him up to the second floor into a small attic room where there was no place to sit, very much like in the office where Franz first met the lieutenant. It was filled to overflowing with stacks of paper, had no shelves and was really small, probably a servants' quarters. More than a token effort would be needed to get this place organized.

The lieutenant shoved a stack of papers tight against the wall and sat down on it. With a short, almost brusque wave of his hand he indicated for Franz to do the same. "I am sorry, but it is worse here than it was in my old office. I am not the most orderly of people, and then with the move . . ." He fished a Lucky Strike from the pack but did not offer one to Franz. After he lit the cigarette and exhaled the smoke, he said, "Okay. You have something for me?"

Franz nodded as he pulled a little box with violet drops he had found on the black market out of his pocket and put one in his mouth. It was laughable, pitiful, and absurd. He could find much-too-sweet violet drops—little girls' candy, sure, but licorice lozenges? No. Nowhere to be found.

Herter smiled sarcastically. "I see you have settled in well."

Franz shrugged. "One muddles through as well as one can."

"Oh, you certainly do that well."

Franz stared at the small poster of Heinz Rühmann and Lilian Harvey pinned to the wall behind Herter. It must have been left by the servant girl who had lived in the little room until a couple of weeks ago. Franz stared and kept silent. He did not want to, dared not offend Herter. Herter was his ticket to a new life. He would learn English, get an American job, he was not too old for that, and then he would have his family join him in the States. How good it sounded. Mathilde would quickly forget all about that other man when they were together in America. No doubt about it.

Herter interrupted Franz's thoughts. "So tell me, then."

The lieutenant sound jovial, almost friendly, and his German had improved with use since they last met, but Franz knew to excercise caution with him. "Our agreement still stands?"

"Of course." Herter looked at him innocently. "Don't you believe me?"

"Sure. Of course." Franz faltered, fearing that his plan to deliver Matthus and his group to the Amis for a new identity and a true blue American passport would not go as smoothly as he hoped.

"Come now, don't keep me in suspense."

Herter was getting impatient, and Franz knew there was nothing else he could do. He had to deliver. "I have ferreted out a group of former colleagues hiding in Berlin. I don't know if they plan to go underground or escape, not that it makes a difference. You'll probably arrest them all anyway."

"You can bet your life on that." Herter clapped his hands. "Great. Who are they? Where can we find them?" He was electrified, determined.

"SS Sturmbannführer Matthus. Kriminalrat Borg, my old boss and several others of various ranks, even another Sturmbannführer. All in all about twenty people."

"Very good." Herter grinned, his eyes aglow with hunting fever.

"Very, very good. Now, where are they? When can we round them up?"

Franz told him about the rear courtyard in Schöneberg. He detailed how to get there and how the area looked. Herter listened carefully, all the while taking notes and asking questions when he didn't understand a street name or other detail.

"Is that everything? Do they have lookouts?" he asked, surprised when Franz finished abruptly.

"I didn't notice any. And if they did have," he added, "you can bet I wouldn't be sitting here. They make short shrift of traitors."

"No lookouts, how dangerous." Herter grinned again, full of anticipation and delight. "Yes, it is child's play. You only have to wait until they are all inside. Then they are in the trap."

"Good work, very good work."

"You're welcome." Franz had to clamp down on himself to keep from jumping up and shouting for joy. He did it. He really did it! He survived not only the horrors of war, the chaos of the Nazis, and now he would survive the peace. He had done good work. He had been diligent and tenacious and everything would get better from here on. "What now?"

In answer, Herter stood up, walked to the door, and roared something into the hall that Franz did not understand. Two MPs came into the room, jerked Franz off the pile of papers he was sitting on, and brutally twisted his arms behind his back.

Franz had no idea what was happening. "What is this?" he demanded. "What are you doing?" He did not struggle, knowing intuitively that struggle would lead to more severe measures. He stared at Herter, bewildered. "What are you doing?"

"I am detaining you," he said with an unapologetic smile.

"What?" It had to be a mistake. "We had an agreement," Franz persisted forcefully. "I deliver the Nazis to you, and you give me a new identity, a new life. You can't just break your promise."

"Of course I can." Herter's quick smile gave way to a look of fury and hate. "I can, just as you and your kind did, or will you tell me you kept all the promises you gave your poor victims?"

"You dirty double-crosser." Bewilderment flamed into indignation. Indignation at Herter. Anger at himself. How could he have been so trusting? How could he have been so naïve? Did he have any other choice? No. Probably not.

"You admitted that you were an official of the Gestapo and a member of the SS." Herter adopted his most bureaucratic, prosecutorial tone as if reading a list of charges, but Franz could hear the tension that lurked beneath the strained coolness. "As such, you are a war criminal, and I herewith officially place you under arrest. You will be transferred to a military court." Tension rose in Herter's throat until he lost control and burst into anger, hate, and resentment. "Do you believe that we would let crimes like those you have committed go unpunished? Do you believe you could betray a few old comrades and everything would be okay, that you could get off so easily? You are a torturer, a murderer. You are scum." He blotted sweat from his brow with a pearl white handkerchief and breathed slowly and deeply in a great effort to regain his composure. Finally, in disgust, he said to the two MPs, "Take him away."

"Stop!" Franz commanded the two MPs hoping to confuse them for a moment if he was lucky. He needed just a minute to make a quiet suggestion to Herter, and to his surprise it worked. The two MPs hesitated and looked questioningly to Herter. Franz had his opportunity, but now he had to say something. He feverishly tried to come up with an idea, reason for the lieutenant not to send him to prison, not to court-martial him, but search as he may, he could come up with nothing. Not a thing. His only thought was of the image of his little white house somewhere in the countryside of America as it slowly, inexorably burst into a thousand little shards like remnants of a shattered mirror.

Herter caught himself, drew a breath and wanted to snap at the two MPs to finally get Franz out of there.

"No," stammered Franz in the last second trying to calm himself. "Don't. Don't let them take me away."

"Oh, no? Why not?" Herter's eyebrows arched with the slight amusement of a game beginning; the cat wants to play with the mouse before he kills it.

"It would be a mistake." Franz grasped for the first thing that came to mind trying to gain time. "Look, you don't know if I told the truth or not. You have to check that out first."

"You told the truth, of that I am convinced. And, if you did lie to me, I know where I can find you."

"You believe me then?" Franz's life, his dream, the mirror shards flashed before him as if they were trying to find each other again, and Herter watched wordlessly until Franz grasped at an idea to sink the hook. "Then you've found someone you can count on. Why take me out of action? I can still be of use to you. I can continue to search."

"Do you think I have not thought of that?" Franz heard the loathing return to Herter's voice. "The danger of you absconding is too great. You should not, and will not come out of this war unpunished."

"But you trust me." He ignored Herter's bitter laugh. "Besides, I am here with you of my own free will."

"You had hopes of getting American papers. But now?" Herter sat back down on his stack of papers and looked at Franz inquisitively. "What would you do in my place? Would you actually trust yourself in my position?"

"In your position, I would have never arrested me. I would have put me off using the papers as reward and sent me out again on a new mission. At least until I came up empty-handed."

"Still, at that point, you would have arrested yourself." Herter made no effort to hide his contempt.

Franz nodded. Slowly. Ashamed. "Yes, probably."

"So, why should I do anything else with you?"

"I think that you are one of the good guys. You do everything differently, everything better than we do." Franz immediately bit his tongue. Why did he say such nonsense, why did he condescend to the lieutenant?

The lieutenant snorted disparagingly.

"It would be a mistake to lock me up now," added Franz.

"Oh, yeah?" A snarl, not speech. Narrowed eyes, a big cat about to spring. He shouted at Franz, "Always the master race? Always the old arrogance? Do you Germans still believe you are superior? Do you still think that you are a cut above everyone else?"

"No." Franz forced himself to remain calm, completely calm. This was it. He had not yet screwed everything up yet, and now was the time to be smart. "I don't think of myself as something better, absolutely not. I never have for that matter. I have only done my duty."

A scornful snort but the lieutenant said nothing. He paid attention.

"Only," Franz held his breath, "tracking down and interrogating people is my work. I have trained for, and done that work for over twenty years. I don't know what you do in civilian life, but you are certainly not an investigator. You probably have this assignment only because you speak German. In that sense, at this point, I am better. I have more experience. Better, not a cut above."

Herter thought deeply. What Franz said made some sense to him. It was true, and he knew that his desire for revenge and retaliation could stand in the way of getting his job done. Perhaps he could use Franz's help.

Franz studied Herter. I have him, he thought. He's uncertain and obsessed; about to lose an important and promising path to uncovering hidden Nazis because of his short-sighted anger and hate for the Germans, and he knows it. I have to be careful. I must build a bridge; a bridge over which he can retreat without losing face. "Send the MPs outside," Franz said quietly, "so we can talk alone. I want to propose a deal."

NINETEEN

He waited for Borg to be alone in the print shop. He had the least to fear from Borg and knew he would be the easiest to manipulate. He waited a while after Matthus, Kleinmann, and the others had left before he slipped into the rear courtyard, climbed over the rubble pile, and knocked on the metal door. He stepped back to avoid being a target should Borg start shooting when the door opened. He waited. Borg did nothing. Franz tried again with the same result, but he'd expected that. He went over to the little hole he used to eavesdrop on the group and yelled into the print shop, "Kriminalrat Borg, open up. I know you are in there." He waited, listening, but nothing stirred inside.

"It's me, Franz Tegge. Don't worry, this is not a robbery." As before, no answer, no movement, no sound. Franz wondered if he should just use the key he made and open the door but decided it would be too risky to just walk in. Borg, probably hiding like a cornered animal, would shoot him.

"Herr Borg, I found you, and this is not the first time. Don't hide your head in the sand. I'm here, and I won't leave, so open up. I just want to talk to you."

Nothing. No noise came from the print shop. Franz wondered if he made a mistake. No, probably not. Borg rarely left the shop so why would he today? He decided to up the stakes. "Come on, do it. I have a hand grenade. It will be very unpleasant if I throw it in there."

The threat worked. He heard the latch grind and watched the metal door slowly open. Franz was careful to hide behind a piece of wall waiting for Borg's head to emerge around the door. His former boss looked around in confusion. "Tegge? Where are you?"

"Flip the door over and show me your hands. I want to see if you have a weapon."

"Tegge, please. What do you expect from me?"

"I don't think anything. Come on, do it."

Borg sighed and did what he was told. As Franz expected he had no weapon, but safe was safe. Franz stood and approached the former Kriminalrat. He looked worse than at their first encounter. The time spent in the dark, buried workshop had kept him out of the cheerful summer sun. His skin had turned sallow and wan, he was unshaven, and his hair hung in oily strands from his head.

Borg pleaded with Franz. "Please, leave. I do not know how you tracked me down, and I do not want to know, nor will I give you away. If the others discover . . . Matthus will pound you into sand and scatter you in the wind. Do you have any idea how much trouble you've made for me by showing up at the lake? My wife should never have been allowed to know where I was hiding. Matthus feared this would happen; that someone could find us because of her. Please, leave. Go, right now!"

"No. I am staying." Franz's voice sounded just as calm, steady and relaxed as Borg's was nervous.

"Oh, no. That will not do. That absolutely will not do." Borg wrung his hands, an unpleasant dry, raspy sound of brittle skin parched by the ever closer fire of fear. Franz saw it in his face, like a blush. "Matthus will kill you if he finds you here."

"Not if you vouch for me."

"Me? No!" He glanced around, confused, searching the back courtyard with obvious panic, afraid Matthus and Kleinmann might be coming.

"Let's go inside. We run the danger of someone shooting us up here."

"No. I don't dare let anyone inside. Out of the question. Impossible. No, no. You must go." Borg stumbled as Franz almost pushed him down the ladder into the shop. Franz closed the door over his head and threw the latch, then followed Borg by the beam of his flashlight.

"This is idiocy. What are you doing?" Borg babbled shuffling through the print shop to the apartment behind it. "This will be the death of you. Of us." Franz followed him.

A single candle flickered in the kitchen. Borg dropped into a chair and buried his head in his hands, filled with doubt but resigned to his fate. He mumbled at Franz, "What do you want?"

"The same as you," Franz said, pulling up a chair across from Borg. "I need to escape, to vanish by whatever means necessary. I must disappear, get new papers, and vanish. "Matthus will not let that happen."

"Why not? Aren't we all in the same boat? We were all SS, now we are disbanded, or should I say terminated? We have to hang together or hang separately. Our honor is our loyalty. Isn't that how it goes?"

"Tegge, I no longer recognize you. A few weeks ago you would never have talked like that."

Borg was right. A few weeks ago, Franz would not have dared to strong-arm his boss. A few weeks ago he would have never faced off against Matthus. Back then he went with the flow, always careful not to stand out or be noticed. He had lived his life as a law-abiding and, he told himself, an ethical man. Now he was prosecuted, hunted like a common criminal. He had allowed himself to be tricked, and scolded, by a German-American who was probably also a Jew or Communist. He had lost everything important to him, everything he had believed in. He had nothing more to lose, he thought. That was what made everything okay, at least so far.

"Tegge, please. I implore you. Go, before it is too late. For both of us."

Franz shook his head. "No."

Borg slumped helplessly. Franz leaned back in the chair and shut his eyes. So they sat and waited.

Time stood still. Franz lost sense of the minutes, or hours, until he heard a dull, hollow knock on the door. Borg jumped up like he had been shot and ran to open it.

Franz listened to Borg. "I can't help it," he babbled trying to excuse himself as he unlatched the door. "I can't help it. He threated to toss a hand grenade. Everything would have been destroyed. We'd have lost everything." Franz couldn't hear Matthus's answer, but it was curt. Footfalls on the ladder and through the print shop moved inexorably, sharp, and determined to the kitchen. Franz tensed up, every muscle and tendon strained, rigid as steel. Now he would find out if his ploy would work. Or not.

Matthus entered the kitchen followed by Kleinmann and the woebegone Borg, still babbling, trying to explain himself like a drunk that can't let a subject go. "I had to open up for him. He made such a ruckus. We would have been exposed. I had to prevent that."

Franz stood up leisurely, clicked his heels, and greeted Matthus even as Borg kept on prattling his excuses. "Heil Hitler, Sturmbannführer."

If Matthus was surprised to meet Franz in his hideout, he didn't show it. "Unterscharführer Tegge," he sighed, "yeah, that was to be expected." He nodded slowly. "Well, it is better if we drop the Unterscharführer, and the Sturmbannführer too, those times are over." He held out his hand and went to Franz, paying no attention at all to Borg who followed with panic in his eyes. "Please give me the hand grenade. None of us has any weapon in here. That is an ironclad rule, you can understand that."

"I don't have any. I am sorry, but that was a little ruse." Franz glanced at Borg who threw him such a crushing, and at the same time crushed, glare that Franz had to curb a smile.

"You understand that we have to check that out." Matthus motioned to Kleinmann. Franz raised his hands. Matthus's henchman patted him down and shook his head.

Franz had been careful, even leaving his bread knife behind. "Do you really think I would be so careless as to walk in here with weapons in my pocket?"

"It was careless to walk in here at all. Tie him up." Kleinmann wordlessly grabbed Franz's arm, twisted it behind his back in a police grip, dragged him back to his chair, and tied him tight. Franz held back a cry of pain and did not struggle. He had figured on this.

Matthus sat down across from Franz. "Now, tell us how you found us. And, most importantly, who have you talked *to* about us?"

A nervous Borg spoke up, anxious to help and erase his mistake. "He told me he wanted to go underground and needs to either escape or get new papers."

Matthus silenced him with a glance and returned to Franz. "Is that right?"

"I thought we are all old comrades, and I could count on you. They are looking for me just as much as they looking for all of you."

Matthus stared into Franz's eyes trying to bore into his mind. He was suspicious, and furious, but maintained his self-control. "Good. Good. We will see what we can do. Maybe. First, though, and please," he sneered menacingly, "tell us the truth. Tell me, how did you manage to suddenly find us here?"

Franz had thought about this question as well. There was no reason to hide it. "You were kind enough to bring me along from the lake. On the bed of the truck, under a couple of blankets and tarps."

For a moment Matthus lost his composure. "You've been watching us that long?" His voice was filled with icy indignation, and fear. Franz heard the fear. He was not only a thorn in Matthus's side but also an opponent to be reckoned with. Good. Very good. "Yes," he replied evenly.

"Idiot. You damned idiot." Matthus poked Kleinmann's chest and shook his head with frustration. "I've told you to be careful. Can I not trust anyone, do I have to do everything myself?"

Kleinmann dropped his eyes. "I'm sorry. It won't happen again."

"And you!" He turned his wrath to Borg. "You babble to your gossiping wife. Dammit. You know women cannot keep their mouths shut." Borg shrunk back into his chair while, to himself, Matthus murmured, "Why did I even let you in?"

"It isn't that bad," Franz spoke and Borg looked at him, almost thankful. "After all, I'm a friend. I belong to the group."

"Ah, yes. You are a friend," Matthus said quietly before whirling to face Franz, moving as if he wanted to cut his throat. "That is for me to decide. Why didn't you announce yourself as soon as you found us?"

"I was afraid. I didn't know if I would be welcome."

"And why now?"

"The Amis are here now. If we don't get out of Berlin or get decent papers soon, they will round us up. The Amis are more effective, more thorough than the Russians. We don't stand a chance with them."

Matthus nodded agreement. "Good. Good. We can believe that."

Matthus spoke softly, and Franz glimpsed a trace of trepidation. The thought had already occurred to the Sturmbannführer, or rather, former Sturmbannführer. Their truck was gone. The Russians he had bribed had been transferred or sent home. Times were becoming difficult for Matthus and his group. Matthus began to pace, then suddenly turned to Franz. "Who have you spoken to about us?"

"With no one," Franz shot back.

"No one. How can I believe that?"

"I'm not stupid, Sturmbannführer."

"Again, drop that Sturmbannführer stuff," Matthus snarled. "I have told you, those times are gone. The cataclysmic maelstrom has past." He resumed pacing the kitchen floor to calm himself until he stopped in front of Franz and sneered, "You know what will happen if you are lying to us?"

"And you know I didn't come here without some insurance." Franz looked Matthus straight in the eye. "No one, as yet, knows about you or your hideout. Yet. That will change if I simply disappear from the scene."

"I thought you came as a friend and comrade."

"Trust is good, control is better. That came from Lenin, of course, but who cares? Where he's right, he's right. Like hell I'd show up here without safeguard."

"And that is?"

"You will see. . . ." Franz met Matthus's gaze unwaveringly. Matthus looked at him like a bug that he would gladly crush but pulled himself together. What did Franz know? What kind of trick was he playing, and who had he talked to for his "insurance?"

"Think about it," Franz added. "If I wanted to turn you in, I'd certainly have cut a deal to stay out of jail, and the Amis or Ivans would already be here."

"Good, good. Good point." Matthus knew he had no cause for his suspicion even though it still haunted his thoughts. Kleinmann and Borg became restless.

Franz forced himself to remain calm, silently thanking his mentor for the training back when he was a young policeman. Back then he would put Franz in tough situations where he had to learn emotional control, to let things develop, wait things out. He had taught him to remain silent. Silent and waiting. Choose his moment carefully. "If you're satisfied I'm not the enemy, you could untie me."

Matthus was jolted from his train of thought and stopped abruptly, almost standing at attention. He shook his head toward Franz. "How did you just quote the enemy? Trust is good. . . . ?" He hesitated, then drew a deep breath and began to explain his thinking. "Look, Tegge. I know you have to disappear. A lot of us have to do that but we," he indicated to the others, "can't help everyone, even if we wanted to. We even have to turn deserving old friends away because we don't have the means. All of us here took, how should I say, precautions. Yes, certain precautions. Even before the end, we learned things, gathered money, and other things of value. We stashed things like weapons and I.D. papers. You understand, help is not a one-way street. So, I ask myself, what does Tegge have to offer?"

"Security. Or maybe I should say a certainty that you, whatever you plans are, can carry them through undisturbed."

Matthus laughed. "This certainty you speak of is a lot surer without you. And sorry to say but it wouldn't be too much of a loss if you regrettably died a hero for *Führer, Volk und Vaterland* even though they no longer exist."

"Yet even though I may have been incautious to come here, perhaps even dumb, I wouldn't be so foolish as to arrive without a safety net; you can't believe that."

"So you would betray us after you are dead. Which is the same thing as betraying us before you are dead. Either way, it would be treason; there is but one sentence for treason." Matthus smiled a sadistic grin as he gestured slitting his throat.

"Yet my death will not increase your security. In fact, just the opposite."

"I'll have to run that risk. We will see how strong your safety net is in the end. Maybe you are lying to us as you did about the grenade."

Franz dared not show his worry even though he had not lied. He was not the only one who knew where he was; still, Herter would wait a day or two for Franz to report on the escape routes, and conspirators. He did have a second lifeline—but how strong that would be was anybody's guess.

"Well, time will tell. For now you will stay with us, just to be sure." Matthus scooped water out of the canister into a kettle, lit the cooker, and put the kettle on. "We'll wait and see and drink calming tea." Matthus laughed at his rhyme, but no one laughed with him. "Kleinmann," he barked, "bring him over here."

Kleinmann untied Franz from the chair and pulled him up.

Franz had a spontaneous inspiration that could go terribly wrong but regardless he needed to keep his freedom of movement. "Perhaps I can offer even a little more than security," he said.

Matthus's expression showed interest. "Yes?"

"You are missing the truck the Russians took back."

"How do you know that?" Matthus snapped at Franz. "I just know it."

Matthus's whole body tensed. "How? Did you overhear us?"

Franz knew Matthus would really like to pummel him but stood his ground, smiling at the former Sturmbannführer. "I'm a trained, experienced detective, remember?"

"Yeah, so?"

"Kleinmann drove it every day, but for the last few days he hasn't. I can add one plus one."

Skeptical, Matthus said, "Okay, let us assume you are right. We don't have the truck. What of it?"

"How would it be if I could get one? Would it serve, how should I say, as a fitting gift to the host?"

Oh yes, it would, thought Franz seeing the hunger in Matthus's eyes.

Matthus tried to cover his excitement. "Probably," he said. "I would have to think about it, and other questions. Until then, you stay with us." He dismissed Franz with a backhanded wave and gestured to Kleinmann who took Franz into the print shop. He carefully tied their prisoner to the machines and left him alone. From the kitchen Franz heard the whistle of the tea kettle.

* * *

Franz sat alone in the dark and thought through his dilemma. He had no idea how to come up with a truck, and he had to get out of there, fast. Maybe their need for a truck would persuade Matthus to let him go but right now, as he sat there, his hands were tied, figuratively and literally. He had to report to Herter every two days, three at the most. If not, Herter would march in here, arrest him with the others, and happily indict them all as war criminals to his great satisfaction.

It had been tough enough to negotiate these few days from Herter so he could learn more. Herter wanted retaliation and very reluctantly agreed he would get little by merely arresting this group. He wanted those behind the plot, loopholes plugged, and routes closed. The deal was simple. Franz would deliver everyone involved, along with how they worked and their routes, in return for an American passport. Just to be sure, the deal had to be carried out step by step, like a prisoner exchange.

Franz did not trust Herter but he needed to cover his back; and he needed allies. But—who could he trust? Who could he work with? His former colleagues had either fled or were in the same boat as he; and besides, he'd never been that close with any of them. He had no friends.

Still, maybe there was someone after all.

The idea had originally popped into his mind while he was coming back from Schöneberg after his hostile talk with Herter. At first he discarded it, but it had refused to be thwarted, pushing itself to the front of his mind, cheeky, like a sparrow picking crumbs from a horse apple. The longer, more thoroughly he considered it, the clearer it became. It was his only choice.

He had turned off Schlossstraße toward Steglitz, and in that moment doubts crept into his thoughts again, staining pristine snow with spatters of mud. No, that would not do, he could not do that. He didn't dare involve his nephew in such things. No way. But did he have a choice? Was there anyone else?

Just a little later, Franz pulled his shirt collar high and ducked his head low as he approached a line in front of a butcher shop near his old neighbourhood in Kniepholzstraße where he had discovered Frieder by fortunate coincidence. It was dangerous to be around there, yet he had to take the risk. Franz looked closely but he lucked out, once more;

besides Frieder, there was no one there he knew. He figured the boy would be standing in line for about another hour waiting his turn. Walking slowly past him, Franz murmured that Frieder should meet him a few blocks further on when he was finished.

He had hurried to the black market in Kleistpark and had even more luck. It took some bargaining and cost a fortune in the cigarettes he had confiscated, but in an impossibly short time he got what he wanted. He then hurried back to meet Frieder.

The boy had already arrived there with a little package under his arm. So, Franz thought, he got some meat. Good. It would have drawn unwanted attention if he returned home empty-handed.

"You have never seen me," Franz said sharply to him. "Never, no matter what happens, do you understand?"

Frieder, his eyes wide and shining, was excited and nodded. This, he knew, was important. He was needed. He hoped to be able to help save the Reich, to defend it against the hated trespassers, and help his uncle, still an Unterscharführer after all.

Franz announced solemnly, "I hereby appoint you a secret agent of the Reich. If you should say anything of what you hear from me or about what you see and do in the next few days, it will be high treason. Do you understand the punishment for high treason?"

The boy nodded earnestly, obedient, filled with a holy sense of duty, and exalted by the honor, and the mission. He would never commit high treason. Never.

"Take this envelope." Franz handed it to the boy in his most secretive, conspiratorial manner and then added quietly, "This is valuable information. Protect it well. We will meet here daily about this same time." They looked at Frieder's watch and Franz thought, hmm, the boy's doing pretty well to afford such a watch as this. He continued, "If I am delayed, we will meet two hours later at Kleistpark, right on Potsdamer. Understood?"

"Either here or two hours later at Kleistpark," Frieder repeated, trembling with the importance, the excitement, and holy sense of duty.

"If I should not be here or there, something has happened to me. In that case, hand the letter over to Sturmbannführer Matthus." Franz described the man and the courtyard entrance to the rubble pile where the print shop was. "Do not go in under any circumstance. Wait at the entrance until Matthus appears, even if it takes the whole day."

"Yes, Sir!"

"Good." Franz turned to go. "And, do not forget, you have never seen me."

"Is that all?" The boy was disappointed that he was only to deliver a letter and that only in an emergency. He dreamed of adventures and of oaths unto death; dangerous missions, assassinations, assaults on the occupiers, and wild partisan raids.

"Yes." Franz felt the boy's disappointment and knew that he had to rein him in. Too much disappointment, too much zeal, too much valiant sense of duty could be dangerous. He had to keep the boy calm, to assure that he would not attract attention. "These papers are a secret command document of great importance. The final responsibility lies with the secret deputy of the Reichsführer SS."

It had worked. Frieder was obviously impressed by the fact that he was a part of a mission that involved such a high position.

"Go, quickly now, go home. Don't make anyone suspicious."

The letter was really just another trick, invented in case of trouble. It was an order, written on official SS letterhead Franz got from a souvenir vendor in the black market. The order commanded Matthus to immediately release Franz and was signed by an SS Standartenführer. Franz hoped he was still alive and that he had not yet been arrested, or had any contact with Matthus or his group. It was a stopgap dodge, a flimsy net full of holes, insurance Franz hoped never to use. In the moment nothing better than this forged ploy had come to him.

Franz heard Matthus, Kleinmann and Borg speaking to one another in the kitchen but could not make out what was said. They were probably talking about what to do with him, whether they could trust him or not. There is nothing more I can do, Franz thought. Now he must wait. The interminable wait. He closed his eyes and tried to sleep despite the awkward position Kleinmann had tied him in. He would need all his strength in the coming days. He would need abundant strength.

TWENTY

Exceedingly good luck brought them to the depot just as the train was rolling to a stop with the door directly in front of them. They pushed it open and charged in through the crowded train cars until they found two open seats and were finally able to really sit. More shoved in behind them and more behind them, squeezing in, crowding those sitting, but they defended their seats, or at least Heidrun did. Karla had been taught to give up her seat to her elders, this time to an older man, but Heidrun defended her place, elbows flailing, feet stomping, careful to protect her treasures, the food they had made this trip to gather.

The foraging trip was anything but a pleasure, but they had no choice. Their ration cards did not provide enough for eight people despite Mathilde's hard work and Hermann's additional food card; so the preacher's wife made her decision. She packed up the flashy red, seldom-worn garnet necklace her in-laws had given her as a wedding present that she thought too provocative and slightly obscene, and dragged her niece to the countryside with the offending bauble in her pocket.

She and Karla had canvassed the farmers, eventually trading the necklace for a few eggs, a little ham, and a rucksack full of new potatoes free from eyes and sprouts. Naturally Heidrun had thought her trinket more valuable than that and indignantly turned down several attempted trades. "Unbelievable," she exclaimed. "It is disgraceful how these farmers take advantage of our plight. They have no concept of neighborly love."

Karla lost her patience. "Stop it, Aunt Heidrun. This whining is senseless. They won't give us any more, so either take what we can get or we will go home with nothing and you can keep your necklace."

"You are crazy," Heidrun gasped her outrage. "Hermann's mother paid over two hundred marks when she bought this thing."

"So? Fifty pound of potatoes costs two hundred marks now." Karla was fed up as they stopped at what was now their sixth or seventh farmer. "You're not going to get any more for it. Understand?"

Karla did not care if Aunt Heidrun scolded her. She didn't want to come along anyway. Why, she wondered, did it always have to be her? Why not Frieder? They let him stay out all day with no explanation so now she had to put up with Aunt Heidrun practicing her parenting skills on her.

On the trip out she let a roguish boy with curly sandy hair reach down from the roof of the train and pull her up. Later, when they were on their way to the first farm, Aunt Heidrun let loose a spate of indignation. She was envious that Karla sat in relative comfort on the roof while she, the venerable preacher's wife, had to stand on the step holding on for dear life. Finally she said to Karla, "You are too young to go around flirting. Keep that up, and you can see from your mother where it will lead."

"What's that supposed to mean?" Her aunt was going after her mother, and Karla could not allow that, even if she understood what Heidrun was inferring.

"Then what is it with the Gypsy that is always dancing a tune around you two?"

"What about him? Mr. Baumgartner is a friend." Aunt Heidrun had no right to talk about her mother like that, no right at all. And, Mr. Baumgartner was no hobo either. No beggar.

"One doesn't make friends with someone like that."

"No, you would rather send someone like that to the gas chamber, huh?"

Silence. Both were stunned by Karla's words. Heidrun gasped. The gas chambers . . . that was horrifying. Heidrun had never wanted that, nor did Hermann or anyone else. She absolutely believed that. Even her brother-in-law, Franz, would never have wanted that. They could not have imagined it would go so far, no one could. Still, it was wrong to get involved with Gypsies, those vagabond people. To make it worse, Mathilde, her sister, was married. Unthinkable.

Karla also kept silent, for Aunt Heidrun had hit a sore spot. As much as she liked Camillo Baumgartner, admired and adored him, as much as she enjoyed how he ignored the rules and she reveled in the ways he was so different from anyone she had known—despite all this, it was extraordinary, unbelievable to think of her mom with a man other than her dad.

Karla leaned against the window, lost in her thoughts while the train slowly jerked through Brandenburg. Heidrun dozed in her seat despite the cramped conditions. Others in the train car did the same, slept or just stared into space. A few held quiet conversations.

They were torn from their slumber, their thoughts, and their conversations by noisy, excited voices in the passageway. Karla instinctively pulled her rucksack with their potatoes tighter to her body. Foragers on the way home frequently had their supplies ripped away from them, lost, never to be seen again.

She glanced at her aunt who held the tote bag made from the summer coat Mathilde had outgrown. Heidrun clutched the bag with their eggs and ham inside and stared anxiously at the car's door. The voices, the clamor, came nearer, yet it was not thieves that pushed through the crowded passageway but GIs. This, too? Now they had to deal with a checkpoint? Damn.

Two American soldiers pushed into the crammed car and were suddenly standing in open space where there had been no space at all. Unlike the Ivans, who offhandedly took whatever they wished, the Amis seemed to have no interest in their food. Appalled, they glanced into the shopping bag of an old woman that sat near the door but let her keep her meager supplies. It was the same with others. They checked passes, looked for weapons, perhaps an escaped Nazi, but not for black-market goods. The women, the girls, the old men in the car got little attention. Still, no one said anything.

As Heidrun held out her ID, Karla looked openly at the soldier. He was young and nodded to her with a friendly smile. She thought he was not so different from the Germans at the beginning of the war when they were well-fed and clothed. Without thinking she said, "Hello," as she had heard the Amis say speaking among themselves. The soldier looked surprised, returned Heidrun's ID after barely glancing at it, winked at Karla and said, "How do you do?"

Karla did not understand the question or how to answer. She was embarrassed but returned the soldier's gaze while a censorious, angry, and exasperated Heidrun glared at her niece. Couldn't that girl keep her mouth shut? When the soldier pointed to the potatoes in front of Karla's chest, Heidrun's worry seemed justified. "Been shopping?" the soldier asked.

Karla, who was normally so fearless and bold, shrank back. What did the Ami want from her? He hadn't been interested in the others groceries; why hers, why now? "Brothers and sisters . . . very little . . ." she stammered in the few English words she knew and gestured how big each child was. "Hunger," she added and rubbed her stomach. The GI nodded and grinned but why? What did he want? The Amis were supposed to be different from the Russians. But maybe not.

The soldier reached into his pants pocket for a packet that he put in Karla's hand. "Take it," he said, "for the kids." He nodded to his buddy who had checked the other side of the car, then the two saluted and left. The people immediately flowed back together behind them like water from two streams.

Karla looked at the packet—spearmint chewing gum. *Kaugummi.* She had already heard other kids on the street talking about it, that the Amis had this thing called *Kaugummi.* Now she could finally try it. Glancing around, she quickly put it away. It was her treasure, she had won it, and she would keep it. Her aunt smiled her patronizing smile; the relief was easy to see on her. "Go ahead," she said, "keep it. It has been a hard day. You earned a little reward."

"Thanks." Karla took out a stick of gum, unwrapped its foil wrapper, stuck it in her mouth, and began to chew, tentatively. At first it was a sudden burst of peppermint-like candy only not as sweet; somehow sharper. She moved it from cheek to cheek spreading the sharp, tingling sensation all over her mouth, swallowed, and enjoyed the aroma like a sudden fresh breeze. She leaned her head against the window and looked at Heidrun playfully. "How annoying that we have to learn a new language every day," she joked.

Heidrun smiled and leaned back wanting to doze off again but suddenly felt something slick and sticky on her fingers. She had broken one of the eggs in her tote bag when she held it so tightly. Egg white and yolk leaked through the paper bag and tote and left a greasy yellow stain on her coat and blouse. She swore under her breath and examined the bag. Her face brightened a little. "Well," she said, "at least it was just one."

"You're lucky," said the old man, who Karla had given her seat to.

"It depends on your viewpoint." Heidrun laughed bitterly. "I have never in my life paid so much for an egg and now it is gone," she moaned, "but what is one to do?"

The old guy nodded. He looked tired and gaunt. He was poorly shaven and dirty. His eyes were sunken. "You don't have to tell me. I have to make the trip every two or three days. Otherwise one can't survive."

"We have been lucky up to now. My husband's parish has helped us. He is a pastor, you know."

Karla discreetly nudged her aunt and shook her head to warn her not to tell too much to strangers, but Heidrun indignantly turned back to the oldster.

"Then you really are lucky," he continued. "At least in that regard. But the church lays in ruins and the parsonage as well. Now we live at my sister's. Three adults and five children. What will it be like when my brother-in-law comes home?"

"Eight people. You have a bunch of mouths to feed."

"You can say that again. We don't have enough no matter which way we turn."

The old man rubbed his chin, thinking. "Maybe I can help."

Heidrun flashed a triumphant glance at Karla as if to say: See, this nice man is ready to help, you can count on my reading of human nature.

"How many eggs do you have?"

"Eleven.—Originally it was a dozen," Heidrun added, still mourning her loss.

"I'll make you a suggestion. I have twenty pounds of peas. We trade. You can feed your family much longer than with a dozen eggs."

"Which is no longer a dozen."

Karla chimed in, still chewing her gum. "What kind of peas? Russian?" It was well known that Russian peas had been stored too long, and if you were lucky they were just rock hard so they could be soaked for a few days and used. If you weren't, they were half rotten, wormy, and full of maggots.

"No, no, not Russian. These come out of the Wehrmacht stocks." He pointed to the sack with the Reich's eagle and swastika printed on it.

"Let me see them." Karla remained skeptical.

"Hush now, you will offend the man. He is no con man." That girl could piss off the world, thought Heidrun.

"No, she is right. These days one can't be careful enough." The old man opened the sack. The others in the car nodded and grunted in agreement. They had all listened in. "Here, take a good look." He pulled a handful of peas out of the sack and let them trickle through his fingers. "See, first class goods."

Karla stretched out her hand, and the man put a few peas in it. Karla looked at them closely.

"Fine specimens, aren't they?" The old man grinned at Karla through his missing teeth, but she was still skeptical.

"Why do you want to trade? Your stomach would stay full longer with peas than with eggs, too."

"Love of neighbor," trumpeted Heidrun. "There are still a few people who don't just think of themselves."

Their fellow travellers glanced skeptically at her. It was difficult to imagine anyone was truly selfless anymore. The old man was almost certainly pulling a scam, but no one said anything. They all had to look out for themselves. Why interfere?

"That's nice of you to think of me like that." The old man hesitated, reluctant to continue, then said, "But I have to admit it is not just 'love thy neighbor.' My wife, you know, she hardly eats anything; she cannot get over all this," he made a sweeping gesture toward the devastated landscape that became worse the further into the city they rattled and swayed on the train. "The only thing she will take is red wine with egg." His voice expressed heartache tinged with hopelessness. "We still have a few bottles of red wine but eggs . . ." His shoulders slumped.

"You see, Karla, it is our duty to help this man. An act of mutual neighborly love. Please," Heidrun said as she held out her bag with the eggs.

He looked out the window, seemingly embarrassed. "I can't take them."

"Yes, you can," she said with confidence. "You yourself said it is also in our interest. We both profit from the trade."

The train slowed coming into Treptow. The man stood up. "I get out here."

"Come on, take the eggs," Heidrun pressed him; she wanted the trade, no matter what. If she got home with twenty pounds of peas and a rucksack full of potatoes, the family would have enough all of next week. That was an accomplishment! What a good ending for this difficult, unpleasant day. And she still had the bacon for Hermann and Frieder.

"Really?" The old man smiled. The brakes squealed and the train stopped. Outside, the voice of the station master loudly called out, "Treptow."

"Yes." Heidrun pressed the paper bag in his hand. "Now hurry, so you can get off before the train moves on," she added like a mother hen. The old man nodded and left.

A woman who had been standing immediately took his seat. Heidrun pulled the sack of peas which the man had left over to her; and stared. There, where the sack had rested on the seat spread a damp stain.

Moisture; that could mean only one thing.

Heidrun frantically dug into the sack and pulled up a disgusting rotting mess teeming with maggots. "No," she whined, "please no. It can't be so." She sagged, stunned.

"That bastard," Karla barked and immediately pushed through the barrage of grins, squeezed through the crowded corridor trying to catch the rat, but he was gone, the doors were closed, and the train was moving.

She saw him on the platform as he mockingly waved to her through the open window. She screamed at him to give back the eggs, but he just grinned a malevolent gap-toothed grin and laughed. Enraged, Karla spat her precious chewing gum at him but missed and hit a blonde lady instead. He vanished into the milling crowd like an evil spirit. Karla stared helplessly at the roiling mass of people, the anger roared in her ears drowning out the caterwauling blonde cursing the rude girl.

Karla returned to her aunt, dejected. Heidrun, normally so resolute, had tears streaming down her cheeks. When her aunt was indignant and self-righteous, or overly strict, Karla hated her but now, to see her like this, she felt uncomfortable. Hoping to console her, she said, "I won't tell anyone."

"That has nothing to do with it." Heidrun's imperious tone was almost reassuring to Karla as Heidrun grimaced and stared in front of her. "That crook. What we could have done with those eggs. . . ."

Karla mumbled to herself, "Pancakes, roast potatoes with fried eggs ..." and her mouth watered.

". . . and now? What have we now? Nothing." Heidrun was shaken by such wickedness in the world and angry at her own gullibility.

Karla stood in front of her aunt, balanced against the seat to keep from falling during the jerky trip, and started sorting the good peas out of the sack and into their linen shopping bag.

"Like Cinderella" commented one of the fellow travellers who had gleefully followed the drama. "The good ones in the pot, the bad ones in your crop."

A woman wearing a hat and white summer gloves asked, "Are you going to eat those wormy peas?" She shuddered at the thought.

"Or the maggots?" a third needled and provoked rough laughter.

"You think this is funny, huh?" Karla bitterly defended herself and her aunt.

"It is not so bad," said an old woman, the only one who had not joined in with the mockery. "If they are not completely rotten, you can still eat the peas. Or roast, grind and brew them as substitute coffee. That way, you can lessen the foul taste most easily, and you can skim off the maggots since they will leave the peas when you soak them. At least most of them."

"The others will be eaten along with the peas," commented the first lady maliciously. "The finest game on the hoof." Everyone laughed again.

And so it went until they reached Bahnhof Zoo where the train ended, and they could finally get off. Despondently, they carried the potatoes, the bacon, the good and the rotten peas home. They didn't have the heart to throw away the spoiled peas. Maybe the woman on the train was right, and they might be able to save something. Hopefully.

Karla watched her aunt shuffle back home, defeated; her shoulders sagged beneath a washed-out face. It upset her to see the status-conscious pastor's wife so downtrodden. She was used to seeing her mother like that, depressed, distraught, or worried, and Mom had to be protected, but not Aunt Heidrun. She was the strong one, solid as a rock.

Karla tried to buck her up again. "You always say, one must look down. There are others who have it a lot worse."

A dispirited Aunt Heidrun merely nodded at the echo of her often-given advice, but Karla would not give up so easily. She pointed out a boy who sat in front of a house that rose magnificently among a desert of stone ruins. The street had been hard hit. Only this one house stood undamaged except for a few places on the stucco façade that could be the result of normal weathering, but next to it, in contrast to this absurdly, miraculously intact building, squatted the lonely and forlorn-looking boy. He absently scuffled his cap from his tousled brown hair and weakly held up a piece of cardboard with *ICH HABE HUNGER* scribbled on it.

"Look there, the boy in front. He is a lot worse off than we are. We are healthy, and we have managed to round up something to eat—good potatoes, and even bacon."

Heidrun forced a wan smile.

"We have so much we can give something up." Karla went over to the boy, reached in her jacket pocket and pulled out her packet of chewing gum. "Here."

The boy just looked at the chewing gum, immobile, stoic, and impassive. Karla wondered if he had not heard or was, perhaps, deaf; a victim of the thunder from guns, the howling bombs, the rattle of flak. He appeared to be about seventeen and was covered with dirt. His face was a mask of pimples and peach fuzz, his pants and shirt were torn, and he wore an old loden jacket. On his sleeve was a band that identified him as a member of the Volkssturm.

"Come on, take it," Karla encouraged.

He looked at her from distrustful, scowling brown eyes. "What is that? I don't need it."

"Chewing gum from the Amis. If you don't want it, you can trade it."

"Don't need anything to trade. Have something myself."

"Why are you begging then?"

"Won't give it up. Can't give it away."

"Why not?"

"Won't do."

"Why won't it do?"

"Simply won't do. Won't do. Won't do." The boy repeated the two words doggedly, in monotone, over and over again, an incomprehensible incantation of unknown power. "Won't do. Won't do, won't do."

Something wasn't right with him, even though he appeared unhurt and spoke very clearly. In spite of that, he didn't seem to be all there. Karla looked at him with sympathy, truly wanting to help but didn't know how. At a loss, she held out the pack of chewing gum again, "Do you want it or not?"

"Don't need anything to trade. No, no, have something."

Karla's impulse slackened with the doggedness of his rejection. She shrugged her shoulders, disappointed and a little angry. She was about to turn away when he opened his hand to show Karla what he had held hidden there.

"No, that cannot be." She stared, feeling the ground had been yanked from under her feet. "That can't be, it simply can't be." She fell into the same sing song like the boy earlier, unable to tear her eyes from his hand.

Heidrun, who had stopped a few meters away, looked impatiently over. "Are you coming?"

Karla could not react. She stood there congealed, paralyzed, and frozen.

"Okay, then I am leaving. Do what you will." Heidrun was too tired and too depressed for an argument. She didn't wait to hear if Karla said anything. She moved on towards home. Finally home.

"Where did you get that?" Karla could still not take her eyes off the dirt encrusted object in the palm of his hand.

"All dead. All dead. All dead."

She felt dizzy. "What did you say?"

The boy seemed unaware of her and continued to chant to himself. "All dead, all dead, all dead."

"All of them? Really, all?"

"All dead. All dead. All dead." The boy began to sway back and forth in rhythm to the words.

Karla sat down next to him. She needed to learn more, had to know, even though she didn't want to. "May I look at it?" she asked. The boy showed no reaction as she tenderly, cautiously took the badge of honor for twenty years of police service from his hand. The badge her dad had worn, the decoration he was so proud of. It glinted in the sun. "Does this belong to one of yours?"

"All dead. All. All gone. No one left." The boy had stopped swaying, but his head still wagged up and down. "All dead."

Tears pierced Karla's eyes. The Gypsy lady was right. Her father was dead. Mr. Baumgartner had only tried to console her. Falsely, a mistake. But, wait a minute. Lots of people wore such badges, and Karla's father was not the only policeman who had been drafted into the Volkssturm. The badge meant nothing, absolutely nothing. "Do you know the man's name?"

"The man? Which man?"

"The one this belonged to."

"Dead. All dead. None left. All of a sudden. Gone. Boom! All gone." The boy laughed madly. "All gone."

"How many then?"

"Don't know. At first many. Then a few. Don't know. All dead. All gone." The boy stopped laughing, gaped at Karla without seeing. He suddenly began to shiver. "Careful, duck!" he shrieked shrilly. "Get down! Get to the rear! Get on the ground. Cover, take cover." Shivering he lay flat on the rubble-strewn ground.

He abruptly jumped back up and cried, "Don't shoot, don't. Stop!"

He was thrown back and forth by imaginary powers that seemed to control his spirit. He winced, raised his hands. "Stop, stop, stop!" He covered his ears and implored, "Mommy . . . please . . . I don't want to die."Tears ran down his face. In a moment he stood still and whispered, "Where are all of you?" He looked around with quick, staccato, painfully stiff jerks of his head. He fell to his knees and crept around on the rubble, constantly groping over the stones, trash, mortar fragments. "All dead, all dead."

Karla, confused, watched him. When he paused she felt her quavering universe catch its breath. She pulled him to her and laid his head on her lap. "Be calm, the war is over, be calm." She cradled him like a baby, stared into the emptiness, and unconsciously stroked his hair. "The war is over. It is long past. No fear. Nobody will do anything to you, no more bombs will fall and no one will shoot at you. You have endured. You have survived." She stared into nothingness; into the ghastly nothingness.

"Ei," the boy babbled in a babyish rhythm to her petting. "Ei, ei, ei." He became calm and turned his eyes to Karla. She brought her gaze back from the nameless, unbearable cold emptiness, returned his gaze and stroked him on his scabbed and pimply cheeks.

"Tell me," she said.

"They were there. Once upon a time, they were there," he said, his head held in Karla's palm. His voice was barely above a whisper. "Airplanes. They came over the river. Fighter bombers. They shot at us with machine guns but that wasn't so bad. We took cover in foxholes. Then came the howling and everything exploded." His whole body began to tremble.

"Stalin's organ pipes," she murmured, more a statement than a question. The boy did not answer. "The river, was it the Oder?"

"The Oder, yes. Silesia was already lost, East Prussia. All already lost. Everything lost. All gone. Everything but blood." He took the pin, the badge of honor out of her hand. "Everything lost. Except for this."

Karla stopped stroking. "Did it belong to one of the men you were with?"

"That?" A noise like an uneasy cough accompanied a beseeching glance. Karla understood and began to stroke again.

The boy's gaze wandered erratically, haunted, darting around and finally settled on the silver pin as if he saw it for the first time. "He who always told us what we had to do. He had such a thing."

"The leader of your troop?"

"Yes, the Führer." He sat half way up and held his arm high. "*Heil, mein Führer.*"

"I don't mean the Führer." Karla pulled him back in her lap. "I mean the one who was your superior. Did he have such a pin?"

The boy looked at Karla. "Dead. Dead too. Everyone is dead."

Suddenly a malevolent image flashed before her eyes. She recalled the last letters from her father sent from somewhere in the Oderbruch, the lowlands near the German-Polish border. In them he was an Unterscharführer, a sergeant, the highest rank in the little troop which included a sixteen-year-old boy from the Hitler Youth, that last contingent of a wrecked, crumbled, mangled state on its descent into a bottomless pit with unimaginable impact. Karla felt bile rising, scorching her throat as if she swallowed glowing shards of iron. Could this boy be him? "What rank did the man have? Sergeant?"

The boy jumped up, clicked his heels together. "Yes Sir, Sergeant Sir. The enemy will not cross the Oder. No way. We defend our fatherland. Cost it what it will. If it be our life."

So that was right. The boy was there, part of a little troop, led by a sergeant who had an honor pin for twenty years of police service which was wiped out. Her throat burned with intense fury. He had not escaped. How many such sergeants could there be? She had to know more. She had to be certain, like a hunter finding his target. "What did the man look like? Was he short? Blonde, like me? Was his hair thinning? Did he wear glasses?" She was unconsciously describing her father.

"Yes, glasses." The boy smiled at her and suddenly did not seem so squalid, so dirty. "Yes, glasses. And not tall."

There it was, certainty; horrible certainty. It ran all through Karla's body, a hellish tingling and an excruciating shudder. She expected tears but she waited in vain. She was an empty, white, bare inhospitable inner landscape under blazing light. Now that she was sure, she felt nothing; like being trapped in a bottle and seeing the world through a thick window pane, clear but subdued.

She needed one last bit of conformation. "Was his named Tegge?" she whispered. "Franz Tegge?"

"Franz Tegge." The boy instinctively whispered, too, and then repeated, "Franz Tegge." After a long pause he added, "Did you know him?"

The imaginary bottle exploded from around her, and tears flowed from Karla's eyes. A man with an overloaded handcart rumbled past, the rumbling droned in her ears. Loud. Too loud. She shoved the boy's head from her lap and stood up. "Yes, I knew him," she cried. "He was my father."

The boy nodded uncomprehending and casual. The word "father" seemed to have no meaning for him.

"I have to tell my mother." Crying, Karla charged off but stopped abruptly and turned around, "Where can I find you? Are you always here?"

"Always here. Where else should I go?" He sounded so unbearably lonesome, so bleak that Karla stopped crying for a second. She had a great desire to simply hug the boy despite her own sorrow. Even though she was confused and distraught, she wanted to help him out of his nightmare, out of his loneliness, but there was nothing she could do. "I will come back," she announced. "I'll bring you something to eat. For sure."

"Yes, food. I am hungry."

Karla tore herself away from the boy, and his confusion, and from her own hollow self. She moved briskly until suddenly the realization that her father was dead broke over her. He would never come home, never hang his hat on the hook or monitor her homework. He would never send her to her room or reward her with bonbons from the off-limits box in the living room cupboard. He would never drag her along on Sunday walks and never again buy her a lemonade in the *Waldschänke*. Karla stumbled ever more quickly over the rubble and began to run. She ran so she would not cry.

The boy gazed after her filled with a yearning. "Franz Tegge," he murmured. He shrugged his shoulders and sat back down on the ground, fumbling with his cap. He spoke the question to himself like a mindless prayer, "Franz Tegge. Who is Franz Tegge?"

TWENTY ONE

If only Franz would return, if only her husband were back by her side, but he was not. Now, as life was, she wanted to, had to get away; away from the confines of their too small apartment; away from the regimented routine of her daily schedule; away from life lived under constant fault-finding scrutiny, even when she was alone. A pastor's family must always set a good example—the unspoken rule. Always. In everything. Every little thing. All the time. No matter what.

Mathilde wanted to go out, had to go out, at least for an evening. This afternoon he had suddenly stood in front of her and asked her. She said yes. Confident, without reflection, without trepidation, without reservation she said yes, as if he had merely asked a small favor. A break from her eternal routine, the rhythm of rising in the morning, working in the day, standing in line in the evening, sleeping in the night. No time to simply sit and gaze out the window or listen to a record. No time for a walk, no time to relax. No time. No time.

Not even time for Karla, Mathilde thought, no; she knew something was bothering her daughter but could not get through to her. When she tried, Karla shut her out, became patronizing and defiant. She had nightmares; she was more rebellious than ever, becoming uncharacteristically untrustworthy, distracted, and bad-tempered. Inevitably Karla and her aunt clashed more and more. Mathilde understood her sister's point of view. Without give and take, and organization it was impossible for so many to live in such a small place. Everyone had to do their chores or they could not survive. She also understood Karla; the girl felt restricted and was bothered by the double standard applied to her while Frieder could do no wrong.

Frieder … He was so secretive. No one knew what that boy did other than occasionally standing in line; so much less than he could have done. They should expect more from a fourteen-year-old.

Mathilde leaned toward the mirror on the vanity in her former bedroom. It had become Heidrun's room now, and all six of them slept there at night. She began to pluck her eyebrows preparing for her evening, an evening out. She felt an excited, happy tingling in her stomach, and not even her anxiety for Franz could dampen her anticipation.

She saw the door move in the mirror and turned to find Frieder standing there, looking at her, his expression calm, focused, and inscrutable.

"What's wrong?" she asked, her tone sharper than intended. "What do you want?" He just stood there, seemingly confused, almost disturbed. He should not be there, he should have knocked. That was the rule of their cramped quarters, and everyone knew Mathilde sometimes used the vanity. They had to respect her privacy.

Frieder acted as if he wanted to say something, but he just shook his head, remained silent, and continued to stand there, looking. She would not allow a fourteen-year-old boy to watch her sitting there in her slip. "Please, leave," she said, "and shut the door behind you. Okay?" He did as she asked, but something wasn't right about him. She watched until the door was closed and sighed. It was hardest for the kids.

She finished plucking her eyebrows, combed and fussed with her hair, her face and, given the circumstances, was pleased with the outcome. There were a few lines around her eyes that spoke of weariness and hard work at the recovery site. All in all her being in the sun and fresh air had done her good. Her skin had a healthy tan glow, her hair was shiny. If only her cheeks could be fuller, but that was how it was for women in Berlin these days. No one had enough to eat, no one had lipstick, no one had silk hose. Who cared? She didn't need hose in July anyway.

Mathilde smoothed her dress, the blue velvet with Brussels lace which had suffered from use because she had to wear it more often than she would have liked. She checked herself out in front of the mirror one more time. If only she had some nice shoes, but she could get through the rubble strewn landscape more easily in her hiking shoes than with pumps. Considering that she wore them to work, they had held up amazingly well. Of course, they were quality German work, pre-war. She grinned at her gallows humor.

Her hand was on the door nob when she suddenly stopped. Why leave the room? She could just as easily wait for him here. It was her bedroom, after all, even though she had vacated it for her sister's family. Yes. She would wait here where she could have a moment, a precious moment, alone. She lay down on the bed—*her* marriage bed— not minding that she crushed the pillow and her hairdo. She would simply lay here and wait until Baumgartner picked her up. She grinned childishly at the thought of Heidrun's displeasure that someone might see the carefully made bed all rumbled. It was silly but she giggled.

She heard Hermann scolding the children in the living room just before he knocked. He demanded to know how long she would be. Mathilde remained silently. Hermann was out of line; way, way out of line.

Earlier, just after she had gotten home from work, he had told her that she should take care of the children since Heidrun and Karla had gone on a foraging trip. He was speechless when, instead of taking the kids from him, she heated water for the tub. He pinched his lips tightly to keep from roaring at his sister-in-law, and, restraining himself, asked if she knew her place as a woman, aunt, and mother. When she ignored him, he complained she was wasting wood that Frieder had worked so hard to gather.

"If he does gather it," Mathilde had answered. "Most of the time he forgets and dawdles around somewhere and usually comes home with nothing." She had then vanished into the bathroom.

The *Herr Pastor* had not calmed down and now stood pounding on the bedroom door scolding his sister-in-law. "I know what you're doing," he shouted. "You are going out with that . . . that Gypsy. How could you go dancing with someone like that? You have not heard from your husband. He is still in the field or a POW camp.

You don't know. How could you?!"

Someone knocked at the apartment door. Mathilde jumped up, ran out of the bedroom, ignored Hermann and yanked the front door open. Her mouth was dry as Camillo Baumgartner tipped his hat in greeting, smiling with those amber-flecked brown eyes.

Suddenly her mood changed. She almost slammed the door in his face, almost stammered that it was all a mistake, that Hermann was right. How could she go out with another man? How could she go dancing with a Gypsy?

But then she burst out, "Wait." Her voice squeaked and quaked like a little girl's. "I'll be right there," she said. She could not send Camillo Baumgartner away after he had made the long trip from Marzahn to get here. To see her! My God, she thought, I'm acting like a silly little girl. We are going dancing, nothing more. Absolutely nothing more.

Mathilde sat down to tie her shoelaces and pull herself together, to calm herself, just as Heidrun appeared in the door. She pushed past Baumgartner into the apartment without saying a word.

Heidrun was alone, looked completely exhausted, and she was having trouble carrying her rucksack. Mathilde was worried instantly. "Where's Karla?" she asked as Heidrun dragged silently past her.

"She's sitting with some boy on the street."

Mathilde was surprised. Her sister's tone was emotionless, none of the usual outrage or indignation that came when Karla misbehaved. Suddenly alarmed, Mathilde asked, "Has something happened?"

"No. What should have happened? We've had a long, hard day and I'm tired." The familiar, almost reassuring irritation returned to Heidrun's voice; however, she didn't seem upset with Karla but with something else. Apparently she did not want to vent her anger at the moment. Instead she headed toward the kitchen but stopped again and turned to glare at Mathilde. She spoke with venom in her voice. "You, on the other hand, obviously have plenty of energy to go out and party."

Heidrun's vitriol pierced Mathilde, laying a shadow on her soul. She left the second shoelace untied, raced through the foyer, stumbled down the stairs and out of the building not caring if Baumgartner followed or not. She had to get away, just get away.

His unexpected touch felt like an affectionate caress. Baumgartner took her hand to help her over a piece of rubble. She felt his power, his strength. A light shudder passed through her like an electric shock obliterating the memory of Hermann, Heidrun, Franz, Karla, everything. His hand on her hand seemed to take the weariness of her day on the rubble mountain off her shoulders, which were so stooped from privations and self-reproach. His touch cast aside the shadows, veils, and haze along with the worry, sorrow, and anxiety that moments ago weighed her down.

She walked arm and arm with him, suddenly carefree and in high spirits, brimming with anticipation as they entered the cellar. Candles cast their dim glow through a heavy cloud of cigarette smoke, its aroma mixed with the odor of alcohol and cheap perfume. It all took her breath away. The dusky room teemed with people; the babble of their voices almost drowned out the music. A piano, bass, trumpet, trombone, drums, and a singer played music that had been forbidden for twelve years. Negro music. Jazz. The room, the people, the music put Mathilde in a surreal, almost detached state of mind.

Baumgartner led her past the doorman, an old, sad man whose eyes had seen too much, into the vaulted room about twelve by twelve meters. The walls were undecorated, bare brick, and there were few furnishings. Mathilde's clouded vision slowly adjusted to the dim, smoky room, and she saw several American soldiers in the crowd. Nervously she whispered to Baumgartner, "Are we allowed to be in here? Aren't American clubs off-limits to Germans?"

The Gypsy artiste still had his hat on, and she had the fleeting thought that she'd never see him take it off, as if he would loose something if he did, something vital for life. He smiled at her. "Did they ask you where you came from or who you are? Did you have to show your ID?"

No, she realized, they had not. She had noticed Camillo whisper to the old man and slip him something. She thought it was a tip, but maybe it was money to keep him from asking questions. That pleasant tingling arose again, racing throughout her body. She was doing something forbidden. She was on the verge of having an adventure.

The music was intoxicating to Mathilde who could barely see the band as the pianist's fingers flew across the keys. She wished she could play with such technique, love, and feeling. Kempf? Who was Wilhelm Kempf? Mathilde inhaled the jazz licks of the trumpet, and the trombone caressed her skin while she felt herself sway to the rhythm of the bass and drums. When the singer began her song, Mathilde heard the sound and felt the lyric rush into and through her. She yielded to a sensuous onslaught and joyously gave herself up to it. The song's chords vibrated deep within her, chords she knew and chords she had never known; chords she carefully hid from herself and everyone. Even though she did not understand a word of the lyrics she was transported by the sensation that this song was about her, her life ringing in the voice of the songstress. Mathilde stood there, listening. She was lost in time and space. She was lost in a happy, blissful delusion.

The sound of Baumgartner's voice found her in the labyrinth of tones and sounds. She returned easily to herself, rejoicing as if she had found a long-lost guest, and heard him ask, "What would like to drink? Champagne, wine, whiskey?"

"Whiskey?" Mathilde had never tried it. That was what Brits and Americans, aristocracy and industrialists drank. "Yes, I'll take a whiskey." Her voice sounded to her as if some other woman was speaking.

She smiled watching him as he snaked his way through the crowd toward the temporary bar. When he was out of sight, she looked at the dancers. About half of the men were in American uniforms while others were in civilian dress. How many came from the States, she wondered, but couldn't begin to guess. Most looked healthy with rosy cheeks and bright eyes. Maybe I'm fooling myself, she thought. Maybe their red faces are from dancing and alcohol.

The women intimidated her. In the arms of the men, they turned, spun, and swept across the bare uneven stone floor dancing free, easy, happy. Why am I here? I don't belong here, she thought; they are all younger than me, better dressed, better hairstyles, more elegant. Most of them wore small, chic high-heeled pumps while she could only stomp around in her hiking shoes like a country bumpkin.

Feeling very out of place, she looked around for Baumgartner. He was working his way back to her with two glasses, his face openly friendly and charming. He did not see any difference between her and everyone else as he handed her a glass. They toasted each other.

The whiskey tasted smoky and burned her throat. His smile was as warm as winter sunshine, his amber-flecked eyes twinkled. He took the whiskey from her, got a new one for himself and a glass of wine for her. "This will taste better to you," he said.

"Thanks, how did you know. . . . ?"

"You should have seen your face." He laughed, took her hand, and led her to the dance floor. "Come."

Mathilde hesitated. She felt shy and inhibited, yet when he put his arm around her she felt his steady grip, his power, and she was secure. He was a calming magician, a shaman who needed only to lay his hand on her to work a miracle. At first he slowly began to sway with her, and she became attuned to his movement with the music. She felt even more secure, and they became more energetic and brave, and her feet followed his every move. She glanced at the other women and saw that she was no different. She felt just like they did. Unconsciously she let out a subdued shout for joy and was immediately embarrassed, and Baumgartner understood that, too.

She laughed. She danced. They tried out new steps, made complicated turns, danced apart and back together. They moved as if they had been together since time immemorial. They moved in rhythm to spectral music that only the two of them could hear, had always heard, even long before they met.

Suddenly the artiste grasped her waist and whirled her into the air. Mathilde felt suspended in time for hours, minutes, milliseconds until she was swept safely back to earth gliding over the raw stone floor, the thick soles of her heavy boots becoming as soft and smooth as silk, a second skin on her feet. Then the music ended, the crowd applauded. The musicians, of course, but also—or so it seemed to Mathilde—the two of them.

Baumgartner released her, and as if in a dream, she followed his moves. He bowed, she did a playful little curtsy. He took her hand in his and laid his other hand on her hip for the next dance, but she signaled with a slight gesture to wait. She pulled off her shoes and tossed them to the edge of the dance floor.

The musicians struck up a new tune, and Mathilde nestled herself in the tightrope walker's arms. The tune went from a melancholy start to an ever faster, more frolicsome rhythm. The tempo of virtually laughing harmonies spurred them on; their surroundings blurred in the frenzy, dissolved in the sound, the indistinct candle light became a blur like the flaming tails of meteors. Breathless in his arms, she skimmed through the room and wished, like the time they had played the piano together in the cellar, that this rush, this high, this luck would never end. Never.

Her wish seemed fulfilled as they paused, drank, smoked, talked, and returned to the dance floor consumed in the vortex of music and movement. There was no yesterday, no tomorrow, only the here, only the now.

A disturbance erupted at the entrance, but Mathilde didn't want to know about it. She wanted to dance on and on, but more and more people left the dance floor and moved toward the entrance as the tumult got louder. Soon the conversation diminished and the music broke off. A cluster of people gathered at the door, some curious and many wanting to leave in case a fight broke out or the military police came. Most had just as little right to be there as Mathilde. All she could see was the undulating crowd pushing and shoving. She could not see the doorman who was being pushed inside by a girl, a young lady who had been denied admission.

Mathilde did not care about whatever was going on at the door—she was upset; annoyed that the musicians had stopped playing, angry that her dream of an evening was suddenly over. She was pushing Baumgartner to leave when she heard a voice, a voice she knew all too well. Karla's voice.

How did her daughter get here? What did she want? No, Mathilde thought, she must have heard wrong. Why would Karla be in an off-limits dance club in the middle of the night? Then she heard a scream, a scream for help. "Let me go. I want my mother."

There was no doubt. It was Karla's voice. Mathilde let go of Baumgartner and pushed her way through the onlookers as Karla began to run toward her mother. Barefoot and sweaty from dancing and wine, Mathilde ran to her daughter and hugged her. "What are you doing here?" The girl stopped screaming, pressed against Mathilde and stammered something Mathilde could not understand.

Mathilde stroked and hugged her. "Karla, calm down. What is wrong? What happened?" But Karla could not be consoled. After hours of searching for her mother, now that she found her, she could not find words. She sobbed on her mother's shoulder while Baumgartner, holding Mathilde's shoes, stood affectionately—attentively—watching as mother and daughter clung to each other.

The crowd began to drift away, the murmur of conversation grew, the musicians began to play again, and everything was the same as before. Everything . . . except Mathilde and her daughter. For them nothing was the same. Karla had calmed down enough to say what she had to say, and everyone could understand, even Mathilde. Mathilde understood but could not comprehend.

The doorman ushered the trio outside. Mathilde submissively allowed Baumgartner to take her and Karla to the door. Once outside in the fresh air, the cool of the night, she grasped what Karla had told her; what she had repeated over and over, "Daddy is dead!"

* * *

They sat on the stoop of the solitary house, a grotesque surviving monolith in a rubble-strewn neighborhood; the house where Karla had last seen the boy.

"You must think I'm crazy, but he was real. This is not just another nightmare. You must believe me. He sat right here. You can't mistake a house like this. I'm sure of it."

"I am sure you and Heidrun saw the boy," Mathilde answered, "but maybe you misunderstood him. You said he seemed confused. . . ."

"I knew it; you think I am crazy."

"I'm not saying that." Ever since the moment Karla had stormed into the club Mathilde felt that every facet of her mind had been on the verge of exploding. She needed to calm both her daughter and herself. She needed to make sense of what Karla had said.

"A sergeant who had been a policeman, who had an honor pin identical to Dad's, who commanded a Volkssturm unit in the Oderbruch that this boy served in. A blond man who wears glasses and is named Franz Tegge. What is there to misunderstand?"

Mathilde was quiet. Nothing, she thought. If it is true, if Karla had not imagined it. Do I believe my daughter is crazy? Shame on me. In her silence she prayed; no, not this, too. Franz dead? The idea tore through her mind like a raging storm. Franz dead! She did not want that, she did not want to know. She needed to sleep, to go to bed, to curl up and sleep; to be deaf and blind. She began sobbing softly, not about Franz but from exhaustion.

Karla misunderstood the tears and wanted to comfort her mother but stumbled onto treacherous ground. "Maybe it is better this way. I mean, because Dad . . ." She faltered. "It could be that he also . . . with the Jews . . ." She could not say it and tried to find a better subject. "And besides," she quickly blundered on, "now you are free for Mr. Baumgartner."

Mathilde abruptly stood and flared. "There is nothing there." Yet, as she spoke she felt that before this night what she said had been true; but this dance . . . More had happened during their dancing, so much more than . . . She shied at the thought like a horse at full gallop running to a barrier too high to jump. She sought her salvation in a normal, motherly gesture and extended her hand to Karla. "Come on, let's go home."

Karla was startled by her mother's outburst, then surprised by her gesture. She reached out to take her mother's hand.

Mutely they trudged through the night toward Steglitz. They were too preoccupied to be worried about patrols or the danger they were exposed to; they did not think of what would happen if the were discovered out in the open during curfew. Several times they heard menacing noises or thought they saw frightening shadows and would instinctively huddle together. In those moments Mathilde wished she had accepted Baumgartner's offer to stay with them and help them search. Mathilde wanted to hear from the boy for herself, and Baumgartner would have been there for her, but she sent him away even though in moments of fear she longed for him.

They reached Kniepholzstraße without difficulty, check points, accidents or assaults, and slipped through the foyer into the dark living room. Mother and daughter lay on the sofa and clung to each other in their uneasy, tormented sleep.

They had not noticed Baumgartner following them through the night, along the rubble covered streets. He was there to protect them, even against their wishes. He was there to be sure that he could believe Karla. He needed to know whether Franz Tegge was dead or alive. He had to be certain.

TWENTY TWO

Franz leaned against a wall and waited for Frieder. It was not the first time that he missed his wrist watch. He had been forced to hand it over to the Amis when they had put him in the POW camp. It wasn't especially valuable but it always ran well; typical German workmanship. He could have used it now.

He asked a passer by for the exact time, but the man looked at him with suspicion and hurried off. A woman he asked had no watch. "The Ivan stole it," she said, and left him standing there with a shrug of her shoulders.

An old man had pity on him. At a price though: He tried to engage Franz in conversation while he ponderously pulled out his pocket watch. He had lost everything of value to him—apartment, books, furniture, clothes, and above all his wife. Franz was pleased when he finally got rid of him. Still, he was far too early and would have to wait a while longer.

He shifted his weight from one foot to the other. Every bone in his body ached from the night he had spent tied to that machine in the print shop. He couldn't handle that kind of stress anymore, but if everything went smoothly everything would soon change. Hopefully. Maybe.

He worried about his future, uncertain of what it might hold. Did he dare to believe in a new life in a white house with a red roof and blue shutters? He wanted it, hoped for it, and he had sworn to fight for it.

Up to now his little shell game was working perfectly. Matthus had fallen for it. Last night different people had arrived, some of them true big shots. They sat in the kitchen and talked, then left, shortly before curfew Franz guessed.

The next morning the Sturmbannführer had untied him—the next morning! Even though the decision had been made the night before. But Matthus had delighted himself with the pleasure of making Franz suffer a little longer before he spelled out the deal to him, "If you get a truck that can carry at least thirty people, along with necessary authorizations and safe conduct passes, you are a member of the party. And yes," he sneered, "we will need a few passports as well."

"Where are we supposed to go?" Franz took care to sound casual.

Matthus just laughed. "Wouldn't you like to know?"

Franz did not react. He sat it out. He waited motionless, expressionless until his face felt like it was made of granite.

Still Matthus would not be drawn out. "Don't worry, you'll find out soon enough," he said as he turned away.

"I have to know for which routes we need the safe conduct passes."

"You will need to get general authorizations, of course. Now get out of here before I change my mind and string you up as a traitor."

It was useless to inquire further. Matthus would not make a mistake or give Franz a chance to get his foot in the door, not even his big toe.

Franz checked for a shadow, but there was no one. They had not given him a minder, neither in the open nor undercover. He did see a man, though he took him to be an American. The Amis kept close tabs on him and the whole Nazi community. Luckily they were real professionals, so inconspicuous, so adept that the group around Matthus had not noticed them, at least not so far.

He hoped it would stay that way. Matthus and the others bought his argument that he could have long since betrayed them had he wanted to. Franz thought them extremely incautious from their point of view. Were he in their place he would have crapped his pants. Oh well, it wasn't his problem.

He had other worries. First, where would he get a truck? Herter would be no help. He had made that abundantly clear when Franz had finally managed to talk to him on a phone which had just been repaired.

So he didn't even start to mention safe conduct passes, authorizations and passports to the lieutenant.

Frieder broke his chain of thought. The boy rushed up to him, breathless. "I am sorry, Uncle Franz, I am late. I thought I wouldn't meet you here anymore and would have to go to Kleistpark."

Franz was jolted from this thoughts. He wondered how long he had been standing there and decided he had to get rid of the boy as soon as possible. He no longer needed the insurance Frieder provided. He needed a truck. The boy could hardly help him with that, and Franz did not need another burden. Besides, the kid had done enough. Anything more would be too dangerous. "I'm glad you're here. Give me the letter I told you to hold for me," he commanded, holding out his hand, but Frieder did not move. The boy looked puzzled, bewildered, and doubtful. "I know you are disappointed," Franz continued. "You would gladly do more for our fatherland. But don't worry, your time will come. Of that I am certain. I will let you know when I need you." Franz glanced around. "I will write on the house wall, here, with the other notes, 'Franz is okay and living with Aunt Frieda.'" He chuckled at his corny little joke.

The boy seemed not to pay attention, and Franz noticed how Frieder was looking at him in an odd way. What he thought to be disappointment was apparently something else.

"What is it?" he asked. "What happened?"

Frieder blurted out, "Karla says you're dead. She found someone who told her. From the Volkssturm. Not much older than me." Frieder was conflicted; upset that he couldn't fight anymore, unhappy that he could not defend the late Führer's legacy, high-strung by the the pressure he was feeling. "He says he saw you blown up by a shell."

All Franz could say was, "What?!"

"Last night Aunt Mathilde wasn't home," Frieder began. Franz interrupted him immediately, "Where was she?" All he could think of were clichés.

Frieder pressed on. "Out. She was out. Went out."

"Went out?" A bad feeling crept over Franz.

"Yes."

"Who with?" Franz became the inquisitor interrogating a delinquent.

Frieder wanted to tell him, but how could he say Aunt Mathilde had gone out with a Gypsy? One of those roving artiste *scum*, a devious, dark-looking man who mysteriously came up with things no one else could get. "I don't know," he lied. "In any case she wasn't there when Karla came home."

Franz took a deep breath and let the subject rest. "Okay," he said. "This boy with the Volkssturm—what about him?"

"Karla saw him on the street when she was coming home from a foraging trip with my mother. That's why she went looking for Aunt Mathilde. But she wasn't home."

"Cut to the chase," Franz ordered. He wanted to know about the boy and about Mathilde. Mostly he wanted to hear about Mathilde but at the same time he didn't. He was not sure what he wanted.

"Karla went out again to look for Aunt Mathilde. Mother told her not to, Father too, but Karla left anyway."

"And? Did Karla find her?"

"I think so." Frieder spoke more softly, huskier, and very nervous. "In an off-limits dance club for Amis."

Franz never thought it possible that this could happen to him. This was the stuff of those trashy novels his mother used to devour. He felt his heart turn to stone wrapped in ribbons of barbed wire. The man, the man he had seen in front of the house. Was he an American? Had his Mathilde, his Mathilde thrown herself at a Yank? Was she a Yankee's sweetheart? The man wore civilian clothes, but there were a lot of Amis in Berlin who were not in the army.

"Karla finally found Aunt Mathilde but not the boy, and Aunt Mathilde didn't believe her when she said the boy had seen you killed."

"Then Mathilde thinks I am still alive?"

"I don't know." Frieder hesitated. "Last night, yes, for sure. Karla had bad nightmares not long ago; she told us crazy nonsense about you being dead and Aunt Mathilde being dead, too, all kinds of weird stuff. That was the night Aunt Mathilde slept over at one of her fellow workers."

"Mathilde stayed out *all* night?" Franz asked tonelessly. What Frieder said reinforced his worst fears.

"She claimed she would not have been able to get home before curfew. So she spent the night at her friend's."

She *claimed* . . . So the boy didn't believe his aunt either. It had come to that already!

"In any case, Karla left early this morning, really early, even before Aunt Mathilde went to work, and dragged this lout home. I had to run to the worksite and tell them Aunt Mathilde wouldn't be there today because she was sick. The foreman complained about it but what could he do? I finally convinced him."

Frieder was obviously proud of his ability to weave a story, but Franz became more impatient. "Yes, and?"

"Well, I was not there to hear it all talked out but when I got back the kid from the Volkssturm was at the kitchen table eating *my* breakfast like he hadn't eaten in weeks!"

Franz ignored Frieder's indignation. He wanted to know how Mathilde reacted. Did she believe he was dead? Had she even wished for it? He asked Frieder, candid and cold. He needed to know, no matter what.

"Aunt Mathilde actually said nothing, at least after I got back."

"Did she believe the boy?"

Frieder dodged the question. "He described you pretty exactly, and he had a badge of honor for twenty years of police service with him. It could have been yours. On top of that, the rank of the troop leader fit, sergeant, and you really were in the Oderbruch."

All that actually made sense. Franz slowly nodded.

"After a while, Aunt Mathilde started crying, and Mother tried to comfort her, but she didn't pay any attention."

"She cried for me?"

"Yes. She eats nothing, drinks nothing, says nothing. Just sits there and blubbers."

Franz suddenly knew what melting ice felt like—tentative, weak, uncertain. Inside everything is cold and hard while on the surface droplets appear, begin to move and drip and rivulets start to run. The hope and freedom previously trapped and frozen in him was beginning to melt.

If Mathilde mourned him as he hoped, he had not irretrievably lost her. Perhaps she really stayed overnight with a friend. Maybe she had really gone dancing with a girlfriend. His suspicions could be wholly baseless.

He had taken her out far too seldom. She had asked him often enough, but he just did not want to. All that would change, he told himself, as soon as they were in America.

"What will you do now?" Frieder asked.

"I don't know," lied Franz. He knew exactly what he was going to do but to Frieder he said, "Please. Just like before you must tell no one that you have seen me. Not a soul. *No one.*"

"Even after this?"

"Especially now. If our enemies think I am dead, no one will look for me. But if you tell anyone the opposite ..."

"... your mission is in danger," replied Frieder hastily. "Understood!"

"Exactly. Now, give me the letter. And remember to check this place now and then as you go by." Franz winked at the boy. "Don't forget," he repeated, "Franz is okay and living with Aunt Frieda."

Frieder reluctantly handed the letter to his uncle. He would have too gladly accepted a new, risky mission for the welfare of the Führer and the Reich, but after a stern look from Franz he disappeared among the rubble piles.

Franz waited a few minutes, then pushed away from the wall and rapidly walked in the opposite direction.

TWENTY THREE

Just after noon Mathilde trudged back to the worksite. Schall could let a half day slide but if someone was gone longer he himself would get in trouble for not reporting it. In that case he would have to dock pay and, worse, cut the rations.

That was not what was bothering her though, not the pay or the rations. She just could not take being at home any longer. She could not continue to brood. Franz's death triggered a furor in her mind, her soul. Just the fact that her husband had been killed in Oderbruch, that she was now a widow, was more than she could bear. Added to that was how she had learned about it. She had been dancing in the arms of another man and, on top of it all, Baumgartner had appeared the following morning to be sure she was well.

She had not answered the door herself but sent Gerhild. When the child returned she announced, "The Gypsy wants to see you."

Mathilde went pale. "Send him away. Tell him I'm sick. Tell him I am in bed."

Gerhild did as she was told and returned to the magician. "This morning," she told him, "a boy came here and told us Uncle Franz was dead. Since then Aunt Mathilde isn't well, and no one is allowed to see her."

"Thank you," Baumgartner said and made a quick, playful gesture. Like magic, a bonbon appeared between Gerhild's fingers and the little girl beamed. "Pass on my best wishes to your aunt. If there is anything I can do, she knows where to find me." He then had left, satisfied that he had learned everything he wanted to know.

Mathilde sat alone a while longer trying to sort it all out but could not. Neither her heart nor her head could accept what had happened. She had spent nearly all her adult life with Franz. She could not imagine it was over.

No. She wanted it all to be as before, at least for daily life. Heidrun and her family would move back to the parsonage, Mathilde and Karla would keep their little apartment on Kniepholzstraße, Franz would come home from work in the evening. But, reality lurked like a thief in the dark byways of her mind and told her it was all a pipe dream. She was trapped. She could not escape her thoughts.

She forced herself up and ignored her loathsome thoughts as if they were garbage she could wrap in a newspaper and throw in the trash. Resolutely, she went to the work site seeking refuge in the monotony of routine as she worked feverishly until the bile of bitterness rising in her throat forced her to run from the line and stand alone where she threw up. "Are you okay?" Lene had followed her.

Mathilde started to answer but again threw up water and bile. She had eaten nothing that day. Lene supported her as she sank to her knees clutching her stomach, retching and gasping for air, vomiting time after time. Sweat broke out on her forehead, and she shivered from cold. It seemed to her as if hours passed until she could finally sit. Lene fetched her some water.

Mathilde drank cautiously, one sip, then another and another. It stayed down. Her stomach had calmed itself.

"I'll take you home." Lene talked like a mother to her child.

"No, no, go on. Just let me sit here a bit."

"What is wrong?"

"Nothing. I must have eaten something bad."

"Or not eaten at all?" Lene didn't even pause for Mathilde's reaction but went on. "You cannot always sacrifice everything. Not for me and not for your bunch at home. You will destroy yourself."

"I could not eat anything. It is better that I give it to someone than to let it go bad, isn't it?"

Lene looked at her, worried. "What if your Russian has left you with something? You know what I mean." She hesitated. "I know a woman, a doctor, no quack. You can give her whatever you can. Sometimes, in emergencies, she does it for free."

"No," Mathilde said, "I was lucky." She stared off into the distance. "I haven't thought of that for a long time. It's as if it happened a hundred years ago, or maybe not at all." She sighed. "No, no, if that was all . . ."

"What is it then?"

Mathilde wanted to tell Lene everything. She desperately needed someone to confide in but shied away from talking about Franz or even mentioning him or Camillo Baumgartner. That was why she fled from home to work. Her needs, her doubts, her conflicting, tormenting nagging thoughts played like rowdy children pushing and shoving in the recesses of her consciousness, and Mathilde refused to play along.

Schall shouted angrily at them, but Lene shrugged him off; turned back to Mathilde. "Look, you have done right by me. If I can in any way help you . . ."

". . . I would have long since asked, for sure. But you can't help me." Mathilde clambered up and started back to the bucket brigade.

Lene touched her arm. "It doesn't matter what's wrong. Take off. I'll tell the Pirate something, and for you, taking one day off is better than winding up flat on your back for weeks."

"Thanks." Mathilde laboriously gathered her things and left. She did not go home.

* * *

Franz was convinced that if she still felt something for him, if she mourned him at all she would come here, to this spot. This was their place. It always had been and still was. Even though it had been horribly damaged, there remained a lingering aroma as if the fragile eternity of their whisperings of love had burned; the buildings around lay in despair, mute sentinels peering from blackened, empty eyes.

A few solitary Russian trucks drove on the streets on which a few years ago traffic had roared and raged. A single streetcar crossed over the square that had once been a major traffic hub. Only one thing had not changed. Now, as before, teeming people bustled over the wide space, always hurrying, seldom aimless. Streetcar tracks had been repaired to some extent.

Franz stood where the regulator clock had been and looked over at the carcass of the police headquarters building. Mathilde would have stood here in better times, at least that was what he imagined. She would have gazed at the entrance while waiting for him; waiting filled with desire, anticipation, and full of love.

The regulator clock had vanished, a victim of the bombs or the Russians. If their love had not vanished like the clock, she would appear. Sometime. She would come here, to their place, the place of their love, to say goodbye to him. He would speak to her and tell her that there was no need to mourn. On the contrary, there was reason for joy, reason for hope. He had only a few things to take care of before they would board a ship and sail off to America.

A Russian patrol neared. As casually as possible Franz stuck a violet drop in his mouth even though the perfumed taste almost made him queasy; he wanted to show the Russians that he was not afraid, that he had nothing to hide even though he quaked inside.

It was idiocy to come here to Alexanderplatz in the middle of the Russian zone. If they arrested him all was for naught and yet—standing here at the risk of arousing suspicion was his only, however remote or irrational, hope of establishing contact with Mathilde. He had to see her. If she believed he was dead, she might turn to that man she had gone dancing with, and that was unthinkable.

The soldiers went on by without noticing him. He watched them go and, when they were far enough away, spit out that nasty violet drop. Why in the world couldn't the black market carry his licorice lozenges anyway? He really missed them but he couldn't get them, no matter how hard he looked.

He would do without. He had to. He had learned to wait. After all the stakeouts he had conducted as a policeman, patience had become his specialty. Patience and tenacity. Even when he was stationed here, at Alexanderplatz, before being transferred to the Gestapo headquarters on Prinz-Albrecht-Straße.

Ten years ago, he thought. Not even ten years ago. Only three and a half thousand days. What had he gotten himself into? He didn't understand any of it, probably never would.

Fear and cowardice? Was it really so simple? Were the German people merely a bunch of weaklings and cowards? Weren't there also the true believers, the fervent disciples? Probably, he thought, but he had not been among them. So indeed, he would have to be counted with the fearful, the cowards; with those who wanted nothing but to protect their personal comfort. Those who did not see any reason to break ranks, to sheer off—until it was too late. Until they—until *he* considered the insanity completely normal.

He was sunk so deep into his bobbing and weaving musings that he almost missed her. She had just gotten off the streetcar that stopped in the middle of the square and looked around. She looks tired, he thought, worn out. No wonder when she stays out all night . . .

He watched her, trying to picture that shy, dreamy yet willful and self-confident girl that he had met in the late twenties when he helped the sexton at her church, and soon married. Was she still there, hidden in this woman, his wife, who would be forty in a few years?

She had been surprised when he asked her to go dancing with him after choir practice the following Saturday. That was after he had summoned up all the courage he could muster. She cocked her head to one side, her brown locks bouncing, and looked at him askance. For a horrible moment he was afraid that she would not only brush him off but not answer at all. As if he were not worthy of a response. Unexpectedly, he heard her soft voice say, *Sure, why not?* And from that moment on, he was lost; ready to propose on the spot.

He looked over at her. Despite her exhaustion she was still pretty. So beautiful, he thought. She looked around furtively as if she no longer knew where the regulator clock had stood; where their special place was. Could that be? Had she really forgotten the exact place, the rendezvous of their love; had she forgotten their love itself?

Then why would she have come here? Why suddenly stand in the middle of the square? She must be looking for him. What else could it be? It was hard to orient yourself in the rubble, and it had been a long time since she last met him here. He sighed and wanted to go across to her, to run to his wife.

But, a man approached.

A man with a hat and flashy colorful vest over a white shirt with rolled-up sleeves.

A man that Franz had already seen with Mathilde once.

Franz steadied himself against the collapsed wall at his back. He was not looking at a ghost. Mathilde was meeting the man she had been with that night at Franz's apartment in Kniepholzstraße. The man with whom, according to what Frieder said, she had gone dancing; the man she might even have, one night . . . Franz banished the thought immediately and recoiled, deeper into the shadows among the ruins.

He was not thinking clearly. He saw the man's face in the light and thought he recognized him. Somewhere he had come across this man before, with the hat set foppishly on the back of his head and the absurd, colorful vest—but where?

He was standing right in front of Mathilde, speaking emphatically, but Franz was too far away. He could not hear what was said, still the situation was clear enough. He was hardly dead and already his wife was billing and cooing with another man.

The more he watched, the more it seemed that Mathilde resisted the man. Try as he might, Franz could not image that Mathilde would rendezvous with another man, a stranger, at this special place; their place! Perhaps they met here by chance, or maybe the man had stalked and threatened her, and she needed help. The impulse to go to her rose in him again, and this time he would act.

He had taken a few steps forward when his memory flared, and he stopped. He had indeed seen this man before—because he was supposed to have arrested him. Franz did not recall the charge, but he must have been a Jew or a Gypsy. Yes, that was it! He looked like a Gypsy.

What was it again that had happened that day? Franz was unsure. The memory was fuzzy, hidden at the unraveled and frayed edges of a picture in his mind that withstood erosion by the powerful river of time. He remembered only one moment branded, etched in his memory like a stigma. The man had once fooled him.

Franz had led his Gestapo to arrest him at the Wintergarten. At the stage door he had whisked past them saying, *But you know me, don't you?* and rushed out of the theatre to disappear in the crowd on the street.

He could not show himself to this man, it was too risky. If he remembered Franz he could endanger everything. The Gypsy would denounce Franz and turn him in to the authorities, and he would loose his dream of the little white house somewhere in the Midwest of America.

It was a just a dream anyway. A pipe dream. Would he ever be able to move into his dream house with Mathilde? She was sensitive, weak, easy to influence. How had she reacted, he wondered, when she learned the truth about what his unit had done; what they had all done, even him?

And, what of this man? The Gypsy was always around her. Had he taken Franz's place even before the false report of his death had reached her? Had she taken the Gypsy's side? Was she still his faithful, loyal wife? Franz had no idea. He did not know what his own beloved wife thought, or what she felt, or even if she still loved him or not.

He tore his eyes from them; the sight stabbed him like a thousand needles. He hesitantly stepped backward until he was sure they had not noticed him and would not. Then he turned and hurried away, his shoulders hunched, keeping close to the wall. He would have to wait longer and observe. He had to be careful, extraordinarily careful.

* * *

The next morning Mathilde went back to the work site at Innsbrucker Platz and moved like an automaton, with pale red eyes and deep lines around her mouth. She had tossed and turned the whole night through. Pictures, scraps of memories, colors, sounds, and smells had flown through her mind. The regulator clock at Alexanderplatz was no longer there. A sentence Franz had spoken many years before came to her, *When will you make those delicious broad beans for us again, dear, with plenty of bacon?* Why did she hold on to that? Why did she hold on to the unfamiliar odors of the Gypsy camp, and why through it all, somewhere in the depths of the abyss of her self, the core of her being, did Mozart still swirl around . . . papada-pàda, papada-pàda?

Questions broke like waves inside her mind; probing questions, thoughts, foolish anxieties gnawed at the foundation of her being. Who was she? A widow? A widow needed a black dress. Where could she get a black dress? Doubt, sorrow, fear, guilt mixed and turned, swayed and tumbled as if she were drunk. How did Baumgartner know to find her at Alexanderplatz yesterday afternoon? What was he doing there? Had he followed her? Why? Was their meeting by chance? Was it a sign?

Confused and almost in panic, she had escaped from him, his words, and his sight. She jumped on the next streetcar wanting only to go home, to be away from Baumgartner, away from Alexanderplatz. Even though he meant no harm, was thoughtful and caring; still she felt hounded. She had not wanted to see him; she had not wanted to talk to him. Not then and certainly not there. Alexanderplatz belonged to her and Franz, at least to his memory. His memory was so strong and alive there, almost overpowering, as if he stood behind her and all she had to do was turn around to see him come to her. Instead, for no reason, Baumgartner appeared.

After laying sleepless on the uncomfortable sofa, brooding, listening to Karla's even breathing, she had gotten up. She heard Heidrun in the kitchen using the nightly power ration to precook food, but she had no desire for her sister's company. She could not take Heidrun's well-practiced attentions. As a pastor's wife Heidrun was unsurpassed in sympathy. Instead, Mathilde had sat in the window and stared out at a tree waiting, longing, praying for morning to come.

She had hoped for an uneventful, comparatively "easy" day at the rubble site, knowing that the monotonous, mindless, uninspiring work would exactly be what she needed in her gray mood. But no such luck for they ran into a steel beam. Everyone was needed to pitch in to uncover it and pull it from the rubble. No one could shirk. It was the hardest work they could encounter; harder still for an already exhausted, groggy Mathilde.

When the Pirate, Schall, finally yelled for the lunch break, Mathilde collapsed where she stood and stretched out feeling as if she couldn't move another inch. Lene sat next to her.

She too looked like she had not slept the night before. She, too, dragged, pale and bent, barely getting through from one minute to the next. "Don't you have anything to eat again?" The concern in Lene's voice could not be ignored. "Did you give everything to the kids?"

"And you? Give everything to Robert again?" Mathilde wouldn't take Lene's snippy tone and returned it in kind.

"He needs regular meals."

"The kids do, too."

Mathilde pulled out a slice of bread out of her pocket that Heidrun had forced on her that morning. She felt ill just thinking about food. "Here. There is even a little margarine on it."

"And you?"

"I can't keep anything down anyway."

Lene hesitated. "Just take it."

Lene took it. She knew she should share it at the least. Mathilde looked terrible and needed food as much as she did, but hunger was more powerful. Lene gobbled it down.

Mathilde smiled weakly as she watched Lene eat. "You are half starved."

"If it was only hunger . . ."

"Robert?"

Lene nodded glumly. "Do you know where Mr. Baumgartner is?"

Mathilde reflexively glanced at the platform with the rope the Gypsy danced on. He had not performed yesterday.

"Robert really needs insulin," Lene said as if Mathilde did not already know. "So, where do you think he is?"

Mathilde recoiled as if Lene slapped her. "How should I know?"

Lene would have laughed but saw Mathilde's alarmed face. "Don't worry. I won't tell anyone," she said trying to calm her friend.

"What are you saying?" Mathilde's alarm turned to misunderstanding.

"I know you're married. Your husband is long gone, believe you me, and I wouldn't kick that guy out of my bed."

Lene touched a nerve and Mathilde, incensed, shouted, "Are you crazy? I haven't cheated on my husband." Her voice cracked with indignation. "What do you think I am? I'm not like that. No!"

Lene tried to smooth it over saying, "I didn't mean that. I was only making a joke. A dumb joke," but Mathilde was too mad to hear and scolded Lene so loudly that the other women looked on amazed. They never heard such shrill tones from Tegge before.

Suddenly, without warning, Mathilde's mood changed and she broke into tears.

Lene put her arm around her. "What is the matter?"

As if comfort had pulled a plug, Mathilde's strength gave out. Meekly, she let her head sag against Lene's shoulder.

"What happened? Tell me."

"Franz is dead."

"Oh . . ." After a respectful moment, Lene continued, "And dumb old cow that I am, I implied that you were unfaithful to him. I am really, really sorry."

"I didn't do anything with Mr. Baumgartner, honestly, I didn't," Mathilde insisted like a little child and sank into silence. Sank, or so thought Lene, into sorrow.

It was not sorrow that flooded through Mathilde, pulled her in and spun her like a whirlpool. It was an exultation, a feeling she had not been aware of, could not be aware of, dared not be aware of. She felt closer to Baumgartner than she was to Franz, even if Franz had been alive. She had almost forgotten how Franz looked and smelled and felt; and at one moment yesterday in Alexanderplatz she had sensed his presence sliding into a hazy fog just as the man, her man, had done.

"I believe you didn't start anything with the Gypsy," Lene said. "I believe you."

"I hadn't even thought of it."

Lene nodded, appeasing Mathilde even though she did not believe her. She had seen them talking together, walking off together, standing together. She would have been very surprised, even disappointed, if something had not sparked between them. It was their business. Lene had other worries, beyond what was or was not happening with Mathilde. She sympathized with her loss, of course, but she had never known the man, and so few returned these days.

"I went to Marzahn," Lene said finally, "but only found the woman who was here with the Gypsy, the fortuneteller."

"Keja?"

Lene nodded. "She wasn't real friendly. She wouldn't tell me where I could find Baumgartner. And I doubt she told him that I asked about him." Lene drank a swallow of water. "Could you try? She's probably different with you."

"No." Mathilde was tight-lipped.

"Please!"

"She hates all Germans."

"But not Baumgartner. He takes to you. You cannot overlook that."

Mathilde thought about it. She finally shook her head. "I can't do that. Please, you have to understand."

Lene jumped up and cried out, "Dammit, this is about saving a life! I need you to find the strength to overcome your shadows of grief and save a life. You can at least try."

Tears ran down Mathilde's cheeks but she did not move.

Lene labored to tamp down the despair that numbed her heart and soul like an anesthetic and made her insensitive to everyone except her brother. She pulled herself together and spoke quietly; continued conciliatory, pleading, despairing, "Robert will die if he doesn't get new insulin soon."

Mathilde said nothing but nodded almost imperceptibly.

Lene saw it and the glimmer of a smile spread over her face. Suddenly, a heavy load seemed lifted from her soul. Mathilde would find the Gypsy and get ahold of some insulin. Robert would have another few days reprieve. She had extended his life for another few days.

In the distance Schall yelled, "Get up, ladies! Time to go back to work."

Lene got up unexpectedly easily. "Come on, we have to."

Mathilde made no move at all, not even to wipe the tears from her cheek. She remained sitting, staring vacantly in front of her.

Lene held out her hand. "I understand, it is all too much for you. We will make it." She smiled at Mathilde encouragingly. "Stand close to me. Then no one will notice whether you are working or just shamming." And she pulled Mathilde up. "Together we will make it. Somehow."

Mathilde shuffled after Lene.

TWENTY FOUR

The following day, Sunday, Mathilde shuffled through an undulating crowd in front of the bombed out ruins of the Reichstag.

Hidden goods were mentioned in whispers, "Ami cigarettes" from one, "Bread" from another, shoelaces and on and on. She shuffled aimlessly among them speaking to no one in particular, looking no one in the eye.

Bicycle tubes . . . nails . . . cold cream . . . The drone was incessant. No one looked at the others, but all were careful, observant, watching anyone they came across, nerves on edge. They would disappear like the wind should anyone sense that the police or allies were about to descend.

Meat rations, sewing needles, bed linen.

Mathilde crossed the square, her head scrunched between her shoulders, her eyes fixed resolutely on her hiking shoes. She kept quiet, not trusting herself to utter what she had to offer, fearing to ask for what she sought. She hoped to meet someone who would just miraculously dangle it in front of her, still she hoped in vain. She would have to take the initiative but dared not. Not yet.

The silverware in her shopping bag, which she clutched anxiously to her chest, tugged heavily. She had to be careful. There were criminals, thieves running around here. She was one of them, a criminal among criminals. A woman who, without remorse, had lied to her superior at work when she covered for Lene; who, without scruple, cold-bloodedly, had passed herself off as a doctor to get through a roadblock on her way to Camillo Baumgartner.

Only here—where she was aware of what she did, what she perpetrated—she glanced furtively, panicky from right to left fearing she might meet someone who knew her, who would finger her. She searched for signs of a raid though she knew she of all people would be the last one who could tell if a raid was about to happen.

Here and now, in the crowd, she had time to think, to be clear about the consequences if she were caught; and here and now her mouth dried up. What would Maman Lisson, what would Heidrun and Hermann say if she, their daughter-sister-sister-in-law, were arrested? Would they stand with her, a criminal? Franz, her dead Franz, would roll over in his grave, except he did not have one yet.

A few youngsters had garnered cigarettes, which they were trying to hawk. For a moment Mathilde thought she saw Frieder with them, but when she looked again he had vanished, or perhaps he was never there. Women pushed baby buggies in which no babies lay but rather pieces of furniture, tools, chunks of coal. No criminals. People like her. People who wanted to survive somehow. Nothing more.

Even Heidrun and Hermann might understand that Mathilde wanted to shop at this site. It was obvious to Mathilde that Heidrun must have found some things here. Even Hermann had to know the additions to their meager rations had come from the black market.

But if they knew what Mathilde was selling, or for whom she did it, they would be apoplectic. Mathilde would sell the good, inherited family silver for a convicted saboteur who had been wounded in a penal colony? They would say he was lucky to wind up there. Hermann would preach and reprimand. The brother of your friend should be happy he got probation, he would say with his finger poking the sky. Heidrun would quickly add that the wretch should be happy and truly thankful he survived at all. She would pray for him.

Mathilde cringed at every sudden movement or loud word and felt as if it was midnight and she moved stealthily across a cemetery. If Mr. Baumgartner were here, she thought, he would know the ropes and help her. She slammed the door on that thought so hard she felt like she had been hit with a hammer. Great God! She had just become a widow. How could she think such a thought?! But then she said to herself Franz would not have helped her. He never broke the law. He had never even run a red light.

Mathilde raised her eyes for a hesitant probe. Food and normal household articles were all around but no medicine. Either she went home empty-handed or she had to stop worrying and ask someone for help. She needed suggestions, hints about where to go. Cautiously, carefully, as inconspicuously as possible she checked out the people around her, but saw no one she thought she could trust.

"Well, who have we here?"

Mathilde whirled, expecting to be arrested, led off and tossed into a Black Maria prison wagon, but it was not there.

"What an infrequent guest in this fine establishment."

"What nice thing do we have to sell?"

"Come, show us." The shopping bag was unceremoniously ripped out of her arms and four hands pawed in it. "Ah, the old family silver cutlery. And what do you want for it? Coffee, cognac, cigarettes?"

"No, no, none of that." Mathilde had recovered from the shock and grabbed her bag back. She almost snickered about the sight of the two that stood in front of her and derisively grinned at her; Roswitha, the mighty Horse, and her little, slender bosom buddy, Minchen Krespe, looking like *Pat & Patachon*, the silent movie comedians from Denmark.

"You can tell us. We dig in the same crap as you." Roswitha punched her in the shoulder, a sign of friendship. Mathilde didn't flinch. By now, she was used to this sort of rough congeniality at the workplace.

"Maybe we can help you." A sly smile appeared on Minchen's pointed foxface. "You don't seem to be doing so well, and if there would be a little commission for us . . . ?"

"What do mean by that?"

"You don't know your way around here. That is as plain as the nose on your face."

Mathilde was uneasy. If they had been watching her for any time at all, others might have noticed too, and that was dangerous. After a moment she decided that she must have help and told them why she was here.

The two were amused, a bit scornful and incredulous. "Tegge, I've always thought you were a little too good for this world," whinnied the Horse, "but still not as dumb! Come on, girl. It's better to get yourself some bacon. You look like a corpse."

"Let her be. It is nothing to us why she wants to give away her stuff. The main thing is that we get something." Minchen reached into Mathilde's shopping bag again and grabbed a silver knife.

"Hold it." Mathilde grabbed the knife back. "When and if the deal is done. Not until then."

Roswitha nodded in agreement. "Fair enough. You're not the type to try and cheat us. Not you."

"So, do you have any idea where I can find insulin?"

"Certainly not here. Come on." The two turned around and headed skillfully and unerringly through the milling crowd, obviously wanting to get away from the Reichstag.

"Come on. Are you rooted here?" Roswitha sounded impatient. And Mathilde followed her. The three of them walked for about ten minutes, through the rubble strewn streets and trash paths until they came to a neighborhood inn close to Potsdamer Platz.

It was a dark room with simple wooden furniture that smelled of smoke, beer, and the polish used on the bar every evening. The upper floors of the building had fallen victim to the bombs during the battle around the Reich's chancellery, but down here nothing had changed for twenty years. Men stood at the bar and smoke and drank beer or schnaps. A few women, a few couples sat at the tables. It was as if nothing had happened, except there were no pickled eggs or the ubiquitous meat patties, the famous *Berliner Buletten*. Not anymore.

Roswitha and Minchen went to an unoccupied table. "So, first you buy us a round of schnaps." Roswitha grinned at Mathilde and motioned to the innkeeper at the same time. He came with the glasses, Minchen and Roswitha knocked theirs back immediately and ordered another shot each.

Mathilde paid but didn't touch her glass. "What happens now?" She didn't want the two drunk on her tab until they had said or showed her how she could get the insulin.

"Hold your horses." Minchen emptied the second glass and looked around the place. At first she seemed to not detect who she was looking for, but then a young man came out of the toilet.

A young man? Mathilde marveled at that. Young men were rare items, they were either dead or still in POW camps, and this one was well clothed on top of everything. He wore a new looking woolsuit, good, shiny brown oxfords and a white shirt, even a neckerchief. Thick black hair fell over a southern looking face. The man gave a short wave to Krespe and went to the bar where his glass was. Minchen got up and joined him.

"Go ahead, drink. It will do you good." Roswitha encouraged Mathilde. "Minchen will get it shortly. She knows what she is doing."

Mathilde waved her off. She wanted to stay sober, she felt ill enough at ease as it was. At the very least, she wanted to keep a clear head. "No, I'm good." After she saw that Mathilde wouldn't drink, Roswitha shrugged and knocked it back for her.

In the meantime Minchen had exchanged a few words with the chic young man at the bar. He casually drank the rest of his beer and then left. Minchen came back to the table. "Everything is okay, Tegge. You will have your stuff in a half hour." She motioned to the innkeeper. "So, now we come to the good part."

The innkeeper brought a new round and they drank. This time Mathilde took one. She didn't want to arouse suspicion, now that Krespe had apparently set things in motion.

The dandy really did come back within a half hour, during which the two unlikely bosom buddies had three more schnaps each and steadily gossiped about Schall and others at the worksite.

Mathilde listened quietly. She could picture how they would have talked about her and Lene had she not been there. For now, though, it didn't matter.

The young man wound his way toward the toilet without looking at the three women. Minchen told Mathilde in a hushed voice to follow him. Mathilde stood up grabbing her shopping bag, but the Horse held her back with her strong calloused hand. "Just a moment." She reached into Mathilde's bag and pulled out a knife. "We have done our part. Time to pay up."

"Not yet. The deal isn't done yet." Mathilde started to take the knife out of Roswitha's hand.

Minchen grabbed Mathilde's hand. "You had better hurry. He doesn't know you and he won't wait forever."

Mathilde turned abruptly and went past the bar to the door on which PRIVY was written in artful but fading Gothic script. What else was she to do? Nothing. She had no choice. She had to take the risk.

She stepped through the door into a long, dark, appallingly smelly hallway in which all sorts of junk stood. At the end of the hall she saw a door with a dirty opaque window under which the word PRIVY was visible in remnants of peeling paint. Mathilde took a deep breath, hurried as quickly as she could down the hall, and opened the door. It led to a courtyard where the toilet was to the right, a filthy open hole that had been cleared of debris, but other than that the courtyard was one giant pile of rubble. Outside it smelled even worse than inside. Blinking, Mathilde looked around.

Suddenly the man was in front of her. He had silently stepped out of the shadow of a still standing piece of masonry wall. Mathilde let out a soft yelp and looked at him with a pounding heart.

"You need insulin?" A smile appeared on his lips, fleeting and furtive, like a rogue who already has the next trick in the back of his head. Mathilde calmed a bit. The man had a foreign accent like a Spaniard, Frenchman, or an Italian; for all she knew he also could have been Bulgarian, Romanian, Hungarian. Still, that didn't explain what such a young healthy man was doing in Berlin during these times. Most foreign workers looked no healthier than the soldiers coming home.

"And you have silver? Show me." He had a friendly, matter-of-fact demeanor that would have been more fitting in a jewelry shop than in this repellant, stinking, obscene caricature of a courtyard.

Mathilde held her bag protectively close to her body while she opened it but then did not—could not—prevent the man from pulling it to him, taking out a fork, inspecting it. He looked satisfied. A little packet slid out of the fine cloth of his jacket, like a chick hatching. Mathilde's heart leapt. The packet looked exactly like the one Baumgartner had given her that night in Marzahn. It also seemed to be the medicine she needed. Still, she had to be careful. Who knew what the handsome southerner had stuck in the container?

She took the little package out of his hand and opened it. Eight ampules, just like new. She tilted the packet to be sure there was liquid in the little glass pipettes. Mathilde caught her breath. All signs were that she was not being cheated. The man took three full sets of silver cutlery out of the shopping bag before he gave it back to her.

He left her with three complete sets, as well as the set without the knife which was basically worthless now that it wasn't complete anymore. She might as well blow it, spend it on something extra, something special. Something to eat maybe? Finally get shoes for little Horst who had gone barefoot through the rubble for weeks without complaint? Or something for herself? Maybe even a pair of silk hose? Treasures, precious objects . . .

Suddenly it seemed to be no problem for her to go back to the Reichstag and buy whatever she wanted. Suddenly the anxiety that had fallen over her seemed laughable. She was strong. She could make it through. She was over the shadows of her past, her upbringing, her languor. She had again leapt past those shadows.

Then she noticed that she was alone in the courtyard. The man had disappeared just as ghostly as he had appeared. But, she had the ampules in her hand, and a portion of the family inheritance was still in her shopping bag. It could not have gone better. Mathilde felt like patting herself on the back. She almost floated, almost danced through the evil hallway back to the barroom. She could have sung the hated Czerny etude, she was so proud of herself.

* * *

As in peacetime, thought Mathilde. As in peacetime? It is peacetime. We have peace, she repeated, averred, and confirmed in her thoughts. It was hard to believe, though, given how the city looked, but it was different here. It was as if the war had never happened.

People paddled in the water, lay in the sun, sat by one another, played cards, and gossiped. The children shrieked and screamed while they splashed in the lake. It became more and more quiet as the sun set and most of them went home for supper—in so far as there was any supper to be had back home. But here, outside, it seemed as if the last six years had not happened.

She had come to Krumme Lanke on the *U-Bahn* together with Lene, just as she used to with Franz and Karla. Except for the Amis having taken over some of the buildings around Onkel Toms Hütte, the subway station where they got off, Mathilde noticed nothing different. Well, maybe the fact that there was no wood anywhere, not even twigs or shavings. Otherwise, they had walked through undamaged residential blocks and some piece of forest to the little bathing beach just as Mathilde had done on so many Sundays before the war. She should have brought the children, Mathilde thought while she relaxed and watched the sun going down. For a minute she felt a pang of guilty conscience that she had only thought of herself, not about the others.

From the inn at Potsdamer Platz, Mathilde had run straight back to Kreuzberg and given the insulin to Robert. "See, that wasn't so hard." Lene assumed the ampules had come from Baumgartner's undiscovered underground source. "He has a crush on you. As a woman you have to use that."

Mathilde had shaken her head in denial. Not her. She would not do something like that. She couldn't do anything like that, but Lene didn't pay attention to her anyway anymore. Instead, she gave Robert a shot of insulin with something to eat, and then, suddenly, she was in front of Mathilde with towels and two swimsuits. "Come on, we are going swimming."

"Swimming?" Mathilde could not have been more surprised if Lene had suggested a trip to the moon.

"Why not? It is Sunday, it is summer, it is warm."

Mathilde gaped at Lene, speechless.

"I know what you think." Lene had held one of the swim suits up to her and nodded. It would fit. "You are tired, you have too much to do, and besides you have just become a widow."

"Since when can you read minds?"

"Thanks for the compliment, but that wasn't hard to see." Lene had exuberantly shoved the bathing suit and towel into Mathilde's hand. "No argument. We have really earned it. Especially you! You are about to collapse on me at any moment." Lene had stuffed her towel and bathing suit in a shopping bag and held it up triumphantly. "I have organized a little picnic for us." With a mischievous look she smacked her pocket, and waved her friend out the front door.

Mathilde had not resisted the momentum. They had taken off, marching through the rubble to the subway line to Zehlendorf. Now they sat here at the Krumme Lanke. They swam and gossiped on a summer afternoon, maybe a bit hotter than usual but nevertheless like many others. They smiled knowingly at each other as they heard hushed sounds of lovers in the bushes. They lay next to each other on the towels, ate pastry and drank wine out of the bottle.

"Where did you get all of this? You don't even bring bread to the worksite." Mathilde's head spun like a carousel from the sun, exhaustion and the alcohol.

"Do you remember Hedwig Strache?"

"The former classmate that works in the social welfare office?"

"She surprised me at my door this morning. With this." Lene waved the wine bottle and took another cookie.

"I thought she was a hard nose."

"Yeah, but above all she is careful to stay in good standing and always come out clean." Lene grinned to herself. "It doesn't matter why, the main thing is that I would have traded all this for medicine, but then you showed up and I thought that we could invest it better. In us."

"Well then—cheers!" Mathilde took another swallow of wine, rolled on her side, propped herself up on an elbow, and let her gaze wander worry-free over the colorful people, the green of the water, the blue of the sky. She dreamed, dreamed of peace, dreamed the last six years had not happened, surrounded herself with pleasant warm dreamscapes. She forgot everything, even Franz.

Then her gaze fell on some kids playing, and an annoying humming came to her ear. She was feeling guilty about the kids, and because she had not gone to church today. As if she caught Mathilde's mood, Lene pulled her up and into the lake where the pang of guilt disappeared in the warmth of the water.

They swam out in the same tempo, gliding along beside each other with similar strokes through the water, in quiet harmony with themselves and the elements.

"I am sorry; I didn't mean to scold you at the worksite yesterday," Lene said over the quiet lapping of the waves, "but I was so worried that Robert wouldn't make it."

"No problem. I understand."

"Thanks for going to Baumgartner. I know that wasn't easy for you."

"I didn't go to Mr. Baumgartner."

"What?" Lene stopped swimming in utter amazement and treaded water instead. "Where did you get the insulin?"

"From the Reichstag."

Lene was quiet for a bit. "I would never have believed that of you. Really not." Impressed, she could only, finally, say, "Thank you."

"It is no big thing." Mathilde smiled at her and noticed that Lene's eyes glistened.

"No, I would not have dreamt you would do such a thing. You really are still water, Mathilde." As if Lene had startled herself and could not maintain the emotional moment, she pushed it away to be replaced by exuberant happiness, the lightheartedness and abandon of playing kids. "And still water runs deep," she shouted as she pushed Mathilde's head under water.

She surfaced snorting water, but Lene's laughter was contagious. Mathilde took a deep breath, dived, grabbed Lene's feet, and pulled her down. Lene defended herself, fought back, and they frolicked and cavorted, splashed and snorted like eight-year-olds.

They finally lay on the bank exhausted. Lene magically pulled a cigarette out of the depths of her pocket, lit it and handed it to Mathilde who took a puff. They smoked together, smoked quietly, engulfed in their own thoughts.

After a while Lene asked, "When did you know?" Again she seemed to sense, to know what Mathilde was thinking; that she thought of Franz.

"When did I know what?" Mathilde asked anyway.

"That your husband is dead."

"I don't know it yet. At least not for sure." Mathilde told her about the boy that Karla had picked up on the street. She told about her doubts whether the boy had really seen Franz. She told her how her head agreed that the details fit and that she should believe the boy. But her heart was not convinced as long as she had not seen the corpse or some other unimpeachable evidence. "I know there are a lot of women whose husbands are missing or who know about them only from some comrades. But . . ."

Lene understood and mourned with Mathilde and hoped with her; still, a question bore into Lene's consciousness.

One word triggered a question that let suspicion germinate, a suspicion she could not suppress. Lene realized she knew very little about Mathilde's husband. She had assumed he was a soldier and in some POW camp. Was that right? Mathilde had seldom spoken of him. Lene just now had heard his name for the first time, and she was hesitant to ask the question that bounced around in her head.

"How old was your husband?" Lene asked the question anyway as the moon's crescent palely appeared in the dark blue evening sky, after most of the others had long since left the beach.

"Forty-two, why?"

"Then why was he in the Volkssturm? Shouldn't he have been drafted long before that?"

The question had to come sometime. Was this the right time to tell Lene the truth?

"Was he sick?" Lene hoped that was the case. "Or deferred?"

"He was deferred."

"Why?"

"He was a policeman."

"Policeman?" Lene had sensed it, had feared it. "Only a policeman?" Mathilde Tegge, the still water.

Mathilde took a deep breath. "When I met him, yes. Later he was transferred."

"So *that* kind of policeman?"

"That kind of policeman."

Confused and contradictory thoughts whirred through Lene's head. She liked Mathilde, this woman who always looked a little dreamy, a little screwy, but in spite of that, pretty special. Mathilde had gone through half of Berlin at night in defiance of the curfew to obtain insulin for Robert. And now, she had bought some at the black market. Who knew what she had used to pay for it? How did all that fit with what she had just learned? How could a woman that Lene Behrendt liked be a Nazi wife?

How had she never seen any sign of that? Until a couple of minutes ago she would have sworn she could smell that kind a hundred meters away against the wind, but she had had no inkling until she heard the word—*Volkssturm*. How could that be? How could something like that get by her? Lene fell silent in dismay, baffled and stunned. She would have given almost anything for a cigarette.

Mathilde misunderstood Lene's silence and her stare. "I understand, you don't want anything to do with me anymore. Really, I understand." Abruptly everything came back to her. Hunger, work, and exhaustion all marched in organized columns into her consciousness, and leading the march was the eerie smile of guilt that waved the white, black, and red banner of the Reich.

Mathilde retreated behind a bush and pulled her dress on. She handed Lene the wet bathing suit and the towel. "Thanks for the wine and the cookies." She turned and started to leave.

There was no peace, not even here where she could not see or feel the war. "Wait!"

"Yes?" Mathilde turned back. "Did you know?"

"Does it make a difference?"

Lene shrugged. "Probably not."

"If I say now that I didn't know anything, you wouldn't believe me anyway."

"Did you know nothing then?"

"Not everything." Mathilde's voice almost failed. "I only learned about the mountains of corpses in the *KZ*s after the war."

Lene nodded slowly. It could as well have been a shaking of her head.

"But does that make a difference?"

Now, Lene did shake her head. "Probably not. Is that why you got the insulin for Robert?"

"Because?" Mathilde didn't understand.

"To redeem yourself? You and your husband."

"That isn't really possible, is it?"

"No, of course not." Lene Behrendt's bitter laugh, sign of her unerring instincts, her sense of justice just now returning to her like tardy vassals.

Mathilde responded to the loud echo of Lene's laugh. "No, no. I didn't get the insulin for that. I hadn't even thought about it, not for a moment, whether you believe me or not." Her voice was soft and cracked as she spoke. "Robert was in dire straits. That is why I wanted to help. Even if you don't believe me, I would have done the same for anybody."

The woman had become alien to Lene. With each word she became more and more distant. She claimed in all sincerity that she did not help Robert for atonement and would probably call it neighborly love, thought Lene. Regardless what she might call it, Lene could not understand.

Could Mathilde lie so shamelessly? Could she have told her what she had told her—without batting an eye, without quavering—if it was not true? That she had helped because help was needed. Lene did not think her capable of lying so shamelessly, could not accept that of her, she was not that brazen. On the other hand, half an hour earlier she would have never dreamed Mathilde was a *Nazisse* either, wife of a Gestapo thug.

Yet, if it were true? If Mathilde really helped because of neighborly love, then what kind of person could be so upright on the one hand and on the other watch as innocents were thrown into jail, tortured and murdered, or sent for punishment to companies where they lost their legs?

Bitterness, anger and despair welled up in Lene, mercury rising in the heat of hate. She wished to hurt Mathilde, to see her suffer like Robert suffered, like she herself suffered. Lene wanted in that moment to hit Mathilde Tegge, to beat her. But she could not. Beating Mathilde would not change anything. Did that make any sense at all?

Mathilde looked sadly at Lene for a moment longer, then turned and walked away. She was sluggish and exhausted and held the secret hope that Lene would call her back. But no call came. She trudged through the little wood again, past the houses and to the subway while Lene sat and stared at the lake. Between the green and brown tree shadows the crescent moon shone pale gray on gray, almost imperceptible.

TWENTY FIVE

Franz was thunderstruck. He had been prepared for a lot of things—but this? No! He had been ready for an argument with Matthus because he had not yet found a truck. He had thought through everything he would say to divert the Sturmbannführer. He had been ready for anything . . . but not this; the print shop was empty.

It seemed eerily quiet when he slipped through the door into the back courtyard where the print shop was. He couldn't say what it was but something was odd; alarming. Gripped with tension, he knocked on the cellar door. He called out but there was no answer. He tried the handle. The door was neither locked from the outside nor barred from inside. Strange. Very, very strange.

He climbed down into the darkness, peered into the emptiness, into the silence, and finally groped his way along the machines into and through the kitchen to the shop owner's apartment. He flipped the switch, the light came on and he stood stock still, breathless and shocked. The kitchen could have been the pride of every German housewife, shiny and clean with everything in its place. Only the light odor of soap suggested that someone had cooked, eaten, and lived here. There was no trace of Matthus or his accomplices.

Franz tore open the cupboards. The provisions were gone. He hurried into the back area, and there, too, everything was as if Matthus and the others had never been there. The raw, cobbled-together bunk beds had been dismantled. The double bed had been made. The whole apartment gave the impression that the owners were on vacation and had, like the decent Germans they were, cleaned and polished everything before they left.

Well, there it was. They were gone. Franz slipped back into the kitchen and slumped into a chair. He stared at the naked bulb in the kitchen lamp and played absentmindedly with the tin that held his one precious licorice lozenge merrily clinking from side to side, thinking hard, where in reality there was nothing to think about. The situation was clear. Franz was finished. Matthus had either found a truck from another source, and they were all on their way to South America or wherever; or they distrusted him so much for tracking them down that they had moved to a different hideout.

Whatever had happened, the result was the same. He had lost contact. It was unlikely he would accidently find them again, so good-bye Hans in Luck, his unreliable patron saint. Lost contact meant lost reward. His ticket to freedom, to the little white house with red roof and blue shutters in the American Midwest had been canceled. Herter already thought him just another useless Nazi and would be happy to toss him into prison.

I have to run, he thought. Where? To whom? He had nothing left; no family, no job, no mission. He had turned himself in to the Amis because he knew he couldn't make in on his own. And what did it amount to, what had changed? Nothing. Everything had gotten worse, disintegrated, melted away. His wife, his dreams, his strength, even his persistence and tenacity had been washed away. He had lost everything.

A noise startled him. Someone was at the entrance. He glanced at the door, but before he could stand to turn out the light, before he could hide, before he knew what was happening, boots stomped, commands were shouted, and two GIs stormed in. They yanked Franz from the chair and dragged him through the print shop into the courtyard. They shoved him into the back seat of an army car and slammed the doors as it sped away.

Franz rubbed his knees, elbows, and shins. Why the brutality, he asked himself. He would have cooperated, he would not have fought.

"Excuse us. The boys were a little exuberant in dragging you out of there, but we must be sure you're not under surveillance. It should look like we arrested you, shouldn't it?" The somewhat rusty Ruhr valley accent was unmistakable.

"Am I not then?"

Herter was sitting next to Franz. He was lighting a cigarette as he spoke and absently held out the pack as if casually offering one to a friend before recognizing his error. He had no intention of offering Franz a cigarette. "Excuse me," he said, sounding more embarrassed than snide though. "I forgot you don't smoke."

"I'll take one anyway." Franz grabbed one and put it behind his ear before Herter could pull the pack away. A cigarette was like gold in a prison camp, and he was sure that was where he was going. Herter looked cross but bit back the comment that was, no doubt, on the tip of his tongue.

"Am I not under arrest?" Franz insisted.

"If it was up to me, you would be." Herter exhaled a cloud of smoke, thoughtful. Franz waited for what would follow, but Herter provided only silence. The car sped through the rubble-strewn landscape.

"Where are you taking me?" Franz finally asked.

Herter smoked two more cigarettes, not offering Franz any chance for more. They had left the printing shop in Schöneberg long ago and driven through the ruins and mountains of debris—always the same, the same—past the Reich's Chancellery in the direction of Wedding.

"Unfortunately not to jail."

Franz already figured that out but hid his impatience, leaned back and looked at Herter.

"You took too long with the truck," the lieutenant finally said.

"Did you arrest them?"

Herter shook his head. "Matthus decided you cannot get a suitable vehicle so you became a security risk."

"How do you know that?"

"Do you think that we would rely only on you?" You could hear how absurd Herter found that idea. "We watched your pristine gentlemen independently of you."

Franz expected that. In Herter's place, he would have done the same.

"We saw they were packing their bags and moving out bit by bit.

We suspected they would not have done it like that if they were about to make a long trip, and we were right. All we needed to do was follow the handyman."

Kleinmann, thought Franz, and almost laughed to himself.

"He was slowed down and distracted by the load," Herter went on, "otherwise he might have noticed he was being followed."

"Do you know where they went?"

Herter smiled condescendingly and ignored the question. "You will accidently meet Kleinmann on the street. Tell him you have a truck."

"Do I have one then?"

"I sure hope so."

Franz stared at Herter who looked straight at the driver's shoulders. What did all this mean? Why didn't Herter just arrest the Nazis?

"You're asking yourself why I didn't snatch them all up and ship all of you to where you belong?" Herter shrugged his shoulders. "Orders are orders."

Franz could tell Herter was not happy and he understood. How often had he been angry when Borg or others told him to do something unreasonable? But that was Herter's problem, not his.

"My bosses think they hit the jackpot with you, like you are some sort of Mata Hari." If it wouldn't have been about him, Franz realized, one could have thought that they were talking like equals, colleagues who griped about an incompetent boss. But they were not equals, and his role was that of the odd one out on a suicide mission.

"Have you heard of the Rat Line?" Herter asked.

Franz shook his head.

"Of course not. We are the only ones who use that term." The lieutenant tapped the driver's shoulder and they slowed down. They were getting closer to their destination. "When your comrades figured out that their glorious Reich was collapsing, they prepared their escape. They knew they would be hunted so they arranged with sympathizers to make it safely out of the country they had brought to ruin. We know the path out of Europe exists, but we don't know where or how. You need to find that out for us."

"I should work my way further into the group and go with them until I know where they are going?"

"We are certain the threads lead to a German cardinal in the Vatican. He provides the SS criminals with the diplomatic passports they need to disappear in Bolivia or Paraguay. We don't know how they get from Germany to Rome. We have no idea who helps them, where they get papers, passports, travel authorizations, or where the depots are hidden. You get the picture."

"Understood. How do we keep in touch?"

"We don't. Not at first. We will continue to watch you, but you will travel through a whole stretch of the Soviet zone where it is impossible for us to stay on you. In Rome, at the latest, you will leave the group and report to the OSS. I will instruct my colleagues, and you will have a code word to identify yourself. You tell them what's up, and we take them into custody in Genoa or Naples or wherever they board ship."

"But our deal is still good? Passports and US visas for me and my family?"

"Do I look like I would break my word?"

Franz wanted to say, yes. That's exactly how you look, but that would not be a good move. If he did well for Herter's bosses, Herter would not be able to make trouble. Besides, Franz assured himself, he would be smart enough to withhold some of what he learned until he was safely in America and sure that the Amis would keep their part of the bargain.

"There, up front at the corner Kleinmann will pick up the guys who want to use the Rat Line for their escape. The rest is up to you." Herter leaned over Franz and pushed the door open. "Good luck."

Franz got out and leaned back to Herter. "But I don't have a chance without the truck."

"There was nothing in my orders about a truck." Herter leaned forward to his driver. "Please take me back to the office." The car took off so fast Franz was almost hurled back as it disappeared behind the next rubble pile.

He understood; Herter undercut the orders by following them to the letter and no more. Franz could expect nothing from him.

* * *

Franz stood there and looked around. He recognized the remnants of Müllerstraße, so he was in the heart of Wedding. How ironic, he thought. SS bigwigs were hiding in the former "Red Wedding," the anti-fascist center of Berlin that had experienced a blood bath in 1928. But irony got him nowhere. He needed a truck and had no idea how to get one.

To start he found Kleinmann and persuaded him to arrange for a meeting with Matthus. He knew they would not let him back into their hideout, so he would meet Matthus at a street corner. Matthus had to believe him again, and it worked out that he did give Franz another chance. Franz told him that he had had a truck but lost it when he went to the print shop looking for Matthus and discovered everyone gone. It was Matthus's fault things had not worked out. The Sturmbannführer growled but did not argue.

Franz got a few days leeway, but that would not help him much. Up to now his attempts to get a truck had been miserable failures. He could not find one on the black market, and those people who made such deals wouldn't fall for a policeman's tricks anyway.

He had tried to steal an Allied truck since a German one would have been useless. Trucks in German hands could be found, but there was no gas for them anymore. They were powered by wood boilers. By the time Franz could get a boiler heated and enough pressure built up to drive off, he would have long since been discovered. No, it had to be an Allied vehicle, but they were closely guarded, one could not just make off with one.

Franz prowled the streets for hours in search of a possibility, an idea, an inspiration. He was increasingly hopeless, increasingly despondent. There were no trucks to be found. Once he saw several English trucks parked at the curb while soldiers play football in a neighborhood field. He thought he could pull it off by stealing one of them but discovered they had taken the cranks with them so there was no way to start them up. I would rather have a left-hand drive American truck anyway, Franz thought smiling grimly. As if he had a choice. I'll take this model, please, and make it a black one, not olive green.

Ultimately, he sat in a bar having invested his cigarette, the one thing he had gotten from Herter, in a few beers. He tried to forget everything; to start thinking anew. What was it Kriminalrat Borg had always said when an investigation was at a standstill? "Let's not make the same mistake flies make. You see how they keep flying against the window pane and don't notice the other side of the window is wide open? Let us sit quietly and see where the wind blows. Then we can tell where a window is open."

Franz felt no breeze. He was caught between a rock and a hard place. The fly could flutter and fight all it wanted—both window panes remained shut.

TWENTY SIX

"As for man, his days are as grass, as a flower of the field, so he flourisheth. For the wind passeth and it is gone; and the place thereof shall know it no more. But the mercy of the Lord is from everlasting to everlasting upon them that fear him."

The mercy of the Lord, Mathilde repeated to herself, is from everlasting to everlasting upon them that fear him. Upon them that fear him. Had Franz feared him? He had believed in God, prayed before every meal and went to church every Sunday, but had he feared him?

Did he fear Him when he was on duty? Duty had priority, no matter what. If push came to shove, Franz had feared worldly men in black uniforms more than God. Mathilde prayed for her late husband. She prayed for mercy and compassion, and that God might forgive him.

"Almighty, merciful God, by Your holy will you have called our brother Franz Tegge from this present life home to You in eternity." Hermann spoke, soft and solemn, always appropriate for the occasion in front of a congregation, just like when Mathilde married Franz. It was as if nothing had happened in the meantime. Hermann stood there in his borrowed cassock, a rock, the rock of God.

Other than Hermann's voice, Mathilde did not pay close attention. She filtered the words he spoke and just watched him. The pastor— shepherd of sinners, comfort and guide for his needy sheep—unalterable and resolute, sympathetic and strong. He did *his* duty. His funeral duty for his brother-in-law.

Mathilde surveyed the small party of mourners. No colleagues—they all were in hiding or under arrest; Franz's parents had been dead for years. He had no siblings or friends.

Aside from Franz's immediate family—Mathilde and Karla, Heidrun and her four children including little Horst who was so proud of his new shoes that he wouldn't take them off even to sleep—only the Trimborns listened to Herman's solemn sermon. The Trimborns insisted on accompanying the grieving widow and her entourage. The former block warden would always and forever consider himself the spokesman and representative for the house community; and of course he had come to attend the funeral with his faithful second, his wife Irma, the worst gossip monger around. The two of them would not shirk their duty.

For once, Frieder was not watching Hubert who wandered around the gravestones as if afraid to be near the group. For once, her nephew was not casting poisonous glances or making hateful remarks but seemed dumbstruck throughout the entire ceremony, staring straight ahead as if he had to struggle mightily to keep from breaking down. Mathilde had no idea Frieder had felt so close to Franz. Who would have thought . . .

Mathilde looked at Hermann again, but could not follow what he said. His words and voice blended into a dark steady melody of sorrow and futility. Suddenly she glimpsed a pale face in the shrubbery at the edge of the cemetery. Franz? It must be nerves playing a trick on me, she thought. Stop it. You need a clear head, you have to be here for Karla, you cannot let yourself go. She shut her eyes to erase the image and when she opened them the image had vanished.

For some reason or other she was only halfheartedly relieved. Her gaze and her thoughts wandered further across the bushes, trees, and other graves but she saw nothing. The only reminder of Franz was the raw wooden cross beside the soft, green moss which covered the gravestone of her captain father. He had died almost twenty years ago.

Twenty years. Mathilde remembered how she had cried at his funeral. Nobody had been able to console her. Accent-on-the-second-syllable-Maman scolded her and sent her home and she was not allowed at the funeral reception because she could not behave. She had been "excessive in her grieving."

Excessive in her grieving. Mathilde waited for the lump in her throat, the heaving in her chest, she waited for the tears but none of that came. It was not that she didn't mourn or that she didn't miss her husband, but she did not feel she was standing at the edge of a void. The void was inside her.

Far from her previous excessive grief, she stood between Heidrun and Karla by the grave and felt empty, shiny and smooth like an overly scrubbed wooden floor. Behind them the little ones fidgeted, cowed to silence by severe looks from their mother, and beside the children stood the Trimborns in their practiced, well-maintained composure.

Mathilde glanced sidelong at Karla to discover that she, too, was not crying. Karla, wearing a new dress Heidrun had made for her out of old diapers she had dyed black, looked relieved, almost satisfied or at least peaceful. She looked as though something she already knew had been confirmed.

Her daughter's lack of grief bothered Mathilde; not that it was wrong. In a way, she, too, had a feeling of freedom. Death had spared Franz from arrest, trial, and punishment, spared all of them embarrassment, abasement, and humiliation; but nonetheless it disconcerted her that Karla did not grieve more for her father.

Now and then Karla pensively glanced at Hubert. She had more or less adopted him since they had met. Almost daily he would show up at their place, and Karla would slip him something from their meager supplies. Mathilde smiled to herself. It was almost as if Karla had fallen in love in a nurturing, motherly way.

Hermann finally finished his eulogy and began to pray the Our Father. Heidrun prayed loudly, reverently, and fervently, in demonstrative devotion. She wore her faith on her sleeve like a beautiful, expensive bracelet she was proud to own. At least that's how it seemed, Mathilde thought, but maybe she was not being fair to her sister.

Mathilde remembered how her sister had come into the kitchen and sat down with her at the table. "Hermann and I have talked," Heidrun said cautiously. Mathilde had wondered what she wanted as Heidrun fiddled with a spoon on the table and finally clearly her throat. Subdued, she continued, "Do you really believe the boy, Hubert?"

Mathilde had asked herself why Heidrun broached this subject as if she just now questioned the truth of Hubert's story. It did not seem false, but why did Heidrun start this now?

"Hermann and I, we think," Heidrun's voice broke, "that Franz is really dead, killed in action. So we are of a mind it would be better for you to accept that fact."

"Is it a fact?" Mathilde was confused. Where was her sister going?

"See, that is really the problem." Heidrun nodded earnestly. She paused again and played distractedly with the spoon. "Hermann and I, we didn't come to our decision lightly, you can believe that."

"Yes?" Mathilde had even less of an idea of what this meant.

"That Franz is dead. Killed." Heidrun repeated. It was difficult for her to say what must be said and hard to convince her sister of what she and Hermann knew to be true, a reality. She saw how Mathilde dragged through the apartment and through the days. She ate very little, didn't wash herself properly anymore, slept in her work clothes. It could not go on. Mathilde had to accept the inevitable.

Mathilde looked at Heidrun without understanding what she said and asked, "What do you think I should do?"

"Go to the registrar's office and have him declared dead. Hermann will hold a funeral service."

"What?" Mathilde was startled as if hearing a sudden noise behind her.

"Create facts." Heidrun pressed her further. "That's the only thing that will help you."

Mathilde stammered, "I'll think about it." She got up and fled the kitchen. She sat at the living room window and stared at the lonesome tree in the courtyard whose branches stretched bare into the sky even though it was summer. A rubble tree among rubble houses.

Heidrun said to create facts, she mused. Create facts?

Was it fact? Mathilde did not know. Was what Hermann and Heidrun figured out right? And, if she accepted the inevitable, would she really improve?

Lene flashed through her mind, Lene who had been her friend, yes, the first real friend she's had in her life even; but after Krumme Lanke all she could expect from Lene was bitter, hostile silence.

Camillo Baumgartner stubbornly defied all limits, all borders set on him; he floated at the margins of her life, her consciousness, and her essence like an insolent, adorable, troublesome elf.

Add to them the constant deprivation, continuing exhaustion, nagging debilitation that gripped her like an iron corset.

Create fact.

Should she create the fact that she was a widow? Widow … Mathilde whispered the word to herself; it did not ring true. War widows, those were others. Up to the last few months, Franz had always come home in the evenings. And even now he wasn't really gone—in a way. Frieder and Hermann wore some of his things, and Mathilde had carefully stored his walking stick in the closet. So this man was suddenly supposed to be dead and never return? Suddenly she was supposed to be a widow? Mathilde could not grasp it though the facts told a clear story.

Karla agreed with her aunt for a change. She was so convinced that Hubert told the truth that she was no help to Mathilde. She missed Lene, especially now. Now more than ever.

Mathilde prayed to God for advice, but He did not answer. Only Hermann, His disciple, and Heidrun, her resolute older sister, answered the call.

Hermann and Hubert escorted Mathilde to the registrar's office. She brought the family register, along with Franz's birth certificate, their marriage certificate, the registration for their apartment that had outlived her husband, and his induction orders to the Volkssturm—her husband's whole life on paper neatly filed and carried in her shopping bag. She stood with them, the imperturbable man, the clearly disturbed boy—an odd pair—in the foyer of the office that smelled of floor wax and waited.

Mathilde was surprised a registrar's office was even open and in working condition, but every day people died or were born, and some even wanted to get married. All this had to be documented, registered, attested. Little by little, the clerks—old men, cripples, women—showed up to work again. They all sat in their jerry-rigged offices and worked. Routine.

Like always. So little had changed. So very little, Mathilde thought.

She was suddenly shocked. Around the corner into the foyer came a small man with grayish blond hair and glasses. She was surprised, excited, elated—wanted to run to him shouting Franz! But then he raised his head, and she recognized him or rather did not. It was not Franz, and the shout died on her lips. She felt Hermann's hand on her shoulder, his attempt to soothe and calm her. She made herself as small as possible under his hand and stared at a spot on the opposite wall.

She asked herself again, for the umpteenth time, is what I am doing right? Am I sure? Am I really sure? They had all talked with Hubert again. They had gathered at the kitchen table, gave him something to eat, although it upset and annoyed Frieder, and questioned him in detail about what happened, when it happened, and how he knew Franz's name.

The boy had seemed confused, distraught, and panicky to start with. But then he answered clearly and precisely. The facts fit. He did not contradict himself. He clearly and convincingly described how a Wehrmacht Lieutenant stepped in front of the little squad, presented Franz and appointed him as leader.

Karla reported again how often she had talked with Hubert about her father. "He could even remember in what way Daddy took off his glasses. He pulled the right bow forward with one hand and sort of twisted them off." It was a characteristic movement that tickled Karla when she was a little girl. "Daddy screwed off his glasses," she said and laughed herself silly each time.

Mathilde had accepted that no, there was no reasonable doubt. As usual Heidrun and Hermann were right. Better to make a painful break now than draw out the agony.

When they finally got to the front of the line and presented their case, the clerk, an older man with white hair and kindly eyes seemed to have no doubt either. Hermann knew him. They talked of old times and shared acquaintances. He presented Hubert who told his story clearly, without contradictions, and the clerk believed him.

"Apparently there is no second witness, if all your comrades are dead?" the clerk finally asked. Hubert shook his head silently. One could easily see how the horrific scene he had experienced went through his mind again. "Then it is needless to ask about dog tags?"

"We didn't have those in the Volkssturm anyway."

"But your husband must have had one?" The clerk glanced at Mathilde.

Yes, she thought, Franz had one like all soldiers, all SS people; the little tin tag hung around the neck so they could identify a man more easily in the event of his death or after having been wounded.

"I didn't know that," said Hubert. "In any case it was senseless to search for them after the mortar attack."

The clerk nodded. Hubert was a credible witness. He had obviously endured so much, and while Franz Tegge had not been reported missing in action or presumed dead or alive his death had now been attested properly. Normally the clerk would have had to wait a year before issuing the death certificate, but this hero's death had been proven.

The white-haired clerk signed the certificate, stamped the seal, and voiced his sympathy to Mathilde before asking, rather out of interest than suspicion, "Why the rush? Most find it difficult to come to grips with the death of a loved one. Is there someone else?"

Mathilde shook her head in vehement denial, perhaps a bit too vehement.

The clerk continued, "Do you have another reason then? Was the deceased with the police?"

"What are you accusing me of?"

"My wife and I suggested it." Hermann assumed his most impressive patriarchal manner and jumped to Mathilde's defense. "My sister-in-law would not have filed the request of her own initiative. She would have acted as most who come here, those poor, poor people. We thought it better to accept God's will." He bowed his head and quoted Paul's letter to the Romans, "For none of us lives to himself, and none dies to himself. For if we live, we live to the Lord; and if we die, we die to the Lord. Therefore, whether we live or die, we are the Lord's."

The clerk was bowled over, nodded sympathetically. He vigorously shook hands with the pastor and the lamentable widow. Mathilde hardly glanced at him but looked at her brother-in-law with reluctant thanks. She had put the death certificate with the other documents in the shopping bag and left the office.

Hermann began to sing Bach's "Now Let Us Bury the Dead," supported by Heidrun and Frieder. The Trimborns joined in with shy thin voices, and Mathilde sang with them while Hermann blessed the unadorned wooden cross. Suddenly she stopped. Tears that had welled up in her finally flowed, the tears which she had waited for since she left the registrar's office. Now, with the hymn, they came to her eyes. She squeezed Heidrun's hand, and her sister returned the gesture empathetically.

The Pirate had been sympathetic, too, and given her the whole day off even though she had asked for just a few hours to get the death certificate. So she had no way out when Hermann insisted she go with him to a friend and colleague who would loan him a cassock for the funeral. His had gone up in flames, along with his church and parsonage.

They had been walking through the summer day slowly, each lost in their thoughts. Mathilde felt Hermann was satisfied with her, and Heidrun would be happy that the funeral could take place. They would congratulate her for her strength of purpose, and she would ignore the stale taste left by their patronizing. She was like a tree or stone or roof at the end of winter when the snow melted and finally slipped off, a burden lifted from her.

She asked Hermann's friend if she could play the church organ for an hour. Hermann thought it a good idea and hoped music would bring her solace. Mathilde said nothing, but wondered. Solace? It wasn't about that at all. This was just a convenient opportunity, and she liked to play. She knew a woman who had just been to the registrar's office to be officially declared a widow would not be denied this favor, and she was right. The pastor unlocked the church and showed her to the gallery.

Slipping off the light summer shoes she had worn to the registrar's office, she trod on a few pedals to get a feel for them. The church filled with music. Almost without volition her hands pulled register stops, her fingers found the manuals, and she played a few runs in different tonal colors. The runs joined with the bass figures and wandered seemingly by themselves to a Bach fugue, to "Pachelbel's Canon," to preludes and variations.

Mathilde knew she played unskillfully, inelegant, and rough. It had been too long since she had had the chance to practice, and her hands had suffered too much from her work. She knew it, but she didn't care. She was alone and heard only what she wanted to hear, not what she really played.

Miss Nebenich had always reproached her for that: Mathilde would dream while playing and imagine she had a skill and virtuosity she would never attain. But little Mathilde didn't care if Miss Nebenich scolded her.

It was the same now, in this church. Franz's death, the worksite, the hunger and exhaustion, the fight with Lene; all of it dissolved in the music and flowed away on the melodies. She could not forget them, but they lost their intensity, significance, darkness, and gloom. Mathilde played and played and embraced her freedom, escaped the pain in her hands, the pressure that burdened her. She played even as the electricity in the neighborhood suddenly failed and the electric bellows no longer pumped air for the pipes; she played on for several minutes before noticing that no notes, no melody filled the church. Only the sounds of dry clacking on the keys and register pulls remained.

"No Mozart today?"

Mathilde was startled and slid to the foot of the small circular stairway that led to the organ seat. She was unpleasantly surprised someone had listened after all, had listened once again. She looked into the brown eyes under the wide-brimmed anthracite-colored hat. It was Baumgartner. As always, the artiste.

"Mozart doesn't play well on the organ." She almost added that every child knew that. She was more stand-offish than she wanted to be, yet still not enough.

"Sorry. I'm a low-brow."

His smile seemed carefree, nonchalant, and somewhat cocky to her. She had avoided him, could not tell him the truth. Also, she should not, would not, and did not want to talk with him about anything else either. Had she not just become a widow? And yet she could not walk away, could not leave him standing there. The music had made her vulnerable.

Finally she gave in. She asked herself, why not? I'm a widow now. I'm allowed to meet and speak with whoever I want; yet, she dallied at the edge of opportunity, at the edge of decision until finally she had to say something, anything. "How did you find me?"

"Your niece told me you were going to the bureau. I," he hesitated, "I followed you. I didn't want to approach you while you were with your brother-in-law. He doesn't especially like me, and I didn't want to risk being told to go away just to keep appearances. And just now . . . I didn't want to interrupt you while you were playing your music."

Mathilde detected some uneasiness in him when his speech faltered. That was unusual.

"Even if it wasn't Mozart?"

"Even if it wasn't Mozart. But it sounded like Mozart."

"You are just flattering me, for whatever reason."

"No." He looked earnestly into her eyes. "You play with soul, with joy. That is far more important than hitting every note."

Mathilde nodded. She did not, could not get into a discussion about music. She kept quiet. She waited. She hid in the passing of time and left the initiative to him.

"Come with me. I invite you to get coffee, real bean coffee; and don't try to tell me you can't. You cannot turn down that kind of invitation."

All possible uncertainty, embarrassment, or anxiety, if they existed at all, vanished and the amber-colored flecks in his eyes sparkled like always.

Soon they sat in a club on Kurfürstendamm, ate pastry and drank real bean coffee. Not only could Mathilde not have turned down such an invitation—she had not even considered it.

A sidewalk café on Kudamm. There was a lot left standing here; not everything, but a lot more than in Steglitz. Were it not for the destroyed Kaiser Wilhelm Memorial Church you could, if you chose your point of view cleverly, make a picture postcard on this lovely summer day that would be like a scene of Kudamm before the war.

In any event, Mathilde would not have been sitting with another man on her own in a café on Kurfürstendamm before the war, if she would have been here at all. She and Franz had always preferred going into nature.

Baumgartner expressed his sympathy for the death of her husband.

"Did Gerhild tell you something about that?" Mathilde had no idea why, but it just didn't seem right to her that he knew about it.

"The little one is innocent. I figured it out. I can add one and one. Anyway, I was there when your daughter burst in on us at the club."

For heaven's sake, thought Mathilde. The evening in the American bar appeared before her like a living picture; she smelled the heat, the sweat, the smoke, heard the musicians, the babel of voices, felt the alcohol, the giddiness, the rush of the dance.

"I know why you avoided me," Baumgartner continued.

What did Gerhild always call him? The magician? Could he conjure her thoughts in his mind and speak them into the airy warm space between them?

Baumgartner lit a cigarette thoughtfully, almost ceremoniously, almost as if he did not want to say what he was about to say or, perhaps, what he had to say? "But we were dancing, nothing more. There will never be more than that, certainly not."

Nothing more than a dance? Of course not. What else? Still, Mathilde felt the stab of pain, then instinctively, in the next moment, reproached herself and shook her head. What had you imagined, you silly cow? It could be nothing more. It wasn't permitted. It would not be anything more. Everything else was Karla's romantic imagination, the illusions of dreams and the nonsense of a fourteen-year-old.

Mathilde stirred in her empty cup, Baumgartner smoked. Everything seemed to have been said, in full. Or maybe not? They sat there, two among many. A couple?

No, she corrected herself hastily. They simply sat there like the many others around them on the postwar Kudamm. Friends, cliques, families enjoying the summer afternoon. Everyone here made the effort to come out of the wreckage of their houses into the sidewalk cafés and to stroll about. They were surprisingly well-dressed, vital looking people who, with the defiance of the survivors, enjoyed their life, sun and leisure; and Mathilde did not believe a bit of it.

Sometime later she raised her eyes and attempted to smile at the man across from her, the other man, the stranger, the friend. She couldn't maintain the silence amid the lively, zestful, animated background noise and tried to make contact. She gazed into eyes that intently, forthrightly and inquisitively observed her, like she was under a microscope.

"So you believe the boy from the Volkssturm?"

His question finally gave Mathilde a chance to talk, and it was as if the flood gates opened. She told him of her doubts, her depression, the emptiness, the sorrow. She spoke about Heidrun and Hermann, how they insisted on creating fact. On and on she talked, and Baumgartner listened, did not interrupt, and seemed to soak up every word she spoke.

When Mathilde fell silent again she felt the change. She felt light, and secure, yet at the same time she thought herself a fraud because she did not mention that Franz had been a policeman, and the kind of policeman he had been. She did not dare to. She could not bring herself to speak it out loud.

Franz was dead. He should rest in peace. Why dump Franz's crimes, deeds, and past on Baumgartner? Why disrupt this special moment with something she had no responsibility for? She knew it was deception; that she should be honest, but she did not speak. She was too much of a coward.

Unexpectedly Baumgartner took her hand, and his hand seemed to her like her own. "I want to say goodbye to you."

"Goodbye?" There it was again, the pang, the blow, the stab, only deeper and more hurtful than she had expected. It was worse than when Baumgartner said there would be nothing more between them than a dance. Yet she said to herself this is why it is best to say nothing more of Franz. He should remember me, me as I am, and not the widow of a Gestapo officer.

"Yes. We are moving on. We took down our stuff for performing today. And since you were not at the work site . . ."

Mathilde was awhirl with contradiction. She felt pain and, at the same moment, bliss. He had sought her out especially to say goodbye. He did not want to leave without a word, a comment. There was a bond between them much stronger than a dance. She knew it; he knew it. Even if he did not want to admit it, he felt it.

"We have to go farther, to search further." He held her hand like a valuable, tender gift. "Maybe we can still find a few people from our families, our *kumpania*, who have survived. We have received reports."

"From your family?" For a second Mathilde had the wild, absurd hope that Baumgartner's closest family had not gone the way of so many others, that they had somehow had come through it. He dashed her hope quickly.

"No." He retreated and pulled his hand away. His eyes hardened to burning suns, merciless and infinitely remote. "There will be no news of my family. They were turned into smoke, part of the air."

Mathilde wished she could help him; that she could somehow lighten or alleviate his burden, sorrow, and anger. Without hesitation she stretched her hand out and pulled his toward her as if it belonged to her. She held his hand, and he did not resist. He gazed at her as if he were starved and she was as his last and only sustenance. If Mathilde needed confirmation of their bond, this was it; a pledge, an oath, a vow.

The amber-colored flecks in his eyes shimmered like polished pebbles under the surface of a gently flowing stream. After what seemed to Mathilde to be an eternity, he took his hand from hers, carefully and tenderly as if he feared hurting her. He turned his eyes, lit a cigarette and watched the smoke. "If you could taste my heart, you would die— so much poison is in it."

He motioned for the waitress and looked again at Mathilde who felt as if the blood in her body had frozen. She struggled to understand as he went on, "I am happy I met you. You've helped me understand my sister, Djidjo. She had fallen in love with a *gadsche* which is why we stayed. We should have gone on. . . ." He broke off, but even so Mathilde understood, and she was ashamed of herself for still not being honest.

The waitress brought the bill, Baumgartner paid it and gave a large tip. Mathilde looked at him and said, "If I can do something, anything to heal . . ."

He smiled warmly and heartfelt. His hate was gone, swept away, eradicated, and Mathilde again felt bound to him in spite of her lies, her shame.

He tore himself away, jumped up and set his hat straight. He turned to leave, then turned back one more time. "If ever there was anyone who could, then it would be you. But, sadly . . ." He shrugged his shoulders and walked away. He had been gone so quickly that, to Mathilde, it had seemed like flight.

The hymn rang out and swept the memory of her last encounter with the Gypsy away. The summer wind painted silver green reflections on the low box-tree hedges that bordered a few of the cemetery paths. "Here he was in fear, there, however, he will recover; in eternal joy and gladness shine like the sun."

Here he was in fear . . . It occurred to Mathilde how well the song fit Franz, how well Hermann had chosen it. Tears still ran down her cheeks. She still squeezed Heidrun's hand, and Karla squeezed hers. She realized her daughter was finally crying, too. She offered her a handkerchief from her jacket pocket, but Karla shook her head slightly and showed Mathilde she already had her own. The two smiled at each other almost conspiratorially and sniffled in synchrony.

"The Lord preserve thy going out and coming in from now until eternity. The peace of the Lord be with our sleeping one and with us all. Amen." Hermann blessed those present, blessed the grave, blessed the cross yet again, and ended the funeral service. He expressed his condolences to Mathilde and Karla. Heidrun embraced and hugged her sister, then embraced and hugged her niece.

The Trimborns shook their hands, murmured words of comfort and said goodbye. Frieder disappeared as well, quiet, earnest, and tense. Heidrun shoved her younger children forward; Gerhild, Horst and little Heinrich lay the flowers they held on the grave in front of Uncle Franz's cross.

Karla joined Hubert as Mathilde stepped to the grave and asked the others for a moment to be alone with Franz, with her memories, and with her sorrow.

* * *

Suddenly the face appeared again. It peered through the bushes behind the grave where she first thought she saw it. Go away, she thought. I don't want to see you. Go away, I'm not crazy. The face did not vanish, and Mathilde shut her eyes, willing it to go away as it had before, but it didn't work. She shook her head. It's a mirage, a mistaken identity like at the registrar's; but no matter what she tried the face remained. It was motionless, and she stared, hypnotized, spellbound.

The face spoke. Its voice was one she had not heard for months, one that was as familiar to her as her own reflection in a mirror. The light Berlin baritone that could be so caustic yet so warm and soft and tender. It called her name. It called to her, and suddenly she saw hands that motioned her to come. The voice, the motions were compelling, and she obeyed. She could do nothing else.

"Franz." She could not believe it.

"Didn't expect to see me, huh?"

She did not understand his tone. She could not understand what was happening. "No," she whispered and stammered. She felt like she was in a dream, a nightmare. She knew something was wrong but couldn't figure out what.

"I wanted to see what it would be like to attend my own funeral."

Now it came to her. Franz shouldn't be here. He was in the Oderbruch, torn into a thousand pieces by a mortar round. He was dead. She had just said goodbye to him and set a cross on the family gravesite; his cross. He was dead, but he stood in front of her. He spoke. That couldn't be; it's all wrong, completely wrong.

"You sure consoled yourself quickly. At least you had the decency to not bring him to the cemetery with you."

She was mystified. "Who?"

"Your Gypsy."

Beware, there is loathing in his voice, she thought. It can't be him. He never spoke like that. But how did he know; does he know about Baumgartner? How does he imagine I consoled myself with him? She felt exposed. Had she sinned, if not in deed then in words and thoughts, in her emotions? It's not true, she told herself, you're imagining things. She took control of herself and stretched her hand toward the face, toward the man, but he moved away. A ghost, it must be a ghost.

"Couldn't get me in the ground fast enough, could you? Well, the two of you probably can hardly wait anymore, can't you?" The ghost talked. It said out loud what she had thought in secret. Therefore it had to be a ghost!

"No." Anguish and contradiction rang out in her voice, but protest against a ghost is useless. "Are you a ghost?" she whispered close to panic, to hysteria.

"No." Now he actually laughed. "No, I am no ghost. Go ahead, grab hold of me." He came a step closer, took her hand and laid it on his arm.

She felt his warm soft skin. She pinched into his flesh until Franz softly yelped in pain.

"Is it really you?"

"Yes, it is really me."

"But . . . ?" Hubert's story; Karla, Heidrun, Hermann, the clerk . . . Were they all wrong?

"Don't worry, it's alright with me. Franz Tegge was out of chances. No future." He pulled her deeper in the bushes. "I have to be careful. If someone should find me here . . ."

His unexpected move caused her to stumble, but she kept her balance and her distance, physical and emotional. If someone found him, then everything would happen that she thought death had spared him from: arrest, trial, punishment. But in this moment, she could not, did not want to think about that. "We all believed the boy," she defended herself. "Even Heidrun and Hermann. If they had not been convinced I would never have gone to the bureau. We would never have held this funeral service."

"Calm down." Franz put his arm around Mathilde's shoulders and drew her to him. She started, and jerked for a split second, but Franz strengthened his pull and she gave in. She laid her head on his chest, shut her eyes, and breathed in the smell of his shirt and his skin. She inhaled the familiar scent of her man, the unmistakable scent of her husband. She inhaled and calmed herself. She relaxed. She was suddenly happy in the familiar embrace and the familiar scent.

"I don't blame you," Franz said. "The boy from the Volkssturm was amazingly close to the truth. Frieder told me everything."

"Frieder?"

"He stumbled across me once, found me by accident, but he seems to have kept that close to his chest."

"He knew all this time that you were alive?" Frieder's dazed stares, even his tension had not been sorrow, but deceit, perfidy, and secrecy?

"Yes." Franz nodded approvingly. You could rely on a German boy. "And he told me what you were doing. Even with the Gypsy."

"I did not betray you." Mathilde almost screamed it.

"Shush." Franz silenced her with a rough gesture. "Are you trying to send me to prison?"

"I have not been unfaithful to you," she whispered intensely, "Really not!" Yet she was ashamed of herself, aware that now she *was* lying. There was more between Camillo Baumgartner and her than there ever had been between her and Franz.

Yet she did not really lie. Nothing had happened between them, nothing would happen. Baumgartner had moved on. He said goodbye and left. Only memories . . . of a dance, of a campfire in Marzahn, of a cellar with an out-of-tune piano, and Mozart remained; these were all that was left of him. "The man saved Karla's life. I just wanted to show my thanks. Nothing more."

"But you went out with him."

"Yes." Mathilde wiggled out of Franz's arm.

"And he brought you groceries?"

"Did Frieder tell you all that? You had a proper little spy."

Franz ignored her remark, the quiet sarcasm, and the light reproach in her voice. "It is true though, isn't it?"

"Yes, I went out with him." Mathilde trembled. She didn't understand it all, yet understood it all too well. Franz was jealous. He wanted and needed to rely on her. If not on her, if not on his wife, then on whom?

"Nothing really happened? In that part you are not lying?" Mathilde detected the anger, the fear in Franz's voice.

"I did not lie," she answered, firmly and clearly.

Franz hesitated purposefully, testing her. "Good, I believe you." He again put his arm around Mathilde's shoulders.

She immediately broke free knowing that it irritated Franz, but she didn't care. She stepped back to the wooden cross. "We don't need this anymore," she said and wrestled it from the ground. She started to break it. "We can use the wood to make you some soup, or a few potatoes," and thought about not having a ration card for Franz. She would have to run back to the registrar's office and cancel his death certificate or she couldn't get a card. But that was unthinkable. He would have to hide. She dared not go to the bureau. Mathilde's thoughts whirled in her mind like windup tin toys out of control.

Franz hurried to her and pulled her back into the underbrush. His chin pointed to the cross in her hand. "Put it back."

"What?"

"Leave the cross standing."

"Why?"

"It helps me. You did me a favor even if you didn't know it." He smiled wryly at her. "It's best it remains. You've never been a convincing liar. Had you known I was still alive . . ." Franz nudged her lightly on the nose. "Now no one will ever look for me again."

The tin figures in her mind stopped whirling, and she became quiet. She understood. Something got through to her and brought clarity where only fog had been before. Her husband had gone from being the hunter to being the hunted. And naturally, nobody looked for a dead man. So simple, so perfect. "What are your plans now?"

"I am going to America."

"What?"

"I am going to America."

To America? What did Franz want to do there? "You can't speak a word of English?"

"I can learn."

"Yes, but . . ."

"I will start all over again. I am not too old for that."

"But how?"

Franz face glowed triumphant. He told of Herter, how he searched for the Nazis; he boasted of his success. The payoff? A new name and a little house somewhere in the Midwest; a little white house with a red roof and blue shutters. He grabbed Mathilde by the shoulders. "Come with me! That is why I am here."

"With you? To America?"

"Yes. You are my wife. When I have turned them in, I will get you and Karla and then off we go over the big pond, to where no one knows us. Where everything that was no longer matters."

Mathilde saw excitement flash in Franz's eyes, excitement she had not seen for so long. He was optimistic with the promise of adventure that only came to him when he discovered new hiking routes across country. Get off the beaten path. What he never did, except when hiking . . .

"Yes. What do you think will happen to me if I'm caught? My life here is over, but in America? Think what it would mean for Karla; the opportunities she would have."

"You want to leave everything behind?"

"What is holding us here? Look around. Everything is *kaputt*. Over there they would give us another chance. We have, after all, learned to work hard. You will see, we can do it." He stroked her arms that hung down like they were no longer Mathilde's. "Say yes! Come with me to America. You, Karla, me, we are a family. We belong together. Together nothing can defeat us."

"No!"

"What?"

"No." It just slipped out again, and she hesitated, then repeated once more, "No. I'm not coming with you." She shook her head and knew why she said it. "I can't."

"You can't?" Franz slyly squinted his eyes. "You don't want to!"

"Do you really believe you can simply leave your life in Germany behind you? Do you believe you have the right to do that?"

"Why not?" He had no idea what she was saying.

"You've seen the pictures; bulldozers shoving mounds of corpses into the grave." Mathilde could not go on, sickened by a wave of sorrow, loathing, revulsion, and horror that swept over her, pulled her down, swept her along. "You knew about all that. You sent people to the camps."

Franz weakly said, "I obeyed orders," not really believing it himself. As if his excuse did not suffice, he continued, "Look at me." He forced her look him in the eye. "Yes. I could have refused. I didn't have to transfer to the Gestapo, but then I wouldn't have been promoted, we wouldn't have gotten the apartment, or trips to the Baltic, or been able to buy a gramophone, and . . ." Accusingly, he added, "You never said no to any of those things. Please, you must believe me. Please. I am not a monster," he said, imploring as if he was kneeling.

"I am not the one you should ask for pardon," she said.

"At first it really was only criminals, spies, and saboteurs." he said.

"All the Jews, the Gypsies, and I can't imagine who else. They were not all spies and saboteurs," she replied, shaking her head.

"When I understood it was too late. I could not believe it, just like you. How could German police, German officers be capable of something like that? As what was happening became clear to me there was nothing I could do. If I'd said anything, I would have been tossed into a concentration camp, too."

Mathilde heard the despair in Franz's voice and said softly, "I know. I know you are no monster. You know I believe that." Her husband had never been a Nazi. He believed in God his entire life, not the Führer, not the Party or the German race. At most he believed in doing his duty, like so many others. "Still," she persisted, "it won't work. It is impossible."

"What happens if I turn myself in? I wind up in prison. I might even be executed." Mathilde gasped aloud, and Franz quickly talked on, undeterred. "In any case I have no possibility of atoning for what I have done, not here, no chance at all; but over there . . . ?"

Mathilde hesitated. She looked at Franz, looked for a long time. "Yes, perhaps," she finally said. "Maybe it is the right thing for you to do. It probably is. I hope it works out for you, but for me? I will stay here." Without being able to say exactly why, she knew beyond doubt that she would never, ever go with him and disappear, no matter what he might offer, even a palace.

Franz slumped but was not surprised. He had expected it. "You're lying to me. It is because of the Gypsy."

"No," she said quickly, then thought and added, "Yes. You are right. But not in the way that you think."

"What then?"

"It just won't work. It would be wrong." She could not explain what had changed between them. She searched for words to tell Franz the truth—he had a right to know, but the words . . . the words would not come. How could she explain what had happened between her and Baumgartner? She didn't know herself. It was intangible, indescribable, but nonetheless there. It existed, a living, breathing, feeling presence even though it was likely she would never see Baumgartner again. He was still there. He was stronger than her wedding vows to Franz. "So much more than houses have been destroyed."

"I understand. You've dumped me. Simple as that. Times have changed and the formerly persecuted is somehow better than a has-been policeman who had the bad luck to be on the losing side."

"No, you are wrong. That isn't it," she said but she could not get through to him. Her protest was weak and tame and probably sounded more like agreeing than disagreeing.

What Franz heard was rejection, just as clearly as if she yelled at him and beat him on the chest with her fists. "Goodbye," he said, wanting to disappear in the underbrush. He paused once more. "I have but one last request. Let me rest in peace. I'm dead. It is best for all of us if it stays that way." One last time he stroked her cheek with an excruciating, infinitely lonely gesture. Then he vanished without a trace, just like he had never been there.

Mathilde had not taken part in his farewell, she had observed it like a spectator. After a time, she turned around, returned to the grave and rammed the cross that she still held deeply back into the ground.

TWENTY SEVEN

The knocking did not stop. He tried to ignore it, but it drilled into his brain, into his pain. He pulled the stinking blanket he had found, who knows where, over his head trying to escape from the noise, the light, the morning and his consciousness. The knocking did not stop.

Finally a barely audible voice cut through the pounding and stabbed into his eardrum. "Uncle Franz, wake up. Uncle Franz!"

Frieder? What the devil was *he* doing here? "Go away. Scram!" It sounded more like a bark, a growl, or a yelp than a human voice.

Frieder recognized the voice anyway. "Uncle Franz, I'm glad you're there."

Yeah, I am here, thought Franz and answered with another grunt. Yeah, I am here but I would rather be somewhere else, totally different, far away, not even in this world.

"Uncle Franz, are you okay?"

No, he wasn't okay. He was in bad shape. The bottle of bad booze he had bought in the black market last night and had drunk, more or less straight down, had rewarded him with a fierce pounding head, nausea, and a fuzzy, clammy sensation on his tongue. He rarely drank, and last night the booze had put him out of commission. It was still paralyzing his brain.

That was what Franz wanted. He wanted his numbed mind feeling nothing, hearing nothing, thinking nothing; only to wait until morning, or noon, or night, or morning when he would go to Herter and end it all, or not. Maybe he would just do nothing. He would pull the cover

over his head and do nothing. Now there was this pesky kid at his door. He ought to vanish, go away. How the devil did he know where he had crawled to anyway?

The car where Franz spent the first nights had been taken away along with the rubble it was buried in. As the removal brigade got closer, he took his paltry belongings and moved to a hole where he had nabbed two Communists years before. A small gap in a cellar wall led to a little niche that had originally been part of the house next door but was no longer accessible from there. That's why it did not show up on any floor plans. The cellar room in front of the niche was full of trash and junk that hid the gap. Franz had accidentally found a pretty secure hideout. So how on earth did this annoying youngster find it?

"Uncle Franz, come on, get up!"

The brat had no mercy. Obnoxious as hell. He wouldn't give up. Franz threw off the blanket, shuffled to the improvised door that he had secured with an iron bar, removed it and shoved the door open.

Frieder pushed in and looked around the tiny hideout. The only light came through a crack in the wall. "You look awful," he said. "Has something happened?"

Franz turned on the boy, not even thinking about answering him. "How did you find me?"

The boy saw the schnaps bottle that lay next to Franz's chair and the situation was clear, at least to Frieder. "You were careless," he answered. "I followed you. You didn't notice."

"Yesterday?" An unpleasant, mortifying feeling of embarrassment came over Franz, like a faux pas in his mother-in-law's home, the Captain's wife with the French name. He did not want a witness to his defeat.

"No. A while back. Just after you moved out of the car."

"You knew about that, too?"

"You didn't expect that of me, huh?"

No, Franz really had not expected that of Frieder. He had actually not noticed anything, but it didn't matter. No matter who knew about him now, it was all the same, it was no longer important. "Why are you here?" He pushed the boy aside, grabbed a water container and drank greedily. He splashed the rest of the water on his face.

"You shouldn't drink so much."

Franz thought the kid sounded just like his father, the oh-so righteous pastor Hermann. Damn it all, why couldn't this pain in the neck just leave him in peace?

"I thought we fought together. And I haven't seen you for a few days. You didn't show up at any of our meeting spots. I kept looking for messages from you—Franz is okay and living with Aunt Frieda, remember?"

Was he seeing things, or did the little devil actually wink at him? "We don't have any more meetings. Not since the mission was completed. I told you that." Franz held his head. Gall rose in his throat. He must not, could not get upset.

"Don't you want to fight any more? Are you giving up?" That was the end of winking. Frieder passionately whispered, barely able to speak. "Do you want to break your oath? *Meine Ehre heißt Treue...*" he started to recite the SS code of honor—my honor is called loyalty.

"Take a look around, kid. The war is over. We lost. It's all finished. The oath doesn't mean anything. There is no more struggle."

The boy's eyes widened in horror. Such zeal, such enthusiasm and loyalty, Franz thought. All of it wasted.

Frieder did not give up so easily. "What about Sturmbannführer Matthus and your comrades? I was supposed to hand them the letter just a little while ago. Secret orders of the Reich. They are still fighting, aren't they? You're still a member, aren't you?"

"Matthus?" Franz laughed softly and discovered that even the roots of his hair hurt. "Do you know what Matthus is planning? He wants to get out of here. He wants nothing to do with the fight, do you understand? He wants to disappear to South America. The only thing he is organizing is his escape, and I am supposed to help with it."

"That coward!" Frieder declared with fury. "He'll get his." A Sturmbannführer deserting? Mindboggling. The boy's eyes bore into Franz with the glare of a fanatic who would hang any disloyal scum from the nearest lamp post without blinking. "Are you going with him? Are you helping him, this betrayer of our beloved fatherland?"

Franz looked at him. So much hate, he thought. "No. I am not helping him. I would if I could, but I cannot."

Frieder almost spit his accusation, "Then you are just as much a traitor."

Traitor, thought Franz bitterly. What was left to betray?

"I did not expect that of you," Frieder whimpered in disappointment. "Really. Not of you." Contempt and revulsion shook the boy like a seizure.

Franz knew he had to pull himself together. Even if there was nothing left to betray, even if nothing mattered he had to intervene for his nephew's sake. He grabbed Frieder by the lapels of his jacket and suddenly realized that it had once belonged to him. So Mathilde started giving away his things, he thought. Well, why not? They belonged to a dead man, but this dead man still had a responsibility. A responsibility to this foolish boy.

He forced Frieder to look him in the eye. "What Matthus is doing is the only sensible thing left to do. The battle is over. The war is lost. All that is left is to survive. Do you understand? There is no more *Reich*, no more *Volksgemeinschaft*, no more *Partei*. Whatever they taught you in that school means nothing. We have to make it through all of this. All of us. That is the most important thing to do now. Do you understand?" He released Frieder as pain wracked his head, the desperate appeal he had just made to the kid echoing in his skull. Survive. That was what was important, for Frieder, not for himself. Franz wanted the boy to understand, needed him to understand.

"Okay. I understand. We have to hide. Go underground. Save the most valuable members of our community so the idea survives."

Franz shook his head in dismay, disbelief, and resignation. The dumb kid understood nothing, absolutely nothing, even though he had seen the chaos, the destruction and misery for himself. Still, it meant nothing to him. But maybe it was a start, maybe he could save the kid if he could at least get Frieder to stop fighting and lay low or, if not that, escape.

"Can I do something to help Matthus?" Frieder asked.

"You?"

"Yes. You said you would help him if you could but you cannot. Maybe I can so that what we believe in can survive."

Franz laughed, a joyless, toneless laugh like the clang of a cracked bell.

"And you," Frieder went on. "You belong to the group, don't you? You want to escape too, right? You can't hide forever."

Good, thought Franz. Very perceptive, very logical. The kid is bright enough, he'll make his way in the world but this, right now? This was too much for the boy to handle. "You are fourteen. What do you think you can do?"

"I have my contacts."

He's cocky, thought Franz, like only a fourteen-year-old can be. A kid who believes he has the world by the tail. Enviable, maybe, but so hopeless, foolhardy, futile. "Contacts?" He tried to minimize the sarcasm in his voice. "Allied soldiers who buy belt buckles, party symbols, and swastika armbands from you?" Franz grinned at the surprise on the boy's face. "You are not the only one that spies on the other. So, now. How could your 'contacts' help? Go home, boy. Leave me alone."

"Is this nothing?" Frieder pulled a Walther PPK out of his pocket. "It's not a piece of junk like you find in the rubble. It works." He pulled the magazine out of the weapon. "Look here. Ammo."

"Are you crazy? Do you know what will happen if the Russians or the Amis find you with that? They will stand you against a wall and shoot you." He took a quick step toward Frieder trying to take the pistol from him, but the boy dodged.

"Don't worry. I wouldn't normally carry this around, but I thought you were in trouble."

Franz groaned and held his aching head. "Trouble. You're going to have more trouble than you can handle. Give me that thing. Now." He stuck his hand out.

Frieder calmly stuck the Walther back in his pocket. "I can get more weapons. Anything you want. Even hand grenades."

"I don't need weapons. Forget about weapons, the war is over. How many times do I have to tell you?"

"Sure. I understand." Frieder grinned. "What do you need? Passports? Visas?" He's a kid playing a game, Franz thought. A damn big child in a damn dangerous game that is going to get him killed. "Naturally those are a bit more difficult," Frieder continued, "but if my buddies or the GIs can't get it, I can always go to the Gypsy."

"The Gypsy?" Suddenly it was very, very quiet until Franz, perplexed, repeated, "The Gypsy?" He sounded puzzled even though he knew exactly which Gypsy Frieder was talking about.

"The guy that always visits Aunt Mathilde and always brings something with him. Groceries, cigarettes, and the like. I'm sure he has a source for other things."

"Oh. Oh yes."

Franz barely contained the hatred that raged from the core of his being like a caged animal slamming against the bars to escape. *The guy that always visited Mathilde.* Mathilde, *his* wife.

"Don't you want to tell Aunt Mathilde you are still alive?" The boy tried to anticipate what Franz was thinking. "This guy wants something from her. I have said that all along, and now she thinks she is a widow . . . ."

Franz made an unconscious gesture and the boy broke off. Stop. *Stop,* Franz screamed to himself. "Yeah, yeah, whatever you think."

Frieder did not understand why his uncle was reacting this way, so for a little while they just looked at each other. Then Frieder blinked and looked down. Uncle Franz certainly knew what he was doing, didn't he? Besides, there was something more important for Frieder. His mission. He wanted to help the group around Sturmbannführer Matthus escape so they could build an underground organization in South America or wherever. It was the task he had yearned for. "So, what do you need, Uncle Franz?"

"You really want to bring in the Gypsy?"

"I know they are untrustworthy trash, and we would have to keep close watch on him but he can be useful. We have to get help where we can. We can't afford to be picky."

"No, no," Franz replied. "I have nothing against using the Gypsy, nothing at all." He would have to offer the Gypsy money, he thought, a lot of money. No matter. He could get that from Matthus without much trouble. Then, when it is all done, that damned Gypsy will be caught up by the Amis along with all the others. Franz played the plan through his mind and indulged himself for a moment with the happy vision of this scum who stole his wife from him going for the deal. "Do you really think this guy can get passes and a truck?"

"Passes for sure. But a truck? I don't know," Frieder said, doubtful. "That's a large order, but we have to try."

"Not we. You." He dared not encounter this guy. He knew the Gypsy would remember him from their first meeting when he had escaped capture *and* would realize Franz had recognized him as well. "I cannot go out where I can be spotted right now. It's too dangerous."

"What do I tell him that I need the truck for?"

"You will think of something. It has to be done quickly. Tomorrow evening at the latest." Panic shot through Franz's brain. What if it was already too late? Had Herter already rounded them up? Nervously he rubbed his face and eyes with both hands. He had to call Herter. Somehow he had to delay him. Maybe he could get him to wait until he had a definite place and time, a when and where for all the Nazis to be caught just as they were about to escape.

If it all worked, he thought, Mathilde would see that her fine Mister Gypsy was a common thug who helped hunted criminals escape while Franz delivered them to justice. Maybe she would reconsider and come with him to America; come with him to America and the little white house with blue shutters, or green or yellow shutters. Whatever she wanted. As far as he was concerned, she could paint the house all the colors of the rainbow.

Off with you boy, hurry." Franz pushed Frieder to the gap. "If you pull this off," he said proudly, "you will have earned yourself a medal."

TWENTY EIGHT

Mathilde passed buckets up and down the line—full down, empty up, full down, empty up—a monotonous, unconscious, painful routine. She said not a word. She just passed along the buckets, one full down and one empty up, on and on. The women around her chattered and laughed, but Mathilde said nothing. Even the Warhorse and Krespe joked with her and for once they were friendly, not malicious. If she wanted to sell more silverware on the black market they had selling tips for her, but Mathilde did not answer. She just passed the buckets along; silent, alone, unapproachable.

Earlier she had asked Schall to put her in another group away from Lene Behrendt. Shall understood and gave her a nod. Fights among his workers were a daily thing. He was surprised about Tegge and Behrendt who seemed to be close, but he would never understand women. For the time being he sent Behrendt to work with the wagons hauling away debris. Tegge looked like she would collapse at any moment.

Mathilde passed buckets along and remained dreary, unconscious and mute until finally the work day ended. She took her shopping bag with the empty tin for buttered bread—the empty tin which Franz, the once dead and now living Franz who haunted her thoughts, had carried to work each day—and an empty beer bottle for water and lumbered off in the direction of home. But first she would stop at Färber's, the produce store, where hopefully she could get something that was on her ration card.

Leaving the mountains of rubble she suddenly saw Lene standing alone looking at her. She fought her first impulse to run away. She stopped and stood just like Lene. They looked each other in the eye, and Mathilde saw something beyond all the disbelief, all the revulsion. What she saw was melancholy. Sorrow.

Sorrow? Did Lene regret their lost friendship, as Mathilde did? Neither spoke a word; soon Lene turned and walked away. Mathilde's shoulders, her head, her hands hung slack and almost lifeless as she went on. She was deluding herself.

"Mama." After a few steps the bright though raspy voice of a girl cut through the tangled mass of mixed thought and suppressed emotion that Mathilde carried with her, making each step a grind.

"What are you doing here?" Mathilde made no effort to conceal her surprise.

Karla ran up to her trying unsuccessfully to sound happy. "I thought I would meet you after work today."

"You have never done that before."

"Aren't you glad to see me?"

Mathilde thought Karla looked confused, upset. "Sure," she said but she felt uneasy. Something had happened. "What's going on?"

"Nothing, why? I just happened to come by."

"Really? Just happened to?"

"Don't you believe me?"

"Honestly, no. But if you don't want to tell me, then drop it. I am too tired to try to drag something out of you."

"It is nothing." Karla linked arms with her mother. "I just wanted to be with you. I thought you would like that."

"Thank you." Mathilde wondered if she might think the girl upset because of her own distress.

Karla tried to start over. "Can you guess who I just met?"

No, Mathilde thought, I am not wrong. Something is going on with her. "No," she said as casually as she could. "Who did you meet?"

"Mr. Baumgartner's troupe. They are moving on."

"I know." Karla looked surprised and Mathilde explained, "Mr. Baumgartner told me goodbye. Is that why you came? To tell me that?"

Karla did not answer right away. Fear rushed through her all over again . . . .

The racing coach pulled by four jet-black horses, a figure with clothes flying in the wind is sitting on the coachbox yelling and cracking a whip; advancing on her. It is the big woman with black hair, as before. She comes nearer, high up on the coachbox, but it isn't four horses, only one, and the fine coach is more of a sorry makeshift wagon.

The horse blows its lips and stops right next to Karla. The woman knocks out her pipe and climbs down from the seat. She comes right up to Karla and holds her frozen in place with her glare. Karla cannot move as if she were hexed, and Keja mumbles something in a strange language.

"What do you want from me?" Karla stammers.

"Damn you! Damn you through all eternity. May your womb be barren and childless. May your family die within you. So shall it be or I will die here and now!"

Karla is terrified, certain that her legs will collapse in the moment and she will fall to the ground like an empty grain sack. Unconsciously she speaks aloud, or perhaps the woman reads her mind, "Why are you so hateful?"

"Your mother has bewitched Camillo, seduced and bewitched him. He is not himself."

"Please, leave me alone. You are moving away, far away where nobody can do anything to you."

"He stays. We are moving on and he is staying. He was to come along, then suddenly he is staying." The venom in her voice rushes through Karla from head to toe. Keja strengthens her curse, the *armaya,* by spitting at Karla's feet. She climbs back on her wagon. "Your mother shall be devoured by the rubble if she does not free Camillo. Tell her that." She clicks her tongue, snaps the reins, dashes off . . .

"That woman, Keja, believes Mr. Baumgartner is staying because of you," Karla said to her mother in a sober, almost mocking tone, finishing the brief tale about her encounter with Keja and trying to keep the fearful encounter at a safe arm's length. Mathilde felt giddy, and a light tingle flew through her. What if it was true? She wondered. And what if she had not been wrong with her impression of Lene either? If . . .

"I'm glad that woman is gone. She scared me." Karla kicked a stone along in front of her as she spoke.

"Me, too."

"You know she cursed you?" Karla's voice trembled. "She said that you would be swallowed by the rubble if you didn't free Mr. Baumgartner. . . ."

Mathilde lovingly stroked her daughter's arm. "She wants you to worry. Her curse has no meaning. It isn't real. It cannot work at all."

"She predicted Daddy's death a long time before I met Hubert."

That proves Keja is a liar, Mathilde thought. "Don't worry about the silly curse. It has no meaning. Mr. Baumgartner did not stay behind on my account. Why would he?"

"Because he is in love with you. And you with him."

"Don't talk nonsense," Mathilde snapped at her daughter with a fierceness that could have toppled a mountain.

Karla stopped abruptly, looked at her mother with eyes wide in amazement, and then grinned as if saying, *gotcha*!

Mathilde saw her daughter's grin and heard the echo of her own words, of her brusque tone. She hugged Karla to her, hoping to erase roughness with tenderness while looking over her shoulder into space. "Child, what are you thinking?"

* * *

He looked as lonely as a lightning bug in space Mathilde thought when she saw him. He was sitting at his fire in front of a solitary tent surrounded by a bare landscape. Baumgartner was smoking—of course he was—but other than that he did nothing. It looked like he had been ready to leave when he just decided to sit there, maybe forever. It was comical, and she smiled realizing she looked comical, too. She held flowers in her hand to give to a man. Her, a woman!

Instead of standing in line for groceries she followed an inspiration and bought flowers. It seemed completely natural and appropriate at the time but now, as she reached the bleak Gypsy campground, the idea of coming to Baumgartner with flowers seemed absurd. Suddenly she lost her courage. What was she doing here? What was she looking for?

She debated turning around and leaving when she realized he had already seen her. She was drawn to him like a magnet, this man who looked so lonesome and so vulnerable.

He said nothing as she approached. Mathilde stopped short. Something was different with him, not like the first time she had come. Why? Why was she afraid? Keja, the pipe smoking giant, had left. She would not threaten her any more. Nonetheless she felt frightened as she looked at him.

"Mrs. Tegge," the Gypsy finally said.

He sounded unfriendly, even dismissive to her, or maybe it just struck her that way. Yes, that must be it. She had been imagining things because she was afraid of being rejected, like with Lene. Why would he do that? Why treat her badly in any way even if he had not stayed behind because of her?

* * *

Camillo blinked in the sunlight. It was déjà vu with Mathilde standing right there where a few hours before her nephew had stood. He had the feeling he was frozen in place, but that was not the case. He had gotten up and gone out. He had talked with people and arranged things, yet at the same time in another part of his consciousness those few hours had been frozen, stopped like a broken clock.

The faces he had seen blurred, flowed, interwove one with the other in familiar similarities. Was his mind playing tricks on him? He did not know and did not care. Was it audacity or stupidity that brought her here? Could he have been that wrong about her? Was she really sly and cunning? Or could it be that she had no idea; that she did not know at all? That had to be it. No other explanation made sense. If she knew she would not have come here. She wasn't cold-blooded, or jaded. He realized that, in truth, it did not matter either way. It did not change a thing.

The shock of the boy's arrival still held him in its sway. Keja and the others had packed and were ready to move, ready to take up their lives again. With their status as the persecuted, the victims, they could move freely across the country, trade, make music, and perform their arts. They could search for those who might have managed to survive, and he had planned to go with them in the hopeless hope of finding Djidjo, of finding Sandro. The thought of them almost made Camillo break down. Franz Tegge was dead. The butcher lived no more. He did not need to hunt him anymore. He would have liked to kill Tegge with his own hands, but it was what it was. It was okay. So he thought.

Then the boy had come to him.

At first he had been happy. He thought the boy's aunt had sent him, and for the blink of an eye Camillo toyed with the idea of letting the others go on while he would stay to be with Mathilde.

But the boy had not come from her at all. He presented a cockamamie story to disguise who he wanted the truck and papers for, but all it took was a few quick, pointed questions, like an eagle pecking at a victim, for Camillo to learn that the boy's errand was for his uncle. He had come to ask for help for Franz Tegge, the butcher, Franz Tegge, the murderer, Franz Tegge who wanted to escape across the border with a whole load of other vermin.

The tightrope walker was overcome with dizziness. Tegge was still alive. The butcher's wife had lied to him. She was just as bad as all the other *gadsche*. She had lied to him and to the whole world so that nobody would look for her husband, the murderer. It all became as clear as sunshine on a sunny day.

The woman he had trusted, the woman he hoped could dissolve the burning coals of his hate and end his need for revenge had betrayed him, deceived him. Lied to him!

Camillo was shocked by the mistake he had almost made, how fatally wrong he had misjudged Mathilde, but he gave no hint of it. His reflexes were still sharp, the mask stayed in place, at least enough for the little rugrat in front him. Cool as a cucumber the artiste stared the boy down and came up with a shamelessly high price so that the Nazis would bleed for this; and then he would do them in. He promised the truck, and the boy departed in triumph.

Camillo vanished as well. He had to take care of the truck and counterfeit documents. He disappeared and let the others move on. When he returned they were gone, but an amulet hung on the tent post. It was from Keja. He kissed it gently and placed it around his neck. He was protected. He knew where he belonged even if he was alone.

He had stoked the fire, boiled water, drank coffee, smoked and waited without knowing what he waited for. He was without feeling. He had waited a long time. Now she was standing in front of him holding flowers in her hand and smiling nervously at him. What could she want?

"I brought you these," she said as she knelt and laid the flowers in front of him.

* * *

Mathilde braced herself and took a deep breath. "I've never done anything like this before," she stammered.

Was she here to explain why she had lied to him? He was interested in that, just as a biologist might be curious about the composition of venom sprayed by a viper's bite. Baumgartner relaxed a bit. He offered her coffee and a cigarette.

She took both, lit the cigarette with trembling fingers and almost spilled the coffee. She tried but could not look directly at him. "I love you," she blurted out, her eyes downcast. Then words raced from her mouth as if a pressure valve had been suddenly released. "I know the world will call us crazy," she continued on as the words got easier, unaware that Baumgartner had not replied. "The whole world. Your sister-in-law put a curse on me; my brother-in-law, Hermann, and my sister, Heidrun . . . . I don't even want to know what they think or what they will say. It's okay, isn't it?" She smiled a warm, genuinely happy smile, no longer anxious. "We have found each other, you and I. I know it. You could not go with the others. I felt that as soon as you said goodbye before the funeral. You wanted to go and naturally, you and I, it was completely impossible; you with a German, just like me with a Gypsy, a traveling performer, one of the wanderers. But despite that I sensed it. You, too?"

Did he sense it? No, he sensed nothing at all, not even the memory of a feeling; yet somewhere, in a distant, unimportant vestige of his being, perhaps the feeling was there. A long ago feeling, and not so long ago he had felt it as if through a fog. A hint of feeling, a feeling he must arm himself against.

Mathilde did not care that he remained silent. She was almost relieved that he did not speak or interrupt her. "Something else," she said slowly. "Franz is not dead."

He was dumbstruck. She knew and yet she still came to him? He could not grasp it, but he had not misunderstood; Mathilde Tegge, this warmhearted, tender woman he should have known not to trust, had played a double game with him?

"He went underground for fear of punishment and prison. I did not know until after the funeral. He surprised me. He just showed up and told me I should escape with him but I said no. I could not go away with him, not any longer. Not since I met you." She looked for the amber flecks in Baumgartner's eyes and could not find them. "I love you," she said again, and then she was silent. She sipped the coffee. The cigarette she had not taken a single drag of had burned down to her fingers.

Suddenly he laughed. He guffawed like a mad man, his laughter interspersed with her words which he repeated, "You . . . love . . . me?" He shook as he laughed. "You love me?!" He laughed again, tense. Not mocking. Not affectionate. It was the sound of despair, madness even, and stopped as suddenly as it had begun. Baumgartner sat there silent, calm, motionless.

Mathilde did not know which bothered her most, his laughter, his silence, or the look on his face.

***

Images knifed through his mind; flashes, sights, sounds, all too painful to fully restore from memory.

He sits at a window in front of a table with a large mirror behind it. He has just returned from the stage to his dressing room that smells of mastic and petroleum jelly. He takes off his makeup and looks out the window. Tender green leaves cover a tree in front of the house. A pair of swallows perch in it, resting from their long flight out of the south. Suddenly they fly off disturbed by something.

Men with hats and long leather coats storm into the building, accompanied by black uniforms with knee-high leather boots. At the window, he remains very calm. Later some would say he was ice-cold, and how could he stay so calm in the midst of what was happening?

He puts on his suit, ties his necktie, claps his hat on. He doesn't pull it down on his forehead—as if he has nothing to hide. He leaves the dressing room and walks down the steps to the stage door. Two black uniforms and a leather coat are watching him. The leather coat is blond, small, wears glasses and a badge of honor for twenty years of police service.He does not attempt to flee, rather goes calmly toward the leather coat and the uniforms without hesitation. He doffs his hat in greeting and steps to the door. He is almost past them when the leather coat growls, "Identification?"

He turns around and smiles at the leather coat, "But you do know me, don't you?" He turns again and steps through the door. He moves briskly and purposefully but does not run.

The two uniforms and the leather coat look at each other. "Do you know him, Unterscharführer?"

In a split second the leather coat yanks open the door, darts after him and yells, "Would you kindly stay put?!" Too late. He is lost in the milling crowd on Potsdamer Straße.

Now he runs. Faces, glimpses; people pull away from him not knowing what is happening. They know only that they do not want to be drawn in.

He looks around. Behind him, much farther behind him is a movement in the crowd on the sidewalk. There they are. Far away. They cannot catch him anymore.

Quiet. He sits, stands, sits down again. Why does the conductor not shut the doors? Why does the train not start off? He knows he has to get to Marzahn before the uniforms and leather coats. Hopefully it is not too late to warn the others, but the doors do not glide shut. The doors on the damn *S-Bahn* do not shut.

He knows it is dangerous to travel by train. This will be the first place they will look for him, on his way back to the stinking field where they have him and his people corralled. Still, he has no choice if maybe, please, hopefully it is not already too late. If only the train would move. A woman stumbles onto the platform. Why do we have to wait for her? Surely, she can take the next one.

Finally the train was off.

He runs again. A tie, a step, a tie, a step, over the rails along the railway from the station to the camp along the track, along the rail, which is totally *VERBOTEN*. Besides, to slip is to fall down the embankment. To slip will bring the police to set their dogs on him. He never slips. Never. This is what he does for a living.

Death is already in the camp. He sees the trucks from a distance, and knows. The police have locked down the camp. He knows he is too late. He knows, yet he storms on.

A woman runs, too. She runs away. She holds a child in her arms, her little boy, and she runs away from the uniforms, away from the leather coats that herd the people of the camp to the trucks to take them to another camp, to take them to their death.

She does not want to die. She wants to live. She wants her son to live. She bolts out of line away from the poor souls that clamber into the trucks. She breaks through the rows of guards, and she runs. She runs to the cemetery next to the camp. She runs to the trees and bushes. She runs to the security of the graves.

He sees a sudden movement, a disturbance in the seemingly orderly process. He sees a single small figure move through the lines, the lines behind it starting to spread like an ink spot on a blotter. He rushes down the embankment in great leaps. Hurries to help.

"Stop." One of the leather coats yells. "Stop!" Scraps of words, shards of sounds come to the racing man. He runs even faster. Maybe he can still help. He hopes, prays.

The woman skips and dodges like a rabbit. If she can reach the bushes . . . the trees . . . the cemetery . . . A shot pierces the air. It hits nothing, and she runs. She clutches her child close, and she runs. More shots lash the area.

She falls. He storms on, now only fifty meters away. The noise. The noise he makes does not matter. The uniforms and the leather coat are so loud they can't hear him.

The shots stop. The hunters slow their pursuit. The prey was hit, or so they think. She rises again; maybe she only stumbled, or maybe she tried to fool them by throwing herself to the ground. But there she is, jumping up and running again.

He is startled. He recognizes what he secretly has hoped. It is his wife! She carries his child! The wonderful black hair clings to her forehead. Her expensive colorful clothes are stained with mud and slime. His little son cries in fear. But they are alive! Both of them.

"Philomena, this way!" He has reached the cars, transport for the uniforms and leather coats. He tears open a door. They can escape in one of these cars.

The woman changes direction. One leather coat raises his pistol. It is the short blond with the glasses again; he can tell because the badge of honor sparkles in the spring light. Him again, he thinks. Why him already? How did he get here so fast? The blond leather coat raises his pistol and fires.

The woman stumbles. She screams. Her clothes turn red. He stands stock still.

The universe around him stands stock still.

He hears the whimpering of his son who lies buried under his mother, but it is already too late. Uniforms run past the leather coat, circle his wife and his son. They circle her corpse.

They see him and rush toward him.

"Heart shot, Tegge." In passing, one of the uniforms hits the blond leather coat on the shoulder.

He stands still. His world has stopped turning; has lost all interest in turning.

"Stop!" one of them calls as uniforms and leather coat run toward him. One of them shoots, and he comes to his senses, jumps in the car, and races away. Another shot hits the rear window but misses him. He has not even heard it, neither the shot nor the splintering glass. There is only one sound that rings in his ear—*Heart shot, Tegge.*

* * *

The Gypsy stopped speaking and looked at Mathilde silently. There was no longer any sorrow, nor any sympathy, nor any love in his eyes. All that was there was memory.

Heart shot, Tegge. It rages in his mind to this day. *Heart shot, Tegge.* It will stop only when Tegge pays for that shot.

"So it was no accident that we met?" Mathilde broke their long silence. Baumgartner shook his head. "It wasn't about me?"

Baumgartner hesitated for a long moment and then said, in a voice that sounded as he had just awakened from a dream, "I wanted only to find your husband. The murderer. You just got in my way."

TWENTY NINE

The first thing Lene noticed was the odor. The cloying, putrid, foul odor of a dead body overwhelmed the stench of burned wood, burned metal and burned rubber that lay dormant under everything. The odor clung to the ever present dust. It even topped the fetid stench from when inhabitants relieved themselves wherever they could squat or stand. If the odor was that strong, thought Lene, the corpse must be close.

This morning Schall had put her at the top of the line with the few men who filled the buckets to be handed down. Lene let her bucket drop, crouched down and rubbed her hand over her face. She needed a moment to brace herself.

It would not be the first corpse the women found, not for Lene or the others, and it would not be the last. They were jaded, they had seen death in hundreds of variations . . . but, they were not used to it, Lene as little as any of the others.

Lene bent down and looked at the fragments of rock, debris, and slabs of plaster under which the corpse must lie. She wanted to get on with it but could not force herself to start even though she lived with death every day, or maybe *because* she lived with it. She just could not begin.

Robert's condition had worsened since the insulin Mathilde got for them had been used up and there was no more to be had. She would not turn to Mathilde for help anymore. Hedwig Strache did nothing but assuage her conscience with a bottle of wine and cookies, and there was nothing left for Lene to trade on the black market.

Down at the bottom of the rubble mountain Schall roared, "Hey,

Behrendt! Don't quit on me! Keep going until breakfast!"

"Okay, okay, give me a break," she yelled back to Schall. She dug deeper, pulling stone after stone from the debris and tossing them into the buckets behind her. Maybe she could get someone else to the top of the line and avoid the corpse, she thought. Maybe she could act like she did not see or smell anything. Even as she thought she could work off in another direction to avoid the rotting corpse, she mechanically continued to dig stones from the seemingly endless mound, moving closer and closer to the odor.

When she realized what she was doing it was too late. The stench was overpowering and unbearable, and she could not pretend there was nothing there. This was her job, and the Prussian in her demanded she do it, so she took off her headscarf, tied it around her mouth and continued to dig.

Something glittered. She instinctively dug further. She should report it, there was a procedure to identify and bury the body, but those few times when they had found something valuable like jewelry they had hidden it. It was forbidden but they all did it, though Lene was not sure about Mathilde or Elfriede. Whoever lived around Innsbrucker Platz was not rich. If the women found something it was usually small, a wedding ring or a few coins in a pocketbook. It might buy some bread or a half litre of milk for the little ones. Cigarettes. Or some insulin . . .

She dug. She moved with purpose. A little insulin, a little delay, a few extra days of survival for Robert, a few precious days. A ring, an earring would be a gift from heaven. She tore, she pulled, she burrowed onward. The stench took her breath away, but she pushed on as if she was digging to hell, knowing the horrific sight she would find. Stone by stone she dug toward the glitter, chunk by chunk she pushed it to the side. Filling the bucket was forgotten.

A woman. She found a woman with brown hair, couldn't tell how old. A perm, Lene thought. She had a permanent wave done just before her death! Except for the hair there was nothing undamaged on the body. The face was a mass of undulating maggots, and the rest of the body had been eaten by vermin, one big rotten mess. Lene gagged.

Around what remained of the throat lay a multi-looped pearl necklace.

On her fingers were rings with glimmering stones. What was such a well-to-do lady doing in this neighborhood? A wicked light flashed from one of the diamonds—at least that's what Lene hoped they were, she did not know about such things—and jolted her back to reality.

Her hands shook. She knew that if she wanted to she had to do it now. She also knew that the moment she touched the dead woman, the body, what was left of it, would dissolve, fall apart and slide out of her hands like a wet bar of soap.

Lene took a deep breath and lifted the skull slightly. Without warning the hair and scalp slid off the skull like melted butter. Quickly Lene removed the necklace and let the skull fall. Without wiping it, she put the necklace in her pocket.

She pulled the rings off the fingers slowly, carefully, but could not avoid pulling away scraps of skin and tissue that clung to them. She gagged again, somehow controlled her revulsion, and let the rings vanish into her pocket. Bile burned at her throat, but she held it back. She dared not vomit.

She had to be smart, cool, and strong. Worry and loathing, fear and revulsion tore at her. She wanted to disappear like the corpse into the dark depths, but she had to go on, had to hold on. It was all too apparent that the corpse had been robbed. So, Lene made it look like an accident as she fell against the stone, mortar, and debris she had piled next to the body. "Shit!" She shouted as loudly as she could. She jumped back and the rubble again covered the corpse. Now the face and body were completely demolished, and hopefully all traces of theft erased.

She stood coughing in the middle of a dust cloud.

"Everything okay?" Elfriede called over to her.

"Yeah, yeah. Call the Pirate. There is a corpse here. I had it almost free and then the whole mess fell down again." It took everything she had to sound normal.

"So?" Roswitha crawled over the rubble mound to Lene, dragging her bucket behind her.

Lene heard the suspicion in her voice and steeled herself. "You damn well know how it goes," she said sensing the slight quavering in her voice.

So did Roswitha. Now others closed in as well, curious. As usual though, the Horse reached Lene first. "We share, is that clear?" she murmured sounding sly and greedy.

"There is nothing to share."

"Tsk-tsk-tsk. What will the Pirate say to that?"

"He will say absolutely nothing, nothing at all." Lene forgot all caution, all composure and shouted, "There is nothing. Nothing to share. Nothing to say." It was a mistake.

Roswitha, the Warhorse, was enflamed and ready to grab Lene by the throat. "You got something. I saw you tunnelling."

"Don't you touch me!" Lene yelled, making the others more alert, more suspicious.

"You are probably afraid the rocks that you just stole will rattle, huh?" Roswitha hissed. "We will talk later." Minchen had signaled her that Schall approached.

"Where is it then, my ladies?"

"Here," Lene pointed.

The Warhorse knew to keep her mouth shut once Schall was there. If she blew the whistle on Lene whatever had been taken from the corpse would be confiscated. If Behrendt got away with it she could put pressure on her later. Maybe she would weaken by then.

Schall checked out the hole that had filled again with debris.

"I tried to dig it out and could even see it, but the debris fell back in," Lene explained the obvious.

"It must have looked bad judging by the smell." Schall gave Lene a sympathetic glance. Finding a body had a profound impact on him just as it did for all the others.

Lene nodded.

"You don't look so good either. Go sit a bit." Schall was often really not all that bad. "We will go ahead without you."

Lene turned around and climbed slowly, stone by stone, clump by clump down the rubble mountain. She sat down on a rock and took a swallow of water. Suddenly tears ran down her cheeks. Was it exhaustion, confusion, or horror? She did not know. She carefully felt for the nasty, slippery, smeared jewelry in her pocket. Yes, it was still there and it seemed to weigh a ton. Lene felt the jewels and saw the hair with its brand new permanent wave; the eyeholes, the nose cavity, the mass of maggots that devoured where once cheeks had been. She shut her eyes but the woman's image remained in every tiny horrible, bitingly clear detail.

Lene sensed a hand on her shoulder and shivered. She opened her eyes and turned around.

"I know I can't do much. And if I should leave, just say so." Lene looked into Mathilde's face, recognized her but did not react.

Mathilde waited a moment and then sat down next to her. She waited wordlessly for Lene to say something, do something.

Lene remained motionless. She didn't want the closeness but she couldn't send Mathilde away either. Instead of getting up and leaving, instead of telling Mathilde to shove it, Lene gave in to their bond, the promise of warmth and understanding, and pulled the jewelry out of her pocket as if she were on remote control. She had to share the horror, had to get relief. She held the necklace and rings in her hand so Mathilde could see them and absently wiped the loathsome scraps and slimy remainder of skin from them.

Mathilde had been in enough of these incidents on the rubble mountain to understand. She was genuinely happy. "If you are lucky you can trade that for enough insulin for a few weeks."

Lene heard—and felt—the warmth in Mathilde's voice, but she could not share the joy. She didn't answer for a long while. "I often wish he were dead," she said without looking at Mathilde, "that he had remained in Russia."

Mathilde understood. Lene, the strong one who always fought for her brother, who was unshakeable, brave, and trustworthy, had come to the point where she could take no more. Mathilde understood, and still it took her breath away.

"Robert is going to die anyway, even with the insulin that we might get for this stuff." Lene put the jewelry back in her pocket. "Even if he lives another few weeks, what then? Do you think he will get better in a few weeks?"

"No." Mathilde felt their bond, their understanding, their shared experience. It would never get better, not in a few weeks nor a few years.

Never. She knew that when she had returned from Marzahn, unable to imagine how life could go on. But it did go on. And it would never get better. Never again.

"If he had remained in Russia, he would have been spared the pain, all this misery. Like your Franz."

Like my Franz. Mathilde was startled. She had removed him from her consciousness. Her Franz. Her husband. Now he was only a memory, a figure from another world, another life.

"Franz is actually not dead."

"What?"

Mathilde told the story without worrying that she was betraying Franz or breaking her promise to keep quiet. She talked because she had to. She talked about the funeral and how Franz suddenly appeared afterwards. She talked about his deal with the Amis and how she had refused to go with him.

What she did not talk about was the other one. She could not talk about it, could not share what was too difficult, too humiliating, too hurtful. What she had only imagined?

Lene listened. And Mathilde talked until Schall stood in front of them. "It is nice that you can get along again, my ladies. I would like to bring you a cup of coffee to celebrate the day, but I don't have any. Now, can we get back to work so we can finish sooner rather than later? Okay?"

THIRTY

Hubert followed Karla through the kitchen and bumped into a chair. "Quiet! Aunt Heidrun is sleeping," Karla whispered, energetically wagging her finger at him. Hubert crouched down and stood stock still.

Karla listened at the door but heard only her own tense breathing. Good, Aunt Heidrun hadn't woken up. Karla slipped quietly to the small narrow space between the kitchen cupboard and the wall. She removed the broom, scrub brush, and dustpan that were neatly hung there side by side and laid them carefully, gently on the floor. She stuck her hand into the space and pulled out a loose board from the sidewall of the cupboard. She snaked her arm into the cupboard and between the pots, pans, and plates through to the door latch. She pushed it, jiggled it and opened the door from inside.

She cheerily winked at Hubert, took bread out of the pan that it was kept in, a large roasting pan that was not used for roasting anymore, and cut off two slices, one for each of them. She had picked him up on the street in front of the house and brought him in because he looked hungry again, but the truth was he always looked hungry.

The timing was right. Aunt Heidrun had gone down for her nap just like every day after they had their meager lunch, Uncle Hermann was out, Frieder was wandering around who knew where, Horst probably stood in a line, and the two little ones were playing in the living room. So she and Hubert slipped into the apartment, into the kitchen, and opened the cupboard.

A couple of years ago while cleaning the broom corner Karla had discovered the loose board on the sidewall. Since then she often helped herself to something.

"Another one, please." Hubert was not full. He was never full. Hubert always ate, and ate as much as he could get. He vacuumed down every crumb as if there would never be anymore.

Aunt Heidrun had finally thrown him out after Karla brought him to too many meals. He practically lived with them. "It is impossible to feed him, too," she said. "We hardly have enough for ourselves."

Karla appealed to her Christian charity, but the pastor's wife stood firm. "We gladly donate what we can but we cannot completely support Hubert." For once Mommy had to agree, even if reluctantly, with Aunt Heidrun. Hubert had to leave.

The homeless boy loitered in front of the house, careful to avoid Frieder, who scared him. Frieder would stare at him and make him feel as if he could see right through him. It was very scary even though Hubert had no idea what he had to hide.

Karla felt sorry for him, and he was the last person to see her father alive. She brought him along now and then, and pilfered a couple of slices of bread or zwieback for him.

"Another one, please." Hubert's greedy, pleading eyes looked at her and Karla could not say no.

"Well, okay, but this is the last one." Aunt Heidrun always complained about how fast the bread got eaten, or that there were fewer zwiebacks left over than she had thought. Naturally she suspected Karla but had not caught her in the act, at least not yet. Karla cut another thin slice and handed it to Hubert who wolfed it down. The poor boy, thought Karla.

She went to shut the cupboard again when the kitchen door flew open and Frieder stood in the frame. "I finally got you!"

Karla's and Hubert's heads whipped around toward Frieder. "So that is your trick. You steal from us!" he hissed.

Karla quickly got hold of herself and instinctively relied on her brazenness. "So? What are you going to do? Go tell your mommy?" She abruptly turned away from Frieder, closed the cupboard doors and let the lock snap. She had not replaced the loose board when Hurbert began to whimper. He cried softly and began to tremble. "Shh," she whispered to him. She could handle Frieder, but if Hubert made noise and woke up Aunt Heidrun . . . Karla turned—and caught her breath; she was looking into the muzzle of a pistol that Frieder held in his hand.

"Coward!" Frieder's unsteady hand trembled from the intensity of his anger. "You loser, afraid at the sight of a little Walther! No wonder we lost the war."

Karla's eyes burned with anger, and fear. "Put that thing away. Right now. Are you crazy?!"

"You are the one who is crazy. We starve so this traitor to the fatherland can eat?!"

"Traitor to the fatherland? He was actually under fire. All you did was play a little cops and robbers."

"He gave up." Frieder turned to Hubert again, outraged. "You ran away, you little coward, while I still fight for *Führer, Volk und Vaterland.*"

"Yeah? And how do you do that?" Karla's words were dripping with scorn. "By pulling swastikas out of the ruins and hawking them to the Amis?" It was a shot in the dark, but there was a lot of that going on.

And her shot struck home. "You cannot understand. We need money for our battle."

"Oh? What battle?" Karla stepped up to her cousin. "What battle? Come on, spit it out."

"I'm under orders. I cannot tell. It is a secret command mission. If I tell, it is high treason."

"You can't tell because there is nothing to tell."

"There is!" Frieder's voice became shrill. "If you only knew. You have no idea. And that is the way it must be. We don't need loose cannons like you—and him here," he said, pointing at Hubert with the pistol barrel.

Karla took the quaking, groaning boy's hand and started to lead him out of the kitchen.

"*Halt*! Stay here! Don't move!" Frieder brandished the pistol. "Your theft has to be atoned for."

"Don't preach to us." Karla attempted to push by Frieder.

He thrust the pistol against her chest. "I said, stop!"

Karla shoved the pistol away. "Do you think you can scare me with that rusty old thing? I can find hundreds in the debris."

"This is A-one. As good as new." Frieder was about to lose control. "Stop, this is my last warning."

Karla didn't answer him. She pushed past him and moved into the foyer. A shot.

Karla whirled around, Hubert wailed, and Frieder stood in shock that he had fired the gun. Dust dribbled from the ceiling where a large chunk of plaster had been hit by the bullet. A muffled sound, as if from very far away, came to Karla's ears; Gerhild and Heinrich crying and calling for their mother.

Heidrun bolted in from the bedroom wearing only her slip, her hair undone. She was shocked and furious, her eyes darted back and forth among the three of them before she saw the hole in the ceiling and the weapon in Frieder's hand.

"Go ahead and play, nothing has happened," she ordered Gerhild and Heinrich pushing them back into the living room, shutting the door, and ripping the pistol from Frieder's hand all in one fell swoop, or so it seemed. "What is going on here?" she demanded, ready to begin an inquisition, addressing no one in particular.

Frieder was instantly defensive. "Those two broke into the cupboard and stole bread."

"He's crazy. Absolutely crazy," Karla said, her voice breaking so she had to struggle to get her words out. "He tried to shoot us!"

"I only fired a warning shot in the ceiling."

"How did you ever get a weapon?" Heidrun fixed her son in place. "Talk to me! Where did you get it?"

Frieder stood rigid and defiantly lowered his gaze; and kept silent. Heidrun grabbed his chin and forced his face up. "How . . . did . . . you . . . get . . . the . . . weapon?!"

Frieder still said nothing.

"Frieder sells party insignia and whatever he can find in the rubble on the black market," Karla announced.

"You be real quiet, young lady. Your turn will come. And you," Aunt

Heidrun speared her finger at Hubert, "disappear now! And don't come back. You bring nothing but trouble to this family. Don't ever let any of us see you again."

Hubert jumped at Heidrun's order as if someone had thrown a switch. He stopped trembling, turned awkwardly, opened the apartment door, and went out like an automaton, no longer master of himself. If ever in his young life he had been his own master . . .

Karla watched him go and felt as if part of her consciousness left with him. All fractiousness, all agitation left her with Hubert's exit.

Aunt Heidrun grabbed her son by the arm and hauled him back into the kitchen. She looked around at Karla and said, "Wait here! Don't you dare move from that spot." The kitchen door closed behind her.

Karla felt she too had been transformed into a machine. She obeyed and sat on the floor in the foyer and waited. She stared at the bullet hole in the ceiling. She did not hear when Uncle Hermann came home nor answer when he asked what was going on or why she was sitting on the floor. She was not aware of the subsequent yelling and badgering, of Frieder's moans and wails of protest during the whipping. She did not hear when Aunt Heidrun opened the door and told her to go get her mother. She reacted only when she received a powerful slap on her cheek from Heidrun.

"Will you finally listen to me?" Heidrun said.

"Yes, what is it?"

"I told you to go get your mother."

"Right now?"

"Yes, right now!"

Heidrun was mad as hell, but that wasn't the only thing. There was something new in her voice, something different that Karla could not catch, a worry, perhaps, or a fear? Astonishment about something her aunt could not comprehend?

"Off with you. Go to the worksite and bring her here. We will talk about your thievery later, you can count on that."

Karla had finally run off and now, three quarters of an hour later, stood with her mother in the foyer. Both were out of breath. When Karla had told Mathilde why she was to come home there seemed no real reason to rush. Obviously it was wrong of her daughter to steal food, but they could have sorted that out in the evening. Heidrun and Hermann could deal with their overzealous son by themselves. Yet Karla seemed so upset and afraid of Heidrun that Mathilde finally gave in.

She opened the kitchen door and found what she expected, Frieder sat cowed on a chair and looked like he had been crying. He had obviously gotten a hiding from Hermann. "What is the matter? Why am I here?"

Hermann looked at his son and said, "Repeat to your aunt what you just told us."

Mathilde expected a long circuitous explanation of how he found the pistol and wondered what it had to do with her. She worried for a moment that the boy had found Franz's service weapon somewhere in the apartment, and that was why Hermann was so upset. And rightfully so since it was a death sentence to own a weapon. But, none of them knew Franz had left a pistol here.

Frieder dared not look at his aunt or his cousin. He rasped, "I met Uncle Franz. He is alive."

"What?!" Karla reacted first. "Say that again."

"I met him by accident. A few weeks ago. And then I followed him around and spoke to him again a few times."

"You knew this whole time that Daddy was alive? The whole time?! Even during the funeral and everything?" Karla's voice cracked. First the shot, then this?! "You lied to me the whole time? Simply looked on as my mother and I cried? What a lowlife you are." The furious countenance on her face bore right through her cousin. She hated him. She would hate him for the rest of her life.

Heidrun turned to her sister. "Did you have *any* idea . . . ?"

Mathilde expected Heidrun to continue and say something as if she had known it all along, Hubert lied, you didn't listen to me, nobody ever listens to me . . . But it had been the other way around. Mathilde had not believed it, didn't want to believe it. *She* had to be convinced in the end by Heidrun and Hermann.

Hermann looked at Mathilde in amazement. "You are so calm? Doesn't it surprise you at all?"

"I knew. Franz came to me after the funeral when I was alone at the grave."

Abject silence filled the room. The others looked at Mathilde in disbelief, but Mathilde did not care, she could deal with them or not, as she chose. She was not accountable to them or anyone, except for her daughter. She looked at Karla who was chalk-white and swayed as if she might feint. Mathilde silently implored her, *forgive me!*

"You knew and didn't say anything?!" Heidrun sounded even more offended than usual.

"I had to promise Franz. It was his last wish to me."

"Just like me. I had to swear that I would not betray him. Uncle Franz told me it would be high treason and that he is involved with a secret command operation." Slowly Frieder summoned up some courage again to defend himself.

"Did he tell you what he is planning?" Hermann asked Mathilde. He was angry at his sister-in-law and upset that everyone had butted into the conversation. It seemed to him the whole family was out of control.

"He plans to go to the States. He has worked out some sort of a deal with the Americans," Mathilde replied.

"And I helped him." Even though salty tears were drying on his cheeks and his nose was running, a fierce pride rang in Frieder's voice.

"I beg your pardon?" Mathilde asked perplexed.

"Yes. He needed a truck. And false papers. I got all of that for him."

"You did what?" Mathilde just shook her head.

"Yes." Hermann patted his son, the boy he had just whipped for having a gun, on the head. "He may well have saved your husband's life. The arrangement with the Amis would have fallen through without him."

"Uncle Franz was at a loss. He needed the truck and had no idea where to get it. Then it occurred to me that the Gypsy can always rustle up something." Frieder smiled, proud of being so resourceful.

"Baumgartner? You went to Mr. Baumgartner?"

"Yes. And as greedy as that bunch is, he agreed, of course. He is finding the truck for Uncle Franz."

"No!" Mathilde had to sit down. In a split second she knew what all of it meant. Franz would have Camillo arrested along with the rest of Nazis. Camillo would be considered an accomplice to escape and would land in prison, if not worse. It could not be. It could not be allowed to happen!

THIRTY ONE

She pushed on the pedals as hard as she could. She ignored the pain in her thighs, ignored the pang in her lungs. It was a hot July afternoon, sweat stood on her brow, ran down her back and her legs. She pushed and tramped and thanked God that Lene had loaned her the bike after Karla had fetched her home from the worksite.

Maybe she would be in time. Maybe she could stop the worst. Her initial fear, her panic, her anxiety for Camillo increasingly turned to confusion, disbelief, and surprise. What was wrong with him? She could not understand it. How could the man who lost his entire family to the Nazis help a band of their top thugs escape?

Frieder and Hermann were convinced he was in it for the money. Could that be? This was an upstanding, honorable, candid man. Would he really sell his soul? Was it possible? Had she deluded herself about him because she believed she loved him?

So what? She could not hold it against him even if it were true that he renounced everything holy and dear to him for money's sake. She felt for him, could not erase her compassion. How much must a man—this man!—have suffered that he could hate so much now?

"Somewhere at the harbor," Frieder stammered when she had screamed the question about where the truck was to be delivered.

"Which harbor?"

"Over there at the Großmarkt. The fighters must be around there somewhere."

"Which fighters?"

"The ones that want to rebuild the *Partei* and the *Reich* from South America."

She didn't comment on the supposed fighters and asked, "So at Westhafen, up in Moabit. Don't you know exactly?" The boy shook his lowered head. "What about when?"

"Thursday. I heard something about Thursday. Yes, Thursday."

"Today is Thursday."

"Yes. Today. That could be it. Uncle Franz said something about Thursday."

She could not push him further. Frieder clearly knew nothing more. She hugged Karla, said goodbye, and asked Heidrun to care for her distraught daughter. She then stormed out of the apartment and pedaled off completely focused on what she must do.

She came to Großer Stern. The streets had been cleared so she pedaled on in the direction of Moabit and past the Siegessäule. It had come through the entire war with hardly a scratch and stood—an unreal, almost grotesque sight—between the trees of Tiergarten. The iron arches of Lutherbrücke lay toppled in the river Spree. Beside it moored barges made a makeshift bridge, and Mathilde picked up the bicycle to carry it across. As she stumbled over the planks on barge decks she asked herself if what she was doing made any sense at all. Frieder was not sure of either the time or the place the truck would be delivered. What he knew he had overheard, and the rest he had just figured out.

When she finally reached the harbor her fears seemed confirmed. She looked around, near and far, but there was no truck. The harbor looked just like the rest of the city. Most of the warehouses on the three basins that stretched from the canal along Seestraße toward Moabit were destroyed. Cranes lay wrecked on the wharves, one crane blocked one of the basins. Only a few people worked on the rubble to master the destruction.

Slowly and carefully, Mathilde walked the bike along the wharf. Finally she sat down on a chunk of rubble.

What in the world am I doing here? How could a delivery happen here? Impossible! It was difficult, at best, to get to Moabit in the first place. Why had she not thought of that before? The bridges over the canals and the river Spree had been destroyed. A truck could not even find its way here. Frieder must have gotten it wrong, misunderstood or something.

She wanted to scream when she thought about it, but she was exhausted. She sat there on the rubble, too worn out to stand up, too shattered to ride home. She wasn't too tired to feel despondent, despair, and trepidation. She could not stop the inevitable. It had to happen.

Little by little the workers left, the sun cast its last orange glow across the western sky. Mathilde knew she should go home. She could do nothing here but wait helplessly. She should go home and take care of Karla.

She made a deal with herself. She would wait a while longer, until the crow that was perched on a pile of debris across from her flew off. She waited. The crow flapped its wings and flew away. Mathilde just sat there.

"I hoped that you would come." The voice behind her was familiar.

She whirled around and saw him. "Franz?"

"So the boy blabbed?"

Mathilde nodded. She felt hot, muggy, as if a fog had settled around her.

"That's what I expected," he said very satisfied with himself. "I knew how you would react. I still understand how you think and feel."

Mathilde just looked at him, her expression blank, almost a look of pity. He had never understood her, not at all. She learned that when she became close to Camillo.

"You thought the Gypsy would deliver a truck to me here? How? The bridges are all destroyed." He softly touched her brow. "But you didn't think about that with your little bird brain, did you?"

She wanted to say of course she thought of it, just too late, but she did not make a sound. The touch of Franz's finger on her brow burned like caustic lye.

"At first it was just a precaution. I thought to myself, who knows what will happen? Frieder is only fourteen so he should not know all the details. On the other hand, I had to arrange a meeting with the Gypsy, and the boy was a useful go-between for me. And then I had an idea . . . a hunch, really."

Mathilde was watching him. He looks so happy, she thought.

"And I was right," Franz went on. "I thought the kid might gossip, and maybe my little Mathilde will hear and like as not she has changed her mind since we last met. Like as not she has figured out that she could dally with someone like that Gypsy, but nothing could come of it in the long term. Like as not my little Mathilde is sorry she is not coming with me to America. Then I thought, just go check to see if she is there, and lo and behold, here you are. As I said, it was just a hunch, my intuition, you know, but I was right on the mark."

He will try to hug me soon, a horrified Mathilde thought. She was horrified and sickened at the prospect of his touch, but he was still her husband. She had shared her bed and life with him. Now she could not abide the thought of his embrace.

Franz did not hug her. He took her hand, unable to imagine that she might have reason to be here other than to meet him. "I am so happy you've come," he said. He fondled her hand as he had done so long ago. "So happy," he went on. "We belong together, the two of us. I knew you would accept that sooner or later."

Mathilde looked at him aghast? Could he really believe she was here because of him? Yes, she realized. He really did.

"I will send for you," he continued, "for you and Karla. I promise. Once I get to America everything will be different. I'll even buy you that piano you have always wished for."

Franz misunderstood her expressionless face, her silence, her reluctance.

"You don't believe me? You don't want to wait?" He thought for a moment. "Good. You can go get Karla now. No one is allowed to take family, but what can they do if you are standing right there, dependent on me?" He smiled, a masterful, bold, adventurous hero, as if finding Mathilde here had given him a power he never before possessed. "In two hours we will meet at the safe and bank vault factory in Wedding. You know where that is?"

Everyone knew the factory. It was where the supposed burglar proof safes were made, the ones the Sass brothers cracked in the late twenties. Mathilde didn't know quite why, but she asked, "Why there?"

"The Wedding district is in the French zone, and the French aren't there yet. For the time being the Brits administer it, but they don't give it much attention since they are not staying."

"Oh." Mathilde would not be surprised if someone shook her and told her this was all a dream.

Franz stroked her cheek, a gesture she stoically endured, and then went off through the rubble.

Mathilde looked over the water in the harbor basins where the setting sun threw a blood-red swath. His touch had awakened her, drove the last clinging, stifling billows from her head. Her thoughts were clear as the air after a thunderstorm. The *Tresorfabrik* in Wedding was where it would happen. She had to be there. She had to warn Camillo. But she had time.

It would take less than a half hour to get there, and she did not dare arrive too early. She really needed something to drink. Her mouth felt like she was chewing straw. She needed to find a pump. She had time. Franz had to think she was on the way to fetch Karla. She had time. Carefully, thoroughly, thoughtfully she planned how to proceed.

Mathilde stood and was about to push the bike along the wharf when she saw movement the next basin over. A silhouette. A man with a hat. A man with elegant, lithe movements. Camillo Baumgartner! She ran to him, waved and shouted, but the distance was too great. He could not hear her. She jumped on the bike and raced along the wharf avoiding obstacles of rubble. Why the devil did he not look over at her?

* * *

Baumgartner looked down the wharf to the bombed-out buildings of the port authority that had been at the end of the middle basin. He waited for a small blond man with glasses. He would recognize him with or without the badge of honor for twenty years of service, no doubt discarded by now.

He saw the blond-haired man step through a door frame. He looks good, Camillo thought, well fed and unharmed unlike so many others and far better than he deserves.

He had to tamp down the hate, pull himself together to keep from exacting his revenge on the spot. He wanted this man to pay for his crimes, this small cog in the machine that cruelly crushed Philomena and, in all likelihood, Sandro. Baumgartner wanted him, but he also wanted as much of that horrific machine as he could get.

He adjusted his hat to the way he had worn it back then and bowed slightly as Tegge approached. He said, "Surely you know me, don't you?"

Tegge had no appreciation for the irony of the moment. "Where is the truck?" he barked without a greeting.

Baumgartner smiled thinly and grimly. "Not here."

"I see that."

"You must share responsibility. You did not tell me where your people are. Besides, if you wanted me to bring the truck with me you would have chosen another place. A place where the bridges are still standing."

"You wouldn't have brought the truck with you in any case." Tegge sounded sullen, irritated, and resigned.

Good, he knew he held the weaker hand from the beginning. "That is true. I want my money first. No money, no truck."

"You get your money when we have the truck. And the passes."

"No. I get it up front."

"You don't think I would carry that much with me, do you? Not to a meeting alone with you."

Baumgartner feigned surprise. "You don't trust me?"

"Do you trust me?" Tegge countered. The question didn't deserve an answer, not even a scornful laugh.

"That's what was agreed upon," Baumgartner said. "Either you stick to it or the deal is off."

"And what is my insurance?"

"Me. We go together to pick up the truck."

"Declined. Make a better suggestion."

"That is the only one." Baumgartner turned to go with a shrug.

"Wait." Tegge began to sweat even though it was a cool evening. He patted his forehead with his handkerchief, thinking.

"Yes?" Baumgartner regarded him slyly.

Tegge remained mute and thoughtful while Baumgartner crossed his arms and waited. He enjoyed the wait. He enjoyed playing cat and mouse with Tegge.

"And what about the passes?"

"You get them later."

"No. Together with the truck." Tegge tried hard to win some ground, gain some authority, but it didn't work.

"No. The documents are my life insurance."

Tegge looked at him with feigned, mocking surprise.

"Come on. You know what would happen. As soon as you have the truck and the passes, you would kill me. One witness fewer, and you save money. Besides," Baumgartner could barely contain his hostility, his loathing for this man as he continued, coldly, "in your eyes I am inferior. Vermin for whom no man would shed a tear when I was killed."

Tegge could not look Baumgartner in the eye and concentrated his gaze to the side while he nervously shuffled his feet on the uneven ground.

He is giving up, Baumgartner thought. Now he's trying to figure out how to explain it all to his fine comrades. He is just a stooge who bought his way to South America with the promise of a truck and passes. He pushed again, "What now?"

Tegge gave up. "So, how do we make it happen?"

"I receive the money now. Full payment. You and I fetch the truck together. We load your people and drive to where the passes are. I get out and you are on your own."

"And you stay with us until then?" Tegge sounded almost indignant.

Tegge had, no doubt, been told to keep him away from the others, Camillo thought. He was Tegge's risk. He was the reason they included Tegge in their escape. To bring a foreigner to their party, and Gypsy scum at that, had not been part of the plan, certainly not. "Yeah. One of them drives while I sit next to the man in charge. That way no one gets any funny ideas."

Tegge concentrated on the lightly rippled gray surface of the water hoping for inspiration to find a way out of this mess. Finally, he nodded his head in agreement.

"Where is the money?"

Tegge patted his pants pocket and Baumgartner held out his hand. Tegge flinched defensively. "On one condition."

"You're in no position to make conditions."

"I need two more passports and two more passes." Tegge would not to be deterred by Baumgartner's malice. Instead, he seemed invigorated and strengthened. "For my wife and my daughter. They are coming, too."

Baumgartner thought he saw triumph in Tegge's eyes. He had won his wife back. Well, why should he care? Yet, he did. He felt a bitterness that rose in him, knowing she was, again, involved with this hangman's helper and that she wanted to escape with him. In that case it was just fine with him if she wound up in prison with her chosen man.

"Done deal." Baumgartner said brusquely. "I will get the papers. They won't be perfect in this short a time but they will do."

Tegge reached in his pocket and pulled out a thick envelope. Baumgartner tore it open and counted. At least the Nazis didn't try to cheat him on money.

"Okay. Let's go." Baumgartner put the money away, and the two men left the harbor.

* * *

Mathilde had hid when she saw Franz meet with Baumgartner. She could not let Franz see her if she wanted to warn Camillo so she crouched awkwardly behind a railroad car that stuck out of a bomb crater and watched the two men. She could not hear what was said. When they disappeared through the rubble of the port authority she stood up, her hand supporting her sore back.

Once they were out of sight, she quickly walked the bike through the rubble until she found a path that she could ride on. There she got on and rode off toward the safe and bank vault factory in Wedding.

When she arrived she was surprised to find the halls in the back court were almost undamaged, as was the factory owner's residence across the street. That meant a lot of people without a roof over their heads would have found shelter here. Would the people wanting to escape with Franz hide here, of all places? Perhaps. Maybe they had chosen this place for that exact purpose, she thought; to hide in the crowd, to remain undetected.

It grew dark with no sign that the Nazis were anywhere around. Nothing, absolutely nothing suggested anything unusual would soon happen.

Mathilde pretended to read the notices posted and written in chalk on the broken walls of a house while she snuck a look around. Around the intact factory apartment houses lay in various stages of ruin, like hundreds of buildings in Berlin, like thousands in Germany. The unavoidable dust drifted everywhere along with the ever-present stench of decay.

Mathilde saw nothing notable and brooded. How and where could she catch Camillo alone? She had no idea, no clue, no inspiration. She wondered if she might be able to throw a monkey wrench into the works, but on the other hand that was why she was here. To upset the applecart.

She saw a face watching her, scrutinizing her until there was a glimmer of recognition. The face pulled back into the shadows among the ruins across from the *Tresorfabrik*. She was alarmed. What could it mean? She had seen the man before, but where? Under what circumstance? When?—Borg! The memory bolted through her mind. It was Kriminalrat Borg, Franz's former supervisor. They had met at a staff picnic.

Seeing Borg proved the refugees had not hidden in the factory but across the street. Franz had named the factory as an orientation point. Or, maybe as further feint? Instinctively Mathilde shrunk back to a crevice in the walls between two houses, but there was no time for fear.

A Red Cross truck came around the corner and stopped in front of the rubble patch where Borg had disappeared. Some kids ran to it hoping for care packages, but they were disappointed. Two men climbed out of the cab, Franz and Baumgartner, and shooed the kids away.

Franz looked around, seemingly cautious and alert, but Mathilde knew he was looking for her, searching to see if she had come. When he did not see her he turned away disappointed, went to the rubble pile and vanished at the same spot as Borg had before him.

Camillo stayed with the truck and lit a cigarette. Now. This was her chance.

Papada-pàda, papada-pàda, she softly hummed the beginning of the Mozart sonata with the "Turkish March" in the third movement. Papada-pàda, papada-pàda, the notes floated and swirled around filling the air, building an imaginary bridge between Mathilde and Camillo.

The artiste raised his head, hesitated. He heard the notes.

He did not want to hear them, he tried to shoo them away like a bothersome fly. He pulled his hat down over his brow as if he could isolate himself from her tune, but it didn't work, the fly stayed persistent. Finally he surrendered and looked up and down the street to find the source of the humming.

Mathilde still stood with Lene's bike in the gap between the walls of the destroyed house beside the factory across from where the truck was parked. She stared at Camillo, willing him with all her might, all her power, all her love to see her.

She found his glance, and he found hers, and in that moment she immersed herself in his brown amber-flecked eyes. She did not know if she still hummed the tune. He did not know if he still heard it, had really heard it, could still hear it. The music was simply there. It hovered around them, surrounded them, united and embraced both of them.

Yet the moment, for Baumgartner, was quickly past. The tightrope walker tossed his cigarette away and came closer. The kids who had earlier begged for handouts pounced on the butt and scuffled for it.

"Why are you here? What do you want?"

"Do not trust Franz. He will betray you."

The artiste shrugged his shoulders. He knew that already.

"He has blown the whistle on the escape plan to the Amis. They will all be arrested, and he will be let go."

Now Mathilde had his full attention. "What are you telling me?"

"Please. Be careful. You are in danger."

"Of course," he said.

He didn't appear surprised like she expected. "Go!" she pleaded. "Escape. Now. Right now! You don't have to be here. You already have the money."

His voice turned cold and hard. "How do you know that?"

"I saw it happen. I was there, in the harbor."

Baumgartner looked at her inquisitively, piercingly. "And how did you learn about *that* meeting place?"

"From Franz. My husband," she added at the end. As if she had to explain.

"Ah yes."

She knew what he thought from the tiny pursing of his lips; an unconscious gesture of disappointment. "No, please, you're taking it all wrong. Franz was there by accident."

"Accident?" If ever she had evoked disappointment in him, it was gone.

"No, that's not what I meant. I said it poorly. What I mean is I did not go there to meet Franz, but you. I wanted to warn *you*! You are rushing to your doom."

"Leave me alone." He looked over at the truck.

Borg, Kleinmann, and the others were out in front of the ruins and perusing the area carefully, cautiously. Borg was most careful, but he wasn't searching for Mathilde. He had convinced himself she was a figment of his imagination. One by one they began to climb into the truck.

Mathilde fought against the tears in her eyes. "Is it worth it?" she whispered. "You risk your life? You sell your soul for just a little bit of money?"

"Do you think it is about money with me?" He suddenly looked amused.

"What else would it be?"

He grimaced. "When these pigs are on board I am tossing their plans out the window. I will drive straight to the Brits," he said smirking, his words whirling at her like a thunderstorm. "I will drive the whole load of Nazis right into the barracks yard and give them a surprise. I've told the Brits we are coming, but they don't really believe it. Still, I will deliver them all. All of them, especially your husband. Him above all. The murderer. Did you really think I would let him escape; that I would help him? For money?"

Yes, she had believed it. What kind of fool had she become? How could she have been so naïve as to not realize he would turn the Nazis in?

"I am sorry," he went on sarcastically, "but America or Brazil or wherever you wanted to go won't happen."

"I didn't want to go anywhere. At least not with Franz. Please, you have to believe me."

"I don't believe you at all." Yet, for a fleeting moment, Camillo asked himself if he could be wrong. If she had, as he assumed, made a deal to escape with her husband, then where was her daughter, the girl whose life he saved, the girl he liked and was to have gotten papers for?

Franz looked around wistful, doubtful, and in despair. Mathilde almost felt sorry for him.

Baumgartner turned away, his prey was fully assembled. Time to go. "Goodbye."

Mathilde desperately held onto his sleeve. "No, please, don't go with them. I am telling you the truth, I swear it. Franz is double-crossing you. All of you."

Camillo tried to break free of her grasp. Suddenly, two Russian military trucks from opposite directions rapidly advanced and came to a screeching halt, blocking both ends of the street. Soldiers jumped out and circled the Red Cross truck with breathtaking speed, their machine pistols drawn.

Matthus and Kleinmann tried to run but made it only for a few steps. Shots rang out and Kleinmann, the former SS man, screamed and fell grasping his bleeding thigh. Matthus was grappled by a huge soldier who held him in a bear hug.

Franz was frozen in place, taken wholly by surprise.

Instinctively Baumgartner faded quickly deep into the shadows and pulled Mathilde with him. "The Russians? Why are they here? I thought your husband betrayed us to the Americans."

"I have no idea." She was as much at a loss as he was.

Russian soldiers shouted orders to the other Nazis to surrender. They were lined up spread-eagled against the truck while the Russians searched them for weapons. Kleinmann, groaning, was dragged by two soldiers over to the other prisoners.

"You pig! You damned Gypsy pig!" Franz turned around and bellowed with desperate anger. A Russian soldier slammed him back against the truck, but Franz would not stop. "You damned pig!" he cried again and again into the shadows, but there was no one there. All the neighbors or passersby had bolted as soon as the hated Russians appeared.

Baumgartner pulled Mathilde more deeply between the walls and unconsciously put his arm around her to hold her close and protect her. She laid her head on his chest, half fearful and half sheltered against the soft velvet of his vest. She breathed in the aromas of fire, smoke, and the familiar scent of the Gypsy camp that hung to his clothes.

"You really weren't lying?" Camillo asked quietly, almost tenderly.

"No, I don't lie to you." Mathilde heard an unexpected tenderness in his voice and felt a change through his embrace. Her heart filled with happiness.

She raised her head and looked at him and smiled.

He answered her look and her smile.

They lost themselves in each other's eyes. They did not breathe, they did not move.

They danced motionless among the ashes of their lives in the rubble from the ruins that had fallen around them, and here they wanted to be forever.

Still, the world turned. The moon rose.

When the Russians were convinced Matthus and his companions had no weapons they began to force the Nazis into the military trucks. They treated the prisoners roughly, with the same malice and hate these men had treated the poor devils they had arrested.

"You piece of crap," Matthus ranted at Franz, and Franz had no defense. He was as much in the dark as the others. Why had the Russians appeared out of the blue? Whatever, he thought. He just wanted to climb onto the truck bed, onto the scaffold, his scaffold from which there was no escape.

A loud voice rang out, "Stop it. Stop it! Now!"

The prisoners and the Russians looked in the same direction, all of them confused. An American lieutenant accompanied by a few GIs pushed past the Russian truck blocking one end of the street and went directly to the officer in charge. The lieutenant spoke quietly to him. The loading of the prisoners faltered while the Russian soldiers looked back and forth between their commander and the American officer.

Franz's expression brightened as he saw the Americans come closer. He almost beamed when he recognized Lieutenant Herter, his controller. Maybe he would bypass the scaffold. Maybe it was not the end, at least not for him.

Baumgartner was as baffled as the others watching the arrival of the Americans. "The Amis are here," he whispered to Mathilde, "just like you said. You really are here for me, aren't you?" He hugged her even closer.

Mathilde didn't answer. She just smiled, blissful, jubilant, and happy.

Meanwhile the Russian officer indignantly waved to his men to proceed. He told this damned American—in German, the only language they both understood—that he had no right to stop them.

The soldier behind Franz poked him in the ribs with his gun barrel. "*Dawai*, go, climb on!"

Franz could not move. He looked at Herter, imploring him. "Please," he whimpered, "please, Lieutenant, tell them I work for you. Tell them I am under orders." When Herter ignored him he shouted, "Lieutenant Herter, please! You cannot simply abandon me after all I have done for you."

Herter turned fleetingly and shrugged his shoulders indifferently—or was it regret?

The soldier who had ordered Franz to board the truck looked questioningly to his officer who in turn looked to Herter. "Do you know this man? Is that true?"

"No." Short, clear and to the point.

"Is that so? You know this Ami?" Matthus hissed, beside himself with anger. "You traitor! You will answer to me."

Franz ignored Matthus, his gaze fixed on Herter.

The lieutenant ignored him and turned to the Russian commander instead. Herter wanted those prisoners, he needed this manhunt to be successful; he had chased these damned Nazis for so long that he deserved the laurels. At least that. From the start he had believed that exploring the Rat Line, proving it existed, was absurd. And now all chances to do so were gone. This German was of no use to him anymore.

Franz refused to give up. He tore loose from his guard. "You can't do that. Without me you would never have gotten these people," he shouted and lunged at Herter.

The Russian soldier lifted his weapon. Franz made it only a few steps away when a shot tore through the air. Franz stumbled, staggered, fell, and lay gasping for breath on the ground.

Try as she might, when Mathilde saw her husband fall a short loud cry escaped her. It was as if a spotlight had suddenly been turned on her and Baumgartner. The captured Nazis, the Russian and American soldiers all whirled as one and saw her and the artiste. Even Franz, laying on the ground with his eyesight failing, saw his wife in the arms of the Gypsy.

With a wavering arm and shaking finger, Franz pointed at Baumgartner. "That man bought us the truck and papers . . . and papers . . ." He gasped, spluttered and rattled with his last bit of strength, his last ounce of hate for the Gypsy, the man who seduced, hexed and spellbound Mathilde, his wife; with his last bewildered thought of her, his little Mathilde, his voice broke, his eyes went dark, his arm sank down. Franz collapsed. He was dead.

Even as Franz was dying, Herter and the Russian officer bellowed simultaneous commands. In the blink of an eye a GI and two Russian soldiers started to pounce on Baumgartner.

Mathilde saw the soldiers coming for her and for her beloved Camillo, and unconsciously raised the bicycle like a shield.

"Out of the way!" snapped the GI. One of the Russians said something in the same tone that, she was certain, meant the same thing. Get lost!

"Out of the way!" roared the GI once again. He pushed Mathilde to the side, tore the bike from her hands and threw it on the street.

Baumgartner had long since clambered up the wall in the gap. He was about to swing onto the power line that ranged between the residence of the factory owner and the factory buildings in the rear court.

The three soldiers aimed their weapons at him and roared in two languages, Russian and English, for him to come down or they would shoot.

"Don't shoot!" Mathilde did not understand the words but she knew their meaning. She pounded her fists on the Russian's back and he shoved her away so hard that she staggered.

Still, she had given Baumgartner time to reach the power line. He grabbed it, swung back and forth a few times and, after swinging a complete circle, he suddenly sat astride the line giving the soldiers a clear, simple, easy target.

Herter and the Russian commander almost tripped over each other shouting orders. Their soldiers had the tightrope walker in their sights.

Mathilde could only whisper, only pray. "Camillo, no, be careful!"

The tightrope walker stood on the line.

"Stand still!" Herter yelled up to him. "That is your last warning."

Baumgartner stopped and looked to the left and the right. He saw that he had no chance. The soldiers would shoot him down. He raised his hands.

Mathilde breathed easier. He gave up, a victory, he gave up. It didn't matter if they put him in prison. At least he would survive.

But Baumgartner did not intend to let himself be captured. He reached under his colorful vest and pulled out the envelope with the money that Franz had given him at the harbor. He opened it, turned it over and let the bills dribble down like oversized confetti. Slowly, like snowflakes in summer, they sailed to the ground. For a brief moment the artiste disappeared in the cloud of pieces of paper.

The soldiers were mystified. What was this? What was happening? When the first bills spun to the ground they were stunned. Money fell from the heavens.

The Russians pounced on the cash. They fought over the bills, tearing them from each other's hands. The GI didn't care about the money and aimed again at the tightrope walker, but was pushed and jostled by the Russians diving headlong for the bills, and he could not get off a shot.

Baumgartner sauntered and danced along the line. He even had the audacity, the chutzpah, to bow for Herter, Matthus, and the Russian officer. He tipped his hat in greeting and threw a kiss to Mathilde who gazed up at him full of fear, full of love as he vanished into darkness of the night.

THIRTY TWO

It was pitch black when Mathilde climbed the stairs in the back house where Lene lived. She braced herself on the walls, held tight to the railing, and painfully bumped the steps. There was no electricity, the lighting did not work. The windows were covered with boards and paper, no moonlight found its way into the stairwell.

It was not only dark but also infinitely, almost alarmingly quiet. No children cried, no pots and pans rattled. People had long been asleep. Silence lay like a heavy blanket over Mathilde. Only the steps squeaked, whispering under her weight.

She counted the floors and knocked on the door she hoped was the right one. At first she knocked quietly, timidly, powerless. When nothing happened she knocked louder. Finally she hammered against the door and called for Lene. It made no difference to her who might be disturbed. She didn't care if she roused a total stranger. Whatever. It was all the same to her.

Mathilde finally collapsed in front of the door where she lay on the threshold. Lene opened the door, her hair unkempt, her eyes sleepy. "What's the matter?"

Mathilde looked up, her eyes flickered.

"I wanted to bring your bicycle back."

"Now? In the middle of the night? That could have waited until morning." Lene pulled Mathilde up and helped her into the apartment. "Come on in."

"The bike is downstairs behind the landing. I wanted to bring it upstairs, but I couldn't lift it anymore."

"That's no problem; it's okay there." Lene shoved Mathilde into the foyer and shut the door. She supported Mathilde as she stumbled again and said, "Quiet, Robert is asleep."

"The bike has had it. I'm sorry. It is completely *kaputt*. The handlebar is twisted, the saddle torn off and the luggage rack demolished."

"Did you get waylaid?" Lene led Mathilde to the cot in the kitchen where she slept. She shoved the comforter and the pillow out of the way.

Mathilde let herself plop down on the bed and groaned. "Do you have a drink of water for me?"

Lene poured a glass and gave it to her. She sat on a kitchen chair and looked at Mathilde in the candle light. She looked really bad, like she had been assaulted. Her hair clung to her brow, her eyes were sunk deep into the sockets. She had various scrapes and wounds on her face, her hands, her arms and legs. Her work pants, which were made from a blanket, were torn up to the knee, and her blouse had spots of blood on it. "What happened?"

"Nothing. I just wanted to give you back your bike." Mathilde sounded as if she could not grasp what she was saying. It was as if someone else spoke.

"But . . ." Lene started to say something, started to ask a question but broke off. She knew what had happened. At least she believed she knew; the Russians had arrested Franz. Karla had fetched Mathilde this afternoon from the worksite. What happened after that, who had made a mess of Mathilde, Lene didn't know, but she could figure it out.

Mathilde huddled on the bed and drank the water. She was silent. She began to shiver, uncontrollably. The glass that she held in her hand slipped from her fingers and shattered on the kitchen floor. She made a shrill noise at the smash but was immediately mute again, just stared at the glass shards and the wet spot between her feet.

Lene didn't move either. She simply looked at her friend.

Mathilde threw her hands over her face but could not even cry. She could not talk or think. The last hours were a single vague undefinable expanse in her memory, as lusterless as hoarfrost, as gray as ashes.

"The Russians arrested Franz." Now Lene said it out loud. She hoped that would prompt Mathilde to relate what had happened.

"The Russians?" An iridescence came over Mathilde's face, a shimmer of recognition, a memory seemed to come out of the deep. A sense of the happenings. "A Russian shot him."

"What?"

"Yes. *Bang!* And he was dead." Mathilde no longer stared at the floor but looked Lene straight in the eye. "*Bang!* And he lay there."

Lene swallowed.

"What . . . what made you think of the Russians?" Mathilde asked. There was more surprise and amazement than interest in her voice.

"Because I told them that your Franz was alive," Lene said firmly, defiantly. Still, she looked away. She couldn't take Mathilde's gaze.

"What? You have . . . ?"

"Should I have stood by and watched while he leads a wonderful life in America whereas Robert dies? Or, in the best case, continues to vegetate as a cripple back there? Can't you understand that?" Lene's voice became harsh and rang piercingly through the room as she defended herself. Then she broke off and it was quiet. It was quiet for a long time.

"You have no idea what you set in motion." Mechanically Mathilde pushed together the glass shards on the floor in front of her.

"I'm sorry." After a pause Lene added, "For you. Not for your husband. I can never pardon him."

Mathilde kept quiet and fussed with the shards. Outside the birds began to twitter. She sighed. "In a couple of hours we have to be at the worksite."

Lene nodded.

"Can I stay here until then? I don't think I can make it home."

They lay close beside each other on the cot. Lene had insisted that Mathilde lie down, and Mathilde insisted that Lene not sleep on the kitchen chair. They lay beside each other in the dark gray before the morning twilight. They felt the body heat of the other, the outlines of their arms, their legs, their hips.

At some point Lene asked, "So he really is dead now? Your husband?"

"Yes."

Somewhere a cock actually crowed. "But the other one is alive."

"Yes, the other one is alive," Mathilde repeated quietly and watched spellbound as the cracks around the plywood that covered the kitchen window changed colors. From gray to pearl to the golden bright light of morning.

Gabriele Kosack and **Günter Overmann**, a couple in life as well as work, started out their artistic careers in theater: Günter Overmann as co-artistic director, playwright in residence, and director in various German theaters; Gabriele Kosack as actress. Now writing full-time, they are both novelists and script writers for German television, currently working for the most successful series on European TV—*Sturm der Liebe*—and developing new shows for various German networks. Gabriele's novel *Am liebsten alle zusammen* and Günter's novel *Tauchgang* are available in German language only. *A Dance in the Ashes* was written in partnership, and is their first to be translated and published in English.

Kenneth L. Fitts is a former professor of theater as well as a two-time EMMY-winning television producer and writer. His projects for German television brought him into partnership with Gabriele Kosack and Günter Overmann, which resulted in the creation of two shows for German television audiences.

Roger "Skip" Wightman, retired Sgt. Major, ASA, United States Army. Well versed in the German language, he lived, studied, and spent many years in Germany. Skip enjoyed a deep appreciation for German culture, language, and its people. He volunteered to translate *A Dance in the Ashes* to help his brother-in-law, Ken Fitts, and completed the project shortly before his death in 2013.